REAPER

RuNyx is a *New York Times*, *USA Today* and international bestselling author of romance. Her stories range across subgenres from dark contemporary to gothic to historical to fantasy and more, and are currently being translated into over 10 languages.

Her pen name has a very special meaning to her. When she's not writing, she's reading, traveling, meditating, daydreaming, and most of all, procrastinating.

THE REAPER

RuNyx

PENGUIN BOOKS

PENGUIN BOOKS

UK | USA | Canada | Ireland | Australia
India | New Zealand | South Africa

Penguin Books is part of the Penguin Random House group of companies
whose addresses can be found at global.penguinrandomhouse.com

Penguin Random House UK,
One Embassy Gardens, 8 Viaduct Gardens, London SW11 7BW

penguin.co.uk
global.penguinrandomhouse.com

Penguin
Random House
UK

Published in Penguin Books 2025
001

Set in 9.92/14.06pt Adobe Caslon Pro
Typeset by Six Red Marbles UK, Thetford, Norfolk

Printed and bound in Great Britain by Clays Ltd, Elcograf S.p.A.

The authorised representative in the EEA is Penguin Random House Ireland,
Morrison Chambers, 32 Nassau Street, Dublin D02 YH68

A CIP catalogue record for this book is available from the British Library

ISBN: 978–1–911–74640–9

Penguin Random House is committed to a sustainable future
for our business, our readers and our planet. This book is
made from Forest Stewardship Council® certified paper.

To my parents.
For always having my back, giving me strength and encouraging my dreams.
I wouldn't be who I am without your unconditional love. I love you.

Author's Note

This is the second book of the *Dark Verse* series and picks up directly where the first book, *The Predator*, left off. If you have not read the first book, I highly recommend doing so for a complete reading experience.

This book contains explicit scenes of violence and sexual nature. There are also a few trigger warnings I feel would be fair to warn you about in case you are sensitive to these subjects - panic attack, murder, mentions of rape and torture, mentions of human slavery.

If any of these subject matters make you uncomfortable, please take heed. If you continue to read the book, I hope you enjoy the journey. Thank you.

Book Playlist

The playlist is for Tristan and Morana for both Book 1 and Book 2.

Devil Devil – Milck
Carnival of Rust – Poets of the Fall
Animals - Maroon 5
Closer - Nine Inch Nails
One Way or Another - Until the Ribbon Breaks lyrics
Every Breath You Take – The Police
Eyes on Fire – Blue Foundation
A Little Death - The Neighbourhood
Russian Roulette - Rihanna
Between the Bars - Elliott Smith
Toxic - Sofia Karlberg Cover
Hypnotic - Zella Day
Carry You - Jeffrey James
Bravado - Lorde
Salted Wound - Sia
Crazy in Love - Beyonce (Fifty Shades Cover)
Wicked Game - Ursine Vulpine ft. Annaca
Bedroom Hymns - Florence + The Machine
Cut - Plumb

Fire Breather - Laurel

Broken - Seether ft. Amy Lee

Monster - Imagine Dragons

Demons - Imagine Dragons

Don't Let Me Go - RAIGN

Help - Hurts

I Found - Amber Run

Making Love on the Mountain - The Woodlands

Lullaby - Nickelback

Touch Me - Rui Da Silva Ft. Cassandra

Bleeding Love - Leona Lewis

My Heart Is Open – Maroon 5

Partition - Beyoncé

50 Shades - Boy Epic

Trust - Boy Epic

Dirty Mind - Boy Epic

Walk Through The Fire – Zayde Wolfe ft. Ruelle

You Belong To Me - Cat Pierce

My Love Will Never Die - Claire Wyndham

A Little Wicked - Valerie Broussard

You Should See Me in a Crown - Billie Eilish

Flesh - Simon Curtis

Dinner & Diatribes - Hozier

I'm A Wanted Man - Royal Deluxe

Dangerous Woman - Ariana Grande

Not Afraid Anymore - Halsey

Game of Survival – Ruelle

Shameless – Camilla Cabello

Craving You – Thomas Rhett

Madness – Ruelle

Blood and Muscle – Lissie
Fear and Loathing – Marina and the Diamonds
Black Magic Woman – VCTRY
I Can't Go On Without You - KALEO

"I love you as certain dark things are to be loved, in secret, between the shadow and the soul."

— *Pablo Neruda*

PROLOGUE

The orange glow of the burning cigarette was the only flicker of life in the sheer dark, stormy night.

The man sitting behind the steering wheel looked at the cemetery on his left, his hazel eyes tracking the lovers kissing each other amidst the dead. While he couldn't see the girl, hidden as she was behind the tall frame of her lover, he knew exactly where she was, just as he'd known all these years.

He watched them from the darkness of his car, his window rolled down just an inch to let the smoke escape before it choked him. Not that he feared death, not at all. He just had a purpose, a goal that had been driving him for a very long time. He had lain in wait, day after day, week after week, year after year, taking one metaphorical step closer to his goal.

Taking a long drag into his lungs, he felt the smoke seep into his cells and mix with the ashes of his old life. He rubbed his knee absently, stroking the ghost of a pain that haunted him.

A flash of lightning illuminated everything for one split second. Had The Predator turned around, he would have seen him easily. But one of the best hunters in the mob was distracted by the woman. He was irrational, sloppy. He was emotionally invested in her.

The man watched them separate, watched the younger man bend down to pick up the fallen gun, watched him hand it to her. He watched, silent as the shadows, as the woman followed him to the waiting vehicle.

Rolling the window down completely, the man threw the half-smoked cigarette outside, droplets spraying in his face with the enthusiasm of a reconciling lover, kissing his skin. His eyes drifted to the silver ring glinting on his right ring finger, the skull chiseled down to its last details. It had been made for him a long time ago as a gift. The skull had been his crowning jewel once. Now, it was his ghost.

He'd wondered over the years about the thin line between justice and vengeance. Which side he ended up on depended a lot on the girl. He wore the ring, not for the memories of laughter and friendship, but the reminder of all that he had lost.

It was time to bring it back.

CHAPTER 1

EAVESDROP

The rain was consistently coming down in sheets.

The drops splattered against the windshield and died an instant death, weeping down over the glass as occasional bursts of thunder rent the night sky.

Morana was still on the other side of that window, still looking out at the shower, still removed from the drops trying to penetrate the invisible walls and touch her.

This time though, she wasn't untouched. She'd already been kissed by them, ravaged by them, made love to by them. This time, she was drenched and wet and shivering with the force of the memory of those raindrops caressing her skin for a moment frozen in her heart.

This time, as had been that night in the penthouse, she wasn't alone.

She still hadn't turned her neck to look at him in the car.

He wasn't untouched either. Earlier, she'd watched with rapt fascination as he'd silently gotten inside the vehicle after walking away from her.

The clouds had rolled. The lightning had split. The winds had whipped.

And she'd stood outside, exposed for a long time while he'd gone behind his walls.

But not completely.

Though he'd turned on the ignition, he'd not made any move to pull the car out, soundlessly waiting for her as she'd stood to his periphery and let her eyes linger on the exact spot where she'd made her choice and forced him to make his. Their footprints had been washed away by the onslaught of rain, mud, and grass covering up on the outside what had been a turning point inside her. The deluge had also washed away most of the smudges on her body remnant from the blast and opened the graze wound she had on her bicep. That had worried her slightly, since getting it wet was something she'd avoided last night and now it was completely drenched.

Even as she'd stood feeling and contemplating the tautness in her arm, he'd not once honked the horn, nor opened the door, nor revved the engine. He'd not made a single move to overtly indicate that he'd been waiting for her. Yet, she'd known it simply because he'd still been there, a silent but magnetic presence lingering forcefully in the empty area – a sentient life amongst the death and destruction surrounding him.

Silently, he'd offered her a place behind those walls that sheltered him. Just as silently, she'd accepted. She'd made her way around that beast of a vehicle and climbed right into the passenger seat. He'd simply pulled out of the cemetery.

The warm air blowing from the vent felt good on her clammy, cold skin now as she thrust her palms directly in front of them, letting the heat from the circulation seep into her bones slowly. Allowing her eyes to roam freely around the interior of his car for the first time, she was not in the least surprised at the black leather seats that were now completely doused in moisture, thanks to both their clothes. It was her first time in his car, a gorgeous black BMW she was slightly envious of if she was being honest.

Shaking her head slightly, she turned towards the console, seeing 'Play Music' glowing on the digital dash and raised her eyebrows, wondering for a second what kind of music he indulged in if he even did. Did his taste in music lean towards Rock or R&B? Or was it as eclectic as her tastes? Simple questions that she'd never allowed herself to ponder about him rifled through her mind as she took in the objects surrounding them.

Her wandering, inquisitive eyes came to a halt at a small pendant. It was really small, feminine, dangling on a silver chain that hung around the mirror in the center, a tiny round disk on it.

Without seeming too obvious, curiosity getting the better of her, Morana squinted her eyes and tried to make out if there was an inscription on the flat disk-like shape.

There was.

'Baby sister'

Oh lord . . . it had been hers.

Luna.

Morana felt her heart squeeze painfully, all her newly acquired knowledge making her fall back against the backrest, her gaze falling to the silent man beside her.

He appeared relaxed in his seat, neither of his hands clenching on the steering wheel or the gear stick when he shifted it, his breathing smooth and even. Everything seemed fine. Except for one little thing—he was looking straight ahead with a devout concentration that she doubted he needed to drive, avoiding her eyes since the moment he'd handed over the fallen gun to her.

Since he'd kissed the bejeezus out of her.

Morana let her eyes flutter back to that simple, small pendant, weaving in circular motions with the movement of the car, and felt her chest hurt. That tiny piece of jewelry dancing freely between them – the silver that bore the imprint of and had once belonged to his beloved baby sister – said more about him than anything else ever could. So much pain, so much rage, so many scars . . .

And along with the heaviness in her chest came another epiphany—the car was his territory too. Or else that pendant would never have hung there, so exposed, so pretty, so vulnerable. Its very existence in the car told her it was very, very private.

And she realized – just like he'd done at his penthouse that first night of the rain when he'd decreed she would stay at his apartment rather than leave with Dante – he'd let her into his territory. Again. Even after making a choice she could not even begin to fathom.

The aftermath of that choice still clung to her muscles, still bussed in her blood, still hummed in every cell in her body. She could still feel the cold metal of that gun against the pounding of her beating heart. She could still feel the pressure of those lips throbbing against her swollen ones. She could still feel the slide of that tongue stroking against the inside of her mouth.

A shiver wracked her frame – from the chill or the memories, she didn't know.

Questions swirled in her mind, words formed in her throat and came right onto the tip of her tongue, but she bit them down, unwilling to break the silence. She had just forced him into a spot, and knowing what she knew of him, she understood that he wouldn't respond well to being coerced to talk, not until he'd had the time to process it all.

Or well, at least that's what she would've wanted had she been in his shoes. She was still uncertain about him, about where his brain was at, but she was alive and shivering beside him after giving him a chance to kill her. And that was enough. For now.

The sound of his phone buzzing on the dash cracked through the tensed silence.

Morana glanced towards the phone reflexively.

'Chiara calling'

A slight frown wrinkled her brows before she could stop it.

Chiara? Who the hell was Chiara? And why would she call at this time of the night?

Turning her head towards the window intently, Morana focused on the raindrops cascading down the glass, at the other vehicles on the mostly-empty road, aware of him rejecting the call. Whether he did that because he was driving or because of her presence or simply because he wasn't in the mood, she didn't know.

But a tiny knot in her stomach unfurled, worrying her by its very existence. There shouldn't have been that knot at all. There shouldn't have been any reaction to beautifully named women calling him in the dark of the night. She didn't have the energy for this. This was bad.

Shaking off the thoughts crowding her head, she chose to study his large hand instead as he shifted the gears smoothly, in a way she'd never had the time or inclination to. She took in the huge metallic watch around his strong wrist with a navy dial that looked expensive, the veins that ran at the back of his hand, the sparse dusting of hair that curled right under his sleeve, the long, strong fingers she'd felt inside her intimately. Squirming just slightly, she let her gaze travel lower, looking again at the broken skin over his knuckles, the flesh still tumefied. Though he could've easily done that damage last night on the shower wall, it looked freshly bruised.

She opened her mouth to ask him about it, saw the corner of his lips pull down infinitesimally, and shut up.

Not the time. *So not* the time.

The miles flew by as he drove, weaving the car expertly through the light traffic, and after long, tensed minutes, she saw the familiar gates of his apartment complex, the building rising high into the tempestuous sky, the sea a vision on the far left of the structure.

The two guards at the gates with guns strapped to their hips nodded at him respectfully and he drove down the small driveway to the underground parking. White lights lit the entire space, gleaming on the metal of all the dark vehicles sleeping there. Morana looked at all the cars and wondered for a moment who all lived in the building apart from him and Dante.

Before she could follow that train of thought, he maneuvered the car into his spot beside his beautiful bike. Morana looked at the dark muscle on it, a longing to ride the thing again echoing in her heart, coming from the treasured memory of that first bike ride, from that first memory of feeling truly free.

Her longing cracked open when she heard the door open and turned to watch him jump out of the car, slamming the door behind him, all before she could even undo her seat belt. She got the sense that he wanted to get away from her and again, while it made her a little mad, she understood. Had she been in his place, she would've probably ditched him in the cemetery itself and run away for her precious space. She'd honestly half-expected that from him as well.

And just like in the cemetery, though he reached the private elevators first, he didn't go up but silently waited for her. Morana quietly opened her door and locked it behind her, letting her hand stroke the seat of the bike once, the cool air of the garage making her wet frame shiver as she made her way on brisk feet to where he stood inside the metal box with his foot beside the doors to keep them from closing.

Surprised by the gesture, she entered as he withdrew, and pressed the code for the penthouse. She watched as the doors slid shut, the mirrors on them reflecting both their drenched forms. Morana stared at the picture they made. While he looked put together, his tall, muscular frame encased in that drenched suit and dripping tie, those abs evident against the white shirt plastered to his torso, she looked like death warmed over. Her clothes were slightly torn from the blast, her light-colored top now an odd shade of brown, streaks of dirt and mud marring the fabric and in places, even her skin. Her hair was matted and tangled, half in the drooping ponytail and half out of it, her cheeks were the only spot of color on her face, her eyes huge and slightly red.

The contrast between their reflections at that moment—his darker skin to her pallor; his clean dark clothes to her dirty light; his tall, broad frame to her small, curvy one; the power radiating from his very being, even in a disheveled condition at a moment when he wasn't even glancing at her, prickling against her skin—sent a shiver down her spine.

While the thought of having this man's body against her had merely aroused her until a few days ago—although to a level she'd never understood—it was a chaotic frenzy inside her now. Fascination and lust, compassion and lust, anger and lust, mingled in an ardent concoction she could feel brewing in her stomach, knowing that while now wasn't the time, she would have him again one day— this time as naked as she would be, this time with his flesh against her, his sweat, his scent, his scars rubbing on her as she marked him with hers.

He would be her ruin. And she would ruin him right back.

But now was not the time.

Taking a deep breath to center herself, to give both him and herself the time to process the events of the last twenty-four hours, she peeked at where he stood, remembering the first time she'd entered this elevator with him. He stood leaning against the back wall, mere feet away from her, scrolling through his phone, not once looking up or making eye contact with her. It was odd, this lack of eye contact between them. And now that he was denying her those magnificent eyes of his, she realized how much she'd come to rely upon them to read him.

She knew that he knew that she was watching him. Yet, he deliberately kept his gaze on his phone.

Blowing out a breath, she started rubbing her arms to warm herself, conscious of the slight pain on her wound, when the doors finally slid open, showing her the majestic view of rain and the city outside those windows she'd come to love so much, that always made her breath catch for a split second.

And, then, angry voices reached her.

One loud, masculine. One soft, feminine.

Reigning in her surprise—both at finding Amara there and hearing Dante sound so unlike himself, Morana stayed glued to the spot and looked at the silent man beside her, seeing him finally put his phone down and concentrate on the two people inside.

"You had no right!" Dante spoke, his voice higher than Morana had ever heard, his anger brimming in every word. "It wasn't your story to tell."

"I couldn't just stand aside and let him destroy himself or her!" Amara retorted, her voice still low and raspy but firm enough to let Morana know she meant business. "I've seen him do that for years and I cannot stand it."

"This isn't about you, god damn it!" Dante yelled and Morana flinched. "You want to tell someone how you got that scar? Do it.

Tell them all. But you don't get to tell anyone how he got his, Amara! I told you all of that in strict confidence and you betrayed it. You betrayed him. How. The. Fuck. Could. You?"

"You accuse me of betrayal? God, I don't even recognize you some-times," Amara whispered, the rage in her voice boiling over, her tone a whole world different from how it had been an hour ago speaking of this very man. "Yes, I told an innocent woman who had no part in any of what happened to him about why her life was at stake. I told the truth about him to a woman who makes him so alive, I've never seen him like this before. If by betraying you and him, he gets a chance at a better life than he's had, then I'd betray you a hundred more times! She deserved to know and he deserves a chance!"

"Do not start with this again," Dante whipped out. "It's a fucking simple thing. We trusted you and you broke it. It was his story to tell and he would've told her if he wanted. He didn't."

"Because he's scared it'll change things!" Amara cried out, her soft voice straining. "And things need to be changed, don't you get that?!"

"Not like this."

There was silence for a second before Amara asked quietly. "Are you mad because I betrayed him or because I betrayed you?"

Atta girl.

Morana cheered silently on the woman who'd become her friend, who had knocked a yelling man down a peg with her soft, scarred voice. Something akin to pride filled her.

Before another word could be uttered in the apartment, the hulking man beside her—who'd stilled more and more with every word—stepped out of the elevator and turned right, striding towards the dining area where the voices were coming from. Morana followed quickly, a few steps behind him, biting her lips to keep her thoughts to herself.

She stopped at the edge of the living room, seeing both Dante and

Amara frozen to their spots, inches away from each other but both looking at Tristan Caine with wide eyes. Dante's gaze flickered to her for a moment, taking her in from head to toe, his observant eyes lingering on her lips for a long second that suddenly made her realize how swollen they were. Morana didn't avert her eyes from his dark ones in his troubled handsome face. He shook his head once before moving away sharply towards the window and glaring out at the view.

Amara didn't look at her at all, not for a moment. But stared right back at the man beside her, her spine straight and chin up, no remorse on her face for what she'd done. Morana felt her respect for the woman go up a notch—because being on the receiving end of Tristan Caine's eyes drilling holes into you was intimidating as fuck.

She looked up at him to find him staring back at Amara, his jaw clenched.

Nobody uttered a word.

The tension between the two seemed to climb higher and higher, so much so that Morana debated interfering for a moment. But then she saw his lips move.

"Go home, Amara."

His voice—that voice of whiskey and sin—spoke for the first time in hours, softly to the beautiful woman, a demand and a request rolled into one.

Amara nodded without any argument or explanations, picking up her bag from the counter and walked past them towards the elevator. She came to a halt beside the console and turned to look at Dante as he looked out the windows, her dark green eyes angry.

"Stop being a coward, Dante," she spit out softly in his direction. "It's high fucking time."

Uh oh.

With that, she walked into the elevator and closed the doors behind her.

Okay.

But it wasn't over, it seemed. Morana watched with her eyebrows up in her hairline as Dante fisted his hands beside him, before picking up a vase from the nearest cabinet and throwing it on the floor, smashing it to glimmering pieces. Flinching from the suddenness of the noise, the beautiful crystal shattering loudly, and the broken bits splattering all over the floor, Morana inhaled sharply.

She was too tired, too overwhelmed, to witness anything more emotional in any kind, not until morning. In a way, she was actually grateful to Tristan Caine for keeping his silence and not being the forceful whirlwind he could be sometimes. For now, she needed to unwind lest she resembled that vase on the floor—shattered from a force it could not withstand.

So, knowing it would be better for her to retreat and to leave the men to their mutual brooding and privacy, to go tend to her wound, she stepped back.

Retreating towards the guest room on silent steps, she opened the door and slipped inside, aware of the pin-drop silence in the apartment, the only noise coming from the torrent clashing with the glass windows. Letting out the breath she'd been holding since getting on the elevator, Morana quickly put her phone on charge, headed to the bathroom, and went about turning the warm water on in the bath.

Taking a seat on the ledge beside the sunken tub, she went about cleaning her wound again, hissing as the sting made her already sensitive eyes water, and closed it with butterfly bandages. Then, stripping her clothes, she threw them in the corner, knowing she would never wear them again. The water tested, the door shut, she dipped a toe in the large bathtub and finally sank.

It was like a full-body hug from the best warm water she'd ever dipped in.

The *best* hug.

Groaning at the amazing way the water caressed her sore muscles and kissed her little cuts, she dunked her head once before tipping it back against the tiles behind her, keeping her arms on the ledge beside her, her eyes closed.

She didn't let herself think of anything—not her car, not her cold-blooded murders, not her father, not his attempt to kill her, not the man who'd come for her, not the choice they'd both made, and *definitely* not the kiss that still stung her heavy lips. She didn't let herself relive it—not the rain, not the gun, not the man. She didn't let herself remember it—not the soft caresses, not the hard hunger, not the silent choice.

She just lay there, letting the water be her tender lover who soothed her hurts, cleansed her, and relaxed her completely in its arms.

The thinking could wait until tomorrow. She ignored the string keeping her together, ignored the ache as it pulled taut on every thought, ignored it all. She just lay there.

After long, long minutes, when the water went cold and her skin began to prune, when she was almost lulled to sleep by the simplicity of a good bath after a hard day, she somehow dragged herself out of the tub, pulling the plug, her eyes stinging, the exhaustion and lack of sleep of the past few days catching up to her. All she wanted was to put herself in that comfortable bed, draw the thin blankets over her head, and sleep undisturbed for the next ten years. Minimum.

Sighing, she switched off the lights in the bathroom and walked out to the still-dark bedroom, without a stitch of clothing on, not caring because she was exhausted and not worried because she was pretty sure he wasn't going to enter her bedroom tonight, not after all the avoiding he'd done since the cemetery.

Without another thought, she climbed into the bed, snuggling into the abundance of pillows, a groan escaping her at the plush comfort.

A buzzing noise from her phone made her peek one eye open. It had come to life.

Grabbing it from the bedside table and removing the charger, she unlocked the screen, to see alerts for 4 Missed Calls and 3 Text Messages from Tristan Caine.

Blinking, sleep fading from her eyes, she swallowed, clicking on the texts, seeing her last message to him.

Morana Vitalio: *They should be. After all, I just blew up a car and killed two men in cold blood.*
(Sent 4.33 PM)

Tristan Caine: *Where are you?*
(Received 4.34 PM)

Tristan Caine: *This is not amusing, Ms. Vitalio. Where are you?*
(Received 5.00 PM)

Tristan Caine: *I swear to god ... WHERE THE FUCK ARE YOU?*
(Received 5.28 PM)

Then nothing.

Nerves balled up in her throat, stomach heavy with the very roil of emotions that she'd been trying to avoid, Morana closed her eyes and put her phone back on the stand, turning on her side.

It was almost 10.30 now. Which meant she'd seen him in the cemetery at roughly 9. What had he been doing since that last text?

No. Deliberately shaking herself out of it, she inhaled deeply—the light citrusy scent of fabric conditioner on the sheets filling her nostrils—and told herself to just sleep for the night. There was a lot of time in the morning, to think, to process, to plan. For now, despite the day, she was alive and tired and her brain could wait for a few hours.

Nodding to herself, she almost closed her eyes again when the voices from outside broke into her consciousness. Frustrated, she covered her ears with the pillow.

And then put it down.

The men were talking.

Tugging her lower lip with her teeth, she wondered what they were talking about when the silence in the penthouse aided her, their voices, though not loud, still drifting to her well enough that she could hear it.

"Father called when you were out," Dante spoke.

So, no questions about the emotional health of either, then. *Men.*

The sound of crystals clinking together against plastic told her either of them was cleaning up the mess on the floor.

"Things are escalating back home, Tristan," Dante stated, in the calm, collected tone she'd come to associate with him. "It's getting worse. We need to return."

Tristan Caine didn't speak for a long moment.

Then, his voice rolled over her naked skin.

"Yes, we do."

Morana indulged in his gruff tone for a second, before the words broke through. He was leaving?

That knot in her stomach tightened, an odd kind of panic filling her for some reason. After the past few hours, the past few weeks, after making certain she wouldn't run away when she'd wanted to, he was going to leave the city behind? And her? Right after she'd made the gamble of her life?

Her heart sunk.

Gripping the blankets in her fists, she tried to keep her head quiet and focus on what they were saying.

"Are we going to address the very big elephant in the room?" Dante.

"I don't see one." Blase. Indifferent. Him.

She heard Dante sigh. She was pretty sure that sigh had been his friend for a long time. "What were you doing at that bastard's house tonight, alone of all things?"

That had so not been the elephant in the room she'd imagined. But who were they talking about?

"Paying him a visit," Tristan Caine answered.

Her eyebrows went up at that tone inviting challenge.

Dante didn't disappoint.

"Things are already fucked up for you at the moment, Tristan. In case you've forgotten, someone is out for your blood—"

"Someone always is."

"—and you just keep feeding it fuel. We do not need Gabriel Vitalio going cocky-assed on us right now, not when we're here."

One.

Two.

Stunned.

Morana looked up at the ceiling, stunned out of her freaking mind. He'd visited her father? At his mansion? Alone? *Was he insane?!*

Her brain supplied her the image of his hands on cue—those bruised, broken knuckles that had told her, even as he'd kissed her, that he'd made someone's night hell. She'd vanished and he'd gone to her father's mansion alone and yet made it out? And now had broken skin on his knuckles?

What. Had. He. Done?

Breathing heavy, heart racing like a wild horse out of control, Morana couldn't even begin to grasp the implications of this. She just couldn't.

And yet, there was something else too. A novelty. Because she had fallen down the stairs and he had punished her father. Because she had gone missing and he had walked into the lion's den and burned it and made it out unscathed. The novelty of feeling like this, for the first time in her life, dampened her eyes. Having been alone for all her existence, with the knowledge that nobody would break a sweat if she disappeared, the fact that this man—the man who had hated her for twenty years of his life—had broken flesh made her heart clench in a way she'd never experienced before, in a way she could not understand. Only feel.

Taking a stuttering breath in, she kept listening, her knuckles white from gripping the sheets.

"It's a good thing we won't be here for long then, isn't it?"

A long pause.

"Does that include Morana?" Dante asked quietly.

Morana's heart battered in her chest, hammering with a force that mingled with the inexplicable emotions inside her, as she waited for a response from him, to understand what he would do. Because while he'd given her silence, he'd also given her actions. She needed his actions now.

When he didn't say anything for long moments, Dante sighed again, and her heart slipped. "Tristan, she's his daughter. As much as I understand why she's been here, we can't let this go on. Vitalio might retaliate. And it could end nasty. You know that."

More silence.

"You haven't been focused as much as you usually are on the threat and weeding it out. We cannot afford a full-blown war like this, Tristan. You've been distracted—"

"It's not her fault—"

"Isn't it?"

A pause.

Dante continued. "Look, I don't want her under that jerkwad's roof any more than you do. We have a safe house we could move her to. Maybe get her fake passports, get her out of the country as we did with Catarina and the girls. I will stay back to ensure it all goes smoothly and she's not harmed and—"

"She comes with me."

Four words.

Soft. Guttural. Irrefutable.

The breath she'd been holding in her throat escaped in a rush, her heart pounding so hard she felt faint. Putting her hand on her naked chest, she felt the fast thumping under her palm and took a few steadying breaths, relief and something else filling her.

She comes with me.

Did she want to go? To leave behind the only home she'd known, the only city she'd known, the only life she'd known? She knew she could fight him on this, but did she want to?

No.

Dante stayed silent for a long minute and Morana wondered what they looked like right then, how closed off they were to each other, how hard they challenged the other's stare.

"Father will retaliate," Dante warned in that quiet tone.

Tristan Caine snorted. "Like I give a fuck."

"It's not retaliation against you that I worry about," Dante clarified. "It's her. For doing what he couldn't ever do."

Which was what exactly? she wondered.

"Leave it, Dante," Tristan Caine uttered, his voice a dangerous blade. "He'll know the exact score once we land. Just get the plane ready for the morning."

"Be ready at 8," Dante stated.

"Done."

Okay.

Taking a deep breath, she heard the soft ding of the elevator, indicating Dante had called for it.

"By the way," Tristan Caine called out, "Chiara called."

Chiara Mancini. The phone call. Who was she?

"What for?"

"I didn't answer. Nor will I," Tristan Caine replied. "But if he gets her to—"

"I'll take care of it before we board," Dante responded and the elevator dinged another time, telling her he'd left.

Who the hell was this woman?

Morana turned on her side, looking out the smaller glass windows in her room, watching the rain, and marveled at how drastically her life had changed since the last time she'd been in the same bed in the rain like this. She'd been contemplating jumping beyond those windows then, even hypothetically. Now, she couldn't fathom letting go of something so precious inside her—something that made her feel everything so acutely, something she'd begun to fight for.

Life.

She was alive and she'd never felt it more viscerally as she'd done over the last day. She absorbed the new facts she'd learned about him since the cemetery—that he had a pendant of his sister's still hanging in his car after twenty years, that he'd gone to her father's mansion for some reason alone and beat up someone and still made it out to tell the tale, which told her how utterly feared he was. She didn't know many men, hell any man, who could claim to walk into the enemy's house alone, have a fistfight, and come out breathing.

A shiver rent her spine, and she closed her eyes as the newest fact lingered—that he was willing to take her with him, away from this place that held nothing for her anymore, away from this hell, testing the wrath of not only her father but Lorenzo Maroni. And that he was certain she would be unharmed. She knew it in her bones she would be unharmed. Because even though he'd always talked about killing her, in hindsight she realized he'd not reacted well to her being harmed - both when she'd come to him after her father let her fall down the stairs, and when he'd shot her in the arm to save her. Or when he'd thought her gone and stroked her beloved car.

Her heart clenched at the memory.

Before she could let herself drown, she heard a soft swoosh as the air in the room changed.

The door opened.

Surprise filled her as some instinct, some deep-rooted voice, told her not to move a muscle or open her eyes lest he left without doing what he came to do. What had he come to do? Watch her sleep, as he had once before? Or to talk, which she didn't think was plausible quite yet?

She suddenly became acutely aware of her arms exposed out in the air, of her breasts barely concealed by the blankets, of the one bare leg she'd forgotten to cover, bare to the hip. She felt something electric thrum through her body, her arms breaking out into goosebumps, her toes tingling, making heat travel up that exposed leg, her nipples pebbling hard, one of them almost peeking out over the covers.

Despite that, she didn't move, didn't do a thing to cover herself better, didn't make a motion to indicate she was anything but sleeping peacefully, her breathing even as she regulated them through sheer will, keeping her body deliberately lax.

She didn't know if he still stood by the door or if he'd stepped into the room or if he'd come closer to the bed. She didn't know if he had a better view of her leg or her breast. She didn't even know if the heavy gaze she felt on herself was real or just a figment of her imagination. What she did know, however, was that he'd watched her sleep once before, for how long, from how far, she didn't know. She'd been asleep then. This time, she wasn't. And she wanted to see what he would do if he would reveal something else about himself when he thought no one was watching.

Keeping her inhale soft, her heart thundering in her chest as a clap of thunder sounded outside, Morana kept herself from curling her fingers into her palms, from biting down on her tender lips, from keeping her tremors contained. Her lips felt on fire, the weight of his gaze resting upon them, stroking them with his eyes, opening them in his mind. It could all have been fanciful on her part, but somehow, someway, that same deep-rooted voice told her he was watching her, and that same deep-rooted instinct made her want to arch her back wantonly and let the blankets fall away.

She didn't.

She let her lips feel the singe of those eyes, felt the hunger deep inside her gut, felt the memory of his mouth right upon hers.

Something feral, fervent invaded her belly.

Her heart slammed, pulse throbbing in her ears, an ache blooming in her core, right between her legs, making her skin prickle, making her feel unduly warm under the covers that she wanted to kick off, sizzling her blood with rapture without him even laying a finger on her.

But she stayed still through it all—through that fire coursing through her body, through the lump on her chest, through the emotions in her heart. She stayed still and relaxed on the outside, with the perfection of the mask she'd donned with ease over the years.

Moments passed.

Long, loaded moments.

Short, sinful moments.

With the ease of sand slipping through the fingers.

With the difficulty of a broken clock.

Moments passed.

With heartbeats.

With breaths.

And the air changed again.

He was there.

She knew, with sudden clarity, she knew—he was right before her.

He stood between her and the window from what she could feel, her body turned towards him, her face breaths away from his thighs. She could feel the nearness of that gaze, the proximity of his heat, the musky scent that wafted off his body, that scent—magnified by his wet clothes—that was all him.

The curve of her stomach trembled, hidden beneath the layers, her heart thumping in the anticipation that hung between them, her palms becoming sweaty as she drew all her strength to keep herself relaxed, to see what he would do.

A part of her was disturbed by how deeply he affected her, over the power he had over her body. The other part, however, reveled and gloried in the sensations, on feeling so alive, in a way she'd never thought herself capable.

She didn't understand this. And at the moment, she didn't want to.

She just lay breathing softly.

In.

Out.

In.

Out.

In—

A finger.

His finger, ghosting over her wound.

It wasn't a light touch. It wasn't a touch at all. It just was.

Hovering right over her skin, on the precipice of a cliff but never truly falling, a ghost touch, almost tentative, tracing the butterfly bandages with a butterfly stroke she would never have detected had she been anything but intensely conscious of his every move.

Her heart almost stopped, the skin of her entire arm cackling, perspiring, straining.

The ghost touch disappeared, and Morana almost opened her eyes to call it back, when it reappeared over her jaw, light as the air. That ghost finger, never really touching her, pushed back a strand of her hair and exposed the entire line of her throat and naked shoulder to his perusal. She could feel the pulse fluttering at the base of her neck, a drop of sweat beading on her upper lip as that finger ghosted over the line of her jaw, like the way his gun had traced it hours ago.

The memory of that solid, insistent, cold metal, and the reality of the light, barely-there, soft digit sent a bolt of electricity straight to her core. Her entire being strained towards that almost touch. Her entire body was famished to feel it on her flesh. Her brain was tripping slowly, her control over her faculties getting dazed, her lungs starving for a gulp of air she refused to take.

Only instinct, that bothersome thing, told her that he would vanish if she showed any indication of being conscious. And she didn't want that. Not yet.

This . . . this was . . . *enlivening* her.

The ghost finger traced the shell of her ear.

Her toes almost curled.

It traveled over the terrain of her heated skin, going over the line of her jaw again—and she both cursed and blessed the fact that he didn't touch her, or her skin would have betrayed her charade. It was like eavesdropping on the most private, most intimate of conversations. Her heart thudding, beating almost too fast for her to keep up with it, she pressed her thighs together to find some purchase.

And then, the ghost touch stopped at her lips.

Fragile purchase lost.

Those sensitive, swollen lips, that still bore the mark of his mouth, trembled.

Just minutely, but they did.

Her heart stopped.

Did he feel it?

Still.

Everything inside her stayed still—like a prey scenting a predator.

Everything about him stayed still—like a predator scenting a prey.

But who had been who in the past few minutes?

And had he felt it?

She had her answer within a split second.

The finger withdrew.

He left as quietly as he'd come.

She heard the swoosh of the door. And then it shut again.

She let go.

A huge shudder wracked her entire frame, her chest heaving with pants as though she'd run a marathon, her hands shaking as she threw the covers away from herself, her entire body lit from within with a blaze she couldn't control.

She felt ravaged. On the inside. On the outside.

And he'd not even *touched* her.

Digging her head back into the pillow behind her, her nipples aching in the cool air, she took her breasts in her small hands and squeezed them, gasping as her nipples pebbled harder against her palm, shooting sparks down to the tips of her toes.

He'd never touched her breasts. But for that stolen moment, she imagined his hands—those big, rough hands, strong against her soft flesh, skilled against her nipples. She imagined the callouses on those fingers rub against her nipples when he tugged them, imagined his hands completely engulfing her sinuously, imagined him squeezing her breasts together as she did the same with her hands, her lips parting as little breaths left her.

Feeling liquid, limber, her muscles coiled on the threshold of an inferno ready to consume her, she let her trembling fingers travel down to between her thighs.

And she was *soaked*.

In a way, she'd never, ever been.

Completely, utterly soaking wet.

A little moan left her lips and she turned her face into the pillow beside her, so on the edge she knew it wouldn't take much to send her careening into that abyss of ecstasy.

She slipped a finger inside her, easily. Pushed another in.

The hunger in her walls gnawed at her, spinning out of control. She remembered how he felt inside her—big, heavy, powerful. She remembered how he speared her walls—with focus, ferocity, and fire that set her aflame. She remembered how every stroke hit that spot inside her, how every thrust made her spine curve, how every slap of flesh against flesh drenched her even more.

Panting, she rubbed her clit with her thumb, just once.

And *exploded*.

Gloriously.

Her back arching as she bit into the pillow to muffle her cries. Her entire body coming off the bed for a split second as fire raced through her veins and coiled in her core, blasting in the most dazzling of explosions, blinding her for a second.

It was rapture.

It was ecstasy.

It was delirium.

She fell back into the mattress, even more exhausted, limp, no strength in her body to move a single muscle, slight shivers running up and down her frame in the aftermath.

God, how had this even happened? He'd not even touched her, not made a sound, and yet she'd been dripping wet.

It frightened her. It thrilled her. It enlivened her.

He enlivened her.

Slowly calming herself down, her body much laxer, much more

susceptible to sleep, with the tension in her body released, she flipped and pulled the blankets over her again, her eyes going one last time to the window to look at the rain.

And her heart stilled.

He was there.

In the darkness.

Leaning against the wall beside the window.

Hands in his trouser pockets.

Tie undone, hanging over his collar.

And those magnificent eyes blazing on her.

He was there.

He'd been there through it all.

Her heart stuck in her throat, she looked at that blaze for the first time since the cemetery and felt seared, her entire body flushing under that intensity, upon realizing what he'd seen.

He'd known she'd been playing him earlier, and he'd played her right back.

Blushing till her roots, she held his gaze, her eyes drifting down for a moment towards the big bulge tenting the front of his trousers, before coming back up to his, the knowledge of having aroused him while taking care of herself electrifying her, titillating something reckless inside her.

She knew he wouldn't break that silence, not tonight.

But he was watching her again, despite himself.

That brought a small smile to her lips.

She saw as his gaze followed that smile before she flipped on her back again and cuddled into her covers, closing her eyes deliberately.

She felt his eyes on her for long minutes, but this time her heart didn't pound harder. This time, her heart lay beating in her chest, nestled in an odd kind of comfort she couldn't understand, only feel. She had made it through the day and seen right through him, and he'd made it slightly through his past and seen right through her. And that, for some bizarre reason, comforted her.

She felt him leave as softly as he'd entered, leaving her completely alone in the room this time, the knowledge of his interest, his desire within her.

Almost to the edge of sleep, Morana tried to get her mind to shut down and get as much rest as possible. Because anxiety and anticipation mated in her stomach.

In the morning, the start of something new would begin.

In the morning, her life was going to change.

In the morning, they were going to Tenebrae.

CHAPTER 2

PANIC

The rain had finally stopped, leaving behind clear blue skies and sunlight that spilled into the living room of the penthouse from the huge windows. Bathed in the bright early morning sunshine, the entire city was sprawled beyond the windows, looking fresh, clean, the smeared dirt collected over the days having been washed off from existence, the city having just woken up from its slumber. For that one moment in time, it almost looked pure.

She had lived there for too long to believe that mirage anymore.

Nonetheless, Morana enjoyed the breath-taking view, sitting on the stool beside the kitchen island, sipping freshly brewed coffee, enjoying the calm since the owner of the apartment was still upstairs in his room. It had been a trying day for them both yesterday and the night to match. She didn't begrudge him the rest if that was what he was doing. Since she'd never ventured back into his room again, she could only assume.

Not that she hadn't been tempted, especially after the show she'd unknowingly put on for him last night.

Morana exhaled softly as the elevator dinged, drawing her eyes to Dante as he walked in, looking as put together as she'd always seen him. Dressed in a charcoal gray suit with a darker gray tie that fit his enormous frame perfectly, his hair styled and pulled away from his handsome face, Morana watched him approach her, his dark brown eyes not as distant as they'd been to her, but still cautious.

She wondered if he was worried about her witnessing his momentary lapse of control the previous night after Amara had left. Deciding to be more forthcoming, because while he was trying to protect his own, he'd been nothing but good to her, Morana gave him a small nod.

"Would you like some coffee?" she asked politely.

Dante declined just as politely, coming to the stool next to hers, leaning against it as he regarded her thoughtfully.

"Is Tristan up yet?"

Morana shrugged, keeping her face deliberately blank, ignoring the way her body reacted to the simple name of the man. "I haven't seen him this morning if that's what you're asking."

He nodded. "Good. I wanted to speak to you alone."

So, he could try and persuade her to stay back.

"Okay," she assented, feigning ignorance of what she'd heard last night between the two men.

The clear light glinted off his dark eyes as Morana regarded him over her rim.

"Tristan needs to return to Tenebrae," he started without preamble, his voice strong and firm. "So do I. He wants to take you with us and while I have absolutely nothing against you, I need to explain some things first, without Tristan muddling the issue so that you can make an informed decision."

Morana put the hot mug of coffee to her lips, taking a small sip as gratitude filled her, for this enemy's son who'd shown her kindness when she'd been hurt and who was still giving her kindness, even if for his own reasons. The ability to make her own choices had been denied to her for so long, she treasured it now, and felt a flash of respect for Dante for giving her the tools in that moment.

"I'm listening," she encouraged him to go on.

"Amara told you everything," he stated coolly, even as a myriad of emotions flickered over his face before he reined them in.

Morana nodded, not mentioning anything more.

"And since you're still here, I'm assuming you and Tristan have come to an understanding?" he asked.

"That's really not your business," Morana stated softly, putting a stop then and there to any questions about what had transpired last night between them.

Dante inclined his head. "What is my business, though, is the Outfit. I'll be clear with you, Morana. Someone is setting Tristan up real bad. And it's somehow connected to what's been happening to the Outfit for the past few weeks, just like you found out."

Morana gulped down some more of her beverage, keeping her eyes on the man a few feet from her.

"This is not the time for Tristan to be stubborn," Dante continued, blowing out a breath. "His life is on the line and one wrong move could end it. And bringing you to Tenebrae with him? Wrong move. A few months ago, I would've been fine with it. Would it have been problematic? Hell yes. But we could've worked it out. But right now, with the way things are?" He shook his head, taking a breath before continuing.

"Not to mention, my father," Dante sneered at the word. "You think your father's the shit? Trust me when I tell you, he's got nothing, absolutely nothing, on Lorenzo Maroni. My father would invite you into his home like a gracious host and slit your throat while you smiled back. He's got no love, no affiliation for anything or anyone. Only power, power, and more power."

Morana already hated the man, only from everything she'd heard about him.

Dante took a deep breath before speaking again. "Whatever history you share with Tristan is moot right now, Morana. You're still your father's daughter and still the enemy for Lorenzo Maroni. Tristan bringing you into his territory without permission, without any knowledge, especially after what he did to your father last night . . ." he stopped abruptly.

Her heart started to pound.

"What did he do last night?" she asked, half-afraid of the answer, pulse throbbing in her ears.

Dante sighed wearily, running a hand over his face. "Doesn't matter."

It did.

It did matter. But she didn't bite the question back, not say anything.

Dante inhaled, his huge body becoming bigger for a split second. "What matters is what you want to do. Whatever you decide Morana, know that you'll have my protection either way. If you wish to get away somewhere else, I can arrange that too. If you wish to come, we'll work it out. And if you refuse to leave, Tristan won't force you."

Morana raised an eyebrow, skeptical. "Really?"

Dante chuckled. "Oh, he'll try to intimidate you into going his way. But he won't force you."

"So, he'll let me be if I choose to stay here?" Morana asked, completely serious, wanting to know his thoughts.

Dante mulled over her question for a long moment, his eyes on the beautiful view outside, before turning back to face her, completely serious as well. "He will never let you be, Morana. You both are bound together by things I don't even think both of you understand. However, the question is do you want him to let you be?"

Hadn't she already made that choice last night, standing in a cemetery? Hadn't she already forced him to make his choice too, standing in the brutal rain?

But last night, she'd only been concerned with how it affected them. She'd deliberately not given a thought to anything else.

Morana felt the severity of the situation, of everything she hadn't been thinking about last night, hit her like a truck. Last night, she had been focused solely on her own emotions, guided by instinct, thinking with her heart.

It was time to get her brain out. It was time to see the picture as a whole instead of the tiny portion that concerned her. It was time to weigh these decisions. Because while she may have emotionally decided where she stood last night, in the light of the day, she couldn't ignore how her decisions might affect everything else.

Dante was right. If she went to Tenebrae, there was no saying what her father would do. Though he'd tried to kill her himself, she knew his pride would have taken a serious beating and he would retaliate. He would probably use her leaving as a reason to declare the war the two territories had danced around for over years, possibly accusing Tristan Caine of stealing his daughter.

And that was only part of the equation. She didn't even know how Maroni would react but from the sound of it, his would be worse than her father's response. And with Tristan's life on the line, with someone unknown but well-versed in computers framing him, sending her information about the Alliance and planning lord knew what else nefarious schemes, Morana could feel everything suddenly crash down over her.

Her heart started to race along with her thoughts, flashing one after the other, switching, changing, transforming before she could grasp one completely.

The burden of that responsibility started to suddenly choke her.

She didn't want to be responsible for these people. She didn't want to be responsible for anyone. For the first time in her life, she wanted to be utterly selfish. She wanted to be reckless. She wanted to get on the back of that bike and throw her hands to the wind. She wanted to sleep at night knowing she wouldn't be harmed. She wanted to taste the life she'd whet on her tongue just days ago.

Her heart thumped loudly in her ears, a drop of sweat rolling down the line of her spine, her palms became clammy. Morana turned to the windows, gazing out at the view as her breathing picked up speed, spinning beyond her control, the enormity of everything crashing all around her, pulling her under.

The ability to make a choice that she'd treasured moments ago strangled her. She wanted to choose to get on the back of that bike, not in the driver's seat. She didn't know how to drive it, didn't know how to control the beast, didn't know where to guide it. And she could feel herself heading for the collision, feel the inevitability of breaking everything inside on the impact.

Her breathing went choppy.

She didn't understand this reaction, didn't understand her own body in that moment. It almost felt like she was outside her skin, watching it all in some sort of delayed reaction.

Black slithered around the edges of her vision.

A lead weight settled upon her chest, rendering her incapable of the simple act of breathing.

She felt the half-full mug of coffee slip away from her suddenly nerveless fingers, heard the crash of the ceramic against the floor, even felt the hot drops splatter on her bare, dangling legs.

Yet, she felt numb.

Staring at a space she couldn't even see anymore.

Existing in a place she couldn't feel anymore.

Rushing with the blood she couldn't hear anymore.

Her body senseless, her mind blank, a dark, ugly feeling swallowed her whole as she thrashed against it on the inside, the outside world slipping away from her, the collision coming towards her at break-neck speed.

She heard sounds, everything a buzz around her, tried to make sense of it, tried to place the noises but failed, going under whatever was engulfing her.

Thoughts raced through her and she couldn't catch a single one, spinning inside her own mind until she felt dizzy, her body swaying, the ugly monster trying to bite into her flesh, feed off her, make her go under.

She tried to fight it.

She thrashed.

She gnawed.

She clawed.

It still sank its fangs into her, drawing from her until the pressure on her chest felt explosive, as though she was going to snap and shatter into a million pieces, never to be put together again, those pieces of her lost forever to the inside of her own mind, to the ugliness, the blackness, the void trying to consume her like a black hole.

Physical fingers wrapped around her throat.

The monster eating her reared its head.

She lashed out against the hand holding her by the neck firmly, her nails clawing at whatever they could find, trying to escape from everything, deep, deep into herself.

Her attacking wrists were swiftly gathered in one hand behind her back, the one on her neck giving her head a shake.

"Look at me."

Three words penetrated her haze.

That commanding timbre.

That razor tone.

Whiskey.

Sin.

Morana knew that voice. She knew the baritone of it, reacted to the ice of it. She latched on to that voice, gulping down the smoky whiskey of it, letting it trickle down her throat and into her body, warming her from the inside as tremors shook her frame.

The blackness around her vision receded a bit, the ugly emotion holding her captive releasing its reins.

"Breathe."

She blinked, trying to clear the black away.

Once.

Twice.

The blackness withdrew, leaving behind . . .

Blue.

Clear blue.

Magnificent blue.

She tethered herself to it—to the brilliant blue that looked like burning sapphire, to the dark pupils enlarged in those pools of blue, to the intensity of them focused on her.

She tethered herself to them, not daring to blink lest she drowned again, not daring to look elsewhere lest that anchor was gone.

God, she was cold.

She felt so cold. Down to her fingertips, down to her toes. She felt chills race over her spine yet, try as she might, the ice refused to leave.

The pressure on her chest intensified.

"Breathe."

She felt something strong, something hard, something warm pressed against her chest, moving in a rhythm that was dislodging the rock weighing her own chest down. Morana latched on to it, let herself focus on the rhythm as she felt it right against her chest, and tried to copy it.

The thing pressed against her chest contracted.

Morana contracted hers in sync.

In.

That first rush of air into her lungs nearly knocked her out.

Greedily, without even realizing, she gulped down as much air as she could, never removing her eyes from those blazing blues. She didn't recognize herself in that moment, but she recognized those.

In.

Out.

In.

Out.

"Breathe."

Breathing.

She was breathing.

The blackness fogging her senses receded slowly, long fingers of the monster that had touched her curling away, withdrawing, disappearing as her physical and mental senses joined forces again. The shadows slinked away, retreated, allowing her the clarity that had been misted over.

Slowly, eventually, she came back to herself.

Slowly, eventually, she became aware of everything.

Became aware of him.

Restraining her.

Tethering her.

Surrounding her.

She became aware of her body still on the stool, of her legs spread apart to accommodate his form between them. She became aware of his entire torso pressed deliberately to hers, so she could feel every single breath he took acutely against herself, so she could match his even rhythm and calm her thundering heart. She became aware of one of his big hands holding both of hers behind her back by the wrists, the grip tight but not painful, the angle pressing her chest deeper into his.

A huge shiver wracked her frame.

Fingers flexed on her neck.

The awareness of that large, rough hand wrapped around her throat dawned upon her.

And she didn't feel threatened.

For the first time, even though she'd seen him crush people with that hand at the same spot, as she looked up into those ardent eyes, she didn't feel threatened.

She felt protected.

Safe.

Untouchable.

It was a novelty and for that one moment of weakness, she let herself revel in it.

She had no memory of how he got there, or when he got there. The time between the mug spilling coffee on the floor and now was a complete blank.

What the hell had happened to her? Had there been something in the coffee?

She discarded that thought the moment it came. She'd made the beverage herself.

It was something else.

As she tried to make sense of the past few minutes and catch her breath, his hand started to withdraw from her throat.

And the monster reared its ugly head.

"No."

She didn't recognize her voice, didn't recognize the desperation in it, the guttural need in it.

He stilled, his eyes flaring with something primal, and her heart started to pound, her chest heaving against his, their gazes locked.

Without a word, he firmed his grip.

Something inside her calmed.

She knew she wasn't this needy person. She never needed anybody. But in that second, something deep inside her recognized that she needed him to not move. Not from between her legs, not from against her, not from anywhere. Not until she completely came back to herself.

And at that moment, she let the gratitude for what he was doing wash over her. He didn't have to do a thing. Not a thing. He could've let her drown and let her fade for however long inside her head. She would have eventually clawed her way out, perhaps worse for the wear, perhaps with mental scars that would've lingered for a very long time. He could have let it happen. But he didn't. He'd jumped right into her tempest, caught her, pulled her, and remained there, anchoring her. And for someone who'd never relied on anyone but herself, there was something so profoundly liberating about it, something so, so acute it made her heart squeeze in her chest.

The sound of a throat clearing pulled her out of her thoughts.

Morana turned her head to the side towards the sound, blinking as she found Dante standing there, a glass of water in his hand, his face completely neutral.

Oh fuck.

Flushing to the roots, Morana squirmed on the stool, her ass numb from sitting there too long, being in a position as she was before anyone else making her slightly uncomfortable. She tugged her hands out of the firm grasp, feeling the callouses slide against her softer skin, and reached for the water.

Tristan Caine stepped away, his hands leaving her completely even as the warmth of his fingers lingered, imprinted around her throat in flesh memory. She focused on that imprint, focused on that warmth to keep her rooted.

Gulping large sips of water down her suddenly parched throat, Morana finally took in a deep breath after finishing the glass and centered herself.

"Thank you," she murmured to Dante, returning the glass to him, wiping her palms on her shorts.

He gave her a nod, his eyes slightly concerned. "Are you alright now?"

Morana nodded back, touched by his concern. "I am now. What . . . what happened?" she asked, looking from one man to the other.

Tristan Caine—wordlessly, as was his style these days—walked around the island into the kitchen, dressed in dark cargo pants that hugged his fine ass and a plain navy tshirt that clung to his torso, emphasizing his large shoulders and biceps. He was dressed casually, not like he was planning on going out anywhere soon.

And if she could notice all that, she was definitely feeling more like herself.

She saw him move around in the kitchen, opening the fridge and pulling out a small bar of something.

"You had a panic attack," Dante's even voice made her swivel in her seat, surprise filling her.

"I don't get panic attacks!" she retorted, the idea completely foreign to her.

Dante shrugged offhandedly. "There's always a first time. Your mind's been through a lot these last few days. It was only a matter of time."

Morana sputtered, blinking as she remembered the blackness, the weight on her chest, the inability to draw in a breath, and realized that she had, in fact, had a panic attack, a massive one at that. And that Tristan Caine had, in fact, saved her from her own head.

Something slid along the countertop towards her, distracting her.

Morana looked at the bar of chocolate, her eyes flying towards the man extending it towards her, stunned.

He was giving her chocolate.

Like it was nothing.

Just sliding a bar of chocolate over to her before walking away.

She remembered reading in some magazine about men giving women chocolates. Men who wanted to sleep with said women. He was doing it in reverse.

The sudden urge to laugh overpowered her, a chuckle escaping her before she could stop it. She stared at that piece of chocolate, the sound of her laughter, unfamiliar even to her, ringing out in the large space, making her cheeks hurt, her stomach hurt, making her hurt. Laughing shouldn't hurt. But it did.

She couldn't remember the last time she'd laughed. She couldn't remember what she even sounded like then. She did remember, though, being alone and scared as a child, remembered the days her chest would ache. No one had given her chocolates back then. No one had held her up. No one had done anything for her.

And yet, now she'd had a panic attack, and this man, of all people, had given her chocolate.

To comfort her.

In his own way.

Tears streaked down her face, mingling with her laughter as Morana realized she was losing it.

She was truly losing it.

She was breaking down.

And it felt fucking glorious.

For a moment completely suspended in time, she floated, somewhere between agony and joy, somewhere between sensation and numbness, somewhere between caring too much and not giving a fuck, and it was utter beautiful perfection.

For that moment.

She felt free, not weighed down by demons, by responsibilities, by histories.

One moment.

And then that moment ended.

With a large hand on her jaw and fearless blue eyes holding hers, again, that moment transcended, transformed.

"You don't owe these people a thing."

Low. Rough. Gritty.

Tugging at something inside her.

"And I sure as fuck don't. Don't let them control you."

Morana swallowed.

A vein popped on the side of his thick neck.

"You want to go to Tenebrae?" he asked softly, his whiskey voice deceptively quiet.

'With me', remained unsaid but not unheard.

Morana inhaled deeply, her mind clear of everything but her own desires.

She nodded.

"Then that's that."

He let her face go, leaning back, and looked over at Dante.

Morana took in a shaky breath and glanced at the other man as well, who stood to the side, watching her with a slight smile on his face.

Morana blinked in confusion at the smile, not understanding.

Dante inclined his head, taking out his phone from his jacket pocket. "Then that's that. Let me make some calls."

Without another word, he walked off towards the living room, leaving her alone with the man who'd gone back to being silent, who worked around the kitchen preparing breakfast. Morana watched him crack open eggs with one hand in a bowl while he fired up the pan with the other, every action smooth, every muscle prominent, every line of his body delineated in the sunlight. She watched him work around his space and looked down at that singular bar of chocolate that meant so much more to her than he could ever comprehend.

She felt something unfamiliar lodge itself in her chest. Except for the fact that this time, the unfamiliar wasn't an ugly monster that left her cold.

No.

This time, it was beautiful, almost tentative, and it warmed her down to her bones.

She didn't know what it was. But watching this man with the horrific past, scarred present and unknown future work his way quietly, comfortably around the kitchen after bringing her back from the edge twice within minutes, knowing how important the implication of this small moment was, Morana peeled away the wrapper of the chocolate with trembling fingers, quickly hiding it inside her pocket to treasure, and took a small bite.

The sweetness melted on her tongue, going down her throat, warming her even more.

She felt like herself, only better.

Safe.

In a complete turnabout from the past minutes.

Taking another bite, she watched his back.

"Thank you," she spoke quietly into the space between them, the words wrenched from deep inside her.

Apart from a minuscule faltering in his rhythm of beating those eggs, there was no response from him to acknowledge her words. But she knew he had heard. And if they warmed him even a degree on the inside to how much he'd warmed her, it was enough.

For now, it was more than enough.

With that thought, she went silent, focusing on the heavenly chocolate and the sinful view.

❖

Morana had only traveled first class all her life—some trips during college, two journeys to symposiums and that one impromptu journey to Tenebrae weeks ago that had changed the course of her life. First-class was pretty normal to her.

Which was why she'd been surprised out of her mind when Dante had told them, over a scrumptious breakfast of buttered toast and eggs, that the jet had been ready and waiting for them. She'd assumed, simply because that's how she'd always traveled, that all mobsters had traveled that way as well. Dante had cracked a little smile at that one, telling her the Outfit chartered planes whenever they needed—and they needed, a lot.

Which meant that either her father didn't know the Outfit had private jets (which meant his spies weren't that good), or that he was poorer than they were. Both options gave her a wicked sort of internal glee, for some twisted reason. She liked the fact that her father didn't have all the toys in the playground. She liked it because, to her father, these were the things that mattered.

And he was lacking. That gave her joy.

So, after quickly freshening up and composing herself, knowing she couldn't afford to lose it again once they landed in the danger zone, Morana had packed her meager collection of borrowed clothes, which had reminded her that she'd needed to buy some pronto. She'd also dropped Amara a text informing her of the newest development, promising to herself that she would keep in touch with the other woman. They both needed a friend and they couldn't let other people dictate their lives to such an extent again.

'Don't let them control you.'

He'd been right. She couldn't. Not anymore.

CHAPTER 3

BREATHE

Tucking in her precious laptop and other equipment, that chocolate wrapper pressed safely between the pages of her planner, she was done in fifteen minutes. The first thing, as a matter of priority, she needed to do when she got settled was to shop. She was living on Amara's borrowed clothes that didn't fit her right and it made her realize how dire her situation was.

Going out to the living room, Morana looked at the windows and the view beyond, saying her private goodbye to them. She didn't know when and if she would ever return to that view, and bidding adieu to the place was making her lock the cherished memories, the cherished emotions it had inspired in her. She tucked it safely inside her – the memory of that rainy night, one of the most special ones in her heart, directly related to the windows.

Slightly emotional, she turned towards the elevator, only to find

Tristan Caine leaning against that wall in a suit sans the jacket, watching her quietly.

Something passed between them in that instant – the shared memory of a simple, treasured night.

And that was that.

He walked away as Dante joined them; she followed and within minutes, she was ensconced in the back of Dante's car, heading to the airport, both men taking the front as two other cars followed behind them.

Now, sitting at the almost empty airport lounge as their plane got prepped, Morana watched through the glass doors as both men spoke privately outside the small white plane, a man in the pilot's uniform with them, two of the security detail in the lounge with her.

"Don't react," a heavy voice with a slight accent came from a few feet behind her, pulling her attention.

She almost turned but stopped herself, curious. "Excuse me?"

The owner of the heavy voice continued. "You've changed the game, Ms. Vitalio."

"Who are you?" Morana asked, her attention on the man sitting behind her, even as her eyes stayed glued to the Outfit men still outside.

The man ignored her question. "I'm not your enemy but I know the people who are. And I have an offer for you."

Morana's entire attention snapped to the man. "What do you mean?"

"You find out something for me, I'll give you the information you need."

Morana stayed silent.

"Remember me," the man spoke. "We'll talk later."

Morana looked up and found her eyes snared in the gaze of a predator.

He stood near the door instead of where she'd seen him moments ago beside the plane, his blue eyes inflamed as they caught hers, held hers. In a split second, he took her apart and put her back together with that focused gaze. In a split second, her blood throbbed everywhere in her body, just by the touch of that gaze.

He held her eyes captive for a long second before glancing at the seat behind her. Morana turned, only to find it vacant.

Wordlessly, without looking at her again, he turned around and strode towards the waiting jet with long steps, and Morana followed, a confused frown on her face.

They covered the distance in seconds, reaching the stairs.

And then he did the craziest thing.

He took her hand and helped her up the first set of stairs. As though she was some medieval damsel in distress needing assistance to climb high stairs with a gazillion skirts and not a twenty-first-century woman wearing comfortable jeans and comfortable shoes, being very capable of climbing the low steps on her own.

Morana felt her eyebrows hit her hairline.

Tristan Caine did not open doors or help ladies up the stairs.

At least, he never had until then.

His hand—exactly as she'd known it would be, rough, big, consuming—held hers, as though replacing any other touch.

Just for a second. The gesture was just a split second long before he snatched his hand back, shoving it into his trouser pockets.

Morana didn't say a word, just bit her lip and silently, quickly climbed up, finally entering the jet.

A thrill went through her.

She felt him hop on behind her, his presence huge right against her back as she moved forward, taking in the plush interior. This was her first time inside a private plane and she didn't want to miss a second of it.

The area beyond the door opened up into a small but well-planned sitting space, with two couches nailed to the floor and two armchairs, surrounding a glass table in the center on three sides. There was a minibar behind one of the couches and a TV glued to the right wall, the entire interior in brown and cream overtones. Beyond the sitting area was a small door that was closed at the moment.

Spotting Dante on a couch, his tie loose and a tumbler of whiskey on the table, Morana made her way to the chair before his, placing her laptop on the table, aware the entire time of Tristan Caine ducking his head and moving behind her, his breath on her head due to the closed proximity of the narrow corridor.

"Get comfortable, Morana," Dante invited. "It's a long journey."

Morana slipped off her shoes and sank into the plush armchair, tucking her legs under her.

"No air hostesses?" she asked, confused. Didn't men like pretty women catering to them on these private planes?

Dante shook his head as Tristan Caine walked over to the closed door and disappeared behind it.

A frown furrowed her brow.

"He likes to nap on the plane," Dante explained.

Hence, no outsiders except the pilots.

"He trusts you," Morana commented.

Dante chuckled. "As much as he can, I guess."

The captain called out then, letting them know they were going to take off. Morana closed her eyes as the plane rumbled under her, her nerves getting shot as they always did that first moment of take-off.

This was it.

There was no turning back now.

Her presence on this flight would definitely set off a chain of events, most of which she wouldn't even be aware of until it was too late. She knew that.

The runway became a blur.

Morana glanced out the window, taking in the city that had been her home her whole life, a finality settling upon her. She was leaving behind so many memories, mostly ones not worth keeping – her father, his house, her dead car, her spot in the cemetery, the penthouse . . . some dear, some not. And though she'd only known her only for a few days, leaving Amara behind left a bad taste in her mouth.

And then, they were in the air—one man off to sleep, the other still there.

Looking towards Dante, she found him considering her with his dark eyes.

"I have to admit, you surprised me, Morana," he stated casually, inspecting her.

She raised her eyebrows. "I did?"

He nodded, taking a sip of his whiskey, offering her a glass. She declined.

He explained. "As much as I don't approve of how you discovered the truth, I'm surprised. I had expected a lot of things when I thought about this scenario over the years . . . never this, though."

"By 'this', you mean me tagging along to Tenebrae?"

Dante shook his head. "I mean you staying. Any other woman would have been running for the hills by now. Honestly, I don't know what I would have done had you run. Because he would have chased you, you know."

Morana closed her eyes for a second, her heart beating strong. "I know."

"What are you doing, Morana?" Dante asked softly, the concern in his voice making her eyes flutter open. "As much as I love Tristan, better than my blood, I would never want him with my sister if I had one. I'd be lying if I said I wasn't a little worried—for both of you.

There's something very broken in him and if you're here because you think you can fix it, I'm telling you right now, you cannot."

Morana regarded Dante quietly, a tiny ball of anger coiling in her belly. "I'll be honest with you, Dante. I like you. You and Amara have been incredibly kind to me, at a time when I needed it the most. And that is something I'll always admire you for. But," she leaned forward, flames licking her blood, "what's between him and me is between him and me. As you told Amara last night, if he wants to tell you, he will. You won't hear anything from me."

She took in a deep breath, calming her temper down, reminding herself he wasn't her enemy.

"But because your heart is in the right place," she uttered quietly, "I will tell you this—I don't want to fix him. I want to fix *me*. And he's the only thing that seems to be working."

"So," Dante asked, his voice controlled, hand clenching around the glass, "you're just using him then?"

Morana smiled. "And is he not using me? To fight whatever demons live inside him?"

Dante remained silent. They both knew the answer to that one.

Morana stared at a spot on the table, her voice going soft, her heart drumming softly inside her chest.

"His demons dance with mine," she murmured softly, the truth of that statement seeping into her pores. "That's all I can give you."

She found the other man regarding her with a heavy gaze.

"And if your demons take you like they did this morning?" he asked quietly.

Morana swallowed. "Let's hope his find mine, then."

Dante nodded, exhaling loudly, raising the glass to her in a toast. "In that case, I wish you good luck. You're certainly going to need it with him."

A grin tugged at Morana's lips. "That's how you got him into your corner? Good luck?"

Dante huffed out a laugh, shaking his head, his handsome face coming alive. "Sheer, stubborn luck. I was very wilful back then."

"Back then?" Morana prompted.

His smile dimmed and Amara's parting words to him came back to her. She'd called him a coward. Was he? From what Morana had heard and seen of him, it didn't seem to be the case.

His voice broke through her thoughts, his hand swirling the amber liquid inside the glass.

"I cornered Tristan into accepting my partnership over the years. Wore him down." He looked at her. "He's a lot more stubborn, Morana."

"So am I."

Dante smirked, sipping the whiskey. "This will be fun."

Morana let that slide, looking out the window into the castles of clouds, the silence between them companionable as he began working on his phone and sipped that one glass of whiskey. Morana gazed out at the puffs of white, wondering what it would have been like to have a Dante in her corner when she'd been young, looking out for her, watching her back. Would she have slept better at night knowing he existed? He'd almost called her his sister. Would his friendship, his brotherly aura have somehow made everything else easier?

She truly didn't know. Finding herself suddenly surrounded by people who inspired such thoughts in her, who made her wonder about the what-ifs, Morana both cherished and feared it, like a little colt taking its tentative steps for the first time on shaking legs.

And the fact that these two were now in her corner because of the man they were loyal to wasn't lost on her, even though his motives were still lost to her.

He wanted her alive. He wanted her with him. He wanted her. Period. But beyond that? Could twenty years of intense hatred, twenty years of focus on one singular reason of survival, twenty years of telling himself "one day", really be wiped away in a few days? She didn't believe so. No matter how strong he was, how stubborn, how wilful, she did not think it was possible.

And yet, there she sat, alive. Contrary to her thoughts, he had made a choice last night, a choice antithetical to the last twenty years of his life. There she sat, after being brought back from the edge by him, twice. There she sat, after eating a bar of chocolate he'd silently given her after her panic attack. He watched her like a hawk, claimed her flesh for his own—even with the smallest gestures—and yet he kept a chunk of himself aloof from her, while she kept exposing vulnerability after vulnerability.

Morana truly did not understand him in that moment.

But, to be honest, she doubted he understood himself in that moment.

Taking a deep breath, she strengthened her resolve, promising herself to play it by the ear and trust her instincts. No amount of planning would work with a man as unpredictable as he was. What she'd told Dante had been true. Her demons danced with his. She'd let his lead and follow accordingly.

Blowing out a breath, she unlocked her phone and started checking on her ongoing programs, immersing herself in the place that had always brought her peace, always made sense when the rest of the crazy world didn't—her codes.

Hours flew by, both Dante and she immersed in their works, changing positions, eating snacks, drinking water or whiskey, stretching, and enjoying the joys of being on a private jet.

After a while, when she changed her position and curled her legs under her the other way, Dante's voice interrupted her.

"Before I forget," he said, making her glance up at him. "I need to warn you about some stuff that I'm pretty sure Tristan is not going to think to mention."

Morana put her phone down, her curiosity piqued. "Do tell," she muttered, locking her phone, focusing on the man before her.

He scratched the side of his neck absently and started speaking. "About Tenebrae . . . well, we have a big property by the lake—"

Morana remembered the beast of the property but she hadn't seen the lake the last time she'd been there, distracted by the potential murder she'd been trying to commit. God, it felt like a lifetime ago.

"—it's almost like a compound of sorts," she brought her attention back to Dante as he went on. "There are a total of five wings on the property, including the main house, all unconnected from each other. The only way to get from one to the next is by going through the grounds, and the entire compound is on one of the hills outside the main city."

Morana leaned forward, completely fascinated, trying to picture it all in her head.

"One of the wings is where all the staff lives with their families—the housekeeper and her assistants, the gardeners, as such." Amara's family. "It's a huge one."

Morana indicated for him to go on when he paused.

He leaned forward, his elbows resting on his knees.

"The second wing is the training center."

Morana remembered what Amara had told her about the young boy secluded in the training area, kept away from everyone else. Bile rose in her throat just at the thought of the way he had been alienated and she pushed it down, gritting her teeth.

Dante's somber voice broke through her thoughts. "You are never, under no circumstances, to enter that wing. Nobody who's not a trainer or a trainee is allowed there. You never, ever go there. Not by mistake, not by accident. Is that clear?"

The severity in his voice was effective – it made a knot in her stomach, delivering exactly how serious this was. She nodded her understanding.

"Good," he continued, satisfied. "The other two wings are much smaller in comparison and a little farther from the main house. The third one is mine."

Morana raised her eyebrows. "Yours alone?"

A lopsided smile curled his mouth. "Being the oldest son has its perks."

Morana shook her head. Men.

His face grew serious again. "I have my staff in that wing. My cousins visit sometimes, and you'd be more than welcome to stay there if you like. It has its own security detail as well."

Morana nodded her thanks, touched by the genuine offer, soaking in all the information. "And the fourth wing?"

"Is Tristan's."

Of course, it was.

Dante went on, unperturbed. "His wing is the smallest, area wise. It's a cottage, to be honest. It is also the farthest from the main house and the other wings, right by the lake. He lives there alone."

Alone.

Like an outcast.

Morana felt her heart clench at the thought of this, at his reality, as the enormity of his life day after day dawned upon her. He'd lived on the compound but the periphery. He'd lived with people but as a pariah. They hadn't accepted him and they hadn't let him go.

Hands fisting on her thighs, Morana blew out a breath through clenched teeth at the fury she could feel invading her bones. Another monster rose inside her – a monster she was familiar with, a monster that had made her kill in cold blood to exact her revenge.

She wanted to destroy, to decimate.

The depth of her own emotions staggered her.

Inhaling deeply, she tried to get it under control.

"Go on," she urged Dante, needing to know more.

Dante cracked his neck, stretching his legs, his gargantuan body seeming to take up the entire space. "The main house is where my father lives with his siblings and their spouses."

Morana frowned. "And what about the other sentinels or whatever you guys call them?"

"They all have houses outside the compound but right near the edges. Why exactly do you think Tristan is considered such an anomaly?" Dante prodded her to think.

"Because he's the only outsider in the Outfit to live with the high family," Morana murmured, catching on quickly.

Dante nodded. "Exactly. It's made him a target for many people on the outside looking in, men who've been in the business longer than he's been born but never given the privilege of living with the family."

Morana shook her head, confused. "But why does your father even keep him there? Why not let him live outside like the others?"

Dante chuckled darkly, the sound icy. "My father," he sneered the word, leaving no doubt in her mind as to his own feelings for the man, "prizes one thing above all else—control. Control over his empire, control over his puppets, control over his family. And you know the one person he's never been able to control?"

'You try to leash me, I'll fucking strangle you with it.'

Amara's words of a fourteen-year-old boy came back to her.

"Tristan Caine," she whispered, stumped all over again by the sheer brazenness of him.

Dante's lips twisted. "Tristan Caine."

Morana could hear the same awe she felt in Dante's voice, the fact that a fourteen-year-old boy had told that boss of an entire mob that he wouldn't yield . . .

"I've seen men, grown men, lick my father's boot to remain in his favor, Morana. By the time I was eighteen, I thought there was not a single soul on this earth who could stand up to him. And then Tristan happened."

His eyes closed as he inhaled deeply, evidently remembering. "That's the reason I started sticking with him in the first place – he was fearless. He truly didn't give a fuck at what my father did. In fact, the first common ground we both found was pissing the old man off."

Morana slumped back in the chair, her chest filling with something. "And your father keeps him on the compound because . . .?"

"Because though he would never admit it, my father fears Tristan," Dante stated, a smidgen of respect in his voice.

Lorenzo Maroni. Feared. Tristan Caine?

What the what?

Her thoughts were evident on her face because Dante explained quietly.

"He fears Tristan because Tristan is a wild card. He does what he does, even living under the great Lorenzo Maroni's eye. Every time Tristan disregards my father, it's a very public slap on his face. And he fears what Tristan would do if he left his watch. He's already an unknown. My father fears he'd become truly rogue if he left and took away what he prizes most."

"His power," Morana completed, pieces falling into place. "Wait, so he doesn't want him to become the heir?"

"Fuck, no!" Dante responded vehemently. "That's a rumor started by people on the outside who think Tristan lives on the inside because he's being groomed to take over. My father entertained the rumor only to save his face. Because refuting it meant admitting to the truth, which would make him look weak."

Oh boy.

She had to ask. "Why not just kill him, if he's so much trouble?" The thought left her bitter.

Dante shrugged. "Pride. Power. Who knows? Because Tristan is his most valuable asset? Because it would be admitting defeat if he couldn't control him alive? I don't know."

God.

"Morana," Dante paused for a beat. "For years my father has tried to break Tristan, to get even some semblance of control over him. Torture, blackmail, you name it, he's done it. But it's never worked. No matter what he subjected Tristan to, it always hit a wall."

Her heart ached even as the rage filled her, against a man she'd not even met.

"My father," Dante continued, "is going to hate you. And use you."

Morana swallowed, a part of her afraid, another part daring the evil man to even try.

"I don't have any control over him," she reminded Dante, her fingers balling into fists.

Dante agreed. "You know that. Tristan knows that. But to anyone standing on the outside? You don't have control, Morana. You have something better."

"What?" Morana whispered.

"Influence," Dante stated. "To anyone who's looking at you two, it will be apparent you influence him. Which means it's his choice. That, Morana, is going to make my father very, very upset. Because after everything he thinks he's done, Tristan chose to let a girl influence him—that too the daughter of Vitalio. They have history."

Uh oh.

"You need to watch your back with him at all times," Dante

cautioned, the weight in his voice making her breath hitch. "He will try to manipulate you, use you to get to Tristan. I don't know how but you need to be very, very careful. It will not be easy."

Morana remained silent, swallowing down the bout of nerves trying to attack her.

"And not because he wants Tristan to be the heir. Oh no, that pleasure will be all mine," Dante sighed, rubbing a hand over his face, sarcasm heavy in his tone.

Morana took in his weariness, her heart squeezing in sympathy. "What did you want to be?" the question slipped out of her before she could stop herself.

She waited as Dante looked up at her, his tie loose around his neck, hair disheveled.

He laughed, the sound not reaching his dark eyes. "Truly?"

Morana nodded, curious.

"A sculptor."

Morana blinked in surprise at the answer. Dante saw and smiled, a genuine smile.

"My mother had been a painter," he explained, his voice soft, eyes lost in memory. "One of the fondest memories of my childhood is of sculpting with clay while she painted in the same room. She always used to hum this melody and my hands . . ."

He let his words trail off, shaking himself out of the memory, his eyes hardening again as he breathed deeply.

Morana noted his use of past tense.

Her heart clenched, the urge to take his hand and give it a squeeze acute. But she refrained, knowing somehow that he wouldn't appreciate it.

"As I told you once, Morana," he spoke quietly, "you're lucky to be following your dream."

She was.

Sitting there in front of Dante, while discussing the history of a man more damaged than she'd even imagined, thinking of the friend she'd left behind—the girl who'd been abducted and tortured for days for information, one who still carried the mar of that around her throat, thinking of the lost girls from years ago, of Luna Caine—of where she could be, how she could be if she was even alive—Morana felt truly lucky to be just breathing. Her past was filled only with loneliness and not true horrors, not deep scars, not lifeless agony.

"Do you want a hug?" that voice of whiskey and sin penetrated the space around them.

Morana's gaze flew to Tristan Caine standing beside the door, not a crease on the fabric of his clothes, nothing to indicate he'd been asleep, his face a stoic mask, which did not fit with his words. Surprise filled her at the fact that she'd missed him entering the area. Usually, she never did, her body aware of him in ways she couldn't hope to understand.

She saw Dante's lips curl into a smile. "Fuck off, asshole."

God, they were such *guys*.

There was something incredibly normal about that.

Dante turned to her as the other man pranced to the bar, getting himself a glass of whiskey on the rocks, his blue shirt hugging the muscles on his torso as he moved about, before leaning against the wall and facing them.

"Anyhow," Dante began, drawing Morana's attention again. "Just remember one thing—you'll be Lorenzo Maroni's guest. That means a lot of pretending."

Morana nodded. "I'm good at pretending."

She saw Tristan Caine raise a single brow in the periphery but ignored him.

Dante turned around to pin the other man with his gaze. "All done?"

Tristan Caine gave a curt nod as the captain's voice filled the cabin, informing them to put on their seat belts, as they would be landing soon.

Heart suddenly racing, Morana turned in the seat and hooked on the belt, aware of Tristan Caine taking the seat beside hers, not touching her anywhere but his presence searing her.

Closing her eyes, she tilted her head back and focused on her breathing.

The next hour seemed to fly by.

It all seemed surreal—them landing safely, the wind whipping her hair around in her ponytail as she exited the plane, her thanking the crew, then getting into a town car that waited for them near the strip along with two other cars.

Morana took it all in—the men, the bulge of the guns under their jackets, the beautiful sunshine, the wind, everything as she looked out the backseat of the car to the passing city, absorbing it in a way she hadn't before.

She wondered through it all if he had a bike here as well. If he had a sacred space in his bedroom. If his territory was a reflection of him.

She wondered where she would be staying—at the main house as Maroni's guest or with him.

She wondered about a lot many things as everything seemed to happen in fast forward.

And then the cars stopped.

Morana peeked out from behind the glass, her heart drumming painfully in her chest as she saw the huge wrought iron gate that manned the beginning of the property, lush green grass rolling out far into the edge of a forested area. That beast of an almost—castle loomed farther up ahead the drive

almost ominously, another building farther behind that to the left but nothing else to be seen from this vantage.

The iron gates opened smoothly, four armed men standing near the control room.

Her nerves were shot.

The car went in motion again, moving forward, entering the premises.

Morana felt her heart thundering in her chest as she gazed upon that beast of a house, where everything had been put in motion twenty years ago, where everything had changed course a few weeks ago.

That house had changed her life twice.

And the magnitude of that reality settled upon her like a heavy cloud.

The car slithered closer and closer to the beast.

And then, finally, it came to a stop.

Her heart stopped.

Her eyes locked with his in the rear-view mirror, her inhale stuck in her throat.

"Breathe," he mouthed.

Morana breathed.

They had arrived.

CHAPTER 4

MEET

She was alone.

Sitting in the monstrous living room inside the mansion, Morana was still reeling over how easy it had been to get inside. The sun had been bright when they had emerged from the car. There had been guards all around but no one had reacted to seeing her with the two men. That had surprised her. She had expected to be greeted at the large doors by Maroni and his goons. She had expected guns being pointed and arguments being raised. She had half-expected being told to get lost or to die. What she had not expected was to get out of the car with Dante and Tristan Caine, have the guards greet them with nods of respect, and simply stroll inside the house. What she hadn't expected furthermore was to be escorted by Dante into the living room, have him give her a reassuring nod, and then for both men to disappear. Not that she wanted to be in their company the entire time. She just hadn't anticipated being on her own in the den of the enemy right in the first hour.

It had been twenty minutes since she'd seen the men walk deeper into the house to meet Maroni, she presumed. In those twenty minutes, Morana had taken stock of the room—and there was a lot to take stock of. Lush Persian rugs scattered around the monstrous space that was decorated with polished mahogany wood furniture and plush cushions. The walls reflected the same rock-cut exterior of the outside of the house. The room was a cross between rustic and royal—gray rocks and ornate gold, wood, and silk somehow coming together in a way that somehow pleased the senses while sending a chill down her spine. Maroni's decorator had hit the target for the guests—get them comfortable but not enough to let them forget where they were.

She had also taken note of the cameras mounted at the corner of the ceiling, pointed right at her. Whoever was on the other side definitely got a good look at her leg when she had taken out her knives from her bag and strapped them to her thigh. They were the same knives she had stupidly tried to kill Tristan Caine with—the knives that had been collecting dust in her bag since the night she had gone back to his penthouse. She had never, for some reason, felt the need to bring them out there. That in itself was confounding considering she'd slept with weapons under her pillow every single night under her father's roof for years. Not once in the penthouse though, not even that first night, not on any night since then.

The realization stunned her. Sitting in this living room, on edge being surrounded by unknown danger, she realized just how safe she had begun to feel in the penthouse now that it was gone. She had let her guards down, a little bit at a time when she thought no one was looking. On paper, she should be shaken for finding safety in the territory of a man who had hated her for twenty years. But paper castles were burned in her world every day. Since the night in the cemetery, she had stopped fighting what she felt and accepted it completely. Her acceptance was going to pave their way. They had enough blockages as it was.

The cool blade pressed against her skin in a way that reassured her. She wondered what it said about her, the fact that she found the lethal weapon comforting. Could that be why Tristan Caine somehow comforted her too? She knew herself enough to admit that. His presence, hell the mere knowledge of his existence, gave her more comfort than anything in her life had.

Her stomach grumbled slightly, breaking her musings. And then she realized something else—no one had come to serve her. From what she knew of the Maroni household, they had an abundance of staff and one of their duties was to greet guests. Yet, she'd been sitting there for over twenty minutes and not seen a soul. It was quiet, too quiet.

Heart starting to race, Morana leaned back deeper into the cushions, crossing one leg over the other. It pressed the blade against her thigh as she tried to appear relaxed for the sake of the cameras. A few days ago, she would have entertained the thought that this was a trap, that the Outfit men had suckered her into believing them and brought her here for whatever nefarious reasons. Now, even as the thought briefly flickered through her mind, she discarded it. With everything they had been through, everything that was still unknown, every single reaction she had seen in the two men, she knew they hadn't tricked her.

She did have questions though. From everything Dante had told her on the plane, she had no idea how Lorenzo Maroni would respond to her presence. Moreover, she had no clue as to how Tristan Caine would respond to Maroni's response to her presence. The man was a ticking bomb and only he knew when he would explode from what Dante had told her. She was curious to see them interact, to see for herself the infamous boss of the Outfit and his rumored protegee come face to face. She also wondered if there were people on the compound who cared for him, perhaps without his knowledge, like Dante and Amara did. But most importantly, she was curious about where she would be staying. She knew where she wanted to stay but two things were blocking that—one, it was Tristan Caine's home, his actual home, and he had to invite her; two, Maroni had to be okay with it because for all intents and purposes, she was his guest and she was the daughter of the Shadow Port boss.

The sound of high heels clicking on the marble floors had her eyes going to the doorway. A stunning dark-haired woman came into vision, her tan silk blouse flowing against her curves, tucked into dark straight pants that fell straight to the floor, her long tresses pulled back into a high ponytail. Her beautiful attire made Morana conscious of her simple black and white skirt, matching top and flats, all that she had borrowed from Amara. She needed to go shopping as soon as possible, especially if there were more gorgeous women prancing around the place.

What surprised Morana though was the small gun holstered to her side, in clear view. The woman stopped as her bright green eyes came to Morana, a slight frown between her brows. "Can I help you?" the woman asked, her voice strong but quiet.

Morana wondered how to respond as she stood up. She simply decided on a polite, "No, thank you."

The woman's frown deepened. "Who are you waiting to see?"

Morana remained quiet. The woman took a step inside the room. Sunlight hit her olive skin, making it glisten as she tilted her head to the side. "Have we met before?"

Morana blinked in confusion before realizing the other woman might have seen pictures of her. "I don't believe so."

The woman studied her in a manner that should have been rude but was simply curious. And then her eyes flared with recognition. "Morana Vitalio."

Morana stayed still, her heart starting to pound. She was the enemy's daughter and she was standing alone in the house of Lorenzo Maroni. How could she explain that if the situation worsened? To her surprise, the woman smiled slightly, walking deeper into the room, her arm extended. "I'm Nerea, Amara's half-sister."

Surprised but still cautious, Morana took a step forward and held the woman's hand in hers, giving it a firm shake. Up close, she could see Nerea was at least a decade older than her, fine lines, light freckles, and experience clear on her make-up free face.

"Pleasure to meet you," Morana said, keeping it polite, still unsure of how to read her.

Nerea gave a small smile, as though comprehending her uncertainty. "Amara mentioned that you were coming."

It seemed like she had more to thank Amara for. Nerea glanced down at the sleek watch on her wrist. "I have to rush right now but if you need anything, you can come to me any time. Any friend of Amara's is a friend of mine. She doesn't have many in the first place."

"Thank you," Morana said, grateful but still unsure.

Nerea gave her a warm smile. "See you later."

She walked out of the room on those high heels just as quickly as she'd come in. How was Amara's half-sister a part of the mob if Amara was shunned and her mother a housekeeper? Minutes later, just as Morana was thinking upon that, a group of strange men wearing dark suits entered the room. Some looked at her curiously, some leered, some entirely ignored her. They all went to the back of the room and took their positions against the wall.

Morana perused them all. They were eight in total, all of them in dark suits and matching shirts and ties, guns at their hips. They were all middle-aged, some tall, some stocky. One of them though, one with the leery eyes that creeped her out, was built like a heavy-weight wrestler. His huge frame matched Dante's height with added bulk. The other man that stood out to her was the one who was ignoring her the hardest. He appeared to be the youngest in the lot. He looked straight ahead, his hands folded together at the front. What set the hair on the back of her neck buzzing though was the nasty scar going down the side of his face, from the corner of his left eye right down to his neck, disappearing inside his shirt. It looked like his flesh had been gouged out in slashes. His eyes were vacant.

"Well, well, well," a woman's voice interrupted her perusal and had her focusing back at the door at the woman standing there. If Nerea had been stunning, this woman was *stunning*. Her dark red hair falling around her in gentle waves, a gorgeous navy dress (that Morana would have loved to have) falling to her knees. She had bright eyes that were a cross between green and gold, appearing liquid. Eyes that were examining Morana with a surprising amount of hostility.

Morana stayed silent and kept her expression blank.

The woman came forward, her eyes hardening, and spoke low enough that only she could hear. "I hear you've been creating quite the stir for my man, Miss Vitalio. Do you have any idea what you've put in motion?"

Morana tilted her head even as her stomach clenched. Her man? Dante or Tristan Caine?

And that was when Lorenzo Maroni entered the room.

He was a distinguished-looking man, no doubt about that. He seemed to be aging gracefully, his salt-and-pepper hair cut stylishly, his trimmed beard holding certain gravity up close that she had not expected. The lines on his face were stark, a testament to a hard life, and his dark eyes were impassive. Those eyes came to the woman in front of her, the woman who had somehow shaken her steadiness.

"Go to the back, Chiara," Maroni ordered, his voice gravelly.

Chiara? Chiara Mancini? The same Chiara Mancini who had been calling Tristan Caine the other night? Was he her man? Had she been completely wrong and Tristan Caine had a woman? This woman?

Her stomach bottomed out, a flare of anger pooling in her chest. The hostility wasn't one-sided anymore.

Chiara gave her a small sneer, her stunning face contorting into something not beautiful. Though Morana simply raised an eyebrow outwardly, inside she felt worse. She had assumed just because he seemed like a man who wouldn't two-time that he wasn't. But this was the mob. Men cheated and were cheated on here even with the knowledge of their matrimony. The thought of him being someone else's while he fucked her made her angry. But the thought, the mere thought of him being someone else's while he kissed her the way he had, while he had taken her mouth and shared something real with her *hurt*. God, she'd been so sure of him. Had she been wrong?

As though conjured from her thoughts, Tristan Caine strode slowly, almost lazily, at the back, coming to a stop at the entryway. Those magnificent blue eyes of his came to her, doing a quick check, not missing her hands that had instinctively gone to the weapons against her thighs. His lips twitched, just barely, just enough to have a family of butterflies start samba in her belly at the most inappropriate time. He leaned against the doorjamb, blocking the doorway, hands in his pockets, that shirt stretched taut across his chest, one ankle crossed over the other.

And that was when he locked eyes with hers.

Whatever he saw there had him go still. She witnessed every muscle in his body locked as his gaze penetrated hers with a singular focus, trying to read whatever he was seeing there. Morana deliberately looked away towards Chiara as the woman strolled up to him with a saccharine smile. "Tristan."

He didn't reply. She tried to put her hands on him; he took a hold of her wrists and set her back, his eyes entirely on Morana the entire time. And then he shook his head at Morana, just once, dispelling whatever doubts had started to creep in. She needed to trust him. They had come this far on a certain honesty. She had to trust that. Especially here more than ever.

Turning away, she saw Lorenzo Maroni take a seat on the large armchair. The sun glinted off his hair and crisp suit. His impassive eyes held a flicker of interest though when they finally came to her.

With his men in a row behind him as he sat in that large chair, the scene looked intimidating as hell as she stood across from them. Good thing she had practice with her father. She knew how to swim with sharks without bleeding, and Lorenzo Maroni was a shark on top of the food chain.

She kept her expression clean and her body relaxed, acutely aware of all the eyes watching her, especially the woman at the back who had not left the room. If looks could kill, Morana would've been dead ten times over. Her pulse raced as she waited for a cue from the Bloodhound, her palms sweating, the cool blades that had been a comfort now feeling sharp against her skin.

Someone came to stand beside her. She didn't turn to look but the familiar scent of cologne told her it was Dante. That relaxed her a bit more for some reason.

"Father," Morana heard Dante's cool voice from beside her. "Allow me to introduce Morana Vitalio. Morana, Lorenzo Maroni."

Once done speaking, Dante remained standing exactly where he was beside her, surprising her yet again. The stance wasn't lost on her and it certainly wasn't lost on Maroni. His eyes narrowed slightly at his son's blatant body language, before coming to her.

"Morana," the man spoke in that same gravel voice, raising the hair on her arms. "You have grown up beautifully. I saw you once when you were younger about . . ."

"Twenty years ago," Morana finished. His eyes sharpened on her.

"Dante and Tristan informed me you were staying here as our guest for some time. Is that correct?"

"Yes," Morana nodded. "If you're willing to extend your hospitality to me, of course," she added with a sweet smile that fooled no one.

Maroni saw through it. "Very well. You can understand how that would put me in an odd situation, yes?"

"Of course," she acknowledged.

"As I said, father," Dante interrupted. "She's my guest. I have invited her as a friend and I am willing to extend all hospitality to her."

Lorenzo Maroni glanced at his son. "Even without my consent?"

Dante remained silent for a few beats. "Yes."

It seemed as though Amara's words had gotten to him. Morana wished the other woman could have seen this moment. She stayed silent.

Maroni's gaze flickered to where Tristan Caine was leaning against the threshold. "And you will support that I presume?"

There was no verbal response but something if the tightening of Maroni's lips was anything to go by. In a beat, those lips eased. "Very well. Were you checked for weapons before you entered the compound?" he asked her.

She shook her head, her heart starting to pound relentlessly as the knives strapped to her thigh became heavier. Maroni smiled, his lips curling. He was pleased, the bastard. Without a word, he raised his arm, his elbow on the seat, and gestured at his men. The wrestler in the suit stepped up.

"Check her," Maroni ordered.

Morana's pulse started to rattle. The wrestler moved towards her, his eyes gleaming, his lips twisted in a slight grin.

"Seriously, father?" Dante snorted, his voice tight. "Kids walk around here with weapons, for god's sake."

"They are not the spawn of Gabriel Vitalio now, are they?" Maroni replied, his unwavering gaze on her. "I hope you don't mind, dear Morana. Until I can trust you to be on the compound with my family, you are not to be armed."

That wouldn't do. *Absolutely not.*

The wrestler guy stopped in front of her, extending his large hand straight towards her breast. Morana braced herself, gritting her teeth, years of being touched at her father's table giving her the strength not to slit the man's throat and make him choke on his own tongue. He watched her with those creepy eyes, looking far too excited for a simple body search. His hand was almost on her when, out of nowhere, fingers enclosed around his wrist.

Even though Morana knew the other hand like the back of her own, she turned her neck. Her eyes followed the strong grip, the sinews on his forearms, the hint of his tattoo, the veins and the roped muscles, right up to his face. Tristan Caine's eyes were steady and grip firm on wrestler guy who glared back at him, animosity pouring off him in waves. Morana frowned, sensing some old history between the two.

The wrestler guy pulled on his arm; Tristan Caine's grip flexed but didn't loosen, the strength of it astounding her. It was a big man he was holding, a big man who seemed to be exerting considerable effort to get loose.

"Touch her without permission again," Tristan Caine stated so quietly the impact hit her harder, that voice of whiskey and sin sending shivers of a completely different kind over her spine, "and I will break you."

The room went utterly silent. Morana looked at the other goons to see most of them with their hands on their guns, then at Maroni who was watching Tristan Caine with rapt attention.

"Interesting," he murmured, a smile coming to his face she did not like one bit.

Tristan Caine let the wrestler guy go and turned to face her, giving Maroni and his goons his back in a move that showed both his complete confidence in their inability to harm him and his trust in Dante to watch his back. This was unexpected. She hadn't thought he would come anywhere near her where Maroni could watch, for obvious reasons. That he was not only close but was almost flaunting it in the older man's face caught her unaware.

Morana swallowed, tilting her head back, caught by those blue, blue eyes. He raised his hands in silent question and she nodded, granting him permission. Without removing his eyes from hers, he settled his hands on her shoulders, touching her for the first time. Her chest heaved with an inhale. He kept his touch light as he slid his hand around to her back, running it down her spine. Her body arched, breasts brushing against his torso before she could control the reaction, aware of the many eyes on them.

Once done with her torso, he went down on one knee. Biting the inside of her cheek, she looked down. His large hands traced over her hips, making her heart hammer everywhere in her body. His hands went down and touched her ankle under the hem of her long skirt. Her breath hitched as she fisted her hands to keep them from touching his scruff, her mouth tingling with the remembered sensation of it burning her skin as he kissed her. She saw the responding heat in his eyes as his hands traveled up her calves, his rough fingers caressing her skin for the first time in a room full of mobsters. But it fit given their first time had been in a mob restaurant with mobsters outside the door.

His hands paused on her knee, his eyes molten. She took a deep breath in. He knew exactly where her knives were, had known since he had entered the room. He could have checked her from over her skirt. Yet, he had gotten on a knee and placed his hands directly on her skin without once raising the hem of her skirt from the floor. It wasn't lost on her what he was doing. It was a statement to all the men in the room, to the woman who had tried to claim him, and to Morana herself. It was a statement loud and clear. She was his.

Her chest tight, she watched him, his eyes, aware of every man in the room but completely unaware of any other man, feeling his hand slowly drift up to the inside of her thighs in a move so intimate like they had done it a thousand times before. She felt his hands find her blades and felt him remove them with adept skill, the same knife she had held to his back in this very house that first night.

The air between them thickened. Her core pulsed.

An inch higher and he would feel how wet she was, right in the middle of this room, just for him. He could do it too. No one would see or notice.

Her thighs started to tremble even as she tried to keep her face blank, the ache in her belly growing heavier, clawing lower and lower towards his hands. She could feel her muscles naturally straining towards those fingers, her walls clenching with the need to be filled, to be filled by him. He had never touched her there, not with that gentleness with which he was holding her flesh now. She craved it. She craved those fingers inside her, moving as his lips kissed her neck and his scent filled her nose and his breaths deepened in her ears. She wanted her senses to be filled by him. She ached for it.

And he read all that in her eyes, saw the naked desire painting her eyes. His fingers tightened infinitesimally on her skin. Just a few inches. Just a little.

Her chest heaved. His hand flexed.

She shivered. His jaw tightened.

Swiftly, he got up, the knives in his hands, and turned to face the room, leaving tremors in her body. Besides Dante, everyone was staring. Morana breathed deeply to keep the flush from her cheeks. Tristan Caine took his position beside her, pocketing her blades and pointing his even stare at Maroni.

"I do believe I will enjoy having Morana for a guest, Tristan," Maroni said with the smile that quickly simmered her heat down. Dante had been right. She would have to be careful, very careful with this man. Tristan Caine did not react. Not outwardly at least. She knew enough about the man to discern there was a lot more going on inside than anyone realized.

"How did you meet my son and Tristan, Morana?" Maroni demanded rather than asked. "Tell me, I am curious."

Morana tamped down her emotions and imitated Maroni's smile. "It's a long story."

Maroni's lips pursed. Then, he turned to one of the goons. "Have Antria prepare the guest room."

"No need," Tristan Caine spoke for the first time in a while. "She stays with me."

Maroni shook his head, crossing one leg over the other, settling in. "No, she doesn't."

Tristan Caine didn't say a word, just stared the man down. Maroni stared back. Now she knew what Dante had been talking about.

"Tristan, honey," Chiara spoke up from the back, making Morana's jaw clench at the sudden need to do something violent. "Until Lorenzo has spoken to the right people, he cannot allow her to live that far off the main compound. She has to earn his trust. Till then, she will be a welcome guest at the main house, won't she, Lorenzo?"

"Of course," Maroni agreed, never taking his eyes off the younger man.

Morana looked up at Tristan Caine to see his face completely void of any tell—no clenching of the jaw, no expression in his eyes, no tic in his cheek. Nothing. Seeing him like that suddenly made her realize she hadn't been the only one letting her guards down. He did that too, only when she was watching or with Dante and Amara.

"She stays with me," he stated again.

"Not possible," Maroni refuted immediately.

Just as he opened his mouth to speak, Dante took over. "If she stays at the main house, you give your word no harm would come to her?"

Tristan Caine cut a sharp look at Dante; Dante just shook his head, silent communication between the two men.

Maroni watched the interaction with interest. "As long as she doesn't harm anyone."

Even though part of her was getting furious about being talked about like she wasn't there, she tamped it down, knowing this wasn't the time or the place.

"I'll stay at the main house," she spoke before the situation could spiral out of control, which it was close to doing because she knew the stubborn men won't relent. She was his bone and he had slapped that in Maroni's face; Maroni wanted to take the bone away to make him pay. It didn't take a genius to figure that one. They needed to ride it out.

"Wonderful," Maroni smiled. "Vin," he pointed to the scarred man with the empty eyes, "will escort you to your room. You can meet everyone tonight at dinner."

Morana nodded politely. "Thank you."

Vin headed to the door on silent feet. Taking that as her cue, she turned to the two men—Dante giving her a reassuring look, Tristan Caine still stoic—and gave them a little nod. Wanting to quickly get away from the escalating tension in the room, she hurried to where

Vin was standing. As soon as she was a few steps away, he started to walk again, leading them out the entryway and up the stairs.

Morana looked around the impressive staircase that she hadn't had the chance to admire the first time around. The chandelier glimmered in the sunlight pouring in from the large windows, sparkles dancing over it. The colored reflections danced around the floor, creating an ethereal atmosphere. She could almost forget for a second where she was. Large paintings of vistas were arranged artfully along the walls of the staircase. She examined them all, following the silent man on two floors. On the second floor landing, Vin turned right down a corridor.

"Are there others on this floor?" she asked, initiating conversation and breaking silence.

"No," he responded, his tone curt.

"So, what's on this floor?"

"Guest rooms."

Okay. "Are there other guests at the moment?"

"Some."

Morana sighed. The man was a boatload of information. Following him down the corridor and past several doors, she observed the way he was walking, a slight limp in his left step and wondered what had happened to him. Before she could think more, they came to a stop on the third door that he opened for her. She was about to enter when he pushed his hand in front of her, stopping her.

She looked up at him, suddenly aware that she was unarmed with a strange man on a floor where no one would hear her scream. Muscles tensing, she took a step back as he bent down and quickly removed a small knife from his sock. Without a word, he stood up and held the knife out to her.

Morana looked his scarred left hand and the knife that sat on it, stunned.

Hesitant, not understanding what and why he was doing, she took the knife. "Why?"

The man whispered. "You're with vultures now. They feed off the dead."

A shiver went down her spine, her grip tightening on the knife.

Vin pulled his hand away and gestured for her to enter. "They will be activating the ears in this room soon. Stay sharp."

With that piece of information, he turned on his heel and walked away with that limp, leaving Morana reeling from the entire interaction. Nevertheless, she felt better knowing she had some sort of a weapon. Closing the door behind her, she looked around the spacious room, checking the walls and ceiling for cameras. She couldn't see any but she was certain there were some.

The door locked, she walked deeper in the opulent room done in cream and blues. A queen-sized bed took the center space, a small sitting area across it, a dresser and a chest of drawers in oak wood gracing the other corner of the room. Large windows with a comfortable seat looked out into the sprawling green land behind the mansion. She looked out, seeing the treeline behind which she knew the other wings were, spotting the blue waters of the lake off at the distance.

Had she just exchanged one cage for another? Granted, this one looked less sterile but there was, under a roof she did not feel safe in, planning to sleep with a knife under her pillow at night and keeping the doors locked. There she was, ready to go to dinner that night with a table full of strangers again. There she was, all alone, again.

The vibration of her phone broke through her thoughts. She took the phone out of her bag and opened the new message.

Tristan: *Were you wet?*

Morana looked at the grounds, a small smile forming on her lips.

Morana: *You'll never find out.*

Tristan: *Yes, I will.*

She snorted.

Morana: *I can see the lake from my window.*

Tristan: *I can see your window from mine.*

Heart suddenly beating harder, Morana looked out the window, trying to see where his place was. She saw several buildings spread out behind the treeline and then she remembered what Dante had told her.

"His wing is the smallest, area wise. It is also the farthest from the main house and the other wings. He lives there alone."

Heart in her throat, Morana squinted and tried to find the one building that stood away from the others. And she found it. Right by the lake. Where the other wings were spread out over the west side of the compound, that one lone building stood alone in the east, surrounded by green on one side and water on the other. Half-wild, half-tamed. Just like the man. She couldn't see anything inside because of the distance but just knowing he could see her, that he was still watching her despite Maroni's effort to take her away filled her with a warmth she was unfamiliar with.

He could see her.

Morana realized, watching that little building in the distance, that she'd been wrong.

She wasn't alone.

Not anymore.

CHAPTER 5

OWN

It was almost time for dinner.

A lady in her mid-forties, clearly a member of the staff, had come to the room almost an hour ago with a dress draped on her arm. She hadn't spoken a word, simply handed the dress to Morana when she opened the door and had gone on her way. Baffling as that had been, Morana was more curious as to why Maroni would have sent her a dress and if she should wear it. Sadly, she didn't really have an option. She hadn't packed her own wardrobe when she left her house and all she had on her was borrowed stuff from Amara's closet that was more casual than the dinner demanded.

Staring at the dress—a long, silky number in forest green with full sleeves, a modest neckline and simple back, and a scandalous slit on one side right to her upper thigh—Morana shook her head and took off her bathrobe, freshly showered and clean, and donned the dress. It fit like a glove and that was disturbing, especially because Maroni had sent it to her. She just knew it. The fact that he had stared at her long enough to get a measure of her sizes made the hair on the back of her neck rise and not in a good way. Fighting off a shudder, Morana smoothed the fabric out and debated whether to strap the knife to herself. While keeping it on her would make her feel safer, she didn't have any other weapon and was she searched again, she would lose it. As much as it pained her, she would have to leave it hidden in the room itself.

Brushing her hair out, she carefully applied concealer to cover up the few bruises left behind from the night in the cemetery. That done, she applied her mascara and painted her lips blood red. She'd made the mistake of being in the mansion unprepared once, she wouldn't do it again. She didn't like the insecurity that bopped its head upon seeing the beautiful women, especially when one of them had her sights on her man.

Her man?

The hand holding the lipstick stopped suddenly, hovering in the air as she stared at herself in the mirror, her heart pounding hard.

Her man.

Where the hell did that even come from?

They did not have that kind of a relationship and she doubted they ever would. Even though she had been his long before she even knew him. Even though he had all but claimed her in small, subtle ways over the two weeks. Even though he had touched her for the first time as a mark of her belonging to him (as archaic as that sounded). Her eyes fluttered shut, remembering the sensation of his rough, calloused fingers going up her thighs. Exhale. Her skin pebbled, a delicious shiver coursing down her spine. She was his. By now, probably everyone in the mob knew. She knew. But was he her man?

She inhaled again and got back to her lips, carefully scrutinizing her own face. She was pretty enough, definitely. Though not as visually stunning as Chiara Mancini. But did that even matter? It never had, not to her. She had always been comfortable in her skin, mostly because she had loved her intelligence and her repressed wit that had been waiting for the right person to repartee with. Which was also why she didn't think it mattered to him either. She remembered the way he had simply given her that tight head-shake when Chiara had been all over him, and her lips turned up in a smile.

Fuck yes, he was hers. For however long, damaged and asshole-d, and however he was, he was hers. And good luck to anyone who tried to come between that.

Feeling the strength of that acceptance seep into her pores, Morana gave her hair a final brush with her fingers, stepped into her one pair of golden heels, and opened the door, only to come face-to-face with the she-devil. Chiara Mancini.

Interesting.

The other woman, stunning in a red wrap dress that showed her cleavage just the right amount, gave Morana a smile as false as her eyelashes. Morana didn't even bother.

"I hope you're settling in well," Chiara asked, her voice low and soft. Morana could understand why men who didn't look beneath the surface would fall head-over-ass for this woman. Thankfully, she lacked the requisite body parts to be a shallow dick.

"I'm sure you haven't come up here to ask me about how I'm doing, Mrs. Mancini," Morana said in her most dry voice. "Oh, it is Mrs, isn't it?" she blinked innocently, knowing she'd hit the nail on the head when the other woman's face tightened.

"Yes, I'm married to Lorenzo's first cousin," she gritted out quietly. "Not the most ideal marriage. But then, when does the mob listen when a woman accuses her husband of rape?"

She wasn't lying. Morana saw it in her eyes and her heart, as hard as it had been, softened. "I'm sorry." What else could she even say? Some men got the license to be monsters.

Chiara visibly shook off whatever thought had plagued her and focused on Morana again. "I don't want your sympathy. What I want is for you to keep your distance from Dante and Tristan."

Morana tilted her head to the side, hardening herself again, even as the compassion lingered. "And why would I do anything you want?"

Chiara took a step forward, her hand slamming once on the door, her eyes angry at her. "Because they're the good ones and they don't deserve the shit storm you have created, princess. Neither of them. Especially Tristan."

Morana felt her stomach tighten. "What do you know about what he deserves?"

Chiara smiled. "I know he's fucked me on the regular for almost two years and Tristan doesn't do regular."

Fire.

There was no other word for whatever was spreading through her chest, eating away at her insides. She could feel the burn crawl up her neck, over her cheeks and finally mist in her eyes. But she couldn't let it show, couldn't let it affect her. And that hurt. *Really hurt.* Not that he'd slept with this woman but the fact that he'd done it regularly. Because that implied she meant something to him. Emotionally. And that fucking burned.

Years of practice coming in handy, Morana kept her composure, not even allowing her fingers to curl into her palms, and smiled at the other woman. "Fucked. Past tense, Mrs. Mancini. But I'm the present and the foreseeable future."

Chiara's smile faltered. "He will come back to me."

"Maybe," Morana shrugged. And then she leaned in closer. "Or maybe, I will destroy him for anyone else."

Before the other woman could say another thing, Morana took a step outside. "Now, you've done your due diligence and warned me. I've not heeded it. We both know where we stand and we both know neither will nudge. Either way, I'm hungry so excuse me."

Without another word, Morana locked the door behind her and walked away, not looking back at the woman who had poured gasoline over what had only been a small spark. It was a blaze now, a blaze which wanted to destroy. Him. She would destroy him for anyone else.

For the first time in their convoluted relationship, she took out her phone and texted him first.

Morana: *My vagina just became off-limits to you.*

His reply came almost immediately.

Tristan: *?*

Question mark. He'd sent her a damn question mark. She was seething.

Morana: *Not that it matters. Your regular would be more than happy to welcome you in her bed, I'm sure.*

No immediate reply. Of course. Morana walked down the stairs, barely looking at the paintings on the walls, watching her step as that knot of fire coiled tighter in her belly. Her phone vibrated with the incoming message.

Tristan Caine: *Jealous?*

God, he had to be the stupidest man on the face of the earth.

One did not ask a woman who was jealous as hell if she was jealous. Just *no*.

Morana: *I'll ask you the same after I find myself a hot stud from the buffet in this mansion.*

He didn't reply.

Morana shook her head, trying to shake off the weird cloud over her head and get back that happy mojo. It didn't work too well.

She finally came to the ground floor, the landing almost empty except for two staff members doing their chores. Morana ignored them as they ignored her, walking in the direction of the dining area (that she remembered from breaking in a few weeks ago). Her steps were muffled by the thick carpet lining the foyer and the corridor. The lights were perched on both sides of the corridor like fire-torches, adding an ancient aesthetic to the place. In that warm glow, Morana finally entered the dining room and stopped.

It was empty, except for one lady in the housekeeper's uniform positioning cutlery on the table. Morana looked at that table—long, wooden, and able to sit at least thirty people—wondering if this was the same table she'd been put on as a toddler or if it was another table in another room. That part of the story she didn't know about. And if this was indeed the same table in the same room where twenty years ago a young, innocent boy had been scarred for life, Morana wondered what it took out of him to come into this room regularly and eat on the table where his father's blood had splattered.

It was there, standing in that room full of demons, that the full extent of his torture hit Morana over the head, making her stumble. She caught the edge of the window she was standing beside, her heart shattering for him. To have to sit with people who tortured and trained him, to see them laugh and crack jokes, to quietly get sustenance where your life went to hell ... how did someone ever heal from that?

She turned her back on the room and looked out the window, trying to center herself even as she wanted to weep from the pain she felt for him, for her, for them. Were they truly doomed? What was she even trying to do? What was she doing thinking a man that badly damaged could ever heal enough to be with her? They had ended even before they had begun. And that was a depressing, depressing thought. The conflict inside her ensued, one part of her tugging her to the evidence of two weeks, the other part showing her the impact of twenty years.

Letting out a breath, she watched the endless green ground surrounding the house, ending with the shadow of woods. The moon, a beautiful crescent in the dark sky, played hide and seek with the clouds. A few men patrolled the property on foot with weapons while a few others in suits were gathered around a small bonfire, talking.

"Good evening."

Morana turned around to see a handsome older man walk into the room, dressed in a sharp suit like the rest of them.

"Good evening," she replied quietly.

"I'm Leo Mancini," the man said, smiling. Morana looked him up and down, her eyes narrowing.

"Are you the Mancini who likes to rape his wife or is that a poorer relation of yours?"

The man, who had been smiling until that point, lost his manners. Morana braced herself, standing tall, not looking away.

"Be very careful, Ms. Vitalio," he threatened. The tension in the room escalated, broken only with the sound of people coming in. Morana looked away to the entrance, seeing a bunch of strange men and women, adults and teens, enter the room. She only recognized three faces.

Lorenzo Maroni saw her standing near the window and smiled the smile that made ants crawl up her arms. Morana looked away deliberately, to see Dante enter under the arch, wearing a white t-shirt and jeans, a gun tucked in his belt, his hair wet and slicked back from his strong face. It was the first time she was seeing him so casual. He saw her, gave her a small smile which she returned, glad to have a friend in this strange place.

And then Tristan Caine entered, dressed similar to Dante, his t-shirt black and jeans faded, no gun in sight. She didn't know if that was ballsy or stupid or both. Either way, she couldn't help but admire that kind of confidence. Watching the two men in a crowd of people dressed to the nines, Morana didn't know if this was how they always dressed for dinner or if this was a giant "fuck you" to Maroni and his system. Judging by the disapproving look on the man's face, she would place her bets on the latter.

She was aware of the curious gazes on her as she walked to the seat Lorenzo indicated for her to take. The staff was bringing out the food as everyone took their seats in choreography that spoke of years of practice. She pulled out her chair, strategically placed between a teen boy with dark hair and an older man she didn't know. Her eyes sought out the two people she did know, to see them opposite her side but closer to the head of the table where Lorenzo sat like a self-proclaimed emperor.

"Are you family?" the teenager asked her curiously.

She shook her head. The boy opened his mouth to ask something when a shadow fell over them. Morana looked up to see Tristan Caine standing behind the boy, his face wiped of all emotions, his eyes on her.

He addressed the boy. "Wanna sit with your cousin?"

The boy's eyes widened. "But I'm not allowed up the table."

"You are now. Scoot."

The boy didn't need to be told twice. He was out the seat and beside Dante in all his youthful exuberance. Morana saw Tristan Caine take the seat beside hers, hyper-aware of all the eyes on them, hyper-aware of his big, solid form warm just inches away from her. She swallowed, focusing on her breathing, donning the mask of carefully crafted indifference like this wasn't a big deal at all. Nope. No big deal. Tristan Caine changing years of seating arrangements and sitting beside her in front of everyone—no big deal. She could smell that musky scent that was all him, feel the air every time he inhaled and exhaled softly, feel the sheer force of his presence caress her all over.

Food came. Nobody said a word. He didn't say a word. Morana could practically feel the tension climb up as she kept her eyes glued to her plate like it was the answer to global peace.

"Tristan," Maroni's voice came from the head of the table, loud. The sound of cutlery paused. She kept her head down, aware of the man beside her looking up silently.

"This won't happen again," he warned.

The man beside her said in the same tone. "It better not."

Holy shit. She looked up just in time to see Maroni bristling. Tristan Caine continued eating. Nobody said anything but slowly, they resumed eating. Morana looked down at the soup in front of her, her appetite lost under all the tension in her body. Forcing herself to drink a bit, she almost dropped her spoon when a hand went under the slit of her dress, holding her inner thigh like it had every right to. She knew what he was doing. He was testing her.

Morana relaxed her body, closing her thighs hard, trapping his hand between them, just inches from her throbbing core. He flexed his fingers, the movement sending sensation coursing like an arrow to her center. She didn't open her legs or give his hand room to move. He gripped one of her thighs hard, his fingers prying her legs loose enough to get his hand out. Morana felt the loss ghosting over her skin, knew from the warmth that the imprint of that hand would be darkening the flesh inside her leg. It thrilled her, the knowledge of his having been there, the proof of it marked on her skin, so close. She was wet.

"Morana," Maroni's voice broke through her lust-induced daze, chilling her. She looked up to see the man wipe his mouth with his napkin.

"I've informed your father you're here."

Morana tensed but didn't remove her eyes from the man. "Awesome," her voice came out nonchalant.

Maroni smirked under his beard, looking around the table. "Everyone, this is Morana Vitalio, the daughter of Gabriel Vitalio."

The air around the table, which had been curious but relaxed, chilled at the announcement. Every eye turned to her and she kept hers steady on the man at the head seat. He continued. "She is here as a guest, of course, so everyone will treat her as such. Anybody who sees someone not treat her as a guest will be reported to me."

Morana heard the warning to herself loud and clear in that. Do not make yourself at home.

Maroni went one step further. "She is staying in the guest room on the second floor," he told everyone. "Nobody will bother her. She is her father's daughter, after all."

Her jaw clenched as her hand fisted, the urge to walk up the table and punch the smug bastard in the face acute.

Maroni looked around the table, his eyes coming to rest on Tristan Caine. "And nobody will touch her."

The hand on her thigh returned. This time, she let it stay.

"But you have to be careful, Morana. Accidents can happen anywhere sadly."

Which meant anyone could hurt her and he wouldn't do shit

about it. Morana knew what Maroni was doing. She was caught in that battle between him and the man beside her but she had willingly placed herself there. She knew what she was getting into.

And it was that which prompted her to retaliate. "And what if I want someone to touch me?"

Maroni's eyes flew to her, surprised. He had not expected that. And then he gave her that slick smile that made her want to bash his head.

"Then you will get more than you bargained for, little girl."

Fucking. Bastard.

Her blood boiled. She moved to get up when the hand on her thigh tightened, keeping her in place, telling her to be calm. For the first time through dinner, she looked at him, her anger at everything bubbling over. But the storm she saw in his eyes made her pause. His eyes, those magnificent blue eyes, were trained on Lorenzo Maroni and screamed so much death it sent chills down her spine. She realized she could never hate Maroni as much as this man hated him. And that soothed her.

"I think the only ones you're scaring are the children, father," Dante commented dryly from his place. "Let them eat in peace."

The children, on that note, stuffed their mouths quickly. The adults followed. The rest of the dinner flew by, remnants of tension lingering in the air. And throughout dinner, his hand remained on her thigh, not stroking, not moving, not doing anything except just being. Morana had never experienced it—the way a touch could anchor her. The only time she had come close had been with him when she'd had her panic attack. But this was different. This time she was conscious and aware of everything, her emotions still all over the place, and his touch, not sexual, not sensual, simply a touch, was grounding. It made her realize how hungry she had been for this sensation all her life, how much her skin had craved contact with another and never had it, how much she had desired his normal touch. Just the weight of his hand on her flesh made her feel light, lighter than before.

Done with dinner, the children excused themselves and left the room. Some adults took the cue and skipped dessert to leave as well. Morana wanted to do the same and escape the suffocating area. She didn't because he didn't.

"Did you know you were here quite a few years ago, Morana?" Maroni began conversationally, sipping his drink. "In fact, you sat on this very table and played."

Morana felt the man beside her tensing and for the first time, instinctively, she put her hand on his thigh, hoping for her touch to anchor him like his was doing to her. She felt the tight muscles in his legs and held it firmly.

"Father," Dante warned from the side.

"Terrible day that was though," Maroni continued speaking. "Such a terrible day. Do you remember, Morana?"

She gave him a relaxed smile. "Of course I don't. Unlike you, I'm not ancient, Mr. Maroni."

Dante coughed to hide his chuckle as Maroni's smile evaporated at her dig. "I have been here a long time, indeed. And I have stayed here for a good reason."

Morana retained her smile. "Terror."

"Power."

Morana nodded, pretending to agree. "Senility. One of the signs of old age."

The silence on the table would have been terrifying had she not felt the hand on her thigh give her a small squeeze.

"You forget your place, girl," Maroni spoke, his voice so quiet she could feel his anger.

She was so done with this shit. "Let me make something very

clear to you. I think you mistake me for someone you can push around, Mr. Maroni," Morana spoke, her voice reflecting the steel in her spine. "I'm not. I'm your Pandora's box. So, if I were you, I'd keep me very, very happy and very, very alive. Because once this box opens, your power, your empire, you will crumble and you wouldn't be able to do a thing to stop it."

Chiara Mancini sneezed and Morana's eyes went to her. The squeeze of his hand on her thigh turned sour. Done, completely done with the miserable evening, Morana pushed her chair back, dislodging his hand.

"Now if you'll excuse me," she addressed Maroni.

Without waiting for any of them to respond, she stood up and turned on her heels, leaving the room. She headed outside through the side door for some fresh air. Stepping out on the porch, she looked around to find a quiet place, seeing the bonfire a few feet away to the left and the men patrolling on the right. Turning, she walked around the house, breathing in the fresh air, looking inside the dark windows. The ones that were lit had the curtains drawn over them.

"Be careful of being alone outside."

Morana stopped to see Dante come up beside her, his eyes on the men near the bonfire. "I'm sick of people telling me to be careful."

His huge form relaxing, he took out a cigarette and lit it, taking a deep drag. Morana blinked, surprised. "You smoke?"

"Used to," he said, exhaling a cloud of smoke. "Now, it's occasional."

"What's the occasion?"

Dante's lips turned up in a smirk. "Seeing that beautiful show inside. Thanks, by the way. Keep it up and the old man is going to have a heart attack from the sheer shock that someone aside from Tristan is immune to his power."

Morana chuckled, well aware. "I'll try my best."

They stood in silence for a few seconds, Dante smoking and

Morana contemplating, before she broke the silence. "So what's the deal with Chiara and him?"

"Who?"

Morana rolled her eyes. "Dante!"

Dante cut a glance at her, smiling, before turning again. "You should be having this conversation with him."

"I will. I wanted to know your thoughts," she clarified.

Dante huffed a laugh. "Chiara is a viper—sleek, beautiful, poisonous."

Morana looked away. "She told me she was raped by her husband."

"She was," Dante confirmed. "And then she proceeded to prey on barely legal boys who didn't remind her of her husband. Don't waste your sympathies on that woman, Morana."

That was twisted. And she felt slightly nauseous.

"Well, then," Morana rocked back on her feet. "Thank you for standing up for me today, by the way."

Dante gave her a curt nod. Not wanting to make it weird, Morana bid him goodnight and headed back into the house, completely through with the night. What she needed was sleep, good sleep and when she woke up this nightmare would seem better.

Climbing the stairs, thankfully not encountering anyone else on the way, she went to her room, unlocking the door. She entered, pushing the door behind her. But the sound of wood hitting wood never came. Morana stilled, turning around to see Tristan Caine holding her door open, leaning against the doorjamb.

Oh no. No, nopity, nope. She was not in the mood to deal with him tonight.

Ignoring his ass, she turned again and went to the dresser, dropping her heels on the side. The door shut behind her. Locked. From the way her body was reacting, she knew he was still in the room.

"Nice dress."

Her hands paused over her earring, her eyes watching as his reflection joined hers in the mirror. "Thanks," she responded, taking her earring off. "Maroni sent it as a welcome gift."

His eyes flared in the reflection. Score one.

He took a step closer, his presence almost behind her. "Did you enjoy the buffet?"

Morana inhaled deeply, keeping her eyes on him. "I've only seen the dishes so far. But from what I've seen, I'm certain they taste really good."

Before she could blink, she was pressed against the mirror, her head pulled back with his hand in her hair. Their eyes collided in the mirror, his breath on her neck, warm, soft. His chest pressed against her back, expanding with every breath he took, syncing her own breathing to match. Her heart started to hammer, blood rushing under her skin, her entire being thrilled at making him snap, at making him react.

"Look at all the dishes you want, wildcat," whiskey and sin poured down her ear and dripped into her body, "but the only dish filling you up is right here."

Morana fought back a moan at the way his teeth grazed her ear, his eyes hot on hers. "I don't share."

His hand tugged her head a bit, his nose inhaling her. "Neither do I."

Stalemate. They were both breathing heavily. And then she remembered there were listening devices in the room.

"They can hear us," she reminded him.

"Let them," he stated, his nose running along her neck. "Let them also listen to what I'm going to do to anyone who touches you."

His hand left her hair, coming to the front of her neck, holding her as he did, her pulse drumming against his palm. "I'll break every single finger of the hand that touches you," he whispered, writing death over her skin as she looked at them in the mirror, her nipples hard as though his words caressed them, his big form behind her.

"Then, I will slit their throat just on the surface, letting them bleed and howl while I skinned them alive," he continued, making her shudder both in fear and pleasure, his eyes blazing on her, his hand simply holding her by the throat. "And then I will set them on fire."

She felt owned. "And what if I want them to touch me?" she asked the same question she'd asked Maroni.

His lips twitched, his hand pressing her closer to his body. "You won't."

"How do you know?"

"Because," he leaned into her neck, his lips ghosting over her skin as he spoke, "you come alive only for me."

Morana shivered, her toes curling into the carpet as her jaw trembled. He was right.

Not wanting to be left a step behind, Morana boldly rubbed her hips against his, feeling him harden against her back, and declared. "Mine."

And for the first time since she had known him, she saw a smile crack his face. It was small, just a little curve of lips, but it was genuine and it was there. And it tilted her world on its axis because he had a dimple.

He.

Had.

A.

Fucking.

Dimple.

She stared at it in surprise, somehow thrown by such a simple thing, wondering who had been the last person to see that dimple.

Their eyes, still locked together, had an entire conversation in themselves. His smile dropped slowly by degrees and she shook her head, raising her hand behind her in the mirror, feeling the scruff brush against her palm for the first time.

That pushed him over the edge. His other hand pulled the dress up and over her ass as she bent forward, giving him room to move, their eyes connected the entire time. She felt his fingers between her legs, testing her wetness. She was dripping.

"Clean?"

She felt the weight of that one word question in his husky whisper. She knew it would change things, knew it was one step closer together. Wordlessly, she nodded. He nodded his own answer.

Just as wordlessly, she felt the tip of him behind her. She went on her toes to get level, canting her hips to ease access for him as his fingers left her, going to under her knee and pulling it up. She balanced her foot on the edge of the dresser, with the other held up on her toes with his strength. His other hand stayed steady on her throat as his eyes stayed steady on hers. She realized it would be the first time she would actually see him when he entered her, the first time he would enter her naked.

Anticipation built, her heart thudding in her ears, her skin aware of everywhere they touched and aware of every breath he took.

And then he thrust into her suddenly.

A loud yelp escaped her as the dresser banged against the wall, her mouth opening on a pant as her walls welcomed him in. The fact that there were listening devices all over the room, the fact that he didn't care, and neither did she, the fact that just the banging of the dresser would have made people in the house aware of what was going on sent a thrill down her spine.

Their eyes on each other, understanding passing between them, he pulled her flush against him, his cock lodging itself deeper inside her, sending heat through her body. He pulled out almost completely, her walls quivering with the loss, before he plunged in, harder. The dresser banged into the wall louder. She moaned, her breaths escalating and his roughened, her muscles clenching around him like a vise. His hand left her knee, going to her throbbing clit, rubbing.

Her eyes fluttered close on the onslaught of sensation.

"Name," he growled. Her eyes opened slightly, finding his, confused. "Say my name."

Her heart stopped. She gulped, aware of him pulsing inside her. His fingers flexed on her throat, so big he encompassed it, the sense of danger and safety mingling together in a heady concoction.

"Mr. Caine," she whispered, her eyes glued to his.

He took the skin of her neck between his teeth, tugging. "Name."

"Tristan Caine," she muttered.

He pinched her clit, making her hips rock involuntarily.

"Tristan," she sighed, her hands holding the dresser tightly.

He rolled his hips, almost blacking her out with the sudden movement, touching her magic spot. "That's the name you're going to be screaming for a long time, Ms. Vitalio. Remember it."

"Stop talking and fuck me then, Mr. Caine," she challenged.

He complied. He started to fuck her in the true sense of the word.

The mirror in the dresser started to shake so much it rattled. The sound of the wood plowing a hold in the wall matched the rhythm of him plowing into her. Their eyes remained connected even on that shaky glass as he thrust in and out of her, rolling his hips, alternating. Her walls squeezed him in sync, weeping and clinging to him, the friction inside her spreading fire all over her body. Sweat coated her skin, her shuddering gasps turning into loud moans turning into small screams she could not control anymore.

"Tristan," she panted, urging him on, moving her hips to his, watching him. It was erotic, watching him like that, watching herself like that, both of them dressed but so, so naked.

"Louder," he ground out between clenched teeth.

It shook her. "Tristan," she moaned louder, feeling all the ridges on his cock, could feel those pulsing veins, all naked inside her for the first time. He started to rub her clit harder, his hips picking up speed, her knees knocking against the wood as she balanced herself on the toes of one foott and the knee of the other, his hand around her throat holding her up and level. It wasn't too tight but firm enough to make her feel completely surrounded, completely owned in that moment. She owned him right back, keeping him trapped inside her with every push. Slowly, the fire in her body concentrated on her burning core, her entire body shaking as she started getting light-headed from the overload of sensation.

And then she felt his teeth on her neck. Hard.

She exploded, screaming as her knees buckled, her balance forgotten, her walls releasing like never before, her heartbeats through the roof, so loud she could feel them thundering everywhere in her body. She could feel her own wetness running down her thighs, her eyes seeking his magnificent blues as he watched her come, committing everything to memory.

He pulled out all of a sudden, pushing her down over the dresser, and she saw him stroking his erection in his fist, his face twisting into agonized pleasure as he exploded over her back, his come pooling on the dress. Morana watched, fascinated, still reeling from her own pleasure, listening to that growl leave his chest as he jerked off for a few seconds, milking out every drop, exhaling.

His eyes, which had closed, opened again and found hers. He tucked himself back in, zipping up. Morana straightened slowly, watching as his hands came to her breasts for the first time. Not to touch, no. He still didn't touch her breasts even as her nipples strained towards his palms, aching with a hunger only his fingers could satiate. He never did. He just took the neckline of her dress in both hands and ripped it apart in one go, the sound of the tearing fabric loud in the room. He stared at her for a long minute, his eyes never wavering down to her bra, now completely exposed in the dress that hung on her only by the sleeves.

Gently, silently, he took the sleeves down and pushed the dress to the floor.

"Get rid of the dress."

With that growled command, he turned on his heel and walked out, locking the door behind him with a click.

Morana blinked, all of it too quick for her to process. What the hell had just happened?

Her gaze drifted down to the discarded green dress that Maroni had sent her. It was ripped, tattered and had his semen drying on it. A slow smile teased her lips the longer she stared at it. A laugh escaped her, the situation suddenly funny. Picking it up, she walked to the bin in the bathroom and threw it in. Humming quietly to herself, she turned to wash her hands and looked at herself in the mirror. Her eyes lingered on the red mark on the side of her neck where he'd hickey-ed her. She touched the mark gingerly, the smile on her face full-blown now.

Showering quickly, she changed into her cute pajamas and jumped in her new bed, the knife safely under her pillow, a pillow pressed into her chest. She cuddled into it, thinking about the entire roller-coaster of a day. Her first day in Tenebrae. Despite being in the enemy city in the enemy's house full of hostile strangers, a small bubble of happiness nestled its way inside her heart. Her life, in many ways, was better than what it had been weeks ago. She had found a true friend in Amara and a protector in Dante. And she had found, under all the madness and chaos, Tristan.

Tristan.

Just Tristan.

She exhaled, her heart squeezing at the giant steps they had taken forward.

She didn't know if he would acknowledge them tomorrow or revert to his usual self. She didn't know how Maroni would respond to her words tomorrow. She didn't know if someone would try to harm her tomorrow. What she did know was tomorrow, she would wake up and work on the mysteries that were plaguing her. Tomorrow, she would work out a plan to deal with the sharks better. Tomorrow, she would think of how to deal with Chiara. Tomorrow, she would call Amara and talk to her. Tomorrow.

She might not be safe but she mattered. She mattered to someone. And he had started to matter a great deal to her.

And tomorrow, as they said, would be a new day.

CHAPTER 6

WARM

It wasn't the most peaceful night she'd had but it wasn't the worst either.

The worst had been a long time ago in her father's mansion when one of his men had sneaked into her bedroom. She had been young, yes, but not defenseless. She had smashed his nose with her foot before smashing the lamp on his head. Scared by the fight in her and the noise she was making, he had escaped. To her relief, her father had found out and punished him. To her disappointment, it hadn't been for trying to assault his daughter but for daring to defy his authority under his roof. That had been the first night Morana had put a weapon beside her pillow and every night since then, she had slept with a weapon within easy reach, knowing how unsafe she had been.

The most peaceful night, much to her surprise had been in the penthouse of the man who'd sworn to kill her. It had been the night after her father had shattered her hopes at the bottom of the staircase, the night she had unknowingly sought out comfort and safety in the territory of the one man who should have terrified her but didn't. It had been the night Dante had weaved his way a little into her heart and Tristan had made her feel safety the likes of which she had never experienced in her life. She had slept that night—vulnerable, exposed, hurt and weaponless—with the utter knowledge that she wouldn't come to any harm, not at the hands of anyone, not while Tristan was there.

Tristan.

Morana smiled a bit, the warm feeling in her chest still lingering from last night. He had asked her to call him so, and so she did. Not just verbally but in her own mind. For some bizarre reason, she'd never thought of him as just Tristan. Maybe it had been too personal; maybe it allowed for an intimacy she hadn't been willing to admit to. But he had addressed it last night in clear terms, broken a barrier she had created intellectually between them. The barrier lay broken now, the stamp of his claiming bare on her skin for anyone to see, the sound of his whiskey-and-sin voice demanding his name in her voice.

Tristan.

He was Tristan now.

Her Tristan.

The warmth expanded.

Morana sat on the edge of the window, looking out at the property. The sun was playing hide-and-seek with the clouds, much as the moon had last night. The light shone brightly upon the lush green lawns, the shadows created by the woods at the edge dark. In the distance, the clear water of the lake shimmered, a lone little house standing on its edge, hidden behind the line of trees creating a visible divide between the in and the out. She understood what Dante had meant—Tristan had been on the inside for outsiders but on the outside for those on the inside, essentially belonging nowhere but with himself. She understood why he had that penthouse on top of a building now, where he could see everyone with those beautiful, giant windows but no one could see him, no one that he didn't explicitly invite into his territory. Layered with that knowledge, their first night against the window became even more beautiful to her, the shift in their relationship even more pivotal.

Men patrolled the property, much like they did at her father's house, but much less ostentatious. These men were skilled, sleek. It was evident simply from the way they moved, the ease with which they held their guns. Morana observed them for a long minute before movement drew her eyes to the house at the edge of the lake. She could make out the tiny form of Tristan walking out of the house to stand at the edge of the lake, his hands in his pockets as he stared into the distance. Fascinated by the chance to observe him without his knowledge, Morana simply watched, unable to remove her eyes from his form.

He stood still, almost unnaturally still, so much so he could have been a statue from such a distance and no one would have known. That stillness of his, even as he stood alone, made her realize how *non*-still he was with her. Since the beginning, there had been an energy about him, an energy that had wrapped itself around her time and again. Even when his physical form had been still, his energy had always been in motion—pushing, pulling, circling, holding, attaching itself to her. She didn't know if that had been deliberate on his part or something he hadn't been able to control (though she suspected the latter from his level of frustration with her in the beginning), but scrutinizing him at that moment contrasted.

She saw Dante's huge form walk with agile grace towards Tristan's still one from the trees. She wondered where his wing was as the man joined Tristan. They stood side by side, brothers, in a way their world couldn't understand, and Dante bought out another cigarette from his pocket. She saw Tristan flick a glance at the cigarette before looking forward again. And then they talked about whatever they talked about. All she could glean from their body language was a big, fat nothing. Tristan stayed the way he was, Dante relaxed in his form. The sun shone brightly on them for a long time in the early morning, the chill in the wind drifting inside the window to her arms.

Morana snuggled tighter into her blanket, shifting on the window seat.

The action seemed to distract the men because Tristan turned his head suddenly, looking straight at her window. She knew he couldn't see her any better than she could see him but she felt the heat of that gaze warming her better than her blanket did. A shiver coiling down her spine, the muscles between her legs still throbbed with the ghost memory of last night, clenching with the memory of his flesh snug inside them.

Dante turned to look at her as well. He raised the hand not holding the cigarette in greeting to her. Morana grinned at the gesture, giving him a slight wave back.

Her phone vibrated.

Tristan: *sent an image*

Morana stared at the image of his card, his name, and details clearly visible to her. Confused, she typed out the reply.

Morana: *???*

She looked up at his figure, seeing his face turned down to the phone in his hand, the other hand in his pocket as he typed out the response with one thumb. He must have hit 'send' because a second later, her phone vibrated again.

Tristan: *Buy yourself whatever you need. You either don't have your card or access to your account or you would've done it before Amara gave you clothes.*

Morana stared at the message, emotions conflicting inside her. He wasn't entirely wrong. She did have her cards but it had been the paranoid computer hacker inside her who hadn't wanted to order anything from his penthouse while she had been there and risk alerting her father. Back then, she had still cared. Now, since Maroni had very kindly informed her father already, she didn't have two shits to give.

Morana: *Thank you. This is very thoughtful of you. But I'll use my own card to buy myself what I need.*

She saw him look down at the phone again and from what she could tell, he exhaled or sighed. Then he typed.

Tristan: *Whichever suits you. Yours or mine, doesn't matter. As long as no more clothes need to be destroyed.*

Well, when he put it that way. Morana felt her lips tilting at the implication.

Morana: *I might just have to accept more clothes from Maroni just to have you rip them off, in that case. I enjoyed that.*

She looked up slowly to see his gaze back on the window, on her. Her heart started to pound, just seeing his reaction after that message, seeing the way his eyes didn't move away for a long time. And then he turned to his phone again.

Morana let out a breath she hadn't been aware she'd been holding, feeling her phone vibrate in her hand again.

Tristan: *Buy.*

Morana sighed, slightly deflated by the anti-climactic response. She'd been expecting a text more along the lines of "Me, Tarzan; You, Jane". Her phone vibrated again and she looked down quickly. Surprisingly, the text came from another man.

Dante: *Dear Morana, whatever you just told Tristan, kindly don't again. He is just itching to go punch my father in the face and that would be very inconvenient for our plans. I don't want to get in between whatever you two have going on but please don't egg him on right now. I need him focused. Thank you. Dante.*

A huff of laughter left Morana at the way Dante had phrased the text, the amusement in his tone evident along with the exasperation she could just imagine in his expression. It also restored the warm wave she'd been riding to know that what Tristan wrote and what he felt were very, very different. She wondered how many times she'd "egged" him on, as Dante so eloquently put it. Well, since she was egging . . .

Morana: *Dear Dante, of course. I completely understand. If he knew you were telling that to me, I imagine there's another Maroni he would want to punch. But that's not relevant. By the way, could you please forward me Amara's number? I want to talk to her. Thank you. Morana.*

She had Amara's number. Of course, she did. It was about making a point.

Dante: *He wants to punch me every five minutes. I want to punch him every four. And I know you have Amara's number. Say hi to her for me. Thanks.*

Morana grinned.

Morana: *I admire how much self-restraint you men have.*

Morana: *And I don't want to get in between whatever the two of you have going on.*

Dante: *Touché.*

Energized, and truly happy for the first time to have an unconventional relationship where she could be herself and not worry about it, to have a friendship where she could sass and be sassed in return, Morana felt liberated in a way she couldn't explain. Shaking off her thoughts, her plans for the day materializing, she sent another message to Dante.

Morana: *Since you offered me to come to your wing when I needed, I have three questions. A. Is it tapped for audio or video? B. Is there a kitchen? C. Does it have WiFi?*

She saw Dante's figure talk about something to Tristan. Tristan nodded and Dante typed. Interesting.

Dante: *A. No, there is no audio/visual invasion of privacy. There are security cameras outside the door but none on the inside.*

Dante: *B. Yes, there is a kitchen with a fully-stocked fridge so you can eat. You can also order something from the house and one of the staff will deliver it to you.*

Dante: *C. And yes, of course, there is WiFi. I'm assuming you want to come and work there?*

Morana: *Yes, if that's okay with you. I'd like to catch up on the trail of the codes. With everything that's been happening, it's time to get back on it. So, A. That's great. I'd be more comfortable making calls and working where I knew nobody was listening or watching. B. I'd be more comfortable eating there than order something at the house. Best case, someone spit in it; worst case, it'd be poisoned. C. I'll bring my equipment.*

Dante: *It's good. No one will bother you there. Make yourself comfortable and let me know if you need anything else.*

Morana looked at the simple message, her eyes misting. Blinking the surprising moisture away, she typed.

Morana: *Thank you. I just need directions there.*

Dante: *I'll send someone to escort you.*

Morana: *Thanks.*

Slipping away from the window, Morana quickly dressed into a comfortable pair of jeans and a t-shirt, pushing her feet into flats, glad she'd be able to order her stuff today. Brushing her hair and popping a bright shade of pink on her lips, she put her glasses on and picked up the blade from beside her pillow. Taking her laptop bag from one of the shelves, Morana collected everything important and everything she needed for the day, placed the knife in one of the pockets in the lining of the bag, and zipped it up. Hitching the bag up over her shoulder, she picked up her phone from the bed and headed to the door, seeing the message light flashing again.

Unlocking it, she saw another message from Tristan.

Tristan: *Dante and I are heading out for the day. Don't talk to anyone. Don't head to the main house until we're back.*

Morana raised her eyebrow at the tone of the text, shaking her head.

Morana: *Yes, Mr. Caine. Of course, Mr. Caine. Anything else, Mr. Caine?*

There were a few seconds before his reply came on.

Tristan: *I'll see how cheeky you are tonight.*

Morana felt her breath catch.

Morana: *What's tonight?*

Tristan: *Something that's long overdue.*

Morana: *Which is?*

Tristan: *Your mouth, wildcat.*

Oh my.

Morana brought her free hand up to fan her face, the cool wind doing absolutely nothing for her escalated heartbeats or her heated cheeks incited by two words. Two damn words. Her mouth. What with her mouth? What would he do with her mouth? Would he trace her mouth with his fingers? Eat at her lips with his own? Tangle his tongue with hers? Or would it be more primal? Would he let her mouth taste his flesh? Explore him? Explore the muscles on his chest, trail over his pecs, lick at his scars, kiss his abs, trace lower and lower and lower . . .

Oh my.

Morana could feel her entire body humming with the heat those thoughts infused in her blood, rushing, pulsing, throbbing everywhere. Shaking off her musings, she inhaled deeply and tried to center her thoughts back on track. After a few seconds of deep breathing, when her skin felt like it wasn't on fire anymore, she pocketed her phone and exited her room. Thankfully, she didn't see anyone lurking outside the door.

Locking her room (as though that would make any difference in the Maroni household), she headed to the stairs and went down, anxious to be out and away from the house as soon as possible and into Dante's wing. She had stuff to do today, the least of which involved ordering her clothes and calling Amara. What she'd told Dante had been right. Over the past few days, with everything happening the way it had between Tristan and her, the entire reason for their meeting in the first place had gotten sidelined.

There was still a set of dangerous codes out there, missing. There was still a nefarious someone who was trying to frame Tristan. There was still a mysterious someone well-versed with computers who was sending her random information. And now, there was also something else she knew she was going to look into, without telling anyone—the disappearance of girls twenty years ago. Regardless of her relationship or dynamic with Tristan, the truth that she had been abducted and returned, that there had been other girls who went missing never to be found again, troubled her. She needed to uncover those buried secrets. And if there was any chance of finding Luna, she would. But she could never, not until she had concrete evidence of something, let him know about it.

Lost in her head, she didn't see Maroni coming out of the living room just as she headed towards the main door.

"Morana."

His voice brought her up short. Morana turned to see the man walk towards her, that smile on his face that always sent eerie chills down her spine. She braced herself, her grip tightening on the strap of her bag.

"Mr. Maroni," she greeted in a calm, composed voice.

Maroni stopped just short of her personal space, tilting his head to the side, his dark eyes scrutinizing her. "You know I've tried to reach Tristan for years. Last night was the first time I saw him react."

Morana stayed silent, letting the man speak and observe her, keeping her face clean of every emotion.

Maroni smiled. "It's interesting, isn't it? The things I've done to that boy. Twenty years, I tried to break him. The more I tried, the stronger he became." He sighed. Morana felt her blood simmer as she stayed silent. "Torture, murder. He never flinched. I had begun to believe he was the perfect killing machine. Until last night, when I saw it with my own eyes. I believe I have, at last, found his Achilles' heel. So, thank you for that, Morana."

The venom she felt in her heart for the man reached another level. The smile on his face at the thought of bringing down the man she had come to care for made her instincts rage in a way they never had. How a man like Dante could've come out from this monster was a wonder. Bottling it all up, Morana smiled softly at Maroni.

She saw with some satisfaction that his smile faltered, just slightly, under his neat beard.

"That's where you're wrong, Mr. Maroni," she spoke quietly, her tone soft. "You assume, with your limited mind women only make two good things—wives and whores. I'm neither. What I am is a woman who has been freed from the shackles men like you had bound me to. What I am is a woman who knows that freedom thanks to two good men who've made me believe again."

Maroni opened his mouth to speak but Morana put up her hand, not done, the fire inside her raging now. She leaned forward, staring the man much taller than her down, her voice menacing.

"I'm not a victim. I'm vengeance," she ground out. "Mark my words, Mr. Maroni. I am going to make you pay—for every single scar you've put on Tristan; for every little hurt you inflicted on Dante; for banishing Amara from her home. And for all the girls who went missing."

She saw his eyes widen slightly at the last bit and nodded. "Oh yes. I know you're involved. I just don't know how. But when I do, you will pay."

"You assume you'll live that long," Maroni threatened, all veneer of civility gone from his face.

Morana chuckled mirthlessly. "You say you've never seen Tristan react until last night. Try killing me and then see what you'll unleash on yourself. Just try it. I fucking dare you."

Maroni's hand came up to her neck at her insolence, hovered mid-air, inches from her skin. Morana watched the hand, then looked back at him, staring him down, unwavering.

"You have no idea what you've just done, little girl," Maroni whispered, his eyes lethal. Morana should have been terrified. This was the man who made grown men shake in their pants. But she had witnessed eyes with far more death, far more rage than his.

"I told you not to threaten me," she stated in an equally quiet voice. "You just did. Now, watch as the dominoes fall."

"Respect, little girl," Maroni spat out.

Morana raised an eyebrow. "Long live the king. The king is dead."

Without another word, she simply turned on her heels and walked out the main door, into the beautiful, warm sunlight. Adrenaline still coursed through her body, churning in her gut with the poison of seeing that man breathe after everything he had done. She knew in her bones he had a hand in the missing girls, somehow. He wasn't invincible and she was going to prove it to him.

The silent figure of Vin standing near one of the pillars outside made her halt. Just as he was when he had escorted her to her room, he was quiet.

"Are you my escort to Dante's place?" she asked him, half-expecting him not to respond. He surprised her by saying a simple "yes" in a quiet voice, taking out his dark shades from the pocket of his dark suit and gesturing for her to walk beside him.

Morana fell into step as they walked west on the property as she observed everything around them. Men she'd seen from her window still flanked the property. Long stretches of grass lay between the house and the line of trees at the north, segregating the lake and beyond. Towards the west, she could see two different wings, one painted white and the other not painted but simply red-bricked, set almost at two different corners of the property. The white one was huge, set farther back than the red house. It had a flat roof above the third floor and black, wrought-iron railing on its balconies. The red-bricked house was much smaller in comparison, and had a slanting roof on one side above the first floor, with a simple wraparound porch.

They were headed to the red one.

"The one on the right is Dante's," Vin broke their silent walk, indicating the house. Morana was surprised by the fact that A- he offered the information, and B- he called Dante by his first name. Filing that away for later, Morana took the opportunity to get more info.

"And the white one behind that to the left?" she asked, keeping pace with his brisk steps.

"That's the staff building," Vin informed. "They have apartments inside."

Morana nodded, curious. "And the training center?"

Vin's step faltered for a split second before he picked it up again, cutting her a glance from behind his shades. Morana kept her face innocent.

After a long moment, in which she thought he wouldn't answer, he spoke. "That's in the opposite direction. I would advise you to keep as far away from there as possible."

Noted.

"Why did you give me the knife yesterday?" Morana asked the question that had been bugging her since she saw him. "Not that I'm not grateful, which I am. But I don't understand the motives."

Shutting her mouth, Morana blinked, surprised at herself. She babbled in her head, sure. All the time. But this was the first time she'd slipped into it outside of her mind. She had to be more careful, much more careful.

Vin shrugged. And stayed silent.

Not good enough.

"Seriously," she prodded. "I need to know if you're one of the good guys."

Vin cut another glance at her. "None of the guys here are good, miss. But will I put a bullet in your head? Not unless you don't cross me personally. Who else you cross or don't doesn't matter to me or my gun."

Okay, that was good enough.

Morana nodded, glad to have that equation cleared. They arrived at Dante's place and Vin knocked on the door once sharply. A few seconds later, the door was opened by an older woman with graying hair, a kind, wrinkled face, and Amara's stunning green eyes. The woman couldn't be anyone but Amara's mother. And the fact that Dante had brought Amara's mother to his wing as staff told her a lot more about the man.

Vin nodded at her and Amara's mother and left without a word.

The older woman's face had split into a large, dimpled smile upon seeing Morana. Surprising the fuck out of her, the woman extended her hands hardened by years of hard work and took Morana's, her eyes misting with tears.

"My baby told me you are her friend," the woman told her in an accented voice. "She does not have friends, you see. I thank you."

The purity of the woman's heart touched something inside Morana she'd thought dead a long time ago – the proof of a parent's universal love. Squeezing back the woman's hands with all the emotions rumbling in her, Morana spoke softly, "Your daughter is the kindest, most generous spirit I have ever known. She's been a true and strong friend to me. And she misses you very much."

The woman smiled through her tears and pulled back her hands to wipe them. Opening the door wider, she invited Morana inside.

"Come in, child," she said affectionately, locking the door after Morana entered and leading the way inside. The house was warm – its walls, its drapes, its wooden furniture, the browns and reds and creams just wrapping Morana up in its warmth. The smell of eggs and coffee and patchouli somehow mixed intricately together, the open windows bringing in the soft breeze, the sounds of wind chimes tinkling outside. It felt unlike any place she had ever been in. Warm. Cozy. Inviting.

"Dante told me you would be here," the older woman continued, guiding Morana towards a cozy, plush brown couch and making her sit. Morana sank into the cushion. "Make yourself at home. Have you had breakfast?"

Morana shook her head, overwhelmed by all the emotions. The woman smiled. "I will bring some food and coffee for you. You like coffee, yes?"

Morana nodded. The woman stroked her head softly, in the manner a parent did to their child mindlessly as she had done it countless times before. It was the first time in Morana's memory. She felt her chin tremble.

"Do your work, and if you need anything, call me," the woman turned to leave.

"What do I call you?" Morana asked abruptly.

The woman grinned, her face lighting up and wrinkling. "Zia, of course. That is what Dante calls me."

Morana smiled as she watched the woman go and exhaled. More shaken by the simple encounter than she'd expected to be, Morana saw the tremble in her hands as she pulled out her laptop and other equipment she needed from her bag. Slowly, as she set up on the table in front of her, Morana folded her legs under her and settled in.

The older woman came out with a tray of some delicious looking omelet, slices of toasts and fresh fruit and coffee. Morana thanked her as she placed the tray on her lap and exited, shutting the door behind her, giving Morana privacy. Hearing her stomach grumble because she hadn't eaten properly at dinner, Morana dug into the breakfast with relish. Within minutes, everything was cleaned off the plates and her stomach was happy.

Placing the tray on the floor beside her, Morana sipped her coffee and first things first, did her shopping online. Usually, it didn't take her a long time to shop. She knew her style and knew what she liked to wear. But that morning, she took her sweet time picking outfits that went from the scale of "comfortable enough to veg out in" to "uncomfortable but classy as hell". Zia came in and took the tray away with another smile, which Morana returned. Then, Morana ordered herself lingerie. Good, sexy lingerie with a particular someone and his tendency to rip her clothes in mind. Shoes and make-up went next. Then, accessories. By the time everything was done, it was afternoon. She had spent a lot of hours and dollars but damn, it felt good. Putting the delivery on for the next day, she put in the address for the mansion and stood up.

Stretching, Morana walked towards the window in the living room and looked out at the property from the different vantage. From there, she could see that beast of a mansion uphill in all its glory, and the lawns, and the gates. What she could also see from there was the lake farther downhill and the house on its edge. Though it was still very far, it was closer than the window. She could see it was a brown cottage, see it had one level above the ground but nothing more than that.

Keeping her eyes on the house, Morana brought her phone out from her pocket and dialed the number of the woman she was now starting to consider her friend. It rang twice before connecting.

"Morana," Amara's low husky voice greeted her. Had Morana not known Amara's ugly history and seen the terrible scar that slit across her throat and damaged her vocal cords, Morana would've said she had a voice made for sex. But anything that brutal could not be associated with something beautiful. Or could it?

Shaking off her thoughts, Morana replied will all the fuzzy feelings she felt. "I've had two wonderful greetings here, thanks to you."

Amara chuckled. "That place is a trap. We girls gotta have each other's backs. So, I just thought you might need all the people on your side you can get."

"I appreciate that," Morana smiled. "Thank you. For everything."

"Anytime, Morana," Amara's soft voice came through. After a second of silence, Amara asked. "So, how's Tenebrae?"

Morana huffed a laugh. "The weather has been good so far. The people surprising."

"How so?"

"Well," Morana planted her ass on the edge of the window, playing with the edge, "as mentioned, your half-sister surprised me. Your mom as well."

"I wouldn't trust Nerea entirely if I were you," Amara warned about her half-sister, surprising Morana. "I mean she's always been good to me, loves me a lot. But you're a stranger and she's also harsh. I have put in a good word for you but I honestly doubt you'll see her much. She mostly travels out of the city."

Everything inside Morana thawed at Amara's honesty. "I will. She seemed okay so far but I'll be careful. Your mother, by the way, told me to call her Zia. Is that her name or does it mean something?"

Morana could hear Amara's smile in her voice. "It means aunt."

Aunt. A strange woman she'd never met before had asked her to call her aunt simply because she'd been good to her daughter. She'd never had an aunt. Especially one who stroked her hair lovingly and fed her. The knot in her throat tightened.

"She's a wonderful woman," Amara's voice broke into her emotional musing. "But don't tell her your secrets because she'll tell them all to Dante. She loves that man something fierce."

"Is that because you love him?" Morana asked, before suddenly realizing maybe she shouldn't have said that.

Much to her relief, Amara laughed, her voice strained due to the stress on her cords. "No. Maybe. Who knows? Ma's always loved Dante, even back when my infatuation with him had been secret. I think she just felt motherly towards him after his mother passed."

Morana wanted to ask more about it but didn't, knowing Amara wouldn't share anything related to Dante with her. After a slight pause, the other woman finally asked, "How is he?"

Morana couldn't help her lips from twitching. "Good. He's had my back on multiple occasions now with his father."

Amara exhaled. "That's good. I'm happy to hear that."

Morana hesitated. "Do you know if you can ever return home?"

"No. At least not until either Maroni leaves the throne or Dante marries elsewhere."

"And that doesn't bother you?" Morana asked.

Amara's voice turned soft. "It used to. Not anymore. He can be with whomever he wishes."

Changing the topic, knowing she was digging into old wounds, Morana shifted on the window ledge. "By the way, do you know anything about Tristan and Chiara Mancini?"

Silence. For a long second. Then Amara sighed. "He was her first extramarital affair after she came to Tenebrae. She chose him because sleeping with him would hurt her husband's and Lorenzo's egos the most. Tristan slept with her for that exact same reason I believe."

Morana swallowed. "She implied she was his constant for a long time."

Amara scoffed immediately. "Oh, puhleez! That woman's a reptile." Dante had called her something similar. Interesting. "She wanted you to believe that because she's the kind of woman who is immediately threatened by any other woman. Smarter, prettier, doesn't matter. And anyway, if there was any woman who was a constant in Tristan's life, it was you, even in your absence."

That, in a twisted way, warmed her. She let out a breath of relief. Hearing her exhale, Amara continued in a firm tone.

"Don't let her or anyone else get to you, Morana. I meant what I said. I have never seen Tristan as alive as I do with you. I truly believe you both have the possibility of building something good. Don't let anything ruin that, especially in that place. That house is crawling with people who would love nothing more than to see Tristan burn. So, be strong for both your sake."

Morana took a deep breath. "I will. Thank you, Amara."

"As I said, anytime," Amara replied in her soft, husky voice. "You need any inside information, or just to talk girl talk, I'm here. I'd like for us to continue this friendship, regardless of what happens with Tristan or Dante."

Morana picked at her top, smiling. "So would I."

"Good. I'm going to go now but we'll talk later, okay?"

"Okay," Morana looked up at the sky, a weight lifted off her chest. After saying their goodbyes and planning another call, Morana kept her phone aside and watched the clouds dancing in the blue sky, the grays and whites merging, creating something magical. And she marveled at it. She marveled at everything and everyone she had gained in a few weeks. In the span of such a short time, she had friends, relationships. She had people who would give a shit if something happened to her and she had people she wanted to protect.

It was such an odd thing, this new emotion inside her chest. She grabbed on to it, held on to it, cherished it.

It mattered.

CHAPTER 7

HOLD

Morana silently thanked Amara, once again, for telling her the truth. The fact that Tristan had not been with that woman for long as she'd wanted Morana to believe made her relax. She had been the only constant in his life, even though they were entwined by traumatic pasts. But they did have the possibility of something beautiful. She had sensed it, felt it, tasted it.

On that happy note, she munched on some salad Zia had quietly left for her while she'd been talking to Amara, and finally switched to work mode. The codes needed to be traced. More importantly, any damage that they had already done or could do needed to be contained. She quickly worked on writing another set of codes, as she'd told Dante she would do days ago. These new codes would alert her as soon as the original codes were used and contain any damage they wanted to do.

Along with that, she was also customizing it to backtrack and trace any unique elements of the original codes so that even if it was used separately by anyone, anywhere, she would know. As the person had some knowledge of computers, she didn't want to take any risk.

It took her hours of focused, concentrated work. She had her earphones in, her soothing instrumental playlist on, her glasses sticking to her nose. Zia came and left, not disturbing her once and always shutting the door behind her. Her phone buzzed once but she didn't check. But hours and stiff fingers later, she finally had all the new codes up and running, her trap set. There was only one limitation to her genius—whoever had the codes needed to use them or her program wouldn't be triggered. It would be running for years if that didn't happen. But she was relying on the culprit to use them. Or why else would someone go through the elaborate scheme of having Jackson woo her, steal them from her, and frame Tristan to take the fall for it? They had to use it at some point in time, right? Or what was the point of stealing it at all?

Tired after spending hours intent on the task, Morana stretched, her spine stiff, and cracked her neck, looking out the window. It was already dark, time being flown by at rapid speed while she worked, undisturbed. It was some of the best work she had done.

She picked up her phone to check the message that had come in and saw her father's name.

Father: Are you seriously in Tenebrae?

Morana looked at the message for a long time, wondering if she should reply at all, then decided against it. Fuck him and fuck his agenda. She didn't owe him anything. For the first time in her life, she had something good, even in the middle of chaos. She wasn't going to let him taint that. Never again.

Disgusted, she threw the phone on the cushion to her side and put her feet up on the table, crossing her ankles. Pulling her laptop up on her lap, Morana minimized the programs she'd initialized and opened another window. Seeing her father's name had reminded her of something she had been meaning to look up after she'd eavesdropped on Dante and Tristan's conversation the night of the Choice, as she liked to think of it. Yes, with a capital C. Dante had mentioned something about Tristan Caine going into her father's territory when she'd been missing. And Morana was crazy curious to know what had happened.

Which was why she was pulling up the cameras in her father's study/office that she had installed years ago. He didn't even know that they were there. Morana, as out of the loop as she had been back then, had wanted to be in the loop. And what better way to be in the loop than rig the boss' office. Seeing and listening to conversations not just kept her informed but also allowed her to build ammunition of files against many, many men of their world. Most importantly, her father. She knew of most of the dirty things he was involved in, had made note of conversations and meetings, and filed them away for a rainy day.

Her failsafe.

Closing her eyes at the disappointment and pain he caused her, Morana shook it off and concentrated on the more important matter at hand. Quickly typing in the multiple passwords, she logged into the system and put in the date of the day she wanted the record of. She put in the time after what had been her last text to him and pressed 'enter'.

The screen lit up from the feed of the camera in the upper right corner of the office, showing the inside of her father's study. It was empty. Fast-forwarding a few minutes, Morana pressed 'play' when her father entered, his steps agitated. He picked up his office phone and spoke into the receiver, his voice hard and grainy in her earphones.

"Is it done?"

She knew he was talking about her car, her beloved car, being blown up. Whatever the other person on the line said did not make him very happy. He sat down on his chair and put his hand to his forehead.

"What do you mean the men aren't answering? Call them! I need to know if she's taken care of."

'Taken care of'. *Nice.*

Morana just observed impassively. Her father put the phone down and stared out the window for a long time. Morana would've liked to think there was a hint of remorse, a hint of sadness inside him after what he'd just done to his only daughter, but she didn't think there was. A man who let his child fall down the stairs, who ordered her to be blown up, was not capable of remorse. The only reason he was contacting her now was that Maroni had informed him of her presence and she was ruffling his feathers.

She watched as something outside the window drew his attention. Her heart started to beat faster.

Leaning forward without realizing it, Morana watched, stunned, as Tristan blew into her father's office like a raging storm. No warning, no explanation. He simply strode in like he owned the place, not even glancing at the three men behind him with their guns on his figure, his entire frame coiled tight to spring any second. He was a bomb and he was ticking.

"He just broke in," one of the men panted, explaining. "We tried to stop him but he knocked two guys out."

Morana watched, mesmerized and shocked, as Tristan Caine— no, The Predator—took a seat in one of the chairs opposite her father's, his entire form vibrating with a kind of rage she had never, ever witnessed. Heart pounding, she didn't dare move a muscle as she watched the tension in the room climb higher and higher.

"I remember you, boy," her father stated, leaning back in his chair, his eyes on Tristan. "You shot your father point-blank between the head. A boy your age. That's a hard thing to forget. I didn't place you when we met recently. Now I can."

The Predator simply stared him down. "Where is she?"

Her father smiled the Maroni kind of smile. "And I remember the way you walked to her, wiped the blood off her face."

Morana felt her pulse race, no memory of the incident in her mind but just the thought, the idea of that boy wiping the blood off a baby's face, of him doing that to her, made her heart clench.

"Where is she?"

"And the way you stared at her in the restaurant," her father continued, pretending to be unperturbed by the gaze of a lethal, lethal man on himself. But Morana could tell he was worried. He had a tick at the side of his cheek. "Surprising, no? The women who can attract you? I wanted to get her married to the son of one of my partners. I even had everything planned. But that little whore spread herself good for you, didn't she?"

Before she could blink, Tristan Caine was out of his chair and around the table, his one hand twisting her father's arm behind his back and the other hand holding his face down to the table by the neck.

"Her name," Tristan leaned down to whisper, "is Morana."

Chills.

Morana paused, trying to catch her breath and her stomach dropped. She observed the man she had let inside herself in more ways than one, watched his form frozen on the screen, bent over her father, his lips poised open at the last syllable of her name.

Swallowing hard, she pressed 'play' again. Guns trained on him. Her father whimpered. A thrill shot down her spine as she heard him speak her name for the first time, felt the syllables wrapping around his tongue, heard her name infused with whiskey and sin. Letting out a shaky breath, she watched enraptured.

"Call her a whore one more time," Tristan continued, "and what I did to my father will look like a child's play compared to what I'll do to you."

He twisted her father's arm harder, making Gabriel Vitalio yelp out in pain. He didn't even spare a glance at the multiple guns on him. "Now, I'll ask you one more time. Where is she?"

Her father's words got jumbled because of his cheek pressed flat against the wood. Tristan eased his head a bit.

"She's dead."

Still.

The stillness that took over the room made goosebumps erupt over her flesh, and she wasn't even in the room. She waited with bated breath, her heart in her throat, her eyes glued to the black and white screen.

"You're lying," Tristan spoke, his voice clear.

"I'm not," her father replied. "I gave the order myself."

Tristan slammed her father's head into the table, harshly pulling on his thumb, the crack loud in the room. Her father yelled, one of the men fired. Tristan ducked, took out his own gun, and stared the men down while keeping her father immobilized.

"I don't have any problems with you," he told the men. "Leave now, leave alive. Or die."

She watched as the men hesitated, two of them leaving, evidently aware of his reputation. The third one, trying to be brave, held his gun up. Tristan shrugged, shot him in the shoulder, and pointed to the door with his gun. The man escaped, leaving him behind with her father alone.

Tristan eased up on him and tucked his gun back in his waistband.

Her father looked at him with venom in his eyes. Tristan sat down on the edge of the desk and leaned forward.

"Where is she?"

"Dead."

Tristan smiled, a cold, hard smile without the dimples she now knew he had. "You have nine more fingers for me to break. Then two wrists. Two elbows. Two shoulders. Six ribs I can break without damaging you internally and don't even get me started below the waist. And it doesn't heal well in your age, old man."

He tilted his head to the side, holding her father's hand in his almost casually. "I have the time and patience to make you feel pain the likes of which you've never felt before. Pain that will make you wish you were dead. So, I'll ask again. Where is she?" His fingers poised over the other thumb.

She saw her father's arm shaking, his jaw tight as he looked up at something much worse than death. "I'm not lying. I gave the orders."

"Where?"

"A cemetery behind the airport," her father admitted. "My men have trailed her going there multiple times."

Tristan straightened, throwing away the hand, turning to leave.

"Is she your weakness, Predator?" her father's voice stopped him cold in his tracks. Her father, evidently the stupidest man on the planet, goaded Tristan instead of letting him go. "After so many years, I would've thought she would be the last person you would look for."

Tristan turned, raising an eyebrow, his hands relaxed by his sides.

"You know you're risking war, don't you?"

Tristan chuckled, without mirth. "You don't have the balls for war, old man. You didn't have the balls to protect your daughter when she was defenseless with a gun pointed to her head back then. You don't have the balls now."

Her father stood up, offended for his masculinity. Seriously, how was she related to this pompous, egotistical douche of a man?

"I have always protected my daughter. You were stupid to come here," her father uttered.

Tristan walked back to the desk, leaned forward with his palms flat on the desk. "If a hair on her head has been harmed, I will come back here again. Not quietly, no. This time, I will come to your house, and I will kill you, and I will take my sweet time doing it."

"Don't threaten me."

"I'm warning you. Post as many guards as you want," Tristan said, in that soft, lethal way he had. "And pray she is okay."

"Why do you care so much about her?" her father asked point-blank.

Morana felt her heart stop at the question, her hands shaking as she waited for his answer.

Tristan didn't reply for a long moment. And then he did.

"That's for me to know and her to find out," he said in that menacing tone. "No one else."

Turning on his heel, he walked to the door again, then stopped, pinning her father with that brutal gaze of his.

"Stay away from her, old man," he warned, his voice hard. "Come after her again, I'll come after you."

"Her pussy must be magical for you to . . ."

Before her father could finish that disgusting sentence, he was pinned back into his seat and Tristan punched him hard on his recently healed nose. Blood started to pour out of her father's mouth, making her realize he'd probably broken a tooth too.

Tristan gripped his jaw tight in one hand, and leaned down, almost nose to nose.

"One more word," he said in a tone that sent chills over her body. "Give me just one more reason to cut out your tongue."

Her father stared at Tristan, speechless.

"One word," Tristan urged, the mask fallen from his eyes.

Her father mutely shook his head.

"Now, listen to me and listen hard," Tristan uttered, shaking her father's jaw for emphasis. "She's under my protection. Mine. Nobody hurts her. Nobody talks shit about her. Not me, not you, not anyone. Next time I hear you call her anything less than the woman she is, I will cut your tongue out and feed it to your dogs. Next time I see you anywhere close to her, I will kill you. Stay. The. Fuck. Away. From. Her. Do you understand?"

Her father nodded.

Tristan nodded. "Good. And anytime you forget that, just remember how I killed my father when I was a boy for her. And think on and think of the people I can kill now that I am a man to keep her safe."

Her father nodded mutely again.

This time Tristan Caine left the room.

Morana sat back, *stunned.*

Overwhelmed.

Her eyes still stayed glued to the screen, watching her father make calls and whatnot. She pressed rewind and watched it all again from the start. The entrance, the broken thumb, the threats, the gunshot, more threats, the exit. And then she watched it again, and again, and again, until every stance, every nuance, every word had imprinted itself on her heart. Every word of his hammered onto her heart, cracking it open slowly, until it split in two and let him in.

She could not remember, not once in her life, anyone standing up for her. She had lived with men who were supposed to be strong and lived in fear. She had lived with her father turning the other way when men touched her under the table. She had lived alone, never, ever thinking someday, someone would storm into her father's office, fearless, hurt him, threaten him, all for her.

And he had. Even before she had asked him to make a choice, he already had. Even before he knew that she knew, he had wanted to protect her. Even before she had exposed herself to him the way she had, he had wanted her. That entire interaction with her father—hours before he had found her, only based on their interactions as they had been—had shown her nothing but his fierce protectiveness and the respect he had for her.

A tear rolled down her cheek as she put the laptop on the table. Morana wiped it away, her heart full in a way it had never been. Surrounded in a warm, safe place with a strange woman who had opened her heart to her, with friends in her life and a man who would go to the ends of the earth for her without fear, her heart was full.

Standing up, she went to the window, more tears escaping her eyes—joy, sadness, pain, relief, gratitude all mixing together in a concoction until she couldn't tell one from the other. Staring out into the lawns, she didn't move until she heard the main door to the house open and Dante's voice drifted in. Morana turned to the door, her heart in her throat, and waited for it to open.

It did.

Dante and Tristan walked in, both men still dressed in the same suits as they were in the morning but rumpled now. Dante's tie was askew and Tristan wasn't wearing one. Dante looked at her and gave her a small smile. Tristan just looked at her.

And Morana couldn't hold it in anymore.

Without a moment's hesitation, she ran towards him, and threw her arms around his neck, holding on tight.

She felt his body go rigid with stunned surprise and buried her face into the crook of his neck.

"Dante," she heard his voice rumble from his chest.

"I'll be outside," Dante spoke. Morana heard the door shut behind them.

And then she felt his arms come around her, tentatively, as if unsure of how to hold her. Morana wrapped her own tighter around his neck, standing on her toes, leaning her entire weight into him, pressed into him like that for the first time. His arms, slowly, held her tighter, one around her waist, the other coming up to cup the back of her head.

"Did something happen?" he asked in a quiet, almost soothing whisper, the huskiness of his voice right next to her ear.

Overcome with all the emotion bursting inside her, her eyes leaking, she shook her head.

"You okay?" his tone relaxed slightly.

She nodded into his neck.

She could feel his confusion at the way she was behaving but for once, she didn't care. She deserved to hold someone who cared for her as he did. He deserved to be held by someone who cared for him as she did.

Without another word, he picked her up and moved in the direction of the seating area. Morana clung to the strong muscles in his neck, her legs hanging in the air. He turned, sitting down on the same couch she'd been sitting on and Morana bent her legs to accommodate, straddling him, feeling the gun at his waist press inside her thigh, still hiding in the space between his neck and shoulder.

She could smell his musky scent and his cologne mixed around his pulse, feel the vein throbbing against her cheeks as she nuzzled into him, feel his soft hair against her hands as she ran her fingers through the strands. His heart beat against her breasts crushed to his chest. His warm muscles felt hard against every curve of hers. His pelvis tucked into her hips perfectly.

His arms, tight around her smaller frame, didn't move. Not to stroke, not to explore, not to do anything. She could sense he was half-afraid it would trigger her into something and half-confused as to why she was clinging to him like a koala to his favorite branch.

After minutes and minutes of holding him, and him allowing her to hold him without complaint, Morana pulled her face out of his neck and looked at his Adam's apple, exposed by the unbuttoned collar of his white shirt.

Letting her eyes travel upwards, she finally locked her gaze with his.

Those blue, blue eyes made her sigh softly. They were patient, not in the alert way of predators but in a softer, much tender way. He was waiting for her to explain her bizarre behavior.

Morana moved her hands to the sides of his face, cupping his jaw in her palms, feeling that scruff scraping against her palm in that delicious way and told him, in two words, with every emotion strangling her heart.

"Thank you."

His brows furrowed, just minutely, as he tilted his head slightly to the left, trying to figure her out.

After a minute, he asked. "What for?"

Morana stroked his cheek with her thumbs. "For caring."

He didn't get it. Of course, he didn't. How could he? He didn't know her entire history. He didn't know what he had become to her. He didn't know she'd seen him do what he had done to her father when she had been missing. He didn't get it because he didn't know how it had tilted her world on its axis again, how it had split her chest open, how it had warmed her to the bone in a way she knew she would never be cold or alone again.

And she wouldn't be able to convey it to him, to tell him any of it. So, she did it in the only way she could in that moment.

She leaned forward and pressed her lips to his.

He stilled.

Completely stilled.

His hands tightened slightly on the side of her hips but he sat frozen under her. Morana didn't care. She held him with all the affection she felt for him in her heart, and tilted her head, pouring it into that one kiss. She nipped at his lips, sipped from them, kissed them gently, reverently, giving him tenderness she knew he had never received in two decades.

He let her. He let her shower him and received it. Accepted it. Didn't kiss her back but didn't push her away.

Morana tasted his lips the way she had wished to for such a long time. Tilting her head to the other side, she fit their lips together again, locking them for a moment before sucking at his lower lip, feeling the scruff on his chin rubbing against her skin, the bristles around his mouth burning hers.

Someone knocked on the door.

Morana pulled away from the simplest, most beautiful of kisses and stared deep into his eyes.

"You," she whispered to the space between them, "Tristan Caine, are a beautiful, beautiful man. And my heart beats for you."

The confusion and surprise on his face were priceless. This was not The Predator. This was the boy who had been called a monster for doing the brave thing and left behind alone never to be told he was precious. This was the boy who had buried himself deep inside the stronger man, who could not understand or process her actions or the thoughts behind them. She had reached under the persona and found the man, the boy.

Without another word, Morana stood up. It was proof of his shock that he let her.

She opened the door and Dante looked at her, eyebrows raised. Morana shook her head. He smirked.

"We should get to the house. It's time for dinner," Dante announced, indicating the main door. "We can talk on our way there."

Morana nodded. "Is it okay if I leave my laptop here? I've left some programs running and I won't feel comfortable with them in that house."

"Of course."

"Can we have a moment?" whiskey-and-sin asked from behind her, addressing Dante.

"Another moment?" Dante grinned, before shaking his head and walking out the main door wordlessly.

Morana turned to ask what he wanted to talk about when suddenly, she was slammed into the wall beside the door. She looked up, baffled, barely catching her breath, only catching a fleeting glimpse of the wild look on his face before his mouth crashed down over hers.

Her toes curled into her shoes, her fingers going around his tight waist, feeling the gun tucked to the side of his trousers under her palm. Body catching fire, heart thundering in her chest, Morana caved to him like sand under an ocean wave. His hands fisted in her hair, tilting her head back as he devoured her mouth. This kiss was nothing like the one minutes ago. It was harsh, almost bruising in its intensity, but the undercurrent of something untarnished ran through them. She still felt his confusion in the kiss, but there was something else there too. Something precious. Something she couldn't understand and he was trying to tell her. She parted her lips gladly as his tongue swept through them, dipping inside her mouth before pulling out. His entire body pressed hers into the wall—feet to feet, hips to hips, chest to breasts—as he leaned down and she went up on her toes as high as possible.

Sensations coursed through her body, her blood heated and burning every single part of her from inside out. His teeth tugged on her lower lip; a moan left her mouth. He swallowed it, stroking her tongue with his, tangling them together for a split second before pulling away again. Her hips canted into his, her hands pulling him closer as he feasted on her mouth, his hands firm but gentle in her hair.

It wasn't just a kiss. It was more, much more.

They broke apart for much-needed air.

"Dinner," she mumbled through a hazed mind.

"I'd rather eat you," he murmured back, kissing her feverishly once again. Morana lost herself in the kiss, let herself drown anchored by him. They kissed for seconds, or minutes, or hours, she didn't know. All she knew by the time he pulled back was her lips were swollen and she wanted more. He did too. She could feel it in his body, see it in his blue eyes.

"That's how you kiss me next time," he told her, putting a little space between them.

Morana rolled her eyes. "Thanks for the tutorial."

She caught the flash of a dimple as he turned away towards the door. She tugged him back by his shoulder and planted another one on him. That dimple was to blame. He returned it. Passion burst between them.

Panting, he took a solid step back this time. Morana straightened her clothes and brushed her hair with her fingers. Following him out the door, she saw Dante take note of her swollen mouth and Tristan's disheveled hair.

"Not a word," Tristan warned, slipping back into his usual mask.

Dante just grinned, pushing one hand in his trouser pocket and another around Morana's shoulder as they started walking towards the mansion. Morana saw Tristan glance pointedly at Dante's hand, which the man did not remove. Tristan looked forward again and kept walking. She relaxed into his hold.

The night was quiet, beautiful. The sky was still littered with clouds, the moon still peeking from behind them. Men, who had been visible around the property during the day, became invisible again. Strolling towards the mansion with the two men, Morana broke the silence, announcing, "I had a little moment with Mr. Maroni today. Nothing that I couldn't handle."

She informed them about the conversation, at least parts of it, and about the coding programs she had worked on all day. Leaving out the parts about her watching the camera recording and talking to Amara, she walked, tucked beside Dante, walking beside Tristan. It felt surreal. Safe.

The closer they got to the house, the more she could see both men tense. After a point, Dante dropped his arm from around her and walked into the mansion. Tristan was back to his stoic, cold self as they reached the door. He gestured for her to precede him. She did, still fuzzy in the heart and the body.

They entered the foyer. As the door shut behind them, surprising the hell out of her, Tristan pulled her into his body and looked down into her eyes. His hand came up, his thumb circling her heavy lips where his mouth had left his mark.

"Tonight."

Morana inhaled sharply as she felt the touch throb in her body. She gulped, nodding. He dropped his hand.

"Give them hell," he whispered to her.

She smiled. He stared at her smile for a long, long minute, his magnificent eyes glued to her mouth.

And the most beautiful, precious thing happened.

His cold, aloof eyes warmed.

CHAPTER 8

WARN

Something wasn't right.

The nagging, persistent feeling refused to leave Morana alone as she looked down at her phone, tracking the progress of the programs she had left running in Dante's house remotely. It never, ever took her software so much time, no matter how complex the algorithms. She prided herself on that fact. And yet, it was almost twenty-four hours that she'd let the codes run and the progress, much to her disbelief, was only at forty percent. Forty fucking percent. That just wasn't possible, not unless she had external interference. She had checked for it. There was none. So she just didn't understand what the hell was taking so long that her program was progressing at the pace of a pregnant snail.

Baffled and annoyed at her creation, Morana walked out into the lawns from the house. She was slightly frustrated and not only at the program—also at last night.

The dinner had gone over surprisingly smoothly. There had been some underlying tension of course, but not a single snide remark from Maroni. He had informed her politely about a party he had been planning for a while, a party that would be held tonight, and then he had been quiet throughout the dinner. Maybe that was how he behaved at the table and her first night had been an exception. She didn't know but she had been braced for a wrong look or that smile that rubbed her the wrong way. She had been braced for some underhanded words at her or worse, at the hunter sitting beside her who, by the time they had been seated, had completely wiped away every trace of the man he had been back at Dante's house. Had her mouth still not been burning from the passion inflicted by his, she would have chalked the entire thing up to her crazy imagination.

Tristan had not been Tristan sitting beside her, he had been the silent Predator - alert, watchful. And now that she had seen some of his layers, she marveled at the ease with which he switched back to his default. And not just him. Dante had sobered as well, his grins of ease shifting to smirks without mirth.

The more she got to know both the men, the more she realized just how much of their true selves they kept hidden, so much of which she still hadn't been exposed to. Some could say the same about her as well. But since she knew herself, she knew it was more about not knowing who she was under the entire facade. She was discovering that herself for the first time in her life because, for the first time, she had started to feel the edges of that comfort. Regardless, there was a long way for her to go, to realize who she truly was as she wasn't her father's daughter deep down. For now, she was a confusing mess of things. All she knew at the moment was.

And despite everything, she still didn't trust anybody completely.

She trusted Tristan and Dante more than she had ever trusted anyone but she knew she was still holding some part of herself back, especially when it came to Tristan. She trusted him to keep her safe. She trusted him not to hurt her. She trusted him enough to show him her jugular, over and over again. She was getting attached to him at a rapid rate she couldn't and didn't want to control. But there was a part of her, a rather small but strong part, that told her to hold some of herself back, to not surrender completely. She felt for him, strongly, deeply and truly. The emotion he incited in her came from the most broken parts of her, and yet it was the purest emotion she had felt in her life. She acknowledged that he had the power to emotionally scar her in ways her father had never even grazed. He had the power, that she had given him, to ruin her for anybody else.

And that small part was her failsafe, her just-in-case. Because if that ever happened, if he ever betrayed her and left her for the wolves, she won't succumb like a helpless lamb. That small part of her would let her survive. It would let her build herself back up. That small part was hers, only hers. And she had no clue how to give that to him, even if one day she wanted to. That was just another one of the many reasons for her frustration.

She was also vexed because her shopping was supposed to be delivered by noon and it was already afternoon. Usually, that wouldn't have bothered her but she'd just had a rather rancid encounter with Chiara Mancini in the morning. The stunning woman had reminded her rather nastily (and Morana was assuming she was nasty because she, like the rest of the house, had heard her passionate encounter with Tristan two nights ago after she had warned Morana off him) of the party Maroni was hosting in the evening for his 'business' partners. The party was in honor of some big deal they had made that she was not supposed to know about. And assuming from the first party

Morana had seen on these grounds, she knew she needed to look good, especially if that Chiara woman planned on looking stunning and make eyes at her man. It was a female thing.

She needed a dress.

Another reason for her irritation was Tristan himself. Last night, after his eyes had screamed unnamed pleasures on her flesh, after his mouth had whispered the same promise of pleasure on hers, he had escorted her to her room after dinner and opened her door. And then, for the first time since she had known him, he had chickened out and left her there.

Chickened out.

Tristan 'The Nothing-Scares-Me Predator' Caine had chickened out. Yeah, she hadn't believed it either. But she had seen it in his eyes, those magnificent eyes.

He'd been spooked. She, in all her tiny capacity, had spooked him and he, during the quiet dinner, had had enough time to process whatever shit had gone to his head.

And so he'd backed off. Completely. There hadn't been any texts from him in the morning and she hadn't seen him at all. Not even from the window. And Morana didn't know whether to be annoyed or amused by the stunning turn of events.

She understood needing space and everything because he did have a lot to process and from what she had seen of him, emotional processing wasn't his forte. He reacted more than thought and felt. Or at least he tried to. And it was a good sign that he was so off-kilter with her because he was feeling. So, she was trying to be understanding about it and not pester him like she wanted to. But he needed to get it sorted soon or she was banging down his door.

The noise of a large vehicle pulling up outside the gates broke her out of her thoughts. Morana watched as the gates opened and a white delivery van came down the driveway. Letting out a breath, one of her issues sorted, Morana headed towards the end of the driveway in front of the mansion to greet the guy and sign off on the delivery. She just got there when she noticed the men patrolling the property had stopped. They were looking at her and the van, mostly curiously but all alert. Morana raised her eyebrows. What, didn't anyone shop online around here?

The sound of the vehicle door opening jarred her perusal. She turned to greet the two uniformed delivery men who looked around the property rather nervously.

"Delivery for Morana Vitalio," the older of the two said to her.

Morana nodded, signing off on the device he extended to her. That done, she got to choreographing the two guys into putting all the boxes on the steps of the entrance, watching them get antsier and antsier to get out. She couldn't entirely blame them, not with the way the guards were watching them.

At least thirty boxes later, the men inclined their heads at her and hurriedly got into their van. Hastily, they reversed out the drive and went off at record speed. Morana sighed, realizing yet again that the world so normal to her was, in fact, not normal. Outsiders were absolutely terrified of it unless it was romanticized in stories.

Shaking her head, she looked at the boxes and sighed again.

"I see you're already spending Tristan's money," Chiara spoke from the doorway, eyeing the packages.

Morana rolled her eyes, all pretense of civility gone between the two women. "Green is not your color, Chiara."

Chiara actually looked down at her blue dress before grasping her meaning. She scoffed. "Oh, please. I could have men lining to buy me anything I want. I can do anything I want."

Morana nodded seriously. "Yeah, except leave me alone apparently."

The other woman grit her teeth. "Tristan won't protect you forever, you little slut."

Morana deliberately picked up a package, perusing it, not giving the woman attention. "I don't need his protection, Chiara. That's for women like you. Now shoo. Go lurk like a lizard somewhere else. I have work to do."

She could feel the other woman bristling at her dismissal. She didn't give a rat's ass. Like seriously, how Tristan could ever sleep with that and not have his rather good male equipment shrivel up was beyond her. Chiara slithered away and Morana shuddered. Then she turned her focus on deciding what to do with her deliveries. She could ask some of the staff to help her take them up to her room.

But the few people in sight were already busy with chores, making arrangements for the party, and she didn't want to leave the packages just lying there unattended, not after the money she'd spent on them from her own pockets.

Floundering at what to do, she felt someone come behind her. Whirling around, her package held up like a weapon, Morana narrowed her eyes at the three guys she'd seen near the perimeter, their tall rifles strapped to their backs. They were all taller than her (which wasn't a benchmark because her height was nothing to boast about) but two of them were kinda short and the third, for some insane reason, reminded her of Chris Pine. Shorty, Stocky and Pine were looking at her quietly.

"Um," Morana shook her head at the weirdness of the situation. "Can I help you?" What else did you ask fierce looking guys who patrolled the enemy grounds with guns?

Shorty grunted. "You Caine's girl?"

Morana felt her lips twitch even as she forced herself to keep them straight. "Yes."

Shorty and Stocky nodded in sync and moved to the packages, picking up a bunch of them together. Without another word, they moved into the house. Morana watched them go, baffled, before turning to look at Pine, who simply stood there, guarding her deliveries.

Had she somehow stepped into another dimension? What the hell was going on?

Shorty and Stocky returned, their arms empty, and picked up more of the boxes and went in again. Morana shook her head.

"Not that I mind this, but shouldn't you guys be patrolling?" she asked, completely confused. "Why are you helping me?"

Pine grunted, just like Shorty had, but didn't reply. Okay.

After two more trips, when all her packages were upstairs, Morana looked at the three men. "Thanks."

Grunts.

Men.

They walked away just as quietly as they had come. Morana watched them go, puzzled, making a mental note to ask Dante about the entire episode. There had to be a reason they had suddenly decided to help her out because nobody helped anybody out of the goodness of their hearts. Especially not three men who just grunted.

Moving to head inside, her eyes came to a halt at a lone building far in the distance on the other end of the property. The training center.

She lingered there for a second, tempted to head in that direction but shook it off. There were multiple eyes on her—staff and guards and whoever else Maroni wanted to have her watched. So, with a last glance at the building, she returned to the beast.

Darkness had fallen. It was a moonless night, the stars completely concealed behind clouds. The wind was chilly, drifting in her window that she'd left open. Morana glanced down the window at the manicured lawns. There were strings of beautiful lights on the trees that lined the property, lighting the entire area and leaving the lake and the house behind it in the shadows. Morana couldn't see anything beyond the treeline no matter how hard she squinted.

Due to the possibility of rain, the party was to be held in the hall at the back of the house, a part of the mansion Morana had never been in. Even though she was ready, something was twisting in her gut as she watched cars line up the driveway. Men of all ages in suits, women glittering on their arms like accessories, walked around the well-lit lawns to the back of the mansion, a bevy of staff guiding them through.

Morana watched the who's who of the mob, recognizing many faces, dangerous faces that smiled, baring teeth like baring fangs. The women, she observed closely. Some seemed happy enough to be where they were; some had clean faces and dead eyes. Morana took them all in from her room above, out of their line of sight, and prepared herself for whatever and whoever she would find. Throngs of people came in. The lights around the property glinted off the women's jewelry, gemstones shining in the dark. People had trussed up in their best for an invite by Maroni.

Amongst the light crowd, her eyes caught sight of one man who strode up the driveway all alone, without any partner. There was something dangerous about the way he stalked up the gravel. Morana observed him closely, sensing something about him that reminded her a lot of Tristan. She couldn't make out his height or strength from where she was but he seemed older somehow, at least mid-thirties, his stride confident and comfortable in a way she'd very rarely seen in their world. One of his hands pushed in his dark trouser pocket, everything about the man was dark.

Palms clammy, Morana turned away from the window and walked to her mirror. She'd spent her entire afternoon arranging her new wardrobe that she freaking loved, and keeping an eye on her phone for an update. Her program was at sixty percent and her inbox empty of any new messages.

Morana gazed at her reflection with a trained eye. Having dressed multiple times for her father's dinners, Morana knew how to manipulate her looks to inspire whatever impression she wished the beholder to have. She thought of herself as a chameleon that way. An extra stroke of mascara for some innocence here, a floaty dress for softness there. She knew how to blend. She learned how to stand out. And she enjoyed having people underestimate her because that way she had the upper hand.

That was one of the reasons people rarely remembered her at social events. If she wanted to, she simply flew under the radar. And that was what she wanted tonight. She had planned, initially, on wowing a particular someone and going all out tonight. But for some reason, this party was making her antsy and she was reverting to being invisible. It was safe being invisible. She needed to trust her instincts. Vanity could wait.

It was one of the reasons she had chosen the most nondescript dress in her new arsenal. It was black, with a classy neckline that stopped just below her collarbone and sleeves that went to her wrists. The back wasn't too deep either. The only thing that added something to the dress was the single split that went mid-thigh, only exposing her leg if she moved. Leaving her hair down and her makeup minimal, nothing extra to attract attention, Morana adorned her wrist with a simple gold bracelet that matched her earrings and strapped her only knife to her thigh. Her gold stilettos, though high and uncomfortable, were necessary. Because nothing attracted more attention at a party like this than a woman not wearing heels.

That done, Morana took in a deep breath, and walked out the door, her phone in her hand. Locking the door behind her and nestling the key in her cleavage, Morana descended the stairs. Coming to a halt in the foyer on the ground floor, she asked one of the staff for directions to the room where the party was being held. Guided, Morana started down the corridor leading to the back.

Since she was going through this part of the interior of the mansion for the first time, Morana kept her pace slow, letting her eyes float around, taking in every single detail. The corridor was empty except for an occasional staff or two passing her. It was lined with beautiful paintings, some of which she recognized as classics, some she didn't recognize at all. Almost two minutes into her walk, one wall of the corridor broke into a black door. Morana looked at the door, wondering what lay behind it. She knew that there was no bedroom downstairs. It could be Maroni's office. Or maybe something else.

Knowing this wasn't the time to appease her curiosity, especially since she was certain the room was under surveillance, she kept moving forward, her skin crawling with sudden dread. Unable to explain any of it, she wondered if she should just forget the entire party and simply go to Dante's house and stay there. She was certain he wouldn't mind. But something also told her she needed to keep going.

Preparing herself as much as she could, Morana finally came to a stop as the corridor ended, opening to two large mahogany double doors. She observed the door, the ornate carvings in the wood and the polished brass knobs. Whatever Maroni was, he had classy tastes and not in the flashy way of her father. His entire house screamed of good, refined taste.

Gathering her courage, hoping she would see either Dante or Tristan inside, Morana twisted the knob on the door and pushed it open just slightly, only wide enough for her to slip inside without attracting too much attention. She succeeded. Nobody spared her a glance as she quickly walked to a shadowed corner of the room by a pillar, picking up a glass one of the many waiters had on a tray and leaned against the corner. It was the perfect spot for some surveillance of her own.

Her heart was beating swiftly for some reason she could not understand. Keeping the small tremble in her hand contained, Morana took a little sip of the champagne and let her eyes rove around the place.

The room was monstrous. She could see at least fifty people already inside and more guests coming in through the door that opened in the lawns and yet it felt empty. Much to her surprise, the guests coming in stopped beside the door, handing their weapons over to the staff at the threshold. Astonished, Morana realized it was a weaponless party of sorts. She didn't even know such a thing existed, especially in their world.

And she had a knife strapped to her thigh.

An orchestra played soft music unobtrusively in the background from one corner of the hall, the corner opposite hers. A small clear area, evidently the dance floor, was right in front of the musicians. Waiters milled about with glasses and appetizers held perfectly balanced on silver platters. At the end of the hall, a long table sat, adorned with dishes and servers and seating space. It was a buffet. Lovely.

The decor of the room, like the rest of the house, was tasteful. The high ceiling was adorned with a chandelier that wasn't turned on. Instead, low lights high on the pillars cast an intimate glow all around the room. It felt medieval—the lighting, the people, the ambiance.

Lorenzo Maroni stood near the entrance door, sipping what looked like scotch from a glass tumbler. Morana watched him from her spot, wanting to see the man interact with his people. She watched, with amazement, as grown men went up to Maroni, who stood in his spot like an emperor. Then, they proceeded to take his hand, kissing his fingers. Maroni, in turn, bestowed them with a smile and a few words she couldn't make out. He also took the hands of the ladies with the men and kissed their fingers, like a true gentleman.

Watching him like that, Morana could understand why men and women alike were taken by him. He was charming, wealthy, and powerful. A combination that, when interspersed with danger, swayed people in his direction. This man was the leader of one of the biggest mob organizations in the world. This man reeked with the security of his authority. This man was the Bloodhound whose reputation preceded him.

And then the most fascinating thing happened.

The Predator walked in the door.

For once, Morana forced herself not to become entranced by the man but instead notice everyone else's reaction to him.

The energy in the room crackled. It buzzed over the people, who turned to watch him. Men straightened, women inhaled.

And Lorenzo 'Bloodhound' Maroni lost the security of his authority. The man kissing his fingers had stopped in the middle to watch The Predator stride instead. And Maroni stiffened, an emperor feeling the challenge to his throne pulsing through the room.

It was *fascinating*.

Morana didn't know if the occupants of the room reacted to him the way they did because he was the rumored heir or because he was the anomaly. Or simply because it was him. But one thing was for sure, he incited a reaction. And the best part, he neither thrived on it nor shunned it. It just was.

She finally let her eyes drift to him, watching as he stepped with that confidence he wore like his skin, his body encased in a black suit, black shirt, and no tie. Everyone was wearing a tie. Morana felt a small smile lift her lips at his blatant act of rebellion, her gaze lingering on the skin of his neck and chest exposed by the unbuttoned collar of his shirt. Damn, he wore a suit well.

He didn't stop at the door to hand over any weapons and she didn't know if that was because he wasn't carrying any or because he was confident enough that no one would dare check him. This wasn't the man who had left her at her door last night and high-tailed it out of there as quickly as possible. This wasn't even the man who had slammed her against the wall and left her with swollen lips. No, this was the man who had followed her into the bathroom of his enemy's restaurant and fucked her with his hand over her mouth. This was the man who had touched her against the wall of her father's house. This was the man whose eyes spoke death and trailed life across her skin.

And he got her wet. Both sides of him—the lone boy she had glimpsed yesterday, the intimidating man she observed currently.

Taking another sip to cool down her rapidly heating skin, Morana observed as he headed to where Maroni stood and said something to him that made Maroni harden even more. The older man dismissed the other people around him and said something to Tristan. Tristan took out his phone and typed something, nodding back at Maroni.

And then, as though feeling her gaze, he froze.

His eyes roved around the room before coming right to her in her shadowed corner.

She expected him to take her in, to let his gaze linger on her like she had become used to, to trail those magnificent eyes across her skin and set it on fire.

He didn't do any of it. Instead, seeing her there and seeing she was the one whose stare he'd felt, he simply looked back down at his phone, nothing about his posture changing.

What the hell?

Morana felt her body locking down as her eyes drilled holes into him, fury replacing the electricity, infusing into her blood. She was there, at a party in a place where she didn't know anyone, and he wasn't even giving her his eyes. Morana hadn't realized how much she had come to rely on them, not until he deliberately withheld them from her. His eyes were the one thing he'd never held back from her. Even in their most vulnerable, brutal moments, she'd always had his eyes.

Whatever his reasons for avoiding her, she didn't care anymore. She had exposed herself to him yesterday and then given him space. This behavior angered her. She knew he wasn't rejecting her, just taking his time processing whatever but it still pissed her off as irrational as it was.

Stewing at him and herself for giving him that kind of power, Morana didn't realize someone had joined her until she felt the presence of a warm body beside her. Stilling, her entire body locking, Morana turned to find the man she'd seen from her window, the man who had come alone, standing beside her while looking out at the room.

"We meet again, Ms. Vitalio," the grave, masculine voice spoke from beside her.

Morana was about to turn to look at the man when he told her, "Don't turn. It's a matter of life and death."

"Life and death?" Morana asked, sensing something dangerous.

"Yours, Ms. Vitalio," he returned simply.

Morana looked at him in the periphery, seeing nothing but shadows. "The man from the airport."

"Your new best friend indeed, Morana," the man kept his voice steady. "There is something you need to know."

Morana considered, highly intrigued but wary of him. "Stop talking in riddles."

"Very well," he muttered under his breath.

"Before your boyfriend looks at you and sees me," the man remarked, slight amusement tinging his voice.

Morana almost turned at that. "You know Tristan?"

"It's my business to know things."

"What did you mean by being my new best friend?" Morana cut through the chase, getting straight to the point.

"The enemy of your enemy, Morana," the man spoke quietly. The song changed to another melody. "We share common interests."

"And what would that be?" Morana inquired, keeping her gaze on the swaying couples.

"End of Alliance."

Morana froze at his words. Heart pounding hard, Morana whispered in his direction, "What do you mean?"

The man didn't miss a beat of the music. Morana couldn't feel anyone watching them, mostly because they were in the corner, shielded from the rest of the room, but her heart was racing.

"I mean I'm interested in finding out what happened twenty years ago in this city," the man said calmly right above her ear.

"Why?" Morana asked.

The man stayed silent for a beat. "Personal reasons. You were one of the missing girls and you are looking for the same thing. I have information."

Morana processed what he was telling her. "How can I trust you?"

"You cannot. And you shouldn't," the man stated clearly. "But you're not in my way so you're safe from me."

Morana tilted her head back up and took the measure of him. She couldn't tell if he was lying or not. Morana deliberated.

She felt his lips at her ear. "As a gesture of good faith, let me give you a piece of information I came across," he said so discreetly she could barely make the words out over the music. "Someone at the party is going to try to kill you tonight."

Morana inhaled sharply. The man continued without pausing. "And no, I have not set that up to gain your trust. I simply intercepted the information and I came to the party to warn you."

"Wait, you came here to warn me? Why?" Morana questioned, confused.

"Because I need the truth and you can help me get to it."

She gulped. He nodded. "Live tonight. Find me tomorrow. 459."

"That's your number?"

"Who are you talking to?" whiskey and sin interrupted the man.

Morana turned to see the spot beside her empty. She felt familiar hands go over her hips, pulling her flush against a hard, male body. Morana turned her attention back to the man holding her hips, her mind still reeling from her previous encounter.

"Did you see the man beside me?" Morana interrogated him.

In response, he tugged her hard into his body. The song changed to a familiar tune, a version of *Wicked Games* that she liked. Appropriate.

The hands on her hips held her steady. Morana slowly returned to the present, her own arms going around his neck as they started to move, completely flush against each other.

"What man?" Tristan whispered in her ear, just like the other man had. Except for this time, it sent delicious shivers down her spine, right to her core, that voice of whiskey and sin pouring down her body.

Clearing her throat, Morana informed him. "A man. He just told me there was someone in this room who would try to kill me tonight."

CHAPTER 9

ATTACK

It was fascinating to feel the reaction of his body to the news instead of just seeing it. Morana felt the way the muscles in his body clenched, one after the other, first his hands, then his arms, then his chest and shoulders until he was utterly still for a second. She had seen it happen on multiple occasions but feeling it was different. More intimate.

Suddenly remembering she was pissed at him, Morana took a step away. Or at least tried to, only to be brought right back into his body, his hands going low on her hips in a gesture nobody would miss. He started to move again, their bodies fitting like pieces of a puzzle together.

Morana could feel the multiple eyes on her this time as he moved her around, not expertly but in a raw rhythm that her body somehow followed. Nobody would have called him a beautiful dancer but fuck, he was sexy. With his hips rolling into hers, mimicking a more intimate action, his thigh spreading her legs for a second, grazing against her core before coming back into place, he was sensuality.

The female vocalist breathed *'I don't wanna fall in love with you'* into the microphone. He bent her over his arm, his nose breathing the entire line of her neck. Bringing her back against him, his hands on the edge of her ass, her breasts pressed into his torso, her nipples hardened as his mouth stayed close to her ear. She could hear a ragged breath he took, semi-hard.

Uncaring of the unusual display, Morana inhaled his scent in, the mix of musk and man familiar to her now, comforting even.

"It seems you're done avoiding me, Mr. Caine," she remarked breathlessly, deliberately using his last name.

He said nothing, only his hands tightening infinitesimally on her flesh in response.

Morana sighed, shaking her head. "Next time you need a moment, just tell me. We're honest with each other, remember?"

He didn't say anything. She knew he wouldn't, not when there were people around, unfriendly people, and not when they were watching him like a hawk. He was still The Predator. Only he was doing a very public mating dance, uncaring of those who watched. She didn't understand him sometimes.

The song changed to one she didn't know. His nose brushed against the lobe of her ear, sending blood rushing to the spot.

"Do you have the blade?" he murmured into her ear, like a lover whispering sweet nothings to any watchful eye.

Morana kept her body relaxed in his arms, nodding against his shoulder, pressing her nose into the V created by his shirt.

His hand brushed against her ass. "Let me have it," he spoke, half-stating half-asking.

"Why?" Morana wondered, her mind spinning.

He stayed quiet for a second and then whispered softly, "Trust me."

Oh, she wanted to. How she wanted to. But old habits had her hesitating, debating. If she let him have it, she would be unarmed and he knew it. And he asked for it, despite that knowledge. There had to be a good reason, a reason he probably couldn't share in this setting.

Closing her eyes, her stomach churning, Morana jumped off another cliff. She raised her left leg and wrapped it around his hip wordlessly, his hand automatically coming down to support her thigh. He turned them to the side, hiding her exposed leg from prying eyes, his fingers brushing over the strap holding her knife. Containing the shiver that wracked her body at his fingers stroking her skin gently, Morana held on to his shoulders. She felt his chest rise as he took in a breath, pressing right against her, the air around the side of her head buzzing with his life. With a small jerk, he pulled the knife out from the sheath, his hand disappearing from her thigh.

Morana put her leg back down again just as the song ended.

And felt him press a soft kiss on the top of her lobe.

Before she could even process that tiny action, he stepped back and walked away, leaving her gaping on the dance floor. Quickly controlling her expression, Morana stared at his retreating back, unable to understand what had just happened.

Suddenly aware of everyone stealing glances at her, Morana quickly ducked her head and headed for the door, thankfully not stopped by anybody on her path. Exiting out into the lawns, Morana took off her heels, lifted the hem of her dress and walked out away from the mansion, feeling her toes sink into the damp, dewy grass. The crisp air was refreshing. The sounds of the party faded away into the background as she strolled deeper and deeper into the lawn, heading towards the treeline, mulling upon everything.

A mysterious man had come to the party solely to warn her about a possible assassination attempt. Moreover, he had come because, according to him, they had the same goal - discovering what had happened twenty years ago with the Alliance. And his reasons were personal. Morana genuinely didn't know how to feel about that. He was dangerous, yes, but she hadn't sensed any creepy vibes from him. More importantly, she hadn't sensed any kind of masculine interest from him in her. While they had been dancing close, none of her antennas had been sending any off signals.

And then there was the way Tristan had cut into the conversation. After the way he had avoided her since last night and his snub earlier with the eyes, Morana had doubted he would even speak to her, much less walk over to dance with her. And though he hadn't been Mr. Warmth, he had still oddly warmed her. He had held her not in possession but with the confidence of a man who knew she had given herself to him. The very public nature of that had been interesting though. She couldn't figure out what he was trying to do. She'd thought he would fly her under the radar. Instead, he was beaming the spotlight on her. And somehow, despite the many, many eyes on them, he had maneuvered her into giving up her one weapon, consequently, giving him another small part of herself.

And then he had fucking kissed her ear. Her ear. Like seriously?

Morana touched her lobe where his lips had grazed her softly, rubbing the sensation off. God, the man confused her.

She emerged out of the treeline finally, letting her eyes adjust to the darkness. The lake rippled calmly a few feet from her, the wind dancing over the water in a soft breeze. Morana walked over a few steps, her toes curling into the grass, eyes going to the small house beside the lake.

His house. His home? She didn't know.

Up close, she observed the building. It was almost the same size as Dante's. There was a porch at the front, a comfortable-looking wooden recliner sitting on it, looking out at the lake. Morana imagined him sitting there in the evenings, gazing out on the lake, completely alone, nothing in his life except what he had made for himself. She imagined him sitting there, night after night, watching the same moon she had watched without even knowing about him. He had known about her and she imagined him clinging to her, to the only goal he had in life sitting alone in the dark. She imagined him thinking about her.

Drawn to the house like a moth to a flame, she took a step towards it. Then hesitated for a second, her step faltering. She shouldn't. No. Not without his invitation.

Taking a deep breath, she veered off the path and went towards the lake instead, standing exactly where she'd seen him and Dante standing yesterday. There was something almost peaceful about the place, away from the main house. She turned her neck to see her window from this vantage. The mansion was lit up and her window was very, very visible from where she stood. She could picture her silhouette in the room when he watched from here.

It was as she was contemplating everything that someone came out from the treeline towards her. Someone she didn't know, had never seen before.

Her heart started to pound.

The man she didn't recognize was dressed in black, his blonde hair light in the dark, his cold, dead eyes trained on her along with the end of a gun. Morana swallowed, taking a breath to try and quieten her heart.

"Who sent you?" she asked calmly as if she wasn't looking death right in the eyes. He didn't reply. She hadn't expected him to.

Mind whirring, Morana felt her fingers tighten around the strap of her stilettos. She could use them. Throw one at the gun right as she ducked down. She could then jump in the lake because running won't work. If she ran he would chase, maybe even hit her with a bullet. She would make an easier target running away. The lake would be harder for him to maneuver, the darkness would be her ally. She could easily hide in the murky depths for a while.

As all the plans came and went through her head, Morana kept her eyes steady on the assassin.

Out of nowhere, she saw the tip of a knife press into his neck.

"The lady asked you a question."

Morana watched, stunned, as the assassin reacted to the blade and that voice. Whiskey and sin and death. So much death.

Where the hell did he even come from? She'd been facing the tree line the entire time and hadn't even glimpsed a shadow slinking around. How?

The assassin unlocked the gun. The knife pressed into a point on his throat in silent rebuke, the point the Predator had told her would make her bleed out slowly and wish for death by demonstrating on their first encounter. She saw a drop of blood slide down into the assassin's dark clothes.

"I'm one second away from slitting your throat," Tristan warned, his voice so chilling she shivered. "I suggest you start answering some questions."

The assassin looked at her. "You shouldn't have gone digging old graves."

Before she could even blink, the man twisted his arm, turning the gun and shot himself through the head.

A shriek left her and she clapped her hands over her mouth, shock coursing through her as she watched the now-dead assassin fall, his blood splattered over Tristan. She stood rooted to the spot, her heels falling from her numb hands, as she watched Tristan quickly pocket the knife, squatting down to pat the corpse swiftly.

Morana stayed frozen.

He found a wallet, taking it out and rummaging through it, before pocketing that as well. Suddenly stopping, as though remembering she was still there, he looked up through a face splattered with blood, so much blood, his blue eyes sparking with something cold. Those eyes perused her quickly, thoroughly, before locking with hers.

"Get back to the house," he ordered quietly, without getting up.

Morana opened her mouth to say something but he shook his head, just once, silencing her for the first time. She didn't even know what she would have said. Her mind was blank. Just the idea of staying behind with the body made her feel nauseated all of a sudden.

She swallowed, her eyes going to his house just feet away, lingering, coming back to him in silent question.

His eyes blazed. He didn't respond.

Slightly dejected at still being uninvited, Morana sighed and moved around him and the corpse towards the treeline.

"And text Dante," his voice said from behind her, still quiet. He was in his mode but something was simmering under the surface, in a way she hadn't seen him in before. "Tell him to get here."

Morana nodded, pulling up the contact on the phone, making the call. Dante picked up on the second ring.

"Morana," he greeted, his voice neutral. She could hear the party in the background.

"You need to come by the lake," she told him, her voice so neutral, surprising her. She sounded so calm, too calm.

Dante paused. "You two okay?"

Morana looked at the dead body, then at Tristan, still covered in blood, checking the man's gun. She gulped. "I think so."

"I'll be there in 5."

Dante disconnected and Morana relayed the information to Tristan. He nodded and looked pointedly at the house.

Morana hesitated, part of her wanting to stay and help. But she didn't know anything about taking care of dead bodies and what to do with them. It wasn't her forte. And looking at the blown-out face of the assassin, she never, ever wanted it to be her forte.

"I need you to leave, now," Tristan told her, still crouched on the ground. He needed her to leave. He needed her to go so he could do whatever he had to do. She was a distraction at the moment. Realizing that, Morana nodded and walked back to the house without turning to look behind her, her steps quick. Thankfully, she didn't encounter anybody on the way. Entering through the main door, she climbed up the stairs and went straight to her room, locking the door behind her.

Heaving a shuddering breath in, reaction finally set in. With trembling hands, she took off her dress and jewelry, pushing them off and going straight for the shower. Stepping in, she closed her eyes as the warm water poured over her, the image of the assassin shooting his head off, his blood spraying back all over Tristan, burned in her memory. Scrubbing her skin, as though the blood was on her, Morana shivered in the warm water, her body shaking even as she tried to calm it down.

It was okay. Nothing happened. She was fine. He was fine. She was fine. He was fine.

She repeated it over and over like a mantra, eventually feeling her heart catch its normal rhythm. Blowing out a breath, she shut off the water and wrapped herself in a towel, her brain finally putting the pieces together.

Tristan had set a trap.

Like a true predator, he had taken her knife, perhaps because he'd been unarmed, and left her on the dance floor, knowing she would want to escape and her would-be assassin would follow. Somehow, without her or her assassin even getting the slightest hint, he had followed them, stalked them. And then he'd had the other man exactly where he'd wanted him—on the other end of the knife.

Getting into her new, cute pajamas, a sense of comfort washing over her, Morana got into bed, turning the light off. Her eyes open, she watched the lights from outside play on the ceiling, still surprised at the entire evening, at the meeting with the man who was her 'new friend', at the way Tristan had reacted at the party and then everything that had happened by the lake.

The last words of the man echoed in her head. Words he had said right before killing himself. She was digging old graves and someone, somewhere really wanted to keep them buried. But the thing was, she had no clue what she was digging into and who wanted to silence her so bad that they'd sent an assassin to the house of the Maronis. It didn't escape her attention that anybody gutsy enough to send an outsider in Maroni's property was either really desperate or fearless. She did consider if it was Maroni himself but discarded the idea immediately. If something happened to her, he would be the first suspect for Tristan and Tristan would go rogue on his ass, which Maroni couldn't afford at the moment for some reason. It couldn't be her father, not after the scene she had witnessed between him and Tristan.

And he had protected her, yet again.

She didn't want to be protected but she was realistic enough to know that in the world she lived in, having Tristan's protection was the only thing keeping her alive, especially after the enemies she had made unknowingly. She was grateful for that.

As she stared up at the ceiling, a part of her wished he would have told her to go into his house. She was curious about his space, yes, but more than that, she wanted to be invited where nobody had gone with him. She wanted, one day, to stare up at his ceiling in his bed with his body sleeping beside hers.

But he didn't trust her enough for that, not yet. And honestly, she really couldn't blame him. While she was more open to them, she was holding a part of herself back too. They were progressing but god, they were slow. She just hoped they kept moving forward and not back. She was willing to give him whatever time he needed to come to terms with things, but she had to nudge him to communicate, if not with words then some other way.

Sighing, blanking her mind of everything that had happened tonight and leaving it for tomorrow, Morana closed her eyes and let sleep take over.

❦

Something woke her up.

Morana stayed relaxed, keeping her eyes closed as she let her senses expand around the room. The hair on the back of her neck prickled. There was light in the room—light she could feel at the back of her eyelids.

Nerves taut, a knot low in her belly, Morana opened her eyes just a slit.

The door to her room was open.

Her heart started to hammer.

She automatically reached for the knife beside her pillow and came up empty. Tristan still had it. Fuck.

Without another thought, she extended her hand to the bedside lamp, anything to defend herself, just as a large silhouette moved to her.

She opened her mouth to scream.

And the noise got drowned behind the pillow shoved into her face.

CHAPTER 10

COMFORT

The thing they said about life flashing before the eyes during that moment of reckoning? They lied.

Morana didn't have any flashes, any moments from the past invading her mind in that second, nothing except the most primal need for survival clawing its way to the front as the pillow smothered her. Lungs burning, trying to replenish themselves with oxygen that was deprived to them, Morana struggled against the form holding her down, her legs jerking from side to side. Her noises muffled against the stuffing of the pillow. Her hands tried to scratch and hurt her assailant. Her fingers made contact with leather on muscled arms, slipping, her nails cracking open in the struggle. The pain was diminished by the intense burn in her chest and the methodical numbing of her face.

Panic tried to squeeze itself into her heart and in one split second of clarity, Morana knew she couldn't let panic win. Not in that moment. If she did, the bastard above her would succeed. She would die in her bed in new pajamas while a party went on downstairs. She would die and Tristan would detonate. He would destroy on his path to decimation, people including Dante and Amara and hundreds of innocents who did not deserve it.

She couldn't die. She couldn't trigger it. Not at this stage of her life. She had finally found something worth living for. Nobody could snatch it away from her. Not now. She had to make it. She had to live.

Trembling from head to toe, she extended her right arm to the side where it had been before, letting go of her resistance against the pillow for one second. Immediately, the pressure over her face increased exponentially, the panic for survival burning through her again. She refused to let it win, overextending the muscles of her arm, feeling the strain in her shoulder. She didn't care.

Her fingers made contact with the cool metal of the bedside lamp. Pulling a muscle with the strain, she grabbed onto the handle. Without hesitation, she gripped it tight and blindly swung it wildly in the direction of her assailant.

And missed.

She swung it again, and again, and again, finally making contact with solid flesh.

The assailant took his hands off the pillow to block her weak attack but it was enough. Throwing herself off the bed to the side, gasping loudly for the suddenly available air, Morana fell hard on the floor. Her back arched against the impact, her tailbone bruised. Uncaring about any of it, she looked up at the shadowed male figure wearing a balaclava, coming at her again. Instinctively throwing her right foot up in the air, she kicked him right between the legs and kicked him hard.

Her foot made contact with his groin and the man screamed in pain, cupping his balls as Morana tried to scramble for a weapon. His hand enclosed her ankle and dragged her back down. The frantic fear tried to grab her again and Morana deliberately kept her head cool, letting her brain kick in. Sliding down the floor as he tugged her, Morana spread her legs and trapped his head between her thighs, squeezing for her life. Whimpers left her mouth, her chest heaving as she grabbed the wire connected to the lamp and brought it to her. Her assailant struggled between her legs, the pressure on his skull immense, his intense movement straining her thighs, and everything in between.

Feeling disgusted, Morana brought the lamp down on his skull, hitting him with the end of the metal handle. The assailant bought his hand up to prevent the attack and the glass of the bulb, which had already crashed in her first attack, cut through his palm. Heart exploding out of her chest, Morana panted, trying to dodge his hands as they came to her face, trying to get a grip on her neck, her nose, her ears, all vulnerable spots.

Evading him while keeping his upper half immobile, she hit him again, knowing it was only a matter of time before he picked her up or slammed her into the ground. Her only option was to knock him out before he could get his bearing. With that thought driving her survival, the lamp shaking in her arms, she brought it down again.

Thankfully, this time, he went limp. Breathing hard, Morana slowly crawled back on her hands, releasing him from her thighs, the muscles quivering with the exertion. His body fell sideways and she stared at him, the lamp still gripped tightly in her hands, shuddering wildly as she tried to catch her breath. The adrenaline was hitting the roof of her blood vessels. The roaring in her ears pounded into her skull as she stared at the man's form, expecting him to come to life any second and attack again.

After a few seconds, when that didn't happen, Morana cautiously went closer and gripped the edge of his mask. He was still breathing.

One hand still holding her weapon, she tried to pull up the mask, the muscle she'd pulled in her shoulder screaming at her to stop the activity. Still riding high on the adrenaline in her blood, Morana managed to get his mask up almost to his forehead single-handedly. There was no recognition in her mind as she saw his face. She didn't know him but damn her if she didn't do so by tomorrow.

Standing up on shaky legs, she quickly grabbed her phone from where it had fallen from the nightstand in her struggle. Bringing up the camera, she hastily clicked a series of pictures, the flash blinding her momentarily in the dark. Not once did she hover to analyze his features as she would normally have done. Nothing about this was normal.

The man roused slightly from the multiple flashes, his eyes opening, blinking for a few seconds as he came to grips, his hand going to a head that must have been hurting something fierce.

He saw Morana and immediately reached for a knife in his boot, something the idiot should have done ages ago. Had she been an assassin, she would have simply slit her throat in sleep. But what the hell did she know about assassins? Maybe he had a thing for blood, or maybe he had some kind of modus operandi he operated with. Whatever it was, she sure wasn't going to hang around to test it.

Phone tight in her grip, Morana threw the lamp—that life-saving lamp—at him to divert his attention and ran for the door.

She heard him struggle behind her but she didn't wait to listen. Racing down the flights of stairs, unaware if the assailant was following her, only able to hear the blood rushing through her ears and her own labored breathing, Morana just focused on getting out of the mansion.

Getting to the ground floor, she came to a stop. The sounds of music playing at the back of the house drifted through the blood in her ears and Morana hesitated at the bottom of the staircase, unsure of which direction to go in. If she went to the party, her pajamas ruined, hair disheveled, feet bare, she was sure it would get a lot of attention but she couldn't risk anything. She didn't know if Tristan or Dante would be there or still at the lake or somewhere else. But outside, the guards could be patrolling and they knew she was "Caine's girl". And even though she would be an open target, she had to take that risk.

Decision made, Morana sprinted through the empty foyer and out the doors. The lights around the lawns had been dimmed. She had no idea what time it was but the no moon and low lights were eerie. But good to hide her in the shadows. Quickly slipping into the shadow of the house, Morana hurried towards the west, towards Dante's house. She wanted to, really wanted to, head to the lake but there was a huge possibility that Tristan wouldn't be at home and she'd be a sitting duck outside. At least, at Dante's house, she knew there would definitely be someone to let her in. She hoped. He had told her he had round-the-clock staff when he had invited her to stay and she might very well take him up on that offer now. There was no fucking way she was ever going back to stay in the mansion ever again. She'd move into a hotel or rent out her own place if it came to that. But if she survived the night alive, she was not returning to that room to sleep ever again, Maroni and his brand of douchery be damned.

She heard the chatter from a group of guards near the entrance to the party but she stayed quiet.

And then she heard the main door to the house open again. She looked back to see her assailant, almost one with the dark while she was lit like a beacon with her light pajamas. Abandoning all sense of stealth, her heart thundering with a vengeance, Morana bolted towards the house she could see in the distance down the hill, the small lights guiding her.

The grass cushioned her bare feet, the dewdrops clinging to them making it slippery at her speed. But fuck it, she'd rather die breaking her neck than let that asshole catch her. Thighs burning, both from the sprint and the struggle earlier, her sides catching in stitches, begging her to slow down, Morana just made her way towards the house. Not slowing down, huffing with the exertion, she could see the house coming closer and closer.

Just a bit more.

Her body trembled. A small pebble cut her foot. She cried out, stumbled, but didn't stop. She could feel the cut getting dirty and the blood mixing with the grass underneath her. Her hair stuck to her scalp, the sweat from all the activity coating her skin.

Twenty feet.

The lights got dimmer the farther she went from the mansion. Darkness enclosed around her, fear assaulting her all over again as she realized she could be attacked from anywhere and not see it coming. Her eyes burned and she could feel her body ready to let go. It wasn't used to this, this kind of sudden abuse she was putting it through. She exercised, sure, but never this extensively. Her body wasn't equipped to handle this. She would start training. If she survived the night alive, as was becoming her mantra, she swore she would start training more, just in case something like this ever happened again. She had barely escaped her room tonight by the edge of her teeth. That wouldn't work every time so she needed to equip herself in ways she was strong enough with or without weapons. Like Tristan was. God, she hoped she made it. They had just begun. She couldn't die, not now.

Ten feet.

The sweat on her palms was making keeping a hold of the phone harder. She powered through, her hair a mess, her feet muddy, her t-shirt almost off her shoulder. She had to get there, just get there. Then she would collapse. Then she would sleep and never wake up. But god, she had to make it. She didn't dare stop for a second to look back over her shoulder. The man could be catching up, almost breathing down her neck. Or he could have cloaked himself in the darkness. She didn't know which was worse.

Five feet.

Climbing up the low steps two at a time, she ran to the big wooden door and pounded on it, her fists protesting against the hard, repeated impact.

"Dante," she tried to speak but it barely came out, her whole body shaking. She looked back behind her. This far from the mansion, there were no lights strung in the lawn. Darkness surrounded her and her assailant was in the dark. She had no idea where he was.

Tears forming in her eyes, the pit of her stomach knotted tight, Morana kept pounding on the wood, over and over and over, until she heard movement on the other side.

Suddenly, the door opened and Dante, clad only in a pair of jeans stood there, a gun pointed at her in his hand.

Morana had never been so relieved to see someone in her entire life.

She barely saw the shock on his face before she launched herself at him, her body going completely limp as he pulled her inside, closing the door behind him.

"Morana," she heard him say as she just stood there, her face in his chest, hanging onto his shoulders, her entire body juddering so much she could barely stand straight.

"Morana," he mumbled again and she realized she was sobbing uncontrollably, adrenaline still high in her body.

"Hey, hey, tell me what happened. Morana, are you hurt?"

She tried to speak but the words didn't come out. The sensation of her mouth being smothered by the pillow returned, sobs leaving her throat but no words.

"Dante," she heard someone's voice come from behind him.

"Zia, can you bring me my phone?" Dante said, simply cupping the back of Morana's head in one huge paw, rubbing it in a soothing motion while trying to guide her to walk with the other hand. Her legs were numb, feet stuck to the ground. She couldn't move from the spot.

"I'm going to pick you up, Morana, okay?" Dante told her slowly like he was speaking to a child. "Don't worry, you're safe now."

She felt him bend and pick her up. Morana, for some reason, didn't cling to his giant form, even as she was afraid of letting go, the sounds from her chest finally permeating through all the noise of her blood. Dante carried her somewhere, she didn't see. Her eyes were closed, trying to eradicate the sensations from the attack suddenly assaulting her all over again.

She felt Dante set her down somewhere gently, cushions sinking under her and he pulled back. Morana kept her eyes closed for a long minute, trying to get her breathing under control, aware of all the pain in her body.

"Tristan," she heard Dante speak, her heartbeat spiking again at his name. "You need to get here. Now."

There was silence for a second before Dante stated. "It's Morana." More silence.

"Something happened . . . I don't know . . . Okay."

Morana lifted her eyelids, just in time to see Dante cut the call. He looked even bigger from her seated position and Morana noticed the multitude of tribal tattoos littering across his torso in random, odd patterns. She looked around, to see she was in the living room where she'd worked, her laptop still on the table.

Zia entered the room, coming to her with a glass of water. Morana, her throat tight, accepted the glass and gulped the chilling liquid down only to find both of them observing her. Zia, taking the glass away, stroked a wrinkled hand over her head in a gesture so maternal, Morana broke down again.

"Oh, child," Zia muttered, stroking her hair again while Dante squatted down before her, taking both her trembling hands in his, his chocolate eyes staring into hers.

"What happened?" he asked again, almost gently, and Morana, at that moment, loved him for it. Just his big hands holding hers, his presence, his house—she wished she'd had him growing up. Tears escaped her even more, for everything, old and new, no words coming from her lips. Every time she opened her mouth, she felt the pillow trying to muffle her, her lips and nose crushing from the force.

The door to the room suddenly flew open and Morana flinched, her eyes going to it in fear.

And then the fear left her completely.

Tristan stood there, hair messy, in jeans and a t-shirt he'd put on inside out, his eyes frantically coming to her.

She saw him scan her entirely in two seconds, taking in every single detail, from her feet to her hair. And for the first time, Morana saw his magnificent blue eyes go wild.

He *snapped.*

Like a laser, he strode to where she lay, ignoring everyone else in the room. She couldn't look away. Her heart, which had been exercised too much that night, finally slowed down a bit. She watched him, tears on her face, her entire being collapsing because he was there. He was there. And god, she *hurt* so much.

Just as she tried to move towards him, he reached her. Hands going around her, he plucked her up from the couch and sat down, keeping her sideways on his lap, one of his hands on the outside of her thigh, the other in her hair, holding her tight to him. Her ear pressed against his heart and she could hear how rapidly it was pounding. Listening to it, to the tension in his body personified by the rate of his beating heart, Morana felt her own clench in response to its call.

Relaxing for the first time that night, Morana found the spot between his shoulder and neck again, the one she'd discovered on that very couch hours ago, and pressed her nose, her mouth, her entire face into his warm skin. Her tears wet the spot, her breaths heated it. She felt his hands clench for a second before unclenching again. The hand on the outside of her thigh started to slowly rub the skin in a soothing motion, the hand in her hair pressing her face softly into that spot.

In her mind, Morana replaced the sensation of that cold pillow with the heat of his neck, replaced the smothering of her nose roughly with the smushing of her nose gently. She inhaled him in, letting that smell of him—just musk and him at this late hour—to seep into her bloodstream and replace the adrenaline. She wrapped her arms around his hard, solid body, her fingers holding on to the cotton for dear life as the shaking in her body intensified, the adrenaline finally dissipating.

He held her through it all.

And slowly, after minutes, as her tremors calmed down enough and her blood started to flow more naturally, she felt him press a soft, simple kiss to her ear.

Her lips trembled against the skin of his neck.

His arms tightened around her.

And there, she felt safe. Protected. Like all the assailants in the world couldn't get to her. She knew he wouldn't let them get to her.

"Morana," she heard Dante speak again, softly. She turned her head slightly, looking at him through puffy eyes, her vision slightly blurred.

"What happened?" he asked, his voice urging her to talk.

She swallowed, her throat tight. Focusing on the pulse beating right next to her nose, on his chest expanding as he inhaled and deflating as he exhaled, Morana tried to match her own breaths in sync with his, just like she'd done at the penthouse when she'd had the panic attack. She focused on the life in him, and worked her mouth open, ungluing her tongue. It felt heavy. She felt heavy.

"There was ..." she started, her voice a croak, "someone in my room."

As she had at the party, she felt him go still, every muscle locking against hers. Chest, back, biceps, forearms, thighs. Even his neck. The muscles tensed in one moment of sudden stillness.

"What do you mean someone was in the room?" Dante asked, the anger in his voice breaking through her analysis of the man she was sitting on. Looking sideways at Dante, she spoke, her voice still not Jacksonating for some insane reason.

"Someone was in the room when I woke up," she told them, her voice barely a whisper but loud enough for both men to hear in the silent room. "He attacked. I escaped and got here."

She saw Dante look all over her, his eyes flaring with rage and flickering up to Tristan, whose eyes she couldn't see. It was either staring into his eyes or nuzzling into the warm, comfy spot in his neck. Right now, she chose the neck. Plus the way he was holding her felt *really nice*. Cozy, warm, snug, and safe, Morana suddenly felt her eyelids weighing down on her, her entire body feeling heavy.

She heard Dante say something in a low tone and Tristan's chest rumble but it all sounded muffled as Morana adjusted herself on him and settled in, closing her eyes, drifting to sleep, knowing nothing would be attacking her the next time she woke up.

❦

It was a movement that woke her up.

Panicking, remembering the attack, thoughts of being trapped, held down against her will flooded her mind.

"Shh shh," the soft whisper in the flavor of whiskey and sin poured over her, going into her ears, infusing in her blood, drifting to every part of her body, warming her from the inside out.

Her entire being relaxed. The other memories post-attack came to her then—the escape, Dante's house, Dante, Zia, and finally Tristan.

She'd fallen asleep on him like the little koala she was becoming with him. She couldn't believe she actually fell asleep, not around him, but on him.

The movement continued.

Opening her eyes to see darkness all around her, Morana realized she was being carried by him, one of his hands under her knees, the other around her shoulders. Putting her arms around his neck, Morana tried to peer into the dark but couldn't.

And even though she'd been attacked, despite all the night cloaking them, despite realizing that her assailant could be very near, Morana didn't feel an ounce of her previous fear looking at the dark.

The man holding her was darkness. He was comfortable in the dark, one with the dark, owned the dark. And as long as he held her the way he did, safe in his arms, that dark was hers. It belonged to her. She was comfortable in it, safe in it, one with it. She didn't know where he was taking her. She didn't care. He could carry her to a cave for all she cared. After a life spent fighting for herself, after that night of struggling for survival, this was what she'd fought for, struggled for, lived for. This precious, silent, soft moment where, even on the darkest of nights, she wasn't alone. She had made it to the shore on her own and he was carrying her from there.

She heard his heartbeat again—*thump thump thump*—inside his chest where her ear was pressed. It beat normally now, not the brutal pace it had been earlier.

The wind was cold on her bare arms and legs and a shiver went through her body. His arms pulled her closer to his body, heat radiating from his skin, and he continued to walk. Morana wanted to ask him questions but that would have meant breaking the silence, disturbing the sounds of his steady heartbeats and night creatures, and she didn't want to do that. Even as muscles she didn't know in her body ached and the shoulder pressed into his chest hurt and her thighs felt like they'd been split open, she was restful.

The glow of light made Morana turn her head and look towards the source. It came from a house.

His house.

Surprise hit her as she squinted at the light, making sure she wasn't mistaking it for some other structure. Nope. The same lake, the same porch, the same chair she'd wanted to sit in.

He was taking her to his house.

Oh god.

Oh god.

She felt her heart start to pound again, a major freak out on its way to crash onto her.

Gulping, Morana opened her mouth to say something, this time not knowing whether her silence was because of the attack or the shock. She turned her head to look up at him, and after a few minutes, feeling her steady gaze, he looked down at her. His eyes, shadowed by the little light, locked with hers and Morana felt her fingers clench around his solid neck. She knew the questions were brimming in her eyes and she could see the answers in his.

They made it to the front of the lake—right where the other body had dropped, in fact—and then headed to his porch.

She had to say something.

"Are—"

Before she could get anything else out, he stopped in front of that very comfortable looking chair she had contemplated sitting in, and slid her down his body, right into the chair. Arms still around his neck, Morana looked up at the little light that poured from inside the house, casting his face in shadows. She searched his blue eyes as he looked down into her face, his eyes floating up to her forehead before returning to hers.

He brought his hand up, stroking his thumb over her cheek once, before straightening.

Morana watched as he took out a key from his back pocket, pressed some codes on the alarm on the side, and opened the door. He looked at her, giving her a 'stay here' motion with his hand before going in. Morana felt her brows go up slightly at that. Somehow, she didn't think it was to hide any dirty boxers or something from her. He didn't seem like the type to have any kind of mess around him. No, from what she knew of him and what she'd glimpsed at in his penthouse, everything was in its place in his house. Simple things he could control.

The chair was very homely though. She had been right. And now that she was relaxed in the cushion, the ache in her tailbone piped up in queue with the others. Damn, she needed a good, long, hot bath.

Sighing, she looked out at the lake just as he returned.

Distracted, she watched him approach her and pick her up again. Hands automatically going around him for support, Morana looked at his face, at the scruff littering his jaw, and then at the door.

He headed to it.

Her heart began to race again.

This was big. *Big* big. Huge. She knew it. He knew it. And he was still taking steps towards it.

Taking a deep breath in, Morana watched as he carried her over the threshold, stopping for a second inside to shut the door behind with his feet.

The lock clicked.

The alarm beeped.

She was inside.

Holy fuck.

CHAPTER 11

ENTER

Her eyes looked around the place, trying to take it in. They were in some kind of foyer, the door to her left was closed and one to her right led to a dimly lit living room, from what she could tell. Right before them was a corridor that they were going through, at the end of which were a wide set of stairs leading upstairs.

Morana unconsciously gripped his shoulder as he started the climb straight up, night lighting guiding him through. She could see the walls decorated with pictures of some kind but could barely make them out at his speed and the light. The architecture, she realized as they stopped at the top of the stairs, was similar to the penthouse. The stairs simply opened up into a ginormous master bedroom.

There was only a single bedside lamp turned on. Before she could take in any more details, they were headed to the door at the other corner of the room, the space huge. And after carrying her through from Dante's house to his and up the stairs, he wasn't even breathing heavy. Seriously, what did he eat? After the state of her body, she realized she needed to get on his diet. Stamina of the body would seriously help along with stamina of the brain.

They came through the door into a huge, dimly lit bathroom, much bigger than her own at her father's house or the guest one at his penthouse. The man clearly liked his space.

Morana watched the water steaming in the tub and a groan of pleasure escaped her, just upon seeing it. He was psychic. The scent of lemon and cinnamon permeated the air.

Morana got down from his arms, his arms on her back again to steady her. She leaned into him, and the hands slowly pulled up her t-shirt and stripped her of it. Morana pushed down her destroyed shorts and let them join the floor in a heap.

He indicated the water and Morana, naked as a jaybird but comfortable in that nudity with him, walked to the tub. Careful of her aches and pains, Morana put one foot in, then the other, and lowered herself in. The water, blessed, hot water, wrapped her in the warmest of hugs.

A noise escaped her throat—some hybrid cross between a mewl and a moan. She closed her eyes, ducking her head under the water before coming up, feeling cleaner than she had all night. He had done this before when she'd come to him after her father let her fall down the stairs. He'd been silent but offered her his care, prepped a bath for her. Back then, it had touched her, moved her, surprised her—both his kindness and Dante's. Now, leaning her head back on the edge, letting the water lap at her tired muscles, Morana was surprised to realize she wasn't surprised at this kindness. Somehow, she'd grown comfortable enough to even expect it from him.

She didn't know how to feel about that.

Wiping her face, Morana opened her eyes, expecting to find herself alone.

She wasn't.

Tristan was near the sink, getting a washcloth and some bottles, and coming towards her.

She blinked up at him in surprise, not understanding.

"What are you doing?" she asked softly, watching him.

He simply kneeled on the floor behind her head in answer.

His big, rough hands more at ease with handling lethal weapons slowly wiped over her cheeks, gently, like he was afraid of applying too much pressure. She rubbed her skin more when she removed her makeup. His touch was light, but sure, wiping a soft cloth over both her cheeks, her chin, her forehead.

Morana leaned her head back, relaxing, letting him take care of her in a way she'd never been taken care of and in a manner she doubted he'd taken care of someone in a long time. They both deserved this. This was *theirs*.

Silently, he handed the washcloth over to her and Morana looked down, surprised to find the white fabric pale red. She stared at it, at the muddled shade, and remembered her assailant cutting himself and trying to grab her face. He'd smeared blood over her face.

And Tristan had wiped it.

Again.

Heart clenching, fingers squeezing the rag, she felt her lips tremble as his hands came to her wet hair. The smell of his masculine shampoo hit her nostrils and Morana forced herself to breathe easy. His fingers, his sure fingers, firmly massaged the shampoo over her scalp, lathering up her strands. Morana tilted her head back, groaning at the amazing sensation. His hands paused for a split second before he continued again. He could totally switch careers someday if he wanted. There was something so peaceful in that shared silence, something so reminiscent of the first night she'd spent in his territory.

But she had to tell him the poison eating inside her head. She had to give it to him because he was the only one she knew that poison didn't kill. He would take it, sip it, and still come out on the other side. She couldn't. A life of holding onto venom had slowly started to corrode her from the inside-out until she'd let it out with him.

"I hit him on the head," the words escaped her in a whisper in the silence of the room, given to the dark, to him.

His fingers paused again, waiting for her to continue. She had no idea why she'd spoken, but once it was out, it escaped like a torrent.

"I didn't have any weapon," she spoke softly as he continued to wash her hair, listening intently. She could feel it in the way his fingers moved with her words. "He tried to smother me with a pillow. I somehow got a hold of the lamp and hit him with it."

His fingers twitched. He cupped some water in his palm and poured it over the edge of her forehead. She felt the suds flow into the bathwater.

"Somehow we ended up on the floor and he was between my legs—"

He stilled.

In a much more dangerous way than she'd ever experienced before.

Morana immediately realized her error and hurried to explain. "No, no. Not like that. No, he didn't touch me."

She could hear his breathing, heavier than before, his fingers tightening in her hair as his body remained motionless in that very, very hunter-like manner.

She went on quickly. "I kind of trapped his head between my thighs to make him immobile. And then I bashed his head with the lamp until he passed out."

After a few seconds, he started to wash the shampoo out of her hair again. Morana exhaled in relief, telling him the rest. "I clicked his picture. I'll run facial recognition tomorrow. Anyhow, he woke up and before he could chase, I ran to Dante's. It's a good thing he was there."

He growled softly.

Morana felt her eyebrows hit her hairline but didn't say anything else. She did enjoy his animal sounds, she was coming to realize. She told him the same.

"As much as I enjoy these animal noises, you can speak, you know."

After a few seconds of silence, she thought he wouldn't respond.

"Later."

One simple word uttered in a voice barely controlled. Morana softened, giving him the time and space to process it his own way.

He finished with her hair as she finished with her bath, the water slowly pruning her fingers. After minutes, Morana looked to see Tristan take out a towel and offer it to her. She stood up and took the towel, drying herself as he went out to the bedroom.

Morana drained out the water and exited into the dark bedroom, seeing him ruffling through a drawer beside the door. Taking out a t-shirt, he handed it to her.

"Thanks," she muttered, taking it and tugging it over her head. It fell on her body, almost hitting her knees, wrapping her in his scent. She inhaled deeply. It was the best pajama she'd ever had.

She watched him leave the room and return multiple times, taking something out, bringing something in. After the fourth round, he came to her with a glass of water and pills in one hand.

"Painkillers?" she asked, her eyes on him. His eyes were fixed on his t-shirt on her very naked body as he nodded.

Morana took the pills and drank the water. That done, he took the glass and placed it on the edge of the chest of drawers.

Then he swung her up again and carried her the few feet to the bed. Putting her down on the soft mattress that she sank in, he picked up her now clean foot and inspected it. Then he started to apply the ointment and bandage on the cut where it throbbed, not once looking at her.

Morana watched it all, her heart in her throat. She had glimpsed his scars, seen the mottled skin, the burns, the raised flesh that bespoke some of the most brutal torture, some that she could possibly never imagine. And yet, in that moment, when he took care of her little cut like it was a long gash, something deep inside her, the part of her that she was still holding on to, was given, released, handed over, to him. If there was one thing she had realized over the past few weeks, one thing that had become an epiphany in the past few hours, it was that this man would never have killed her.

As silent as he remained, Morana knew it wasn't because he didn't feel anything. It was because he felt too much and no matter what, she vowed, watching him at her feet, that she would ride it out with him. She had found something immensely precious in their world, a diamond in the coals, a lotus in the mud. And she vowed to cherish it, cherish him, as he deserved. He needed time to open up, to trust her not to abandon him someday, and she would give that to him. He had earned that.

Quickly wiping the one tear that had left her eyes, because she wasn't used to anyone caring enough to fix her wounds, because despite everything he had been through this man had still found it in his heart to care for when she was hurt, Morana pulled her foot back after he was done. She got under the covers and watched him strip his t-shirt and jeans down to his black boxers, throwing them off to the side.

It was the first time she saw his body as it was. Muscles rippled in places she didn't know muscles could ripple. Tattoos and scars littered his torso, front and back, some even down on one thigh. One lone tattoo stretched across his bicep, circling, but it was too dim for her to make it out. But the most noticeable was the confidence he was moving with. In clothes or out of it, this man knew who he was and wasn't afraid of letting people know it.

Morana sank back on the pillows, her heart hammering as she watched him get in on the other side, check his gun on the bed-side table, and turn off the light. And it was such a domestic, normal thing, Morana marveled at witnessing it.

The room plunged into darkness and Morana blinked at the ceil-ing, biting her lip. Her eyes slowly adjusted to the lack of light, some light seeping in from outside the door, allowing her enough to make out shapes.

She turned her neck to trace the shape of the man beside her when she felt one of his hands slide around her neck. It should have felt threatening after the attack. It should have sent panic coursing through her bloodstream after the night she'd had.

It felt anything but.

The palm pressed against her pulse, the fingers spanning her neck, the skin rough against hers—it all anchored her to the moment, to that bed, to him. She felt sheltered, cherished, and so very protected. He tugged her closer, almost until their noses were touching while their bodies remained slightly apart.

She felt his breaths over her face, the heat of his body right beside hers.

And then, for the first time that night, she heard him speak.

"Never again," he whispered, his voice rough with an edge of the wildness she'd seen in his eyes. It sent a delicious shiver down her spine.

"They will die a thousand deaths," he murmured, almost gently as his thumb traced the line of her jaw, "before they ever touch a single hair on your head again."

And then, with that deathly vow still echoing in her heart, he pressed his lips to her fluttering pulse.

"I promise," his lips wrote against her skin.

Morana swallowed, feeling the echo of that promise rushing through her blood. She arched her neck back, exposing it even more to him, sliding her body closer to his. His mouth moved, his lips parting over her pulse, sucking in every heartbeat on his tongue. Heart throbbing along with the rest of her body, Morana slid a hand into his hair, tugging him closer. The motion made pain shoot through the muscle in her shoulder.

She gasped and he pulled back, moving back to his side and tugging her close.

"Get your stuff tomorrow."

Her heart stopped for a beat.

"You want me to move in?" she asked, wanting to be sure, *absolutely* sure, she hadn't misunderstood.

He tucked her face under his in response.

"I've never slept with anyone before," she confessed into his neck, her nose in that happy spot again.

"Me neither," he murmured into her hair.

Fuzzy with that news, thrilled at the knowledge she was going to be with him, Morana smiled. He pressed a soft kiss to her ear. She rubbed her nose against that spot on his neck. They didn't say anything else. They weren't wrapped around each other but their bodies were close. Morana heard as his breathing started to gradually slow down, her own heart finding a rhythm with his.

Tomorrow, she would have to deal with everything that had happened that night – the man and his offer, her codes, her first assassin who had blown his head off, and the second assailant who had accosted her in her bedroom. A bedroom, that she suddenly remembered, was supposed to have surveillance and listening devices inside it. Had that failed or had this been something more nefarious? This, all of this, was much bigger than she'd realized. She would have to talk to the guys about it and figure out what the hell was going on. She didn't know but she would worry about that tomorrow.

For now, she was pressed into a solid, warm body that cared much more for her than either of them had realized. For now, she had another wonderful man in her corner who had handled her with the care she could appreciate in retrospect. Dante had been calm, reassuring and so gentle she felt the place in her heart for him expand.

And he had called Tristan. Who had been silent the entire night until his vow to her. She was in the inner lair of the biggest predator of them all, her jugular exposed to him as she breathed on his neck, in her most vulnerable state. She had bled and he had licked her wounds clean. She had almost tasted death and he had breathed life back into her.

And she realized she'd never, not once in her life, felt safer.

For the first time in her life, she felt home.

CHAPTER 12

DISCOVER

T he sudden jerking of her body woke her up.

Morana opened her eyes, disoriented and confused. The soft bed she was on was strange, as was the dark room. Blinking, trying to remember, she became aware of the weight of an arm around her stomach—a heavy arm. Morana looked down at the limb lying over the t-shirt she was wearing, and followed it to the body it was attached to.

Tristan.

Memories came rushing back. Though she couldn't see him in the dark, she could feel the warmth of his body pressed to her side as she lay on her back. Breathing softly, she allowed awareness to slither through her. One of his rougher legs was lying between her bare ones, his arm lying under her breasts, keeping her anchored to his side. His warm breath hit her hairline, his lips almost pressed against the crown of her head.

It was the first time in her memory that she was being held.

Morana basked in the glow of this moment in the dark. After the night she had had, after the life that she had had, this was the last place she would have thought herself to wind up at. In the home of

Tristan Caine. In the bed of Tristan Caine. In the arms of Tristan Caine. And yet, she couldn't think of anywhere else to be. He had given her a taste of two things she'd never had—safety and home. Both had been concepts, ideas that existed in the lives of people who didn't belong in her world, mirages that illusioned her kind. But he'd been feeding her little doses of both ever since that rainy night in the penthouse, and she was addicted. In the arms of the most dangerous man she knew, she felt the safest she had ever been.

A light sound against her ear broke through her musings.

Morana heard it, and her lips trembled with the sudden urge to chuckle. She pressed them together as the sound came again, softly.

Tristan 'The Predator' Caine snored like a baby.

No wonder he didn't like anyone in the room when he slept; his entire reputation would be crushed. Lips twitching, she turned her face towards him, feeling his exhale on her forehead as her nose pressed into the happy spot she'd discovered between his neck and shoulder.

That was the moment she found out something new about herself—she was a cover hogger. Sometime during the night, she had completely pulled the blanket over to her side, leaving him half in the cold and half in the snuggly warmth. He had simply come over to her side of the bed in the unconscious retaliation. Between his body heat and her conquered covers, she was toasty. Sighing happily, no idea of the time behind the dark drapes that shut out the light, Morana snuggled deeper into him, that musky masculine scent of his flesh wrapping itself around her like another layer of comfort.

His arm jerked suddenly, jerking her body, making her realize it had been the cause of her wakefulness. His breathing changed, getting heavier, his hand tightening slightly on the side of her ribs. Morana tilted her neck back, trying to see his face but only able to make out the silhouette in the darkness. His fingers spasmed on her flesh, his breaths getting shorter. Morana recognized the signs, having experienced them herself on numerous nights, but she'd never witnessed anyone going through a nightmare. She wondered what his subconscious was showing him. With the brutal life he'd led, most of which she couldn't even fathom, she knew she shouldn't have been surprised by this.

Swallowing, her heart clenching, the desire to soothe him acute, Morana slowly placed her hand on his forearm, feeling the muscles flex involuntarily under her touch. No idea what to do, she went with her gut. Tucking her head in, she pressed her lips against his heart, feeling scarred tissue under her mouth, and softly kissed it while stroking his arm.

A low noise rumbled in his chest. His body twitched.

"Shh," Morana whispered, pressing soft kisses on his chest, stroking his arm over and over again. "It's okay. You're safe. It's okay."

His body tensed, the bicep right beside her breasts bunching tightly as his neck moved. Morana patted his arm, nuzzling into his neck and murmuring the same words repeatedly into his skin.

A clock ticked somewhere in the house. Her heart beat steadily—*thump thump thump*—in tandem with it. Minutes passed. And slowly, eventually, she felt his strained muscles loosening up, the grip he had on the side of her ribs easing.

Morana spoke against his heart again, "You're safe. It's okay."

"Leave the bed next time," his raspy voice whispered against her hair. Having not expected him to wake up, Morana tried to pull her face back but his hand, which had been around her torso, came up to the back of her head and held her exactly where she'd been.

She settled in. "Not happening."

"I can get dangerous," he informed her, as though the thought had never crossed her mind. She wasn't an idiot. Morana rolled her eyes but stayed silent.

"I'm serious," his somber tone brooked no argument. "I can seriously hurt you and not know it."

She shrugged. "I'll take my chances."

A frustrated noise left his throat and Morana tilted her head back, bringing her hand to the side of his head, the sensation of his hair between her fingers amplified in the dark.

"You made me a promise last night in the dark," she murmured softly, knowing she had his full attention. "I'm making you one now."

Brushing her thumb over the line of his jaw, feeling the scruff rasping against it, she vowed, repeating his own words. "Never again. You'll never be alone again. No matter how bad the nightmare gets, I'm going to be right here."

The weight of the words echoed in the silence between them for long minutes. His breathing didn't change but his fingers flexed a bit on the back of her head. She knew what this meant to him. She could imagine all the emotions swirling through him, including the most dangerous one of all—hope. Dare he hope that she meant it? Dare he hope after everything he'd been through that he was still capable of hoping? She could imagine because that was exactly the thoughts she would've thought. And they were similar—she and him. Two sides of the same coin, two ends of the same string. She knew what giving this vow meant to her. There was no looking back; they were in this for the long haul.

"Break that promise," he spoke, his voice soft as the underside of a blade, "and I will break mine."

"Which one?" Morana asked, her heart beating faster as the awareness of him shifting closer seeped through.

He tugged her head up, arching her neck back, his nose brushing against her. "To not destroy you."

His lips were right there against hers, almost there but not quite. Her face straining closer to bridge the gap but held back by his hand in her hair. She smiled, knowing he could feel it between them.

"Destroy me."

The dam burst.

His lips crashed against hers in the most beautiful collision, knocking the breath out of her lungs. Everything from the previous night came flooding back—her fear, her close call, her relief at being alive. She could feel it all in the way he kissed her. It was the sensation of reassurance and promise of retaliation combined between his lips and hers. Her arms wound up around his neck, pulling him deeper as he shifted her completely on her back, his much larger form covering hers as he moved his weight on his arms. Their tongues twining, his taste infiltrated all her senses. Morana reveled in the complete, absolute sensation of holding him and having him hold her like that for the first time. Tugging his lower lip between hers, she ran her fingers down his muscular back, feeling all the delineations and scars under her touch, stopping at his very well-formed ass. She had admired that ass in secret multiple times and being able to hold it sent a thrill through her. She spread her legs wider to accommodate him, pulling on that sculpted ass, pulling him in the valley between her legs.

A low rumble vibrated in his chest, right against her breasts, her nipples pebbling harder against his flesh as he devoured her mouth, his boxer-clad hips flexing against her bare form. The t-shirt—his t-shirt—the only garment she'd gone to bed in was suddenly pushed up under her neck. Her breasts, naked breasts, pressed up against his bare chest for the first time. Morana moaned at the sensation, her nipples becoming even more sensitive, shooting heat right to her core.

He pulled back, his chest heaving hard against hers, their breaths labored.

"Fuck," he spoke, slight wonder, slight disbelief in his tone.

Yeah. She felt that 'fuck' too. This whole situation could be encapsulated in that one 'fuck'.

A loud vibration from the bedside table spiked her already rapid heart rate. Morana looked to the source of the noise to see his phone vibrating madly on the wooden surface. She turned back to look at him in the glow from the phone, to see his wild, disheveled hair, and those magnificent eyes focused on her with an intensity that made heat flood her body all over again. She became acutely aware of his hard erection pressed right against her wetness, only a layer of cotton separating them. Her hips rose of their own accord, creating slight friction that made pleasure shoot to the tips of her toes.

The phone kept vibrating as he moved his hips with deliberate intent, applying the perfect pressure. Her head sank into the pillow as her back arched, her fingers digging into his back.

The vibration stopped, plunging the room into darkness again.

His mouth came over hers again. She parted her lips willingly, letting him in, her heart pounding as he slowed them down, a wet spot on his cotton from her, his hand stroking the side of her breast.

The phone vibrated again. He pulled his lips away, his hand extending to the side to pick it up and bring it to his ear.

"Speak," he growled into the phone, sitting back on his knees, the hand at the side of her breast going to her back, bringing her flush with him. Morana wrapped her legs around him, straddling his hips in the most wanton of ways, her entire body vibrating with her arousal.

"When?" he spoke against her neck, his teeth raking down the line, leaving her breathing harshly.

Then the person on the other end of the line said something that made him still in that way of his. Morana pulled back, trying to see him and he let her, laying her back down on the bed gently, his hand resting on her hip. Unable to stand not seeing him, Morana extended her arm and turned on the lamp beside her, flooding the room with a soft glow.

She saw his eyes roving over her entirely exposed body, taking in every inch of her skin and she did the same. He was muscles. His neck corded with them, his shoulders packed, his pecs, his abs, his arms. All wrapped in strength. Morana saw his scars up close and personal like this for the first time but she focused on his tattoos since she'd never had the chance before. She knew there was a small one under his bicep that she could only see the end tails of, a tribal design from the looks of it. How she'd love to spend time just exploring all his marks to her heart's content someday.

Before she could observe the others, he grunted in response to something and his hand moved to right between her legs, where she was spread wide for him. Her eyes flew to his in surprise, locking with those blue ones piercing her to the core as he stayed on the phone, his fingers probing.

A harsh breath left her, the fire which had subsided roaring back to life under her skin, her fingers fisting the sheets under her.

"No, it won't," he said on the phone, slowly dipping a finger inside her wet heat, making her toes curl.

His eyes flickered to her breasts, went to her hands, and returned to hers. She got the message. Uncurling her fingers, she placed her hands over her breasts, holding his gaze, and squeezed. Her walls clenched around his finger. He was touching her both literally and not.

"Get it done." Another finger joined. She tugged on her nipples, the pleasure shooting straight down making her spine curve, a soft moan leaving her lips.

His eyes flared.

"Nothing," he stated, shaking his head at her just once even as his fingers sped up inside her, his thumb joining in to rub her clit. Sucking in a loud breath, knowing she had to keep it quiet without moving her hands from pleasuring her breasts or breaking eye contact with him, Morana bit her swollen lips, her jaw starting to tremble. He saw it, noted it, and attacked with an ardor she hadn't thought possible when he was occupied elsewhere. But she shouldn't have been surprised.

His fingers penetrated, scissored, massaged her walls, withdrew, and repeated. Heat started to unfurl in her belly, knotting into a ball that kept getting tighter and tighter and tighter. His eyes, his fingers, his presence wrecked on her. His thumb rubbed her deftly, pressing with the perfect pressure that was going to make her soar. She knew, just knew he would splinter her apart.

His fingers moved in and out of her, spearing in the same rhythm as his cock would have, her walls clinging on to the digits, weeping for relief. The pressure kept mounting with every second, the knot of fire in her stomach coiling tighter with every shuddering breath, the tremor in her body increasing with every beat of her heart.

"Do it," he ordered, and the whiskey and sin of his voice exploded the flames.

Her eyes closed. Stars burst behind her lids. Head tilting back as her spine curved, her hands gripping her breasts for purchase as her toes curled, her legs shook, and she came on a silent breath. His thumb and fingers didn't stop, extracting everything her body was capable of giving, setting off a series of aftershocks that jerked her body until a whimper escaped her lips, her flesh oversensitive.

Morana came down to earth, panting, recovering, opening her eyes slowly to see him watching her. He brought his glistening fingers to his mouth and licked them. Her tired walls clenched again.

"I'll be there," he stated and abruptly threw the phone down on the bed beside her, his eyes blazing on her, a prominent bulge under his cotton-covered hips.

Leaning forward with lithe grace his body shouldn't have been capable of but was, he trapped her between his arms and hovered over her, the air charged in the space between their bodies.

"I've tasted you now, Ms. Vitalio," he whispered, his gaze locked on hers. "You can't escape me now."

"You don't scare me anymore, Mr. Caine," she replied, her voice breathy.

She saw his dimple make a brief appearance before he jumped down from the bed, heading to the shower. Grinning slightly, Morana moved her limbs again, the aches from last night's attack returning now that the haze of the endorphins was gone. Groaning, she swung her legs over the bed and adjusted his t-shirt, cracking her neck.

The sound of water came through the door and Morana shook her head at the bizarre sense of domesticity invading her. Picking her phone up from the side table, she mentally made a list of all the stuff she needed to get done, first of which was to check up on the software she had left running at Dante's place. She also needed to thank him in person for the absolute rock he had been for her last night. Then, she needed to get info on both her assailants—alive and dead—and discover who had sicced them after her and why. Plus, she needed to find out more about that airport guy and how exactly he had known about the attack.

That decided, she quickly made the bed and went to the window, pulling back the dark, heavy curtains that had encased the room for the night. The lake—clear, placid, beautiful blue—extended for miles and miles on one side, only cut off by the lush green trees at the edge that demarcated the different territories on the property. While it was a stunning view, she also knew exactly why this was the bedroom of Tristan Caine—there was no possibility of infiltration from this side of the property. Anyone on the lake would be a sitting duck and there was no other way to get in from this side without being seen. This was safe.

The more layers she peeled back, the more her heart felt for him. Shaking her head, she turned around towards the room, and a gasp left her. Last night, in the aftermath of everything, she had not paid attention to much. Now, she did.

Early morning rays flooded in through the window, bringing everything inside the room to light. The walls were painted a warm, creamy beige, the furniture deep, dark mahogany, and green was splattered all over, on the bedding, the giant painting above his chest of drawers, and smaller, little splashes. It looked like a forest, nothing like the expected bedroom of a man who had icy, cold penthouses, and a chuckle escaped her.

Walking over to what looked like a collection of small mementos on the chest, Morana leaned in for a closer look. Small, random items littered the few inches but her eyes went straight to the top, to a tiny framed picture of a cherub-cheeked toddler with bright, inquisitive green eyes. Heart clenching, Morana picked up the frame and gazed upon his sister for the first time in her memory. She had a red cap of hair on her head, a wide toothless grin and a red little jumper. Whenever this picture had been taken, she had been happy and grinning at the photographer. Had she shared a room with this little girl? Had she looked at those big eyes? Did she have the memories suppressed in her mind?

Another photo, unframed, at the bottom of the chest, made her blink. She slowly took it out, staring. It was her at her graduation, getting a degree, and smiling. How did he have this photo? Why did he have this photo?

"I need to get dressed."

Spinning around, she hastily put down the photo and watched him standing outside the bathroom, hips wrapped in a towel, studying her. She never understood how a man of his size could move as quietly as he did. He had seen her observing the picture, and obviously, he had known she would the moment he gave her entry to his bedroom. So, she waited for him to react or to say something. Maybe mention something about his sister or the fact that he had kept a photo of her hidden in his house.

He didn't.

Seemingly unmoved, he strolled through the bedroom and opened his closet, taking out a neatly pressed slate gray suit, and put it on the bed. He noticed that she'd made it, paused, then went back to taking out a white cotton t-shirt and a pair of sweatpants. Shutting the door, he lay them on the bed and glanced at her.

"Wear these after freshening up," he indicated the clothes. "And get the rest of your stuff today."

Add to the list—*move in.*

Walking hesitantly towards the bathroom as he towel-dried his hair, Morana paused, not knowing whether she should mention something. Biting her lip, she kept moving and closed the door behind her. The bathroom, which also she hadn't appreciated in the dark of the night, was stunning in the light of the day. Giant windows took the quarter of the front wall from the ceiling, flooding the space with natural light. The clawfoot tub she had used the night before rested against the wall, in front of which was a spacious shower cubicle walled with frosted glass. The theme of the brown and green forest was evident in this space as well.

Whipping the t-shirt off her body, Morana turned to the large granite sink a few steps from the bath and looked at herself in the mirror. Her cheeks were flushed, her hair a silky nest that smelled like his shampoo, her lips swollen pretty. She looked like a woman who had had some loving early in the morning, the only traces of the attack from the night before around her neck. A handprint coiled around her neck like a poisonous snake. Morana traced the bruise with light fingers, the rage for what had happened finally filling her body.

Taking out a spare toothbrush from the cupboard underneath the sink, Morana freshened up and took a shower in record time. Wrapped in a green towel, she went to the bedroom to find it empty.

Add to the list—*find out what happened to Luna Caine.*

Prepped, she quickly dressed in his clothes again, folding and refolding them to make them fit without falling flat on her face, and walked out. The smell of fresh toast made her stomach grumble. God, she was famished.

Following her nose, she lightly went down the stairs, taking the house in, seeing it change. The closer she got to the foyer, the icier it became, until the foyer itself was all whites and grays and blues. Fascinated, the implication of how deeply he hid the core of himself from everyone, and how he had allowed her in, hit her all over again. Taking a left, she entered the spacious kitchen, pretty much a replica of the kitchen at the penthouse, and wasn't surprised to see him cooking. What she was surprised at, however, was how good he looked cooking in a suit. She'd never realized how hot that was until she stood there, taking in his muscular, sharp form scrambling eggs with expertise.

"The kitchen is fully stocked," he told her without even turning around, letting her know how attuned his senses were to her. "Zia brings in the groceries every Saturday morning. There is a list there," head tilt towards the fridge, "so anything you want, just write it all out."

The toaster pinged and Morana moved to take care of it.

"Butter?" she asked him.

"Salted."

Nodding, marveling at the ease with which they moved around the space, she got the toasts ready on the plates, moved around the island counter, and hopped on, deja-vu from the penthouse hitting her. She could get used to this. "What about housekeeping?"

He turned the gas off, serving eggs for both. "Zia. She has keys so she comes in twice a week to take care of it. I'll get you keys tonight."

Taking a seat opposite her, he passed her a glass of orange juice and took his coffee. Morana raised her eyebrow. "And the bedroom?"

He looked up, those eyes of his glinting in the morning light coming from the windows. "Stays locked. I take care of it myself."

"So, he cooks and cleans?" Morana chewed on the delicious eggs. "A man after my own heart."

She saw his lips twitch, just as she'd intended, and felt something warm take root inside her belly. "But since I will be your roommate, duties will be shared."

"Anything else, Ms. Vitalio?" he stared at her, his voice dropping dangerously close to sin in the whiskey. It did things to her, that voice of his.

She leaned forward, feeling brazen. "I'm just getting started, Mr. Caine."

"I thought I finished you off pretty well." He sipped on the juice, his tongue coming out to catch a drop at the side of his lip. Her eyes tracked the movement before going up to his. Her throat went dry.

"Eat," he instructed and Morana complied, knowing it wasn't the right time to play that game. He had badass mob stuff to do and she had nerdy mob stuff to do. They didn't have the time.

His phone buzzed and he took it out. Whatever text he saw had him gulping down his drink in one go.

"I need to leave," he informed her.

Morana nodded. "Don't worry about the dishes."

He gave her a slightly blank look like dishes had been the last thing on his mind until she brought it up, and she felt her cheeks flame.

"Lock up after yourself."

With those abrupt words, he was gone. No 'have a nice day, darling,' or 'I'll be home before dinner, sweetheart'. Nope, not for him.

Her phone vibrated.

Tristan Caine: Stay safe.

Smiling, Morana dug into her breakfast.

CHAPTER 13

SOURCE

Morana: *You too.*

Opening another window, she quickly texted Dante.

Morana: *Would it be possible to have a pair of shoes delivered to Tristan's place from the mansion? I kinda didn't think of them last night.*

Dante Maroni: *Of course. I'll have them sent in 10 minutes. Drop by my place afterward.*

Morana: *Thanks. See you in a few!*

Finishing her breakfast, she cleared up the dishes and organized the kitchen, perusing through the list on the refrigerator, seeing

Tristan's handwriting for the first time. The strokes were surprisingly straight, the scrawl masculine and bold. Shaking her head, being careful on her feet and being light on them, she pocketed her phone and hurried up to the bedroom, shutting the door behind her. Two locks clicked into place and she headed to the main door just as a knock came.

Swinging the door open, she found Vin on the porch carrying a shoebox with him. He didn't even blink at her wearing what was clearly Tristan's clothes.

"Good morning," Morana greeted him with a slight smile.

He nodded, silently handing the box to her, stepping back and waiting. Morana frowned. "Um, I'm sure you have better things to do."

"I'm supposed to escort you, Ms. Vitalio," Vin informed her in a quiet voice. "Orders."

"Whose?" she asked, taking out her simple, comfortable black bellies and slipping them on her feet.

"Mr. Maroni's," he replied succinctly.

"Which Maroni?"

"Dante."

Nodding, she stepped out into the fresh morning air as well, making sure the door was locked behind her and the alarm was on. That done, she started towards the direction of Dante's house, Vin silent behind her.

"Did you go into my room to get the shoes?" she asked, both to break the silence and because she was curious.

"Yes, Ms. Vitalio," he said, facing forward. Morana studied the grim man, definitely younger than Tristan but older than her, his hair cropped so near to his scalp it was almost shaved, and she tried to picture him ruffling through her very feminine closet for footwear.

"Call me Morana, please," she corrected him. "Was the room organized?" she asked, going on a limb. If Dante had sent the man to her room and Tristan's place, then clearly he trusted him to an extent. And Dante had earned her trust, so by extension, she was going to treat Vin as one of the good ones.

"No," he said, his eyes flickering to her before going straight ahead. "It was a mess. Things were not in place."

This meant that aside from the evidence of her struggle, someone had trashed the room as well. But to what end? In rage or search of something?

Walking the sprawling lawns in broad daylight was such a vast contrast to running through it in the pitch black. The mansion loomed in the distance, as always, like a beast. There was activity around it, clean up from the party of the previous night perhaps. Morana turned her eyes towards Dante's house instead, the place that had been her haven, her refuge in her time of need. The warmth in her heart expanding, she quickly climbed the steps and knocked on the door, aware of Vin standing back.

After about a minute, Dante opened the door, dressed in his staple dark suit and tie, his hair swept away from his gorgeous face, high-lighting his beautiful bone structure. His dark eyes roved over her clad in Tristan's clothes that hung on her, and crinkled in amusement.

Morana rolled her eyes and stepped into the house.

"Give us a few minutes," Dante nodded to Vin. Vin inclined his head and walked off to the mansion.

Closing the door behind him, Dante pulled Morana into a light hug, holding her shoulders gently. "I'm glad you're okay."

Chest tight, Morana wound her arms around his huge form tightly, inhaling the scent of his cologne. "Thank you for last night. It meant a lot to me."

He pulled back, looking down at her seriously. "Last night should never have happened. But I'm glad you felt you could come here, Morana."

Morana smiled, her lips trembling slightly and he gave her a squeeze, leading her to the living room. Taking her place back on that couch that she had claimed, she watched as Dante typed something on his phone and took a seat opposite her.

Clasping his hands together loosely, his demeanor somber, he finally spoke. "Tristan and I talked last night about what happened. We're going to take care of things on our end. You, in the meantime, need to get on to the software. All of this is way too closely timed for me to believe it's coincidental."

Morana nodded. "Agreed. I'll be looking at stuff on my end, don't worry. I have a few questions though."

"Shoot."

Morana pulled her phone out, opened her gallery, and clicked on the image of the unconscious assassin she had taken. Turning the screen over to him, she asked. "Do you know him?"

Dante glanced at the screen for a long minute before shaking his head. "Haven't seen him before. Send me the picture though. I'll check up on it."

Picture sent, Morana brought up her next question. "Did you see the man talking to me last night?"

She saw Dante's eyebrows hit the hairline. "What man?"

"He warned me about the assassination at the party last night," Morana told him. "I didn't see his face or even what he looked like."

Dante was shaking his head even before she finished speaking. "No one could've entered the party without an invitation."

"Not to rain on your parade but I did a few weeks ago," Morana pointed out sheepishly.

Dante grinned. "You did. I'll have a look at the cameras later. But be careful of this guy."

Morana shrugged. "He's had plenty of chances to kill me and he hasn't. On the contrary, I think this is the crack I've been looking for and I'm willing to take a chance even if you or Tristan don't like it. You're big boys. Deal with it."

Dante sighed, shaking his head. "I still don't like it. Take Vin. He is your security for now at least until whoever wants you dead is caught."

Morana huffed. "That'll be quite a few people. Oh, and do you mind arranging my stuff to be moved to Tristan's place? I really don't want to step back into that pit right now."

Dante stood up, a small grin playing on his face. "You moved in quickly. Shouldn't you wait a bit, see if this is the man you want to spend the rest of your life with?"

Morana picked up a cushion from beside her and chucked it at his head. Dante laughed, his face creasing in a way that would stop a hundred female hearts in its tracks. She could see why a young Amara had been infatuated with the man.

"I'm happy for you two," he said, walking to the door. "Zia is at the mansion. I'll ask her to get the stuff packed and moved here. You can take it back to Tristan's with her."

"Thank you, Dante," Morana called out to his disappearing back.

"Vin's gonna be here," he called back.

She heard him close the door, heard his footfalls as he left, and then slowly settled into the silence of the house. Cracking her neck, her shoulder twinging just slightly, Morana pulled her laptop across the table towards herself and turned the screen on.

Her programs that had been progressing at a shockingly slow rate were at ninety-four percent. Satisfied, but still suspicious, Morana logged into her system and opened her software for facial recognition, uploading the assassin's picture and hitting search to run in the background. Then, she got digging into all Tenebrae Outfit related news dated back twenty years ago. A killing here, a robbery there, nothing too conspicuous and nothing too alarming. She sat on the couch, reading article after article, news clipping after news clipping, and finding nothing that could hint towards the end of the Alliance. This was surprising because usually when alliances broke, there was always a brief period of bloodshed that followed in the wake of the dissatisfaction. Twenty years ago though? Nothing. Spotless. Unreal.

Annoyed but intrigued, she changed the settings and started going through the reports on the missing girls. There were many, way too many, for it to be okay. Wild theories linking the disappearances to serial killers and pedophiles, to conspiracy theories about aliens with particular tastes in human girl babies ran rampant in the reports. The multiple cases, though well-investigated, were still open but sitting cold after so many years, rotting in the back of some shelf. The facts were mysterious—baby girls up to 3 years of age vanished. Some from parks, some from homes. One girl had disappeared from her pram in the split second her mother turned to check her bag on the street. Another had been playing outside with her sister while their mother kept an eye on them from the kitchen. One second they had been there, and the next both were gone. Cases after cases, stories after stories, unbelievable but true, went through her screen.

By the time Morana finished reading the last one, her gut was churning and eyes burning with rage. She knew for a fact two stories never made it in the reports. Two girls.

Luna Caine, disappeared from her bedroom in the middle of the night, a bedroom that had been impossible to get to without waking up her protective brother; and she, Morana Vitalio, disappeared and returned. While the media and police never connected the cases with the mob, Morana knew they were. There was no reason, other than the fact that she was the daughter of the Shadow Port Boss, why she was returned and others were not.

Morana opened up her systems and checked on her programs one by one. With facial recognition running on the man who had

assaulted her at night and her older programs tweaked to find information about what was going on, she took a deep breath and opened
up her tor window. It was called the darknet for a reason after all.
What could not be found in the normal World Wide Web usually
always existed in the shadow net.

Morana had specialized her tor window and cloaked it in layers
with not one but multiple VPNs that bounced her signal to all over
the world every second in real-time. This was what made tracking
her or her footprints almost close to impossible. She didn't engage in
finding things through that part of the net though. Not just because
it was dangerous but because the things she was forced to see while
browsing made her sick to her stomach. The depravity ran unprece-
dented and unchecked.

It was one of the reasons she had waited so long to venture into
the shadow net. But there was no other choice now. She was dead
certain she'd find some clues, some answers there.

Opening up the cloaked window, Morana tuned out everything
else around her and quietly fed in her keywords. Although she wasn't
sure exactly what she was looking for, she knew the starting point was
Tenebrae twenty years ago and the missing girls. She pressed enter.

Almost immediately, a stream of results flooded her screen rapidly, popping up one after the other. Morana kept her attention on
the screen, her gaze flying back and forth over the words, saving and
discarding data at a speed that marked her as a genius.

Suddenly, a dialogue box popped up on the side of her screen with
a message.

imreaperoo: *you're missing a keyword.*

Morana froze, surprise at the message making her shake her head.
This shouldn't have been possible. Forget just finding her under the

cloaks of her online identity, forget tracking her down at the speed at which her signal was flying all around the world, it should have been impossible for anyone to even discern what she was doing there. Absolutely impossible.

Yet, the message blinked at her, seemingly innocent.

She quickly clicked on the message to see the online id of the person who'd sent it, a grudging seed of admiration filling her because they flew through all her security. Her security was the shit.

A black and white skull made the icon, the negative space behind the skull making it pop on the screen. Still stunned over the fact that this reaper person had found her and made contact, Morana decided to play it by the ear and quickly typed back a response.

nerdytechgoddessoo: *which keyword?*

She waited for a heartbeat and saw the reply pop up.

imreaperoo: *flesh trade*

Morana felt her breath catch for a long second, the implication of those two words making her heart sink. No, god no.

nerdytechgoddessoo: *who are you?*

The clock ticked on the wall behind her as she waited for the reply on the black screen.

Tick.

Tock.

Tick.

Tock.

Tick—

*imreaper*oo: *a friend.*

Morana didn't know what to do with that. Another message came through before she could decide how to proceed.

*imreaper*oo: *i have my reasons for helping you.*

Morana typed quickly.

*nerdytechgoddess*oo: *what are they?*

*imreaper*oo: *i want you to find the truth, morana*

So, he knew who she was. Morana stared at the message, an unfamiliar feeling settling in the pit of her stomach. She didn't understand it. A frown creased her forehead as her fingers moved.

*nerdytechgoddess*oo: *i already know the truth*

There was a pause before the reply came.

*imreaper*oo: *there's still much you don't know*

Goosebumps erupted on her arms at the last message. She rubbed her skin to settle it, her chest heaving without even realizing. Trusting her gut, she wrote out her message.

*nerdytechgoddess*oo: *i want to meet you*

The cursor blinked five times before his – and she assumed it was a man – replied.

imreaper00: *when the time comes*

imreaper00: *for now, use the keyword*

nerdytechgoddess00: *what will i find?*

His reply was cryptic.

imreaper00: *sources*

Sources of what? Before he could disappear, there was one thing she absolutely needed to know.

nerdytechgoddess00: *how did you bypass my security?*

She waited and waited for his response but nothing came. Frustrated at not knowing that, she went back to the keywords and modified them – *'tenebrae' + '1990s' + 'missing girls' + 'mafia' + 'flesh trade'*

It was with apprehension that she added the keyword, hoping against hope that this was a fluke and she wouldn't find anything that pointed to anything like this. The families, to her knowledge, had never traded in the flesh. It didn't make sense. This would access an entirely different part of the net, a darker part of the net that she'd never ventured to and it scared her slightly.

The search slowly loaded and a barrage of new information slammed her. Her eyes scanned through the data feverishly – girls gone missing, girls being auctioned, girls being sold, and so much more disturbing news that made her flesh crawl. However, none of the data talked about girls below the age of 10. The information, as disturbing as it was, didn't have anything to do with the missing girls from Tenebrae.

Sighing, she pushed away from her laptop and got up from the couch, stretching out her muscles, giving herself distance to think about it. Walking to the window that overlooked the lake in the distance, Morana took in the house she would now be living in. It looked serene, almost peaceful. But the man who occupied it wasn't. He wouldn't be until the truth about his sister came to light.

There was a reason why the man online had wanted her to add 'flesh trade' on to the list of her keywords. If it wasn't important, she doubted he would have gone to the trouble of tracking her down and getting in contact with her, whoever he was. He knew her name and he knew something about the girls.

A ping from her laptop made her take a quick look towards it. Going back to the couch, Morana sat down and saw all the results for the search she'd run. Fingers on the keypad, she browsed through the headlines, bylines, and any names at a breakneck pace, her sense of urgency increasing the deeper she went into it. Each piece of information had a certain username attached to it in the place of source.

The man had told her she would find sources.

Diligently getting to work, Morana filtered articles by the sources and allowed the system to accumulate it in sections. Ten seconds later, most of the articles sorted down under one source name – Distance Y.

What the hell was Distance Y?

Before she could follow that train of thought, a ping from one of her programs diverted her attention. Her customized facial recognition was complete. Pulling up the program, Morana didn't find any hits on names but her software had found two other pictures of the man caught on public cameras, one in Shadow Port and one in South America. She sent the image to both Tristan and Dante's numbers and waited for them to reply. They didn't.

A low ache started to form right behind her eyebrows. Pulling off her glasses, Morana pressed the heel of her palms into her eyes, groaning in frustration at the way things were going. She had more questions than answers and every time she felt she was close to something substantial, it slipped through her fingers. Gritting her teeth in frustration, Morana stared at the ceiling for a long minute, contemplating her next course of action.

She made a call.

CHAPTER 14

PROCESS

Tenebrae was a city blessed with natural beauty. Bisected by a long river that merged into the ocean a few hundreds of miles away, it was located right at the foot of some stunning hills that were peppered with beautiful lakes. Unlike the coastal, wet weather of Shadow Port, Tenebrae experienced all seasons – snow in the winters, sunny days in the summer, and the best fall in the country.

Looking at the browned leaves crunched under her new boots, Morana stood at the railing of the very public pier, holding the disposable coffee she'd bought from a vendor across the street. Her light beige jacket kept her warm enough that she didn't feel the chill in the afternoon sun, hiding the small gun she'd taken from Dante's, her hair pulled back into a braid she'd quickly put together in the car as Vin drove her. He was there somewhere, watching her back as Dante had instructed him to do. The silent man was soon becoming one of her favorite people.

The ferries crossing the river honked their horns, people buzzed around her, and Morana stood, alert and aware, waiting for the man she'd contacted to shed some light on her questions.

As though in answer to her thoughts, she heard the familiar, grave voice behind her, "Don't turn."

Though tempted, Morana refrained and simply nodded, keeping her eyes glued to the buildings in the distance on the other side of the river. She felt the man come into her periphery beside her, but couldn't make anything out.

"I wish I could say nice to meet you," Morana quipped.

"You want to know why I contacted you, Ms. Vitalio?" the man with the grave voice began.

Again, Morana nodded. Out of everything, she was most curious about this.

"You are key to a puzzle I've been trying to solve. I believe we can help each other out."

"And how will I do that?" Morana asked, her voice calm as she kept her gaze focused straight.

"Find the information about what was happening here twenty years ago."

"And what will I get in return?"

"Whatever answers you need."

"And you will give me those in exchange?" Morana asked, confirming.

"Yes."

Pondering on that for a second, Morana took a sip of her coffee. It was actually pretty good. "Why should I trust you?"

"You shouldn't," the man replied without hesitation. There was no inflection in his voice, nothing in his tone at all—just the grave baritone that spoke of experience far beyond her years. "But we're on the same side for now, just looking for the truth."

"What are your reasons for interest in the end of Alliance?"

"What are yours?" he shot back.

Morana felt her lips curl. "Alright, then. First question – how did you know someone was going to try and kill me?"

She saw the man lean his arms on the iron railing in her periphery and caught the dark clothes he was wearing. "Information is important in my line of work," Mr. Grave casually elaborated. "Someone put a hit out on you, a pretty expensive hit if I might add. I just told you in goodwill."

A baby cried somewhere on her left. Morana knew Vin was somewhere behind her as well.

"I appreciate you giving me a heads up," Morana thanked the man.

"There's no reason for you to be wary of me, Ms. Vitalio," the man stated plainly. "I have nothing against you or The Predator. You're his woman and I have no wish to make an enemy of him."

His woman. Well, she was, wasn't she?

Morana shook her head. "What's Distance Y?"

The man beside her paused, "You got to them pretty quickly."

She'd had help from someone. Was it this man? Before she could ask, he answered her. "It's the Syndicate."

It was an anagram. What the hell.

"What's the Syndicate?" Morana asked, her confusion mounting. "Is it involved in why the girls went missing so many years ago?"

"You're very smart," the man complimented her, straightening. "Follow that lead. This is where I leave you. When you have information, contact me."

Morana shook her head, her questions unanswered. "Are you the reaper guy? How did you get past my security?"

The man paused. She had a sense he was surprised. "No,

Ms. Vitalio. I'm not. But thank you for what you just told me. It put quite a few things in place."

Morana waited for a beat, her heart slowly starting to pick up the pace. "What did I just tell you?"

"That he's alive."

Before Morana could ask anything else, the spot beside her was empty. She turned around in a circle, trying to find his retreating form but there were too many men in dark clothes and too many people milling about for her to place a man she'd not even seen properly. Shaking her head at herself, she gazed out at the river again, her heart settling with the one question that had been answered.

The girls who had gone missing were a much bigger problem than she'd anticipated. Whatever this Syndicate was, she needed to uncover it. And whoever this Reaper was, she needed to find him.

❀

The sun was setting by the time Morana sat in the Range Rover Vin had driven her in. While she'd told Dante she could drive herself, the fact that it was a new city and she was an unwelcome Maroni guest had made her gladly accept the help she was getting. Vin was a nice guy so far, quiet but alert, and she liked his company.

In fact, she had told him about wanting to train a little more, especially in self-defense and surprisingly, he had offered to help her out "if you so wish". She wished very much indeed. If nothing else, the hit on her had made her realize she couldn't always rely on her luck to get her out of a hairy situation. Next time, there might not be a house she could run to, a safe space she could take refuge in. Starting tomorrow, she was going to make her muscles scream curses at her.

She watched as Vin navigated through the city traffic, through the honking cabs and pedestrian crossings, her eyes taking in a city so different from the one she grew up in, and not just weather-wise. Shadow Port was more laid back where Tenebrae was all hustle and bustle. They finally moved out of the central city area and headed towards the plush green hills where the Maroni mansion was nestled.

Bringing her phone out of the pocket, Morana opened the text she'd sent Tristan about the meeting, seeing it still hadn't been read. After the night they'd spent together, the morning they'd had, she had expected him to have checked up on her at least once. That he hadn't told her he was either too busy doing whatever he was doing or he simply hadn't processed that he was now in a committed relationship. They'd have to talk about it.

The car ascended, turning with the curves of the hill as the city slowly dropped below, the river snaking through it in the distance. She had missed observing all of this the first time in her nervousness, her brain being focused only on its anxiety. This time, being more relaxed, she could take in the beauty and the spirit of this city and see why it had been a crown jewel for so many decades.

The wrought iron gates of the mansion opened automatically as they got closer to the top of the hill. Vin nodded at one of the guards at his station and in they went, the long driveway stretching, the huge rock-cut mansion as always reminding her of a castle buried in the woods of Scotland.

"Your luggage and packages have been moved to Mr. Caine's wing," Vin informed her as he stopped the car in front of the mansion. "You'll find everything in the living room."

Morana smiled, her heart warming at the thought. Though this didn't feel like home to her yet, she was glad she was going to be with him. Thanking Vin for her time, she alighted from the car and saw Lorenzo Maroni watching her from his study window. She didn't know if it was him who had tried to kill her or not but whatever the case, she wasn't under his protection anymore.

Knowing it would piss him off, she gave him a cheerful wave and watched him frown. Lips curving, she turned and headed to the small cottage beside the lake in the distance, to the house of the man who had been kept to the fringes of this world.

It was dark and the lake seemed quiet, serene. The single-story cottage, built of stone and wood, was lit up. Walking up the porch steps, Morana twisted the knob and entered, the scent of cooking tomatoes and basil leaves wafting from the kitchen.

With a smile, she shrugged out of her jacket and entered the open living room to check on her stuff, only to come to a halt to find the pissed off man sitting on the couch, in his white shirt unbuttoned at the collar, his blue eyes on her. Why the hell was he angry?

"Well, hello to you too, my dear," Morana said sweetly, draping her jacket on the arm of a chair, looking at her one suitcase and many boxes of her new wardrobe. "Thank you for checking up on me today, especially after last night." Opening one box, Morana saw her unpacked accessories and kept talking. "It was so sweet of you. This morning was special to me too, and I'm so happy that it was special to you as well. My heart was warmed by—"

"Who was he?"

The soft question from right behind her broke her ramble. Morana turned around, to find him so close his exhale warmed her forehead. His eyes locked on hers, the fury in them a fire. But it wasn't the anger that gave her pause. It was the slight hurt she could see in them, the one he was trying to hide by the clench of his jaw, which simmered down her own immediate anger.

Placing her hand over his heart, she felt the slightly escalated heartbeat under her palm.

"Are you jealous, Mr. Caine?" she asked softly, a slight smile on her lips.

Just as she'd expected, he closed the space between them. His hand went to the back of her head, wrapping her ponytail around his fist, tilting her head back. Tingles shot from her scalp down her spine, her nipples standing to attention as her pussy clenched. It amazed her how this man could simply breathe on her and her body would ready itself for him.

"Don't fucking push me," he muttered softly over her lips, his eyes still completely holding her captive. "You went to meet a strange man in a strange city without telling anyone about it. You talked to him and you came back in a fucking good mood. Who is he?"

"You do know you have nothing to be jealous about, right?" Morana asked reasonably.

He tugged her ponytail in answer, his other hand going to her ass and pulling her closer. "Who. Is. He?"

"I don't know," Morana replied honestly.

He paused. "You don't know?"

She shook her head, stroking the hard muscle of his chest softly. "I wasn't going to hide this from you. You just weren't replying to my text so I thought I'd tell you after. We need to talk about that, by the way."

"You went to meet a man you didn't know?" he asked, disbelieving.

"He'd contacted me once before," Morana clarified. His eyes darkened. She continued, unfazed. "He said he had some information and that's why I met him. He did."

Tristan leaned down, his lips hovering beside her ear, his scruff rubbing against the side of her cheek. "You're not helping yourself."

Morana rolled her eyes, her breaths escalating. "Calm down, caveman. You're being an asshole."

His lips made contact with her skin just below her ear, his tongue tasting her skin. "What I feel isn't jealousy, wildcat." His lips slid down the side of her neck, kissing the skin like he never had before. "It's knowing you're mine and knowing I still have to share you with people. It's a burn in my chest. It makes me want to put you over my shoulder, take you to a cave, and fuck you until you forget everything but how I feel inside you."

Breathing harshly, feeling his lips stop at her shoulder, Morana challenged him like she always did. "Why don't you?"

Before she could take another breath, he had her backed against the wall, picking up her weight with one hand under ass. Morana grabbed his broad shoulders and wrapped her legs around his hips, feeling his cock press urgently between her spread legs.

Taking a hold of his shirt where it was open, Morana jerked on it, sending buttons flying as it ripped open, his chest and abs becoming visible to her. His hands tore down the fabric of her new top from her body until it gaped open in the middle, leaving her in just her bright pink lacy bra. She thought he would slow then, slide the straps of her bra down maybe. He didn't. He just tore through the lace until her bra hung in tatters, her breasts exposed to his eyes, her nipples hard like bullets. They felt heavy, aching.

And then, for the first time, his hands cupped them. Morana felt his touch in her pussy, her hips automatically grinding against him as her head tilted back, eyes closing.

"Eyes," he uttered one raw demand, making her open her eyes and see him. They had denied this to each other before, denied each other so much before. But now it was slowly being bared, this new intimacy between them.

Locking her own hazel eyes with his electric blues, Morana gripped his hair at the back of his head, urging him on. His hands – big, rough, skilled – the same hands that had once wiped the blood off of her, squeezed her breasts together, his fingers skillfully plucking at her nipples, the pressure almost painful but so good her panties were a wet mess.

He ground his hips against her over their clothing, his cock almost bruising against her clit with such delicious pressure she felt her limbs tingling.

"Oh fuck," she moaned, baring her throat to him, her pulse fluttering as her heart tried to keep up with her body.

"Give me your mouth," she demanded and saw a flash of his dimple.

"Greedy little thing," he murmured, still leaning back and watching her, his hands wreaking havoc on her breasts and nipples as he rhythmically started to fuck her over their clothes. "Say my name."

"Tristan," it escaped her on a whisper, her own hands exploring his bare chest. "Please."

"Fuck," he cursed, right before he slammed his mouth down on hers, his hips intensifying the pressure. The feel of his tongue sliding against hers, his hands pulling and kneading her breasts, his cock rolling against her aching core became too much for her. She crashed against the wave cresting inside her, her toes curling in her boots and her thighs tightening around his hips as her spine curved, her orgasm surprising her with its intensity. She felt him lose his rhythm as he groaned into her mouth, his hands leaving her breasts to go under her ass, grinding her pussy closer to him.

Breathing hard, he broke their kiss, leaning his forehead against her. She could feel her heart stuttering, trying to calm down. It was over within minutes.

"I've never come in my pants before," he murmured in the space between them.

Morana felt a chuckle leave her, as it turned into a full-blown laugh. "Me neither."

"I'm not sure my lack of control around you is a good thing," he stated, untangling her legs from around him. "I need a shower."

Morana straightened her glasses and pulled her clothes back into a semblance of decorum, as he turned towards the stairs and climbed up quickly. Her eyebrows hit her hairline as she saw the speed at which he was running away, sighing because he needed to learn to process shit. She already had her hands full.

But well, he'd given her two pretty good orgasms in one day so she could be nice.

Shaking her head, she grabbed her bag of toiletries and followed him up at a more leisurely pace, pretty sure he wasn't going to be expecting what she was going to do. Entering the bedroom, she quickly stripped and headed to the bathroom as the sound of the running water filled the space.

Opening the door, she stepped inside and saw him in the glass cubicle, bare to the eyes and vulnerable. It wasn't lost on her that this was exactly how he'd found her back in the penthouse. But she didn't go to him. Instead, she wrapped a towel around herself and opened her bag.

"You realize we're in a relationship, right?" she called out casually, enjoying the view in the mirror from her spot.

She saw him look at her as he ran his hands over his shoulders. He didn't say anything. She continued.

"Relationships work with communication," she went on. "I don't mind that you're not the most talkative guy in the room, but it means that when shit gets in your head, you tell me about it so we can have discussions like adults rather than retreat and deal with it on your own."

He kept looking at her through the glass, his eyes intensely focused on her. She knew she had his attention. Taking out her face wash, scrub, and a divine mask she'd found thanks to a link Amara had sent her a few days ago, Morana put down her glasses and tied up her hair in a bun.

"I know you're not used to explaining your thoughts to anyone," she went on, slowly wetting her face. "And I'm not asking you to.

What I ask is for you to share whatever you're feeling with me. Be honest with me. I'll be the same. That's how relationships work."

"From what I know, you don't have a lot of experience in relationships," he said over the water, his tone slightly defensive. "In fact, your one ex was a thief who sold you out."

Morana locked eyes with him in the mirror. "And I let him die, didn't I?"

Point made.

She saw his lips curve slightly and slathered her face with the berry-scented wash, cleaning her skin. "Point is, you know I'm in this for the long haul. I know you're in it for the long haul. Let's just make the long haul easier for both of us, what do you say, hmm?"

She saw him turn off the shower and wrap a towel around his hips. Washing her face quickly, she exfoliated, his eyes locked with hers on the mirror.

"And if I don't?" he asked quietly. Morana felt her heart pound slightly but she kept calm, slowly opening the jar for her mask and applying it with her fingers to her face.

"You will," she stated plainly, seeing his eyes flare in the reflection. "Because deep down, Mr. Predator, you're a good man who has been waiting all his life to be able to share with someone. You just need to trust in this connection, trust in me enough."

She saw him take in her muddy blue face, his lips tipping up on the sides. Leaning forward, he pressed a soft kiss on her head, their eyes locked in the reflection, and said the two words that made her heart melt like the goo on her face.

"I'll try."

CHAPTER 15

EXPLODE

Sharing her space with a man was an odd kind of experience. For all her bravado about 'this-is-how-relationships-work', Morana was pretty sure she sucked at it. Well, not that the man in question had ever indicated that but who knew. He kept a lot of shit to himself anyways.

Morana saw him move around the kitchen preparing breakfast like he did every morning for the last few days that she'd been there, sitting on the stool that she'd claimed on the island, sipping her fresh orange juice. His back under the blue t-shirt moved as he sliced through some fruit.

Her eyes narrowed.

Something was off. She didn't know what it was, couldn't put her finger on it, but she just knew. Since she had moved in five days ago, she had settled in and he was trying to settle with her. They slept beside each other. Occasionally, he had nightmares but not often.

They woke up wrapped around each other. But for over five days, the man hadn't made a move on her.

At first, she'd thought that was because he was giving her space but realized that was stupid. Tristan Caine had bulldozed into her space, there was no way he was being a gentleman now. He was taking his own space but he wasn't distant. He cooked for her, talked to her slowly about his day, and asked about hers, sent her at least a text throughout the day. She now had her stuff in his, now theirs, closet and cupboards. The brand of chips she munched on when working occupied the kitchen drawers. He knew her entire limited skincare routine, for goodness' sake. They were the epitome of domesticity.

But he hadn't touched her or initiated any kind of intimacy since that day. And it bugged her. She missed the spectacular orgasms but more than that, she missed the fire he ignited in her senses.

And even though he hadn't made a move on her, he'd been marking his territory. Like just two days ago, she'd been in front of the lake with Vin in her new training clothes, letting the other man teach her how to get out of an attack from the back, when Tristan had walked into the clearing and stood there, his eyes blazing, watching every way the other man had touched her clinically.

And though he hadn't objected to her training, he had been there the entire session, letting the other man silently know that one wrong move would have him drowning painfully in the lake. Morana kind of wished he had taken over training her himself, but she knew why he hadn't – because then they wouldn't train.

Honestly though, it was too much to expect a man like him to adjust that quickly to not only sharing his space but sharing his space with her. She was his Achilles' heel. She was his kryptonite. And just because he didn't want to kill her anymore didn't mean everything was hunky-dory between them. To a guy who had never lived with anyone, he was actually doing better than one could hope. He was just getting used to living with her and there was still a chasm between them Morana didn't know how to breach.

They'd get there. One thing she could definitely say about living so far away from the mansion – no bumping into other people. Morana hadn't seen Chiara or any of the Maroni family except Dante in days and she was happy for it. Zia came every three days to the cottage with all the groceries and chatting with her was one of the highlights of Morana's day.

Hopping down from the stool, Morana went to butter up the toast beside her man, marveling for a moment at how small she felt barefoot next to him.

"Is there something you'd like to tell me, caveman?" Morana asked, calling him by the nickname she'd taken to using on him, one she knew he really liked in that lizard part of his brain.

He glanced at her. "Not that I'm aware of."

"Hmm," Morana huffed, wondering how to come out and ask him straight up why he hadn't wham-bammed her.

Before she could figure out how to voice that thought, a knock sounded on the door and Dante walked in, dressed perfectly as always in a sharp dark suit and tie, his dark hair slicked back away from his gorgeous face.

"I was half afraid I'd have to bleach out my eyes if I walked in," he quipped, unbuttoning his suit jacket and taking a seat on the stool she'd just vacated.

"Shouldn't have walked in then," Tristan quipped from beside her.

Morana gave him a look that he returned innocently and turned to smile at Dante. "Oh, there's nothing eye-bleach-worthy going on here. Nope."

"Oh?" Dante asked, his eyebrows climbing his forehead as he looked at Tristan for a second before settling his brown eyes on her, a grin on his face. Morana felt herself flush. It had been happening more often lately, her brain-to-mouth filter slipping. She didn't understand why.

"Any leads on the Syndicate?" Morana changed the topic without any subtlety, asking the question she was pretty sure she already knew the answer to. Since her meeting with the grave mystery guy, she and the boys had been working relentlessly to unearth some kind of evidence about whatever this Syndicate was, and surprisingly had found nothing. Not even Dante and Tristan, with all their shady connections, could find anything or anyone who had even heard of it. The ghost-group or organization, whatever it was, was good.

"Actually, there is something," Dante said, surprising her.

Morana held up a mug in silent question and Dante shook his head. Heartbeats fast, she settled in opposite him and felt Tristan come to stand behind her, his hand on her waist as he considered Dante. "Tell me."

"I have an informant," Dante directed his eyes at Tristan before looking back at her. "The assassin, who tried to kill you, if his information is correct, was hired by this Syndicate group. He has another lead and wants to meet tonight somewhere public. I've told him to come to one of our clubs."

The voice of whiskey and sin came from behind her. "I'm coming with you."

Dante nodded. "I want you both to come actually."

Morana frowned. "Not that I mind, but why?"

"Because," Dante explained, "I can't be sure someone isn't keeping an eye on us. If they are, I want them to see nothing but us taking you out for a night in the city. Who we meet there, we control. You and Tristan can actually have fun while I get the meeting done."

Morana turned her neck and looked up at the man behind her. "I think at this point in our relationship, you should know I don't like wearing heels."

She got a flash of dimples.

***

Somehow, she still hadn't seen his tattoos.

She didn't know how he'd done it, given she saw him shower and slept beside him, but one way or another, his tattoos were still a mystery to her. Promising herself to solve them soon, Morana checked out the hotness that was Tristan Caine in dark jeans and black Henley, the sleeves pushed up his muscular forearms, bunching in a way that was making her neglected core pulse with every heartbeat. She should probably just masturbate at this point and make him watch. Now, that was a good plan.

She sat at the back as the two men sat at the front of Dante's Range Rover, the vehicle humming pleasantly as they zipped down the hill towards the city, another car following them.

Over the last few days, Lorenzo Maroni had been absent at dinner but she knew he'd been at the mansion. She'd seen him often enough and sometimes, she caught him watching her with an odd look in his eyes – like he was privy to a secret she didn't know. It gave her the creeps. Her father was absent as well. She was sure he knew where she was but she hadn't heard a peep from him.

Morana had video-called Amara in the evening while getting ready, to chat but also to touch base about Shadow Port and if everything seemed okay. Amara had mentioned something felt off, and Morana had to agree. The woman, her friend, seemed genuinely thrilled that she had moved in with Tristan. Morana had been tempted to discuss her relationship issues with her but didn't know how to. It felt so new to her.

That was when Tristan had told her they had to go. And gone they had.

Dante, dressed as casually as his mob brother, broke through her thoughts. "I've been thinking about the man you met, Morana. I suspect who it can be but I'm not sure. If he is who I think he is, I think we can trust the intel he gave you."

"So the Syndicate exists?" Morana asked. "I'd honestly started to think we were chasing ghosts."

"Yes, I'm beginning to think a whole lot is happening here that we don't know about."

"Then, it's time we do."

Dante exchanged a fleeting look with Tristan that she caught. Not mentioning anything, Morana simply asked questions about the city and Dante answered her, Tristan unusually quiet, as they made their way to the club.

In the old warehouse district just like in Shadow Port, the club was called Mayhem. *Nice.*

Morana saw the neon sign from afar, a long queue outside the doors indicative of the good business. Dante parked in the lot and they got out, Tristan opening her door and offering his hand like the gentleman she didn't know he could be. Wearing the heels she hated and a dark blue shimmery halter dress she loved, Morana took a hold of his hand and got out. In her heels, with her hair in a high ponytail, red lips, and her rectangular glasses, Morana looked good. She knew she looked good.

But the way his eyes roved over her with that territorial possession? It made her feel good.

Splaying a possessive hand on his arm, she walked with both the men into the club, the music suddenly pounding into her pulse. Each hard beat drifted off her heart, sinking into her blood, heating her system. She could see the dance floor full of gyrating bodies, the neon lights playing hide-and-seek with all the exposed flesh, a bar on the side lined up with more people.

Unlike her last time, she knew this time she would have a good time.

Dante's hand on her shoulder brought her attention back to him. He nodded to Tristan and smiled at her, before walking off to the back of the club for the meeting.

A weird feeling in the pit of her stomach, Morana shook it off and turned to the man beside her, pointing to the restrooms. Tristan nodded, his eyes still on where Dante had gone, and she knew he was distracted. Leaving him to his brooding, Morana quickly escaped to the bathroom. After doing her business and fixing her lipstick, she headed out again into the crowd, trying to locate her man.

Her eyes scanned over the crowd, only to come to a sudden halt at the bar. He sat there with a drink and a red-haired siren all over him.

Morana stayed still, her heart drumming, observing what he would do, watching as the siren put her hand on his arm exactly where hers had been, and watching as he didn't shake it off. She watched, the sinking feeling in the pit of her stomach worsening, his face blank of all expression as the siren slithered against him.

Fire infused her veins, filled her belly, sizzled her insides.

She didn't understand this emotion, never having dealt with it in her life. She didn't understand how to react. Gripping her phone, unsure of whether to walk up there and punch the siren or walk off and cool down, Morana took in a deep breath, trying to clear the haze of red.

As though sensing her gaze, his eyes came to her. He didn't do anything, didn't move, didn't look away, just waited to see her reaction.

And Morana got pissed.

Spinning on her heels, Morana weaved through the crowd and headed straight for the doors on the side that was closest to her. Pushing open the latch, she stepped out in the empty alley between the club and a warehouse and shut the door behind her. The cool air was crisp in her nose as she inhaled a lungful of it, her hand shaking with her annoyance.

She didn't know what kind of a game he was playing but she wasn't here for it. Fuck him and fuck him twice for trying to test her. She'd been nothing but open and emotionally unguarded. And she was pissed because he was being a hypocrite – daring to let another woman put his hands on him when he couldn't stomach her meeting another man even platonically.

The door opened behind her and the air changed.

Morana started walking away, not even turning to acknowledge him.

She felt his hand on her bare shoulder, turning her around. Shaking with her fury, she looked up at him, surprised to find his eyes amused.

"Sheath your claws, wildcat," he murmured softly.

Morana growled, pushing him into the wall, glaring at him. "Don't play these juvenile games with me, Tristan. I will cut you open and eat you alive."

He looked down at her, his eyes searching hers, a softness in his gaze. "There she is."

Morana frowned, not understanding. But she breathed deeply.

"What was that?"

"I just wanted to see something," he explained.

"What?"

"If you burned as I burn with the need to claim you. That I wasn't alone in the fire."

Convoluted as it was, the explanation calmed Morana a fraction. Insecurity, she could deal with that. She had to remind herself they were both new at this, him more so than her. Keeping her eyes on his, Morana pushed him into the wall and put her phone in his jacket.

His brow furrowed at the action and Morana didn't explain,

sinking down to her knees on the rough ground and unbuttoning his jeans, doing something she'd been dying to do to him for days, putting across her message in a language he would understand, once and for all.

"You wanted to know if I burn with you?" Morana asked, pushing down his jeans and taking out his semi-hard cock, looking up at him to find his attention rapt on her.

She licked him at the tip, tasting his salty flavor, and stated. "That's fucked up. You're fucked up. But you're mine."

He got harder and she licked him on the underside. "Every" lick "fucked up" lick "inch of you."

His hand fisted around her ponytail, holding her head as he pushed inside her mouth, her lips wrapping around him. She took him as far back as she could and pulled back, keeping her eyes on his, her hands on his strong thighs. He opened his mouth to say something, his blue eyes flaring in a way she'd never seen before, and she took him in her mouth again, hollowing her cheeks and applying the pressure she'd read worked wonders in magazines.

His hips flexed, his hand tugging at her hair even as he still controlled how much she could take. "You keep looking at me like that and I'll come under a fucking minute."

Fuck, that felt good. The power she felt in that second, knowing who he was, seeing his control fray at the edges inside her mouth made her feel good.

"Say my name," Morana mumbled, sucking just his tip and flicking her tongue against the slit, not breaking their eye contact. Anyone could come out and see her on her knees, taking her man into her mouth, his fist wrapped around her hair, and it made her fucking wet.

His thumb stroked over her cheek as his breathing labored. He didn't say her name.

Wrapping her fingers around his thick base and jerking him off, marveling at the fact that this huge thing had been inside her, Morana pulled back completely, her eyes watering and not just because of the pressure.

"I don't just burn with you, Tristan," she said, her voice shaking. "I burn for you. And I don't know what I have to do to prove it."

He groaned, his eyes closing. "Fuck, Morana."

Heart pounding, she took him in her mouth again and got back into sucking him off with vigor, feeling him slowly lose control as his hips started to jerk.

"Pull back if you don't want to swallow," he warned. She didn't. Her own breathing hastened with his, and then he exploded in her mouth with a low growl. Throat working, swallowing down every last drop of him, Morana mentally patted herself on the back for a blow-job well done. The gods of oral would be proud.

Opening his fist, he let her hair go and tucked himself back in, pulling her up.

Morana straightened, brushing off her stinging knees and ignored the wetness between her legs, looking at a spot on his chest, suddenly feeling slightly embarrassed. But they had to talk about this.

"I don't like that feeling, Tristan," she addressed him, not looking away from his chest. "I want to be able to walk into a room and know, without an iota of doubt, that the man I have claimed is *only* mine. I know that's not how things work in this world. I know that men and women play around with others, that loyalty is a luxury not everyone can afford. I know. I just don't like it."

Swallowing, she put her hands on his chest and slid her eyes up to his, to find them singularly focused on her, and felt a shiver go down her spine. Would she ever get used to his intensity, to the sheer magnetism of that attention?

Inhaling deeply, she continued. "I just, I really like you Tristan Caine, as messed up as you are."

One of his hands settled on her hips, the other coming up to her neck. "My loyalty is not a luxury for you, Morana. It's a gift and it's yours. You never have to walk into a room and question that."

Morana felt her mouth quiver as she went on her toes, pressing her lips to her happy spot where his neck and shoulder met. "Thank you."

She felt him press his mouth against her hair. "I won't test you like that again."

Morana felt her lips curve and pulled back to look at him. "So are you calling me by my name now or do I have to get on my knees to get that?"

Before he could say a word, a huge explosion rocked the ground underneath her feet, knocking her into his chest. He immediately shielded her behind his body and Morana whirled to see huge flames lick up at the dark sky from the back of the club.

In shock, seeing the gigantic blaze with wide eyes, Morana barely nodded as Tristan pulled out his gun and handed it to her.

"Stay here!" he yelled at her and then he ran towards the fire, leaving her alone in the alley suddenly flooding with people escaping the club.

It was chaos.

Morana mingled with the crowd and ran to the parking lot at the front, to see people screaming and getting out and away from the burning building, unable to understand what had happened. Her eyes found Dante's car and she jogged to wait there, hearing the sound of sirens in the distance closing in, shaking her head in disbelief as sounds of people talking and shouting filled space around her.

A huge shiver wracked her body as she kept her eyes glued to the explosion site, no idea of how many people had been injured. The gun heavy in her hand, she cursed herself for not even having her phone, looking around to find a familiar face. She couldn't. Everyone fromg the Outfit had run to the back to help out.

"Did you see how the door exploded out?" one of the girls near her was talking excitedly with her friend. "It was mad!"

"I know!" the other sounded shaky. "I hope no one got hurt though."

Morana hoped so too.

After what seemed like hours but was probably only minutes, she finally saw Tristan heading back towards her, his face and clothes darkened in soot, his eyes cool, aloof.

Morana took a step forward, the pit of unease in her stomach yawning wide as she looked behind him, her heart stuttering. She saw Vin and two other guys, in a similar state, head towards the car as well.

"What happened?" she voiced as he came closer, trying to make out his expression.

It was stone.

Something was bad.

She looked around for Dante.

Looked back at Tristan.

No.

Fuck no.

"Tristan," she gripped his arm, shaking him, her eyes watering. "Where is Dante?"

He shook his head.

No.

No.

God, no!

He just meant Dante was busy managing the fire and wouldn't be coming with them. That's what he meant.

"Will he come later?" she asked, her voice breaking with hope.

God, no. Please no.

"We need to go," he said, his own voice hard, closed-off.

Morana looked at the flames lighting up the sky and started to walk towards it.

A hand gripped her arm, turning her sideways.

She looked up at him. He shook his head once.

Tears streaked down her cheeks, a long, painful wail leaving her chest as she collapsed into his arms, sobbing for a brother she'd only had for a few days.

CHAPTER 16

KNOW

There were always two types of destruction. Reading history, one could analyze the decimation of any empire and slot it in two. One type was like a house of cards – one piece went missing and the whole fucking thing crumbled to the ground instantly. The other type, the one harder to pin down and slower to take action, was like the dominoes—one only saw the final piece fall but not see the trail of pieces piling one after the other behind it.

Watching the mansion driveway fill with cars from the window of the cottage, Morana couldn't pin down which type this was.

Grief overtaking her heart, she stood alone at the window because Tristan had more important matters at hand – like trying to find Dante's body. Her heart might be filled with grief but her emotions had calmed down enough for her to pause and think. She needed to think because if there was even a sliver of hope, she was clinging to it.

Morana replayed the entire scene in her head over and over again.

She and Tristan had been in the alley when the fire had broken out, the cause for which was under investigation. Three bodies had been recovered from the back, burned beyond recognition, and Tristan had thought one of them was Dante. But was it?

She looked down at her phone and mulled it over. Dante's phone was disconnected and had been recovered at the site. A body with his clothes and watch had been recovered as well but it could be someone else. He had been acting oddly enough for her to question everything. It was entirely possible that she was clinging to false hope but she couldn't, couldn't, accept the fact that the man who had become her protector and family could suddenly be taken away from her. She wouldn't accept that without concrete evidence.

The mansion was ablaze with lights where Lorenzo Maroni had, it seemed, called the entire Outfit after getting the news about his oldest son. They all thought he was dead – Morana wasn't sure. She hadn't even been able to question Tristan before he had dropped her and taken off.

Not knowing what she could do, Morana just observed as men got down from the cars and decided she needed to listen in on the meeting.

Opening up her laptop with purpose, she quickly found the microphone she'd installed surreptitiously in the study one morning and activated it, plugging in her earphones to listen better as she watched out the window.

"They found his body," a man spoke into the room and Morana gripped her laptop, her heart suddenly pounding. Maybe listening in wasn't the best idea.

"This is bullshit," Lorenzo Maroni roared in Morana's ears. "I don't believe this."

There was silence for a beat before one brave man spoke, "It can be hard to accept, Lorenzo. It's a shock to all of us. He was your heir. You'd groomed him all your life to take over. But it's his body. I checked the proof myself."

Maroni huffed out a laugh. "That is exactly why I know it's not him. He's got all you morons fooled."

Another voice chimed in, "We need to have a funeral, Blood-hound. People are shaken. Our enemies have their eyes on us. His body is in the morgue. We have to keep up the appearance."

There was more silence before Maroni addressed someone. "Is it him?"

Whiskey and sin confirmed her worst fear. "It is."

A loud sigh left someone and Morana shut down her laptop, her hands shaking. It was a fluke. For sure, it was a fluke. Because if Dante was dead, there was no way Tristan could be so calm. Or could he? He had seen so much death, killed so many people – he could stay calm in the face of death, even of a loved one.

The sudden vibration of her phone made her jerk, her eyes widening as she saw the caller id.

Amara.

Fuck.

Fuck.

Fuck!

She shouldn't answer. She really shouldn't talk to Amara right now. But the other woman had told her so many truths; it was the least Morana could do.

Fuck.

She answered and stayed silent, not knowing how to even begin.

Her friend stayed silent for a long minute before her soft, raspy voice asked quietly. "Is it true?"

Morana swallowed, giving her the truth, her own voice shaky. "I don't know."

She heard Amara inhale sharply on the other end. "What happened?"

"There was a fire at the club," Morana told her, gripping the phone tightly in her hand. "I don't know what happened exactly but his phone was there and they found a body with his clothes and watch."

"But?" Amara urged, her breathy voice pained.

"But I don't know," Morana confessed. "Until I can talk to Tristan myself, I don't want to believe anyone."

"What's the alternative?" Amara asked, her voice slowly calming down.

"Maybe someone abducted him?" Morana suggested.

Amara chuckled but the sound wasn't amused. "You don't just abduct Dante Maroni, Morana. He's too smart and too skilled for that."

Morana looked out the window, letting the wheels in her brain turn. "So you mean to say that if he's alive and missing—"

"—then he's done it deliberately," Amara completed.

"Well, shit," Morana sat down on the couch, flummoxed. "But why would he?"

Amara stayed silent for a long minute. "I'm done caring, Morana. You've been a good friend to me. Thank you."

The flat tone in her voice suddenly startled Morana's heart with alarm. "Amara—"

"Take care, Morana."

The line went dead.

What the hell?

Morana redialled the number, only to find it unavailable. Reasoning with herself, Morana tried to calm her heart down and allow Amara to have her space to process everything. She couldn't even imagine what the other woman must be going through, and she needed to chill and not make it about her.

Exhaling a long breath, Morana locked up and headed upstairs, thinking on what Amara had said. She stripped and stole a t-shirt from Tristan's side of the closet, quickly washing her face and brushing her teeth. If Dante wasn't dead then he had disappeared deliberately. Why? Why hide that from her and Tristan?

Her hand paused with her brush in her mouth, her bright hazel eyes slightly red-rimmed and wide behind her glasses as she considered that. Could Tristan actually be in on the plan? He had been acting a little the past few days, and his reaction at the club had been stony. But why hide all of that from her?

She spit out and smacked her hand to her forehead as it clicked.

Maroni and the entire household had seen her get out of the car. She had been distraught and crying and holding on to Tristan's arm as he'd walked her to the house. It had been genuine pain because she had believed that Dante had gone.

Done with her routine, Morana flew down the stairs barefoot and rushed to her laptop, her brain churning and settling pieces together. She might have been entirely wrong but it was highly unlikely. If Dante was alive, as she believed he was, he had disappeared for a reason and she bet her entire savings that Tristan knew about it, and they hadn't told her simply because her reaction had to be genuine for the onlookers.

Hoping against hope to be right, Morana opened her systems, shadowed her address, and dived into the darknet. Typing in 'tenebrae outfit + fire', she pressed enter and got hit with the news.

Clicking on the first link, she scanned the article.

The heir to Maroni empire dead in fire
In a turn of events that has left the underworld in shock, Dante Maroni, the oldest son of Bloodhound Maroni, has died in a freak fire accident at one of the Outfit clubs in the Warehouse District area . . .

Going back to the results, Morana scanned the other links of news, finding the same story over and over again, until a link at the bottom got her attention.

My mobsters, did this end the Alliance? Give me your thoughts.

It was a recent blog post, more of a conspiracy theory kind, and Morana clicked on the link, her heart pounding.

My father was a soldier in the Tenebrae Outfit for many years before he passed away. As you know, my interest in the mob came from him. Though I never followed in his footsteps and because I'm a nerd, I've always been curious about the Alliance and its demise.

Riddle me this - if there are three partners of an equal team and two are kings then who's the third?

We theorize that the Alliance existed for so many years between Tenebrae and Shadow Port. But my father told me there was a third partner in the deal. Could it be that the Alliance ended because he got out of the equation? If he was so important, then who was he? Another king from another mob family?

I'll tell you what my father told me — the man took care of both the kings and buried their secrets. That's why they protected who he was.

What do you think? Is it plausible? Leave your thoughts in the comments.

Morana stared at the post, her heart drumming in her chest.
Three partners.
If there were three partners – one Lorenzo Maroni, one her father, then who was the third?

She was close. She knew she was close to the answer, she could feel it in her gut.

It was all connected somehow – the codes, the missing girls, the Alliance.

And the third man was the key.

She was lying in bed in his t-shirt and panties, staring up at the ceiling in the lamplight, when the door opened and Tristan came in. His face – exhausted, covered in soot – made her heart stop.

His eyes came to her, saw her awake, and he tilted his head to the bathroom.

Morana frowned, getting up. "I need to—"

He put his finger to his lips, pointing to the bathroom, taking off his clothes, throwing them in the hamper in the corner. Not that she minded him naked, but she didn't feel like right now was the time for it.

"I can't talk right now," he stated. His voice was flat as he headed to the bathroom and indicated for her to follow. Without another word, she quickly walked to the bathroom and closed the door behind her, seeing him standing under the spray. He looked at her standing near the sink and motioned her closer with his finger.

Confused as hell and not understanding anything, Morana took off her clothes and stepped under the warm spray in front of him, trying to read his blue eyes. He leaned forward, lining his mouth next to her ear, and spoke quietly.

"They've bugged the house."

Eyes widening, Morana gripped his slippery biceps. "What do you mean?"

"I just found out," he told her. "I'll need to check for bugs in the bedroom but until then, I didn't want to risk talking there."

Morana quietly took a dollop of his shampoo in her palm and rubbed them together, lathering them as she waited for him to continue. He sat down on the marble bench in the shower so she wouldn't have to tiptoe too much, his head the height of her neck. Massaging the shampoo in his scalp, she wondered if he'd ever had anyone care for him like this.

His eyes closed as her fingers dug into his scalp, his breath leaving him. "Dante isn't dead."

"I know."

Blue focused on her. Morana smiled. "Once I calmed down, it was pretty easy to figure out. You guys had been off for a few days. And I get why you didn't tell me, as much as it sucked. You needed my response to be authentic."

He stared at her for a long moment, the admiration in his eyes unmistakable. "Fuck."

Morana stroked his head, running her nails over his scalp. "I know my smartness turns you on."

"It does."

"Tell me next time though," she told him seriously. "I'll give an academy-award worthy performance but don't pull this shit next time."

He simply nodded. "It wasn't my idea. Dante wanted to do it this way."

Well, that definitely did make her feel better. Tristan stood up silently, washing off the shampoo, the suds running over his back.

Morana, finally, saw his tattoo properly. On the left blade of his shoulder, a tribal tattoo of a wolf howled at a full moon, the detailing of each stroke of black amazing. Tracing her finger over the tattoo, her heart clenched as she realized what it represented.

Luna.

She walked around to stand in front of him, the wall at her back, and let her eyes trace the rest of his scars and tattoos. A bullet marked his right bicep, hitting a skull in the middle. A phrase went down his left side, right beside his abs.

And so the night will end.

Morana traced the phrase, her fingers lingering on the slashed scar underneath the hard muscle. Moving up to his left pec, right above his heart, there was a symbol she didn't know the meaning of. She touched it with her fingers, looking up at him in question.

"One day," he whispered quietly between them, the two words filled with so much her heart squeezed.

Morana swallowed, asking a question she dreaded. "What if the day never comes?"

He shook his head, sending water spraying out. "It will. Whatever the answer is, I will find it."

Morana didn't know how to tread through this conversation so she tabled it for the moment. She wanted to find answers too, for him and for herself. But what if the answer wasn't what he'd hoped for? Would he be able to cope? Would he be able to survive?

Her chest ached wondering about it.

"I can see the questions in your eyes," he said softly. "But I know, I know, she's alive."

Morana felt a tear go down her cheek, mixing with the water. "Then, we will find her."

He looked at her for a long minute before slowly pressing his lips to hers. It was soft, simple, but it made her heart clench.

Pulling back, he pressed his forehead against hers, his mouth slightly trembling. He gritted his jaw to tighten it and Morana saw, pressing her hands to his face, holding him. They stood there like that for long minutes, before he suddenly pulled away, shutting the water off and handing her a towel.

Morana inhaled deeply and dried herself while he did the same, then followed him naked into the bedroom. He handed her a fresh t-shirt without a word that she quickly donned, and put on a pair of boxers before pulling open a drawer and bringing out a scanner.

Getting into bed, Morana saw as he ran the scanner through every inch of the room, finding only one bug near the door. Opening the window, he threw it out into the lake before closing it again and sliding into bed beside her.

Morana followed, settling against him, her breasts squashed against his chest, her legs twined with his.

"Who bugged the house?"

"I don't know," he whispered. "I'll have to find the rest tomorrow."

Morana looked up at him, her brain working. "Could it be Maroni?"

He shrugged. "He's never done it before."

"You've never lived with anyone before," she pointed out.

"That's true," he squeezed her around the waist, pressing a small kiss to her ear lobe. "We'll deal with that tomorrow."

There was silence for a few minutes before she asked him, "Why did Dante do this?"

His chest moved as he inhaled deeply before responding, "He's had to go underground."

"But why? He's Dante Maroni."

"Precisely," he muttered, his finger drawing some pattern on her shoulder. "He's an excellent extractor of information but there's some information he can get better without his name."

Morana's heart stopped and she leaned up on an elbow, looking down in his blue eyes, her hair falling over them. "Is this about the Syndicate? Is that the information he's gone to get?"

She saw his lips twitch slightly as he pushed a lock of wet hair behind her ear, the gentle gesture surprising her.

"Yes," he confirmed her suspicions. "He's going to infiltrate the Syndicate."

Morana felt her jaw drop. "Are you serious? How the hell will he even do that? Will he be safe? How will we know anything?"

"He'll be fine," Tristan pulled her down back to his chest. "And we have a signal to get in touch. But nobody can know. It is important that everyone, especially Maroni, believe that he's dead. Or he could be in danger."

Morana nodded, understanding the gravity of the situation. "Shouldn't we tell Amara though?" She'd have wanted to know in her friend's shoes.

Tristan shook his head. "Dante told me not to. She will have eyes on her, especially now. Nobody can suspect anything."

As much as it pained her, Morana understood that. She just hoped her friend forgave her when things settled down again.

The dark room, his warm scent, his steady heartbeat slowly soothed her heart. The weight she'd been feeling the entire evening gradually dispersed from her chest as she snuggled deeper into the crook of his neck and shoulder, finding her happy spot. He pressed a kiss to the top of her lobe, squeezing her.

Long minutes passed and Morana was almost on the verge of drifting off when his voice broke through the hush.

"I was given this cottage since Maroni took me under his wing," he began quietly and Morana got to attention, listening as he shared something so close to his chest with her. "When I was young, I used to lie here some nights after a training session, and I wanted to die."

Morana felt her breathing stutter, her arms get tight around him but she didn't dare move, didn't dare do anything to break the moment.

He continued, his finger drawing loops on her back. "There was always a gun in the drawer, and I almost ended it some days. You know what stopped me every time?"

Morana shook her head.

"Thinking my sister would always wonder why her brother didn't love her enough to live for her. I couldn't leave her with that."

She felt her eyes burn, her heart hurting for the ache she heard in his voice.

"But that day seemed so far away and I was so powerless. Every day felt like too much," he spoke softly into the dark, his voice barely audible. "So, you know what I wondered about?"

Morana shook her head again, her throat tight, her chest heavy.

"You."

Her heart stopped.

"Some days, I thought about how I would find you when I grew up and kill you, different ways I would kill you," he went on, baring his mind to her, chuckling darkly. "Some days, I imagined someone else getting to you and how I would kill them. Oh, how I killed them. And some days, when it got really fucking sad and I wallowed in self-pity, I thought of how you'd smiled at me and I wondered if you'd smile at me like that after seeing the monster I was becoming."

Morana pulled back and put her hand to his jaw, her eyes locking with his in the little light from outside.

"Do you still think about killing me?" she asked point-blank, ready if he did.

He stayed silent for a beat. "No," he shook his head once.

Morana breathed. "Do you still imagine someone getting to me and killing them?"

"No," he repeated, his voice sure.

"Do you still think about my smile?"

He watched her for a long moment, his eyes lingering on her mouth, before pushing his face closer to hers, his hand coming around to her neck in a hold her skin knew intimately now.

"I think about a lot of different things now but don't mistake me for someone soft, Morana. Whispered words in the shadows aren't who I am. I'm still a monster."

Morana searched his eyes, feeling his palm resting against her steady pulse, suddenly realizing that was why he always held her neck – to feel her heartbeat under his hands. A slow smile curled her lips, her palms cupping his jaw, stroking it, his scruff scraping over her skin.

"When I was young and alone in my room at night, with a father who didn't like my existence and no mother and no friends, just my overactive imagination and my brain, you know what I used to think about?" she murmured, never breaking their locked gaze. "When one of my father's guards sneaked into my room and I had to fight him off—" his hand tightened on her neck in reaction but she continued, "—wallowing in my loneliness and self-pity, you know what I would dream about?"

He waited for her answer, never moving those intense blue eyes from hers.

"A monster," she whispered between their lips. "My monster. One who could keep me safe and kill the other monsters who wanted to hurt me."

By the last word, his mouth slammed into hers as he turned her under him.

"You always fucking had him, wildcat."

And then he ravaged her like the monster he claimed to be.

CHAPTER 17

RETURN

W alking down the cemetery holding the hand of her man, while pretending to mourn for another man who was in her heart, wasn't her idea of a great morning. However, given everything Tristan had told her, Morana had appropriately donned a simple black dress and put on some makeup to make her face appear paler. She kept her eyes down behind her glasses, her hand on the inside of Tristan's arm, impressed with his performance.

He was stoic enough that had she not known him, she would have been convinced that he was hiding some deep sadness and just didn't want to talk about it. As it was, being the outsider of the Outfit as he was, he hung back during the funeral.

They had done a closed casket ceremony, burying the burned body that was 'Dante'. Tristan had told her in the car that the body had belonged to one of the traitors who had been close enough in the physique department to Dante to pass off as him.

Dante was completely underground in the meantime.

Morana had tried calling Amara again that morning, just to check up on the other woman and found her number disconnected. Zia had dropped by too, her eyes saddened, and asked Morana about her daughter. And it was really starting to worry Morana.

She stood back at the edge while Tristan went ahead to speak with someone, watching everyone.

Lorenzo Maroni was rigid, understandably, while people paid their respects and offered condolences. She recognized Lorenzo's cousin, Leo, with Chiara on his arm, her face tear-stained. Whether they were genuine or fake, Morana didn't know.

Amara's half-sister Nerea stood in the back next to another soldier, dressed sharply, a lone woman in a man's world. Morana wondered about her. Other members of the family, children included, stood with sad, confused faces. The rest of the Outfit slowly milled around, most of the men with expressions meant to resemble sadness. There were more people than she'd been expecting, the funeral much grander than she'd realized it would be. But then, Dante Maroni was a brand.

It made her realize she'd never asked Dante about any siblings. She knew through rumors that he had a younger brother but he'd been missing in action for many years. She made a mental note to ask him later.

In the cool breeze on the hill, Morana watched Lorenzo interact with everyone, trying to pinpoint what it was about the man that bugged her so much. It was an eerie thing, the way he looked at her sometimes like he had secrets about her.

The sound of a car door slamming shut brought her attention to the man sauntering down the hill to the gathering, surprise filling her.

Her father was there.

He paused for a second where she stood, his eyes moving over her with hidden disgust before he proceeded to where Maroni stood below. Morana, now removed enough from the man that he didn't affect her as much, tried to analyze why he reacted to her like that. Tristan watched her father with focus while the older man ignored him and headed straight for the boss.

Morana was too far away to hear what was being said but the men shook hands and then walked a little ways off to talk. If her father was there to talk about her to take her back, he could think again. If he was there for business, it would be curious given the timing of it all. Maybe he was just there to pay his regards but she didn't believe it.

Watching them both openly, Morana's eyes did a scan of the area and came to a halt on a man on the opposite hill, behind a tree. From the vantage of the funeral procession, nobody would be able to see him, hidden as he was. But she, still standing on the hill, could make out his silhouette.

His face was hidden under a beard, and he was leaning on some type of a cane, just hiding behind a tree and watching the two men she had been watching. Frowning, she quickly opened her texts.

Morana: *There's a strange guy at my 5 'o'clock watching my father and Lorenzo.*
Morana: *You can't see him from your spot. Come stand by me.*

She saw Tristan look down at his phone before he casually walked up the hill to where she stood. Finding a spot beside her, he nonchalantly ran his eyes over the place she'd seen the man and Morana turned to see the man watching them now.

He was too far away for her to make out anything about him but she could feel his eyes on her, a shiver going down her spine.

"You know who he is?" she asked Tristan quietly.

"No," he replied, his voice calm. "But he's watching us."

"I know."

They stayed silent for a few minutes as the procession continued below. Dark clouds gathered in the sky, casting a doomed glow over the hills and though it was fall, the winds were cold. Standing there silently, Morana found her gaze drifting to the strange man over and over again.

"Anyone suspects anything?" she asked, her lips barely moving.

He stood stony beside her, his mask on, speaking equally quietly. "Everyone suspects something, they just don't know what."

Morana huffed a silent laugh at that, looking down at her father, who was talking to Lorenzo Maroni with his head bent.

"He might be trying to take me back," she commented, studying the body language of both the men. "Not out of any love, but for his pride."

"He has no pride," Tristan noted beside her. "He won't be able to take you, not even over my dead body. You're too smart for him."

Morana glanced up at him, her heart softening at how much respect he had for her intellect.

It wasn't something she'd expected but the more he told her little things like this, with no pretense or guile, the more she felt herself bloom on the inside.

"Thank you," she murmured softly, squeezing his forearm.

He shrugged. "It's a fact. You're smarter than most of these men put together, and I don't just mean with your tech stuff. Anyone who denies that is stupid."

"You're not stupid."

He turned to look at her, his blues locking with her hazel. "I'm the smartest of them. I claimed you long before any of them had a chance."

Heart fluttering, Morana looked back down with a slight smile on her lips. It slowly died. "You know we'll have to talk about that day someday, right?"

He didn't respond.

Morana stayed silent, letting it go. Pushing him when he was just starting to slowly open up would be irresponsible. He would talk when he was ready, if he was ever ready.

"I came across a very interesting theory the other day about the Alliance," she started, changing the topic to more neutral ground. "It mentioned how the Alliance broke because there were, in fact, three parties involved and one of them got out. Have you heard anything about that?"

The silence from the man beside her stretched for long, long minutes, to the point that Morana had to look up at him, just to make sure he'd heard her. His eyes were staring into space, somewhere far away. She didn't know where he'd gone but wherever it was, it was unpleasant.

Sliding her hand into his, she interlinked their fingers, hers smaller and softer sliding against his rough, abraded, longer digits. Squeezing tightly, she kept her eyes on him and waited for him to come back to her, "Tristan?"

He blinked, looking down at her, suddenly aware of his surroundings. He scanned the hills once and then took a deep breath in, showing her a flicker of vulnerability she would never have been aware of a few weeks ago. Not saying a word, he quietly retreated into his own mind and Morana let him, knowing this perhaps wasn't the time or place to ask.

One of the men from the gathering called Tristan and, after giving her hand a small squeeze like a secret while his face remained completely expressionless, he walked down with the coiled grace of the predator he was notorious for, his body encased in a black suit and black shirt.

The more she got to know him, the more she realized how deeply he felt these little things and how expertly he pretended not to.

After a few minutes of observing everyone, Morana felt someone else come to stand beside her. She glanced up and saw Lorenzo Maroni there, alone, without her father.

"Walk with me, Morana," he demanded and walked uphill towards the cars without giving her a chance to respond.

Cautious but curious, Morana sent Tristan a quick text and followed after the older man, finding him standing alone near his town car as he waited for her. Morana quietly moved to him.

He opened his jacket and brought out a cigar, sniffing it once before cutting it.

"The cigars were a gift from one of my associates," he began without preamble. "That associate was, just the other day, telling me about someone looking deep into our business."

Keeping his eyes on the casket far below, he lit up the smoke. "That wouldn't be you, now, would it? After the way you threatened me, I'm inclined to believe that."

Morana watched the large silver ring on his index finger that hadn't been there before, the skull face polished and detailed and considering he was attending his son's funeral, oddly jarring. "I have no idea what you're talking about."

The older man watched her with eyes that saw too much. "Where's Dante?"

Morana blinked in surprise and looked down at the casket pointedly.

He chuckled. "I've been doing this for far longer than you've been alive, little girl. I know that," he indicated the wooden box, "isn't my son."

Morana stayed silent, not sure what he was playing at, and why he was asking her.

Lorenzo Maroni's eyes crinkled, his handsome face creasing with lines of age as he looked at her with dark eyes that held stories beyond her imagination. She could feel the full force of his experience in that one pointed look and it took everything she had to keep her spine straight and head high as she regarded him back neutrally.

"I can see why Tristan is smitten," he commented, his voice almost soothing. "You have fire. I respect fire. But there are greater powers at play here, little girl. Bigger than you or me. I don't think you even realize the things you set in motion for your selfish needs."

Morana bit the inside of her cheek to keep from asking him any questions.

"You tell me what my son is up to," Maroni took a deep pull of the cigar, "and I'll tell you why you were returned."

Morana was tempted to find out why, but not that tempted. Blinking innocently, she played along. "So, you admit to having a hand in my return to my father?"

Maroni laughed, exhaling a cloud of smoke, his thick neck cording above his shirt. She could see where Dante got his looks from.

"You were a pawn to control your father," Maroni took a deep inhale of his cigar and blew out a puff of smoke, the minted tobacco scent invading her lungs. "I never imagined you'd become a problem."

Morana laughed without humor. "My father never loved me enough for you to control him."

"Oh, he loved you," Maroni smiled, the malice in his eyes evident. Morana stared at him, confused at his words.

"Why did you call me here?" she simply asked, shoving her hands in her coat pockets.

"To offer you the deal," Maroni threw down his cigar, stubbing it with his toe. "You're living in my city, on my compound, with my soldier. I'm not threatening you, just telling you. You don't want to make an enemy of me."

Morana stayed silent as she watched him get into the car and stepped back, not understanding half the shit he'd spewed. One thing was for certain though – Lorenzo Maroni was scared, of whom she didn't know. Otherwise, there was absolutely no way he would stoop down low enough to offer someone like Morana any kind of deal.

She found that very, very interesting.

✥

The beeping of her laptop as soon as she entered the cottage in the afternoon startled her. Quickly hurrying to the systems she'd left running, Morana took her laptop outside to the porch, taking a seat in the chair, with a beautiful view of the lake and the surrounding hills in front of her and the mansion on the right in the distance.

Sliding off her flats that she'd worn for the funeral, Morana curled up on the chair and logged into the system, trying to locate where the beeping was coming from.

And what she saw on her screen stunned her.

It was the codes.

Her codes.

What the hell?

Someone had sent her the codes, the original codes, that she had written and Jackson had stolen and Tristan had been framed for, the codes that began everything. Looking at the attached message, she clicked on it.

imreaper00: *i believe these belong to you. impressive work.*

What the fuck?

Who the hell was this guy? And how did he not only bypass her security but found her codes?

nerdytechgoddess00: *where did you get these?*

The screen remained blank for the next few minutes as Morana felt her heart pound. If she had the codes, that meant they hadn't been copied or used. She'd encoded them with a self-destructive algorithm for that. But why would this strange guy, who was clearly extremely skilled with tech, return these to her? Why give her clues to the missing girls and Syndicate at all?

A message came in.

imreaper00: *it's time we meet.*

He went offline.

Morana, first and foremost, checked through the codes that had taken her over two years to write. It was dangerous in the digital age, with the power to deface anyone and anything at any point of time. It was especially dangerous for mobsters with skeletons in their closets.

It took her a few hours to check and recheck every single line, trying to see if they had been tampered with at all. She found nothing. They were pristine, unused, exactly as they'd been when Jackson stole them.

Pushing her laptop to the side, Morana looked up at the cloudy sky as the hours passed and tried to make sense of everything.

One – someone had hired Jackson to steal the codes she'd been working on for two years, someone who knew they existed in the first place, and framed Tristan for them so she could be led to him.

Two – after she had been led to him, someone had started to send her anonymous messages and clues about their history, the Alliance, and her history that she hadn't been aware of.

Three – she had gone down that rabbit hole and someone had led her towards the Syndicate and once she started looking into it, her codes were returned.

All of these things could have been done only by someone tech-savvy. And now she was thinking all of this was done so she could be led to the Syndicate in the first place. Stealing the codes was a fluke, this was the real target. Someone wanted her working on this.

Whoever this guy was, there was a reason he wanted her attention.

imreaper00. A username but who was he? The grave mystery man from the airport had thanked her for telling him he was alive. Was he supposed to be dead?

The questions were starting to give her a headache.

Dusk settled around the lake and Morana went back inside, feeling a little lost as to what to do now. After getting changed and settling down on the couch, she did what any self-respecting closet nerd did when she got bored. She watched Netflix.

⬥

After a few episodes of her newest obsession and countless snacks, Morana was happily vegged out on the couch in a Netflix-induced stupor she had sorely missed. She had needed the break, needed the space, needed the distance from her real-life shit. Her life had suddenly become too adventurous over the last few weeks and there was only so much a girl could take before breaking down hysterically. And she couldn't break down hysterically because the man she lived with needed her to be emotionally stronger as he let go inch by inch. Maybe in a few years, she'd treat him to it.

That was how Tristan found her, lying down on the couch and watching shirtless Henry Cavill take a bath, her mouth slightly open.

He cleared his throat.

Morana paused on a very good shot and raised her eyebrows at the hot man behind her who could give Henry a run for his money.

"You think it will ever go away?" he asked, his voice deliberately low in that tone that made her belly flutter and clench.

Morana opened her mouth, about to reply but it went dry as he threw his jacket to the side and rolled up his sleeves, coming around to where she was.

She sat up, but before she could move more, he took a hold of her legs and tipped her back, pulling her to the edge, sinking to his knees before her. Heart thundering, her core pulsing with need, Morana watched as he pushed her t-shirt up over her breasts, her legs over his shoulders, his lips closing around her nipple.

A noise escaped her at the wet heat of his mouth, her back arching as she ground her growing wetness against him, trying to find the right friction. His teeth tugged at her nipple, pulling it deep into his mouth before giving the same attention to the other, his eyes on her.

"Not that I'm complaining, but wow, this is, oh fuck," Morana babbled as he ripped the seam of her panties and threw away the scrap of fabric, a flood of heat invading between her legs. His hands went down under her ass, cupping them as he thrust his hips against her. Bending down, he trailed light kisses down her belly, making her suddenly conscious of her little folds of skin. He didn't even pause, going south to inhale her, his teeth sinking into the side of her thigh.

"Please," Morana begged, tugging his hair, pulling him closer.

"Tell me this isn't temporary," he demanded, his mouth an inch from her weeping folds.

Morana nodded. "It isn't temporary."

"Good," he murmured, his words heating her flesh right before he pressed his mouth into her, tasting her for the first time. Morana saw stars for a split second, her thighs jerking around his head as he held her down, his magnificent blue eyes holding her captive.

And she felt his tongue rapidly flick out over her clit.

Her back came off the couch, her breathing labored as he started to eat her out like a starved man seeing a feast for the first time.

He wreaked havoc on her pussy with his mouth.

She was never the same.

❧

Long after her body was sated and limp and they were in bed, Morana traced the frown lines on his forehead and told him about the codes, asking him about his day. It was normal, so normal she'd never thought they would have something like that and she was half-scared it would be taken from them.

"You asked me about a third guy today," Tristan muttered, his fingers drawing inane patterns on her shoulders. "It reminded me of a conversation I'd heard that day."

Morana stopped at his eyebrows, looking into his eyes. "The day—"

He nodded wordlessly. Morana waited for him to go on, knowing anything about that day was thin ice. She didn't know how he would react to something about it.

"Your father and Maroni had been sitting at the table," he reminisced, that faraway look entering his eyes. "Your father threatened Maroni and he subdued your father by mentioning another guy. 'Remember what happened to Reaper,' or something like that, he said."

Morana stilled.

Her heart stopped for a second.

She scrambled up and looked down at him, unable to believe if it could be that simple.

"Reaper," she shook his arm urgently. "Are you absolutely sure that's the name he mentioned?"

Catching on to her urgency, she saw him sit up as she hurried out of the bedroom and down the stairs to where she'd left her laptop.

"Yes, I'm sure," he trailed after her, his voice slightly confused. "What's going on?"

Morana quickly pulled up her chat window and turned the screen to him, her heart beating a mile per minute. "Could it be that easy?"

She saw him read the chat and see the username, saw his face harden as his eyes came to her. "You never mentioned him."

Morana waved it off. "That's not important. The point is, could this be the same guy? The guy I met on the pier said something about him being dead."

Tristan stared at the screen longer, frowning. "It could be but I don't know. I've never heard of any Reaper in the Outfit, even in passing."

Silence ensued for a long minute while they considered it, their eyes clashing.

"Let me make a call," Tristan told her. He went to a drawer and took out a burner phone she'd never seen, leaving the room to go outside, shirtless as he was. Morana followed, standing on the threshold, the chilly wind cutting against her bare legs and arms, the lake completely quiet in the night.

She saw him press some buttons as he turned to look at her, putting the device to his ear.

"I have something," he said quietly, and Morana felt her breath catch. "Ever heard of Reaper?"

There was silence as he listened to whatever the guy on the other end was saying, his frame coiling tighter and tighter. Minutes passed, and unable to stand it any longer, Morana stepped off the porch and onto the grass, her bare feet feeling the cold, wet dew, and walked to stand in front of him.

"When?" Tristan asked, looking at her. "Fine," he said and disconnected, breaking the phone in half and throwing it into the lake.

"Who was it?" Morana asked, curiosity killing her.

Tristan looked at her for a long second before staring out to the lake. "An informant. He wants to meet."

"What are you not telling me?" she asked, pulling him to face her.

He took a deep breath, his eyebrows slashed over his forehead. "There was one Reaper, a long time ago, but he and his family died in a fire."

Morana winced, her lips pursing. "You think it's him?"

"I don't know," he stared off into the distance, his hands fisting beside him. "I'm more interested in why, whoever he is, wants your attention. Bad enough to get the codes and return them to you."

She pondered on that for a second. "Maybe because of the same reason I was unique to you twenty years ago. I'm the only girl who came back."

Tristan shook his head, his eyes distant. "I never understood that you know. I'm glad you came back safe but why? It wasn't because your father loved you, that I know for sure."

'Oh, he loved you.'

Maroni's voice interrupted her thoughts.

"Maroni said something to me today," she informed him. "About there being a reason why I am the only one who came back. Maybe he was playing with my head."

"Maybe," Tristan mused.

They both stood at the edge of the lake, lost in their own thoughts, with more questions than before.

CHAPTER 18

ENTRUST

Amara was officially off the radar.

As Morana looked at the lake and hills surrounding it at barely six in the morning, she worried about that. It had almost been a week and she didn't know what the hell to do.

Her morning had been pretty bizarre as well. Tristan had received a call and he'd been out the door in less than five minutes like his ass was on fire, telling her to track his phone if he didn't come back in an hour. How he knew she had a tracker on his phone in the first place, she didn't know. But he had left and Morana had busied herself dressing and clipping the extra gun he kept in the living room drawer to her jeans and watched the time while standing out on the porch.

At this hour, the hills were misted with a dense cover of fog, the sunlight muted but cutting through it. The cold wind played through the strands of her hair and the scent of early morning dew and flowers permeated her surroundings. She had never been in a place like this. For a moment, she felt transported back in time to another era, the sight before her ancient.

A shiver traveled down her spine and she clutched to the modern technology in her hand, her phone, and reminded herself not to get spooked. She looked down at the screen, at Tristan's tracker, and saw his dot about half a mile away from her location.

Exactly after fifty-three minutes since he'd left, her phone vibrated with a text.

Tristan: *Come to my location. Quick.*

Morana: *On my way.*

She locked up and followed the navigation, heading into the woods on the other side of the cottage. Though he was just half a mile away, Morana followed the path that felt longer, her breathing better than it would've been thanks to her training with Vin daily.

After about a few minutes of no sounds except the wind on water and birds chirping, the tall trees gave way to a small clearing at the base of the hill, the cottage hidden behind the thick foliage.

Morana saw Tristan standing there, his arms folded across his chest, talking to a man she wouldn't have recognized but for his size.

Dante.

Covered in beard and wearing a shaggy, loose gray shirt the old Dante wouldn't have been caught dead in, his hair messy around his face, he was barely recognizable as the once perfect Dante Maroni. Before Morana could stop it, her feet were flying across the clearing as she crashed into the man she'd thought she'd lost, the man who had become important to her.

Big arms wrapped around her in a bear hug unlike any she had ever experienced and she hugged him tightly, smelling hints of his spicy cologne contrary to his appearance, and had to smile despite herself. You could take Dante Maroni out of the clothes but you couldn't take the clothes out of Dante Maroni.

"Good to see I've been missed," Dante's smiling voice rumbled as he slowly patted her back in reassurance. Morana pulled back, blinking up at him with eyes that burned even as she couldn't stop smiling.

"Are you okay?" she asked, looking over him. Though he was smiling, his usually warm brown eyes were, not cold exactly, but off.

"He's fine," Tristan said from behind her, his voice slightly off. "Stop fussing over him."

"Go stand with him before he decks me, Morana," Dante rolled his eyes, his tone deliberately light. "I'd hate to bruise his pretty mouth, out of concern for you of course.

A laugh burst out of her. God, how she'd missed him.

Stepping back, Morana didn't turn, just stared at him. "You sure you're okay?"

A genuine smile grazed his lips under the beard. "I will be."

Morana nodded. "Any leads? Should you be here?"

Dante shook his head, pushing his hair back over his head and Morana watched it fall back again. "I'm working on something but can't tell you much. Have you talked to Amara? Is she fine?"

The wind whooshed around them as Morana considered him seriously. "No, I haven't. She hasn't been reachable since she got the news."

"She thinks I'm dead?" Dante asked, his eyes narrowing.

Morana shook her head. "No, but she disconnected. I've been giving her space but it's worrying me now."

Dante looked up at the sky as though asking for patience, muttering something like, "the things I do for her," before looking at Tristan. "Find her while I get this shit done."

"On it," the man behind her said.

Morana looked at both of them before Dante squeezed her shoulder. "I'll see you guys soon."

Nodding, she watched him silently move and disappear into the woods, a man his size moving with the grace one wouldn't expect from his body. She looked around the place she stood in, before turning to her lover.

"What is this place?"

"This is where I used to escape sometimes," Tristan said, his head tilted to the side. "Dante followed me here one day, stubborn bastard, and it became our spot."

Morana tilted her head to the side, eyes locked with his. "Did he seem a little off to you?"

"He's in the zone," Tristan spoke quietly, taking a step closer to her. "Listen, I have to go out of town for a few days. It's a lead and I'll tell you if it pans out."

Oh, she didn't like this. Didn't like the idea of him going away at all.

He was on the same page. "With Dante gone, I don't trust anyone here. I want you to check into a hotel for the night."

Morana saw the seriousness in his eyes, blinking. "I've slept alert for years before I met you, Tristan. I'll be fine."

"I don't doubt that," he rubbed his thumb over her lips, his eyes intense. "But I need to be able to focus on my task and not worry about you."

"You'll worry about me?" Morana asked, her voice cracking. She forgot sometimes in the flood of her own emotions that he felt for her too.

He didn't say anything, just pressed his lips to hers, answering her without words. "Check into a hotel anonymously. Don't tell anyone where you're going. Vin will drop you off."

Morana nodded, preparing herself mentally, an ugly feeling unfurling in the pit of her stomach.

"If something happens to you, caveman," she told him, looping her arms around his neck. "I'll kill you myself."

She saw a flash of his dimple before her eyes closed and her mouth got busy.

❈

The hotel she checked into was the same one she'd stayed at the first time she'd come to Tenebrae to kill Tristan weeks ago. Smack in the center of the city, it was a tall, luxurious building that catered to the wealthy and vetted every guest that checked in. Booking herself a room was a breeze for her.

Walking into the opulent lobby, her heels clicking on the polished marble floor, a red wig hiding her dark locks, Morana dragged her small suitcase behind her, holding a few clothes and her tech stuff.

"Trina Summers," she introduced herself, giving her false name confidently. The lady behind the reception smiled and handed her the key card. One stay at this hotel was going to put a dent in her savings but once things calmed down, she was sure she'd be able to work again. While she knew Tristan had money, she wanted to be able to pay for her life herself.

Keeping her eyes alert, Morana looked around the lobby inconspicuously and saw all the people, so many of them clueless about the underbelly of the criminal world she lived in. A few suspicious-looking men lingered here and there, and while she kept her eyes on them, she didn't pay them too much attention.

Walking to her room on the eighteenth floor, Morana wondered about how it had only been weeks since her life had been thrown into chaos, since everything she had known had crumbled. She was in a strange city with no anchor except the one man who had once hated her, the one man who was slowly beginning to trust her now.

That was big for him. She knew, because to him, the fact that she was staying with him mattered. He'd been abandoned and left behind all his life by those he'd loved. It made sense why he would be wary of opening up but damn if she wasn't determined to sneak her way there.

Lost in her thoughts, Morana reached her room and called up room service. Setting up her laptop and router, she ate her noodles while surfing the darknet. Searching for information on the Syndicate was like looking for a specific needle in a needle-stack. Now that she had the codes, she was more relaxed and less burdened about the information. She still had questions but the urgency had left her and honestly, it made her much more productive.

She browsed through conspiracy theories and articles about both the Alliance and the Syndicate, spent hours poring over them and finding quite a bit to make her own theories. She knew enough to theorize that the Syndicate was involved in flesh trade and the end of the Alliance had been connected to it. Was it because the parties hadn't wanted to partake in the trade? Given everything she knew, she surmised there was a high chance that the girls who had gone missing had somehow been masterminded by the Syndicate. It would make sense.

Over the next two days, Morana spent her time checking her phone for a message from Tristan (which didn't come and that really worried her), trying to call Amara and not getting through (which worried her even more), and trying to find more clues. She mostly stayed in her room, going down to the hotel restaurant in the evening to have dinner and people watch, making sure nobody could recognize her even if she saw someone familiar.

On the third night sitting at the table and eating her chocolate fondue, a waiter brought her a note.

Morana opened it.

Come to the empty warehouse on the Riviera on Tuesday at midnight.
It's time we meet. Come alone. You won't be harmed.

– The Reaper

Morana whirled around in her seat, trying to locate who sent it. The lavish restaurant was half-empty. Locating the waiter who had delivered the note, she questioned him about it.

"A man left it at the counter for you, ma'am," the young man informed her.

"What did he look like?" she asked him, her heart racing.

"Well-dressed, ma'am," the waiter tried to remember. "He had a dark beard and wore glasses. Oh, and he had a cane."

A cane. Was it the same man from the funeral? What were the odds?

Morana gave the waiter a small smile, thanking him, and quickly paid the bill, hurrying to her room. Once inside, she sat down on her laptop and hacked into the hotel security system, zooming into the footage at the restaurant in the last hour and watching closely near the counter, adrenaline fueling her.

She saw, on the black and white grainy feed, as a lean man limped over to the counter, leaning heavily on his cane. He handed over the note to the woman behind the counter and watched Morana for a few minutes, before he turned to leave, his face wincing with every step.

Morana zoomed in on his face, trying to remember if she'd ever seen him before, but unable to place him. Something on his hand caught her eye and she zoomed in there, enlarging it. It was a ring. A skull ring? She watched the footage multiple times, before finally giving up and getting ready for bed. Wearing her new pajamas, the checkered shorts and 'nerdy is the new sexy' t-shirt that was extra soft, she slid under the covers and thought about this man and why, if he had found her with her disguise and her anonymous name, hadn't he come and talked to her tonight. She'd been just a few feet away, eating and she'd been alone. He had considered it but hadn't. Why? That was what confused her.

Things were getting very interesting.

❧

It was a body sitting down beside her hip that woke Morana. She turned in bed, a scream leaving her throat at the large form looming over her.

"It's me," the voice of whiskey-and-sin poured over her, immediately calming her racing heart. Without another thought, Morana launched up at him and wrapped her arms around his neck, her relief at finding him okay overpowering anything else.

"I missed you something fierce," she murmured against his neck, her nose nuzzling into that happy spot, inhaling the musky scent of his skin. Her first indication that something wasn't right came when his arms didn't come around her. Over the last couple of weeks, he'd gotten good with her surprise hugs, always a little taken aback but tentatively returning them.

Turning on the lamp beside her, she pulled back slightly, looking up into his face.

That was the second indication.

His face was haunted.

She'd never seen him like that.

Morana's heart slammed in her chest, her eyes searching his. "Tristan?"

"Don't," he whispered. "Don't ask me anything right now."

As much as she wanted to, Morana listened. She had to get him out of whatever dark place he was in. Nodding, she slowly unbuttoned his shirt, only to have his hands come up to stop hers. She looked at him in question.

"You shouldn't touch me right now," he told her, his blue eyes so dark and so pained she felt her throat tighten.

"Trust me," she whispered back to him in the same voice, asking him for the entirety of everything she had given him. He waited for a beat, his eyes on the pulse in her neck. Letting her hands go, he gave her assent to continue.

Morana breathed in and slowly opened his shirt, realizing that he wasn't looking at her. She could work around that. Pushing his shirt off his torso, she quietly got up from the bed.

"Lie down on your stomach."

He hesitated, before toeing off his shoes, putting his gun on the table, and taking off his trousers, lying down on his stomach in the middle of the bed.

Morana looked at his back for a second before taking out a bottle of one of her favorite unscented oils from the drawer. She had no idea why he was like this but she had to do something. Had he ever let go in his life? Had he ever simply been told it was okay to not be okay? Ever felt the gentle touch of a loved one in all these years?

Climbing on behind him, spreading her legs and straddling his beautiful ass, Morana took in the view of his entire muscular back laid out before her. He had come to her – broken and messed up, he had found her. The fact that he was there and not at his house, that he'd found her even in this headspace and not headed to the cottage, told her enough.

Without a word, Morana poured out a generous quantity of the oil on her palms. Rubbing them together to warm them, she leaned forward and slowly spread it out over his shoulders, telling him through her very touch that she saw him, accepted him, loved him for who he was, however he was.

A shaky breath escaped him in a rush and Morana continued to slide her hands over him. The tight knots of his muscles there were rigid. Working them out gradually with her thumbs, she heard another breath leave his chest before he could help himself. Her heart hurt, imagining how he had never had this before. His bruised body had never been shown affection, his bruised soul had never been told it was beautiful.

Pressing her lips to his wolf tattoo in a wordless declaration, Morana felt her way down each and every muscle on his beautiful back. She saw a few scars littered here and there, the stories of which she was sure she'd find out someday, but for that moment, she worked silently.

"It was bad," he said into the pillow, his voice muffled. "I shouldn't have been there."

Morana wondered what he had seen that got to him so bad. She let him talk, kneading the muscles at the base of his spine, digging in with her thumbs.

"I want to hurt something right now," he growled. "And I don't want it to be you."

She felt her heart stutter. "You won't hurt me, Tristan."

He let out an ugly laugh, suddenly flipping so she landed on the side of the bed.

"You have no idea what I'm capable of," his eyes were ablaze. "I killed my own father. Shot right here," he pointed to the middle of his forehead. "Do you even realize what that does to you?" his voice escalated.

Morana watched him, her eyes widening. "Tristan—"

"And that was just the beginning for me," he leaned in, trying to intimidate her. "The things I have done, the blood on my hands will never wash off. What the fuck are you even doing here? Just cut your losses and walk away."

Morana felt her breath hitch, not understanding what the hell was going on with him but very, very scared of the way he was walling her out. She took in a deep breath, fighting to keep calm. He was unraveling and she needed to keep him together right now, for both their sakes.

"And if I walk," she tilted her head, keeping her voice even, "you'd let me go."

The stark pain in his eyes told her everything she needed to know. "Then, shut up."

He sat back on his knees, his hands holding his head. "I never meant to kill him," he whispered, his voice hoarse. "I need you to know that. I just saw you and saw what he was going to do. I only meant to stop him. I didn't know, I didn't—"

Morana moved, her heart bleeding for him. Placing her hand on his arm, she straddled him, pulling his face into her chest and his body started to shake. "She left me alone with these monsters after that. She left me to fucking fend for myself with nobody. I wasn't a monster then. I was so fucking lost—"

He *broke*.

Morana held him through the pain, her own eyes tearing up as he cried in her arms. She didn't know what had caused him to break, didn't know what had triggered him into heaving like the little boy who had been left hurt and alone in a world too cruel for him. She didn't know and she didn't care about anything right now except he had sought her out. He needed her acceptance. He needed her unconditional love to heal like his own was healing her. She doubted he even realized that he loved her, or that every action of his cemented that fact in her very soul.

Clutching him to her heart as his body shook in her arms, she rocked him silently, holding him as he had never been held, whispering sweet, soothing words to him, telling him she was there and she was never going to leave him.

The sounds coming from him broke something inside her, the rush of fierce protectiveness engulfing her so acute. She didn't know if she held him for minutes or hours, if the night had passed or still remained. She just held him, pressing soft kisses to his head, loving him as he deserved to be loved, as he should have been loved for so many years.

"What if she is dead?" he asked into her collarbone, his voice rough and so agonized she doubted it would ever be completely gone. She knew who he was talking about.

She tugged his face back, and looked at him. His eyes, his beautiful, electric blue eyes, were red-rimmed and swollen, the tears in them precious gifts he'd shared with her.

"Do you truly believe that?" she asked him, stroking her finger over his eyebrow, wiping away an errant tear.

He shook his head tightly.

"Then we will find her."

His jaw trembled again, everything he was feeling in his heart naked in his eyes, and Morana softly pressed her lips to his, accepting every word that hovered on them but couldn't make it out. He wasn't there yet. She didn't know if he would ever be there. But she knew. And that was enough for her.

"Have you ever been made love to, Mr. Caine?" she asked him softly, knowing she would have to lead him. He wasn't strong at processing emotions, never had to be, and her mere existence in his life was forcing him to slowly confront so much he had buried for so long. Expecting him to understand emotional nuances and express them would be wrong. The damage to his psyche might be something he never recovered from. Morana knew that. And she would be there for him, every step of the way like he was for her with his little touches that anchored her in moments of doubt, with his little chocolates she found throughout the day that warmed her heart, with his little looks at her when he thought she wasn't aware.

"No," he answered, swallowing.

"Then, allow me," she whispered, slowly pressing her mouth against his, taking a hold of his lower lip between her teeth and tugging at it. His hands speared into her hair, holding her face in place as he kissed her, pouring everything he felt into that one kiss. Their lips met, tongues tangled and parted. Her oiled hands slid down his chest to rest on his racing heart, feeling the strong beat under her palm.

She pulled back, looking him right in those blue eyes and telling him the words he should have been told a long time ago.

"I'm so in love with you, caveman."

She saw his eyes flare slightly, his hand coming to rest around her neck, gripping her firmly. "You can't take that back," he warned her fiercely.

Morana shook her head, not breaking their gaze. Taking out his cock from his boxers, she pushed her panties to the side and rose on her knees, letting his tip enter her folds. Even though she wasn't as wet as she should've been, this moment wasn't about the sex. It was about more. It was about acceptance.

She took him inside her, her mouth opening slightly as her walls clenched and unclenched to accommodate him, burning slightly, her eyes never once moving from his. His hand squeezed her neck slightly, holding her even as he held on to her.

"I'm not going to take it back," she told him, her breathing heavy as he seated himself inside her completely.

"I mean it, Morana," he threatened her, his eyes so alive she felt buzzed. "You cannot take it back. Do you understand me?"

"I won't," she reassured him.

He moved her ass, the position placing him so deep inside her she couldn't stop her breath from rushing out. Hip to hip, chest to chest, heart to heart. The hand on her neck never moved. Neither did his eyes.

"Tell me again," he demanded, jerking her again.

Morana looked into his gaze, seeing the lost boy and the lovable man, both of whom he kept hidden from the world, and told him. "I'm in love with you, Tristan Caine. I don't expect you to say it back. I don't need you to. I just need you to keep on loving me."

He pressed his forehead to hers as she rotated her hips slowly over him, their bodies, their beings, their minds so connected in that moment they were the same.

The night continued, and he showed her everything he felt that he couldn't say.

CHAPTER 19

ENTRUST

Morana looked at the man sleeping beside her in the hotel bed in the soft morning light, soft snores coming out of his mouth, his entire frame so relaxed no one could imagine the turmoil that lived under his skin. She knew their journey forward wasn't going to be easy. He was never going to be completely emotionally okay. The trauma he had gone through, most of which she didn't even know about, would manifest itself in different ways through their lives.

But she also knew he loved her.

He wouldn't have come to her last night otherwise. He wouldn't have sought her out over and over as he had. He wouldn't have felt the need to keep her safe with himself as he did.

He loved her, and he would probably never be able to tell her so.

And she was surprisingly okay with that.

She'd rather he look at her the way he did for the rest of their lives. She'd rather he cook for her the way he did every morning. She'd rather he hold her neck like he did when she was old and gray.

He had given her a home, somewhere she belonged, just as she was. Be it his penthouse or the cottage or this hotel room, he was her anchor. She was never going to be alone again.

Dropping a little kiss on his bicep, she frowned at the tattoo, seeing the skull closely. It was the exact same skull, with the same design, as she'd seen on Maroni's ring.

"Tristan," she mumbled, patting his abs absently.

"Hmm," he hummed, his voice roughened from sleep.

"What does this skull mean?" she asked, pointing to his arm.

She saw him blink his blue eyes open, slowly getting alert. "It's an Outfit thing. Most soldiers get this when they're taken into the fold. Why?"

Morana traced it with her finger, her mind racing. "And who in the outfit will have this on a ring?"

Tristan paused for a second, considering. "Maroni has one. Anyone else would have to be someone in one of the high positions."

"I think that's who the Reaper was," Morana scrambled out of bed, rushing to her clutch where she'd stuffed the note.

She returned to bed, seeing Tristan leaning back on his elbows as he watched her curiously, his eyes lingering on her t-shirt for a split second before he asked for the note. Morana handed it to him, waiting to see what he said.

"You're not going alone."

That was predictable enough. "I know. It's Saturday today. I was thinking maybe we should stake out the place tonight, just prep work. He could actually be there beforehand and we don't-"

He cut off her words, swallowed the rest of her plan, and asked her to prove that nerdy, indeed, was the new sexy.

❧

Tristan decided to walk them to the location that evening, wearing a casual black t-shirt and jeans he'd paid one of the hotel attendants to buy from across the street. Morana, although pleasantly sore between the legs, walked happily beside him towards the pier, watching all the people and the buzz, listening to all the chatter of children, street vendors, and excited tourists. Were it not for the gun she could feel under his t-shirt, she would believe he was just a guy strolling through the tourist spot with his lover on a weekend.

Morana enjoyed every second of it, spending time with him in a way she'd never thought she would. She asked him if it was okay to walk around like that without any security, and he'd just given her a look that shut her up. She forgot sometimes, knowing him as she did now, that to the outside world, he was still the feared Predator.

Looping her arm around his waist, tucked into his side, Morana thanked god she'd packed her comfortable flats as they crossed the busy pier.

"You know we should do a picnic one day," she mused out loud, going where he was leading. "And maybe actually go to a restaurant."

"We've been to a restaurant," he reminded her.

Morana flushed, remembering that time in *Crimson*. Fuck, that had been hot. "I meant to eat."

His lips didn't even twitch but she sensed his amusement as he glanced at her. "I wouldn't mind going to a restaurant for exactly what we did."

"Me neither," Morana admitted, feeling her face heat. "Maybe we could actually eat this time too."

"You know we already live together, right?" he pointed out.

Morana sighed. "I've just never been on a date, okay? All I had was dinners with my father at the table and at least one guy trying to grope me."

She felt him tuck her in closer to his side, pressing his lips to the top of her ear lobe. Morana felt a little smile tip her lips and continued asking him questions as they turned from the pier, following the river, but the crowd started to thin.

After a few minutes, Morana felt his body snap to attention as the location came into view. She looked around, seeing the secluded, old warehouse building made of wood and cement. It looked almost dilapidated in the falling night.

Tristan bent down and took out a spare gun from his boots, handing it to her silently. Morana nodded, appreciating the gesture and the fact that he trusted her ability to watch both their backs, and indicated the building.

She watched him switch to his predatory mode, and shook off her appreciation, focusing on the task at hand – scoping the place out.

Sliding into the building through an opening in the door, Morana entered after Tristan into the cavernous, dim space.

It was empty save for a chair to the side and some boxes stacked together. A very odd, unusual place for a meeting.

"I see your curiosity got the better of you," the words came from behind her.

Morana whirled around, her gun pointed at the man limping out from the shadows. She felt Tristan come up behind her, his own weapon aimed at the stranger.

"Put those down, kids," the man waved the gun away, his voice raspy from disuse or smoking. He stepped out into the light, his eyes coming to her. "I'm not going to hurt you, little doe."

Morana tilted her head to the side, frowning. "Do I know you?"

His eyes crinkled, taking her in. His face was weathered and creased, half-covered in a thick dark beard, his eyes behind round, wire-framed glasses.

"You were at the funeral," Morana thought out loud, lowering her weapon. An eerie feeling settled in the pit of her stomach.

He simply turned and headed towards the single chair, "Your timing isn't the best, I admit. We might get interrupted. I have a meeting here soon."

"Who are you?"

He didn't answer, just limped to the chair. Morana turned to Tristan, eyes alert, and found him frowning at the man as well, his gun still up.

"I saw you," Tristan spoke, his eyes narrowing in recognition. "You were there. A few years ago at-" He stopped.

The man chuckled, collapsing into the chair with a groan. "Do go on."

Morana looked between them, confused. The cool draft in the warehouse raised goosebumps on her arms.

The man smiled, his hazel eyes alight with humor. "He's talking about your graduation, Morana. He was there. That's where he saw me."

Surprise flooded her as she looked at Tristan, to find him staring straight at the man.

"Why were you there?" Morana asked the older man.

"To see you," the man rubbed his knee with his right hand, the silver skull ring glinting on his finger, a replica of the one she'd seen on Lorenzo Maroni's hand.

"Are you Outfit?" she asked him, pointing to his hand.

The man twisted the ring and gazed up at her, something akin to reverence in his eyes. "I was once, a long time ago."

Morana slowly lowered her gun to the side, her heart bursting. "Are you the Reaper?"

The man smiled, the lines on his cheeks creasing in a way that wasn't bad. His hair, a shock of salt and pepper, was shabby. "I am the Reaper."

"Why did you call me here? Why not talk to me at the hotel?" she asked him, taking a step closer to where he was seated. She felt Tristan move behind her.

"Because I had to meet you," he told her. "Someplace we can talk alone." He gave a pointed look to her lover. "Please put your gun down. I'm not going to harm either of you."

For some odd reason, Morana believed him. Lowering her gun completely to the side, Morana perched down on a wooden box in front of the man and considered him steadily. "I have questions that I feel only you have the answers to."

She felt Tristan come to stand behind her silently, present but letting her lead.

"Let me tell you a story first," the man began, clearing his throat to get his voice working. "I'm afraid we don't have much time."

Morana nodded.

"About twenty-three years ago, I was a soldier of the Outfit and a happily married man," he started, his brown eyes flecked with green on her. "It was a rarity, believe it or not. My wife, she didn't know much about this business or what I did."

He took a deep breath, twisting the ring on his finger. "This ring was a gift from Lorenzo. It was only for the three members of the Alliance – Lorenzo, Gabriel, and I. While they were the leaders of both the families, I was the one who collected all the data on businesses and operations. I had all the information about the enemies. I dealt in secrets and that made my friends powerful people."

"I know that," Morana nodded, interested in finally getting some answers.

He tilted his head to the side, blinking at her. "Of course," he shook his head. "Everything was going well. I was happy. My wife was pregnant with our second child. That's when I stumbled upon a secret one of my friends had hidden."

Morana leaned forward, intrigued.

"Lorenzo had become a member of a global Syndicate," the man told her quietly. "The Syndicate traded in children."

Her throat tightened as she turned to look at the man behind her. "You don't have to be here."

Tristan looked down at her, the hunger for answers in his blue eyes matching hers, and prompted the man to go on. "The missing children."

Morana put her hand on his thigh and turned back around to the older man, finding him watching both of them with something close to contentment in his eyes. He shook it off, focusing on the story.

"The children were taken from different cities at too young an age, and groomed to become slaves, those that survived anyway. Many died."

She felt Tristan's thigh muscles bunch under her palm at that, and gave it a squeeze. Her skin crawled, knowing she'd been one of those children. "Maroni was supplying children?"

"He's the reason my sister went missing?" Tristan asked over her question.

The older man looked at Tristan with his eyes full of regret. "No. Your sister was all Gabriel. I'm sorry."

Tristan inhaled sharply. Morana felt shame and pain coil in her belly. God, what evil monsters preyed upon *children?* Her father was one of them.

The man continued. "I didn't know how long it had been going on, but I didn't want to be a part of that. Although Gabriel was involved in only a few operations, Lorenzo had his hands in many. He was the real danger. I called both of them and threatened to expose him if he didn't stop. I was a fool, thinking they'd been my friends."

Morana felt something heavy settle in her gut. "What happened then?"

The man studied her, staying silent for a long, long moment. "The Alliance was broken. I stepped down and Gabriel got scared and decided to go his own way. All businesses split. But Lorenzo never trusted anyone. He took Gabriel's daughter as insurance for him to keep his mouth shut."

Morana breathed through her nose and stayed quiet.

He continued, his voice bleak. "He then attacked my wife in our home and murdered her and our baby."

Hand flying to her mouth, Morana gasped at the horror the man before her had suffered. "I'm so sorry," she spoke, her heart aching for him.

The man chuckled, "Oh, I wish that was all he'd done."

Morana was half-afraid of hearing more.

"He took my other daughter too," the man spoke, his eyes sharp on her. "At first, he put her in with the other missing children, but then he got another idea to ensure Gabriel stayed quiet."

Morana's heart started to thunder in her chest, her breathing uneven. She felt Tristan's hand come down on her shoulder.

"He gave her to Gabriel to raise," the man told her quietly, "so he could look at her and remember the extent of Lorenzo's wrath to those who go against him. In exchange for his silence, his own daughter would live. His wife never accepted it was her own child who came back and left him, poor thing."

Her hands started to shake, tears gathering in her eyes as her entire life flashed before her eyes, everything suddenly falling in place. Her father's disdain of her, her mother's absence, every callous word she had heard in that house, how her father had enjoyed seeing her suffer – it started to make an eerie kind of sense.

Morana swallowed, "I . . . don't . . . I" she stammered.

"You're her father," Tristan put into words what she wasn't able to. The man smiled softly at her. "You're my daughter, Morana."

She stared at him in disbelief, knowing in her heart that he wasn't lying but unable to accept it. "Is that even my real name? Or was it her name? Gabriel's daughter?" she asked, her voice climbing.

She felt the hand on her shoulder give her a squeeze, and the older man, her real father, shrugged. "It doesn't matter. You're Morana."

Morana exhaled, tears streaming down her face. "Do you know if she's alive?"

He shook his head and the pain inside Morana deepened. *How?*

Morana wiped her tears and asked the question she knew was on the forefront of Tristan's mind. "Is Luna alive?"

They held their breath as her father said ruefully. "I truly don't know."

Gathering up her courage, Morana straightened her spine. "Why didn't you take me back?"

"I was too injured when all of this was happening," he told her, rubbing his knee. "I didn't know what had happened to you until after a few months, and by then, it was too late. For all intents and purposes, you were a Vitalio."

Morana felt her lips tremble. "Why didn't you try to contact me before?"

He shook his head. "As long as they thought I was dead, it was safer for you. I kept my eyes on you though, giving you what little protection I could from afar."

Her heart clenched.

"I know I don't have any right to be, but I was very proud when you went on to study technology," he told her, the smile on his face a ghost of who he must have been. "You get it from me. You're so much better than I was at your age."

The pride in his voice, the pride she had never been on the receiving end of in her entire life, twisted something inside her chest. Morana searched his face and found the resemblance to her, in the hazel of his eyes, in the way his nose tilted slightly upwards. She felt her eyes fill up again and shook it off, asking the question that had been burning inside her for days. "Why steal the codes? You were never going to use them. Why frame Tristan?"

He straightened his leg, a slight wince crossing his face. "I needed to make you and Tristan cross paths."

Morana blinked, surprised. "Excuse me?"

Tristan's hand tightened on her shoulder.

Her father chuckled, the sound genuine. "Oh, you think I was the only one keeping an eye on you? The boy was always there. He caught me a few times, didn't you, Tristan?" her father directed it at the man behind her, looking at him over his glasses in a gesture Morana recognized in herself.

Heart stuttering at this new piece of information, Morana tried to remember any moment in her past when she'd felt watched. She knew he had a picture of her. But was that all he had? Did he have more? How long had she been watched? She had been watched, not by one but by two people and she didn't remember a single incident?

"I knew what he'd done to protect you once," the man deliberated. "And I knew, with the way he kept his eye on you through the years, that he would protect you again when the time came."

"The time for what?" she croaked out, her mind barely hanging on to everything.

"Justice."

A shiver going down her spine, Morana clenched and unclenched her fists, considering this man before her. The hollow warehouse echoed the emptiness in her stomach as everything she had known about her life crashed down.

"So, let me get this straight," she leaned forward, watching him with an even gaze. "You had Jackson steal my codes and frame Tristan all so I could find him? You were matchmaking?"

The man, huffed a laugh. "It sounds a little silly when you put it like that, but it worked didn't it?"

"He wanted to kill me," she told him.

"I did," Tristan confirmed from behind her.

The older man shook his head. "I think you didn't recognize it, Tristan, and I don't blame you."

He remarked to Morana, "The men in this world don't love like normal men, little doe. Their love is more intense than any other. He fell in love with you as a boy and as a man. And watching it happen has been the only peace I have found in years, knowing you will be loved and cherished and protected after I'm gone. I needed to give you that."

Pulse throbbing with his words, her throat tight with unfamiliar emotions, Morana shuddered, shaking off the severity of his voice.

"Who has been trying to kill me?" she asked him, trying to understand everything.

"The Syndicate."

"Why did you send me towards the Alliance and the Syndicate then? Shouldn't I have stayed away?"

"You can't stay away. You're involved already because of who you are, and I had to prepare you for the truth," he stated simply. "If you weren't prepared, your mind wouldn't have been able to cope. And I wanted your relationship to be successful."

Morana shook her head. "And what am I going to do with all this truth? What is the point?"

The man, her father, smiled indulgently, looking from Tristan and back to her. "You'll do what you want to do, Morana. This world needs people like you to stand up for those who can't do it for themselves. There are so many lost children who cannot find their way home, so many parents who grieve for their babies. The pain of that is unfathomable, my little doe. You don't know the agony that goes through a father when he loses his child, never to find her. Help them."

A throb started in her temples. "How? I don't know."

The man leaned forward, about to say something, when the sound of a vehicle stopping outside made him straighten. He looked at both of them and uttered one word, "Hide."

Uncertain, Morana picked up her gun and felt Tristan pull her up, guiding her to the side, hiding behind one of the pillars. Putting her back to the pillar and shielding his body with hers, she saw him lean to the side and watch the door. Morana twisted her neck and watched the scene herself.

Lorenzo Maroni and her father – no, Gabriel Vitalio – walked into the space, both dressed in suits. Morana saw her father, her actual father, simply smile at them and greet them like old friends. She realized she didn't even know his actual name, or hers. She didn't know about her mother or her unborn baby sister.

Breathing through the pain invading her heart, Morana simply took strength from the man standing pressed into her, took courage from his presence, and kept her eyes on the scene and focused on it. She could break down later.

"Well, well," Lorenzo Maroni guffawed. "Look who turned up from the grave. I thought I'd buried you, old friend."

"Always the theatrics, Lorenzo," her father commented, sounding amused.

Lorenzo chortled. "You should've left the sleeping skeletons alone."

"Why did you call us?" Gabriel cut through the bullshit.

Her father shook his head. "I wanted to ask about the trade. Weapons and children these days, isn't that right, Lorenzo?"

"Not this old tune, Reaper," Lorenzo looked down at his friend's cane. "You remember the last time you threatened to expose me?"

"Very clearly," her father stated. "You're not the only ones I called for this meeting."

Morana watched, surprised, as Dante stepped into the warehouse and leaned against one of the pillars, casually smoking a cigarette. "Hello, father."

Tristan inhaled above her, his heart still steady against her ear. Morana felt her own start to palpitate. She had a bad feeling about this.

Lorenzo Maroni looked slightly startled for a second before he recovered. "Good to see you, son."

Dante gave an empty smile, one like she'd never seen on his handsome face. "I wish I could say the same, especially after seeing the results of your depravity the last few days, father."

Lorenzo stilled before turning to the Reaper. "Why call us here?"

Her father leaned on his cane and stood before him, his body lean in front of Lorenzo's stock. "To tell you that for the last few years, I have dismantled your business. To tell you that I have been planning this for over twenty years. You are true evil, Lorenzo. And you don't deserve to live."

Before anyone could move, her father twisted the top of his cane off, bringing out a hidden blade, and sliced it across Lorenzo Maroni's throat. Morana barely contained a gasp, her fingers fisting in Tristan's t-shirt as he took aim and steadied his gun on the scene, watchful.

"That's for Elaina," her father stated, his voice cold. "That's for killing my love and my baby, for taking away my little girl, Lorenzo."

Dante simply smoked in the corner, seeing his father gurgling, seeing his knees shaking, seeing his crisp white shirt turning an ugly red.

Maroni fell forward on her father, taking out something from his own pocket. It was a blade that he stabbed him with as he went down.

"No!" Morana whispered before she could control it, her eyes widening.

Maroni clutched his neck, trying to talk, his eyes popping out. Her father held the gaping wound on his chest and continued talking through labored breaths. "This is your justice," her father went on, bleeding out. "You bleed to death while your son watches without remorse. That's what you've created."

Gabriel, who had been staring at his old partner in shock, suddenly bent down and shook the dying man. "Where is my daughter?" he demanded, shaking him. "Is she alive? Damn you, Lorenzo, tell me where is she?!"

Maroni gurgled, choked, his eyes bulging, and fell limp to the ground. At a few minutes after midnight, Bloodhound Maroni died in a pool of his own blood.

Morana observed all of this in stunned shock. All of this happened not ten feet from where she stood.

Tristan twitched against her. "Stay here," he whispered into her hair before stepping out into the melee. She saw as Dante glanced up to see Tristan come out, his eyebrows raised but otherwise silent. He threw his cigarette away. Both men stepped up to her real father in sync, bending down to see his body.

Dante patted his chest clinically and took out an envelope, exchanging a look with Tristan.

Her father croaked out something that Tristan bent to listen to, before he and Dante stood up and walked to the warehouse door, talking quietly. Morana didn't know what was in the envelope and at the moment, she didn't really care.

Gabriel continued to shake a dead Lorenzo, asking about his daughter's whereabouts.

"We both know the pain of losing a daughter," Gabriel muttered on his knees in Lorenzo's blood. "Except you know your daughter is safe and I don't. Now I never will."

Her father didn't answer.

Gabriel started to laugh, the sound gaining volume, becoming more and more hysterical.

Morana stepped out from behind the pillar, watching him, aware of both Dante and Tristan turning around to watch him as well.

Tristan looked at her, and shook his head. "Let's leave, Morana."

Gabriel's eyes fell on her and he laughed. "Morana, the little whore in his bed."

He stayed on his knees in the blood, grinning like a madman. "You aren't my Morana! I don't even know who the fuck you are!"

Morana raised her gun and pointed it to his head, her heart hurting. "Did you kidnap girls and trade them twenty years ago?" she asked, her voice shaking.

But Gabriel was too far gone to answer her.

"My Morana is lost. My Morana is gone. My Morana doesn't even *exist!* And me? I would kill you every day I could. I want you to feel the pain my girl was feeling somewhere; I want you to bleed as she bleeds. I want you to question why Daddy didn't love you like my baby must have wondered."

Morana stepped forward, her heart bleeding, hurting, for a girl she had never met, for herself, and for all the other girls who had been brutalized by these men. "Did you kidnap girls twenty years ago?"

She was aware of Tristan's eyes on her, of Dante watching the scene alert, but she couldn't look away from the eyes of the man she had loved as her father for so many years.

Those eyes darkened as they came to her and his laughter got worse.

"You fucking whore," he spit at her feet. "You don't deserve to be happy, not when my baby isn't."

"I was a child," Morana told him, her eyes burning. "An innocent child."

"And I was a father!" he screamed, spittle flying from his mouth. "I was a father to a beautiful baby girl who was replaced overnight! Gone! And you took her place. You're not her! You'll never be her!"

"Did you kidnap girls twenty years ago?" she continued asking relentlessly, her arms shaking with the strain on her mind and her muscles.

He stood up, taking a step towards her, the hatred in his eyes burning her, not answering her question. "Every time I looked at you, it reminded me of my baby. How she must have suffered. How she must have cried for me. You didn't deserve her life."

Morana felt each word assault her like a bullet, finding its mark, digging into her skin.

In the second that it took her to process his words, Gabriel took out his gun and pointed it at her head, his dark eyes unhinged on her. "Oh, he has a gun on me. He might kill me but I'd get my shot in. And I'd hit right between the eyes."

Morana stared at the dark hateful eyes, unmoving. "Did you kidnap Luna Caine?"

"I've been crazy for a long time but I had to pretend, for the sake of my daughter, for the hope that one day Lorenzo would tell me where she was."

Morana elevated her own arm, pointing it to his forehead.

Tristan's calm voice came from her right. "Don't do it, Morana."

"Oh, do it, Morana," Gabriel's voice mocked her name. "Your father is dead. Your mother is dead. I will kill your lover too. And your children—"

"Don't let him get to you," Tristan's voice came from the periphery, cool and collected. "I've got him. You don't want to do this."

"Oh you want to do this, don't you, Morana," Gabriel cajoled, his eyes feral like she'd never seen before. "You know if you have daughters, I will steal them—"

"Morana, don't listen to him—"

"—and put them in the trade. Just like I did twenty years ago—"

"I've got him, don't do it."

"Stop it!" Morana screamed at both the voices coming at her, her hands shaking, her entire form trembling with pain and rage that just kept accumulating inside her body. She felt the ice and fire battle inside her, taking her from cold-blooded detachment to burning fury in moments.

"Did you take Luna Caine?" she bellowed at Gabriel, her voice breaking.

Gabriel laughed. "Yes, I did!"

It happened in a split second.

Before she had even realized it, her fingers had pulled the trigger, the recoil hitting her hard, the sight of a gaping hole in the head of the man who had been the only father she had known all her life.

A tormented howl left her throat even as her knees collapsed.

"Fuck!"

Arms came around her, pulling her up even as her eyes looked at all the death around them. Lorenzo Maroni lying in a pool of his blood, his throat slit. Her biological father, a man she had known only for ten minutes but one who had protected her all her life, dead with a slight smile on his face, his shirt soaked in blood. Gabriel Vitalio, a man who had gone mad after losing his daughter, a monster, her father, killed by her.

Morana took it all in, and blacked out.

CHAPTER 20

AFTERMATH

It was the sound of low voices that penetrated her consciousness.

Blinking her eyes open, Morana looked up at the familiar ceiling of the cottage living room, and tried to sit up, her head hurting. A glass of water appeared in front of her and she took it, gulping down the cool liquid down her parched throat, looking up to see Tristan staring at her solemnly. Her eyes moved to the other occupant in the room, Dante, who watched her just as solemnly.

Suddenly, everything came rushing back to her. Taking in a big lungful of air, her chest suddenly tight, Morana looked at the both of them, blinking her tears away.

"Are they all dead?" she croaked out, putting the glass on the table in front of her.

Both men, to her relief, nodded their heads. Dante elaborated, "There's going to be a shitstorm."

Morana focused on her breathing, so much colliding and collapsing inside her she didn't know how to think about any of it. Things were freezing. Her blood was cooling. Ice was slowly slithering into her veins. Nodding once, she stood up, needing space, needing distance, to bury it all.

"I need a shower."

Without waiting for their response, she calmly walked out of the room and up the stairs, going to the bathroom and locking the door. She gripped the granite counter with her paling knuckles, leaning on her arms, looking up into the mirror to see her reflection staring back at her.

Who was she?

Who the fuck was she?

She didn't have a mother. Her real mother had brutally died with her sister in her womb. Her father hadn't told her her name in the few minutes they'd spent together. Her father, who had been on a quest for revenge for two decades, had watched her for years and felt proud of her. And the man she had loved all her life as her father, the man whose approval she had longed for, had been an evil monster who had destroyed so many lives. She had killed him.

Her biceps started to shake, her reflection blurring as her breaths became harder to take.

A knock sounded on the door behind her.

Morana opened her mouth to reply but no sound came out. She stared, wide-eyed, at her own reflection, trying to call out but her throat closed up, a ball lodging itself there, suffocating her.

"Morana, open the door," whiskey-and-sin came from the other side. How could she face him? How could she when her father had destroyed his life and taken his sister away, sending him spiraling into the dark? What if she looked into his eyes and saw real hatred for herself? She couldn't take it. Fuck, she couldn't see him. But she wanted to turn around and twist the knob open. She needed to. She couldn't move.

The knocks became more insistent. "Morana, open the fucking door!"

She really, really wanted to. She wanted to fling herself into his arms and have him tell her that he didn't hate her. But how could she face him?

"I swear to god if you don't open this damn door right now . . ."

Ungluing her fingers from the counter, she managed to turn around and found her knees locking together. Black spots danced in front of her eyes, her lips parting to take in much-needed air. She couldn't breathe.

She heard a loud thump, then another before the door crashed open and his furious form stood there.

"Jesus—" He took one look at her and swooped in, picking her up in his arms and carrying her to the shower, turning all the faucets on and sitting down on the bench with her in his embrace.

The cold water jarred her system, jerking her body. Morana buried her face in his neck, finding that spot right at the juncture of his shoulder, and tried to gulp in some air.

His arms tightened around her and he kept her close. "It's okay. It's just a panic attack. It'll pass. Just focus on my voice and breathe with me, Morana."

She did. She focused on his voice, on the whiskey that got her drunk and the sin that made her feel alive. She breathed with him, feeling the slow expansion and deflation of his chest and matched hers to him.

Her mouth trembled. "It should've been me."

"What do you mean?" he asked softly, getting entirely wet with her.

"Your sister was with me. She should have been here. The real Morana was supposed to be here. I wasn't. I don't even know who I am."

A hand fisted in her wet hair and pulled her head back firmly, another wrapping around her throat, demanding her attention.

Morana closed her eyes.

"Look at me," he ordered, squeezing her neck once.

She didn't want to. She was scared of looking at him, didn't he know that.

The grip on her neck tightened, and she opened her eyes, staring at his throat.

"Eyes," the demand found its way through the fog.

Slowly, heart thundering in her chest, Morana looked at him.

And found those beautiful, magnificent blue eyes looking at her with anything but hate.

"You are exactly where you were supposed to be," he told her, his voice leaving no room for doubts. "I know exactly who you are."

"Who am I?"

"Mine."

Morana felt her chin quiver, her eyes burning.

"You might have been born with another name but you are Morana. My Morana. You're the girl I killed for and you're the woman I'd die for. You are mine and you are exactly where you're supposed to be. Don't ever question that again, do you understand?"

Morana did, she understood his words, but her foundations had crumbled, her entire life shaken, her future a blank. In that moment, sitting in the cold shower with him fully-dressed, looking into his blue eyes, there was only one thing that mattered.

"Don't hate me again."

His hand flexed on her throat. "Do you know why I enjoy holding you like this?"

She shook her head.

"I can feel your life under my hand," he stated, his eyes burning on hers, his fingers locking her life to him. "Your body, your life, your heart – they're all mine now. Trust me to keep all of them safe."

And Morana collapsed into his chest and broke down for everything they had lost, both of them holding on to the one thing they had found.

※

"I want things to be clear going forward," Dante elucidated, looking around at each of the men and few women in the room, his gaze dark. "I will be taking over all businesses starting next week and I want you to come forward and report directly to me about everything you were keeping under the rugs for my father. That's not how things are going to work now and if you have a problem with that, there's the door. Get the fuck out."

Dante had changed. She didn't know what had happened or what he'd seen in the envelope, but the man with the easy smiles was heading towards an explosion she didn't think he was aware of.

Morana watched him across the table in the mansion, sitting there not in the capacity of his friend but as the surviving Vitalio heir in the West. The rest of the Outfit men gathered around the room, both in shock of Lorenzo's death and Dante's return from the afterlife.

Tristan sat just as gravely beside him, his sharp eyes not missing a reaction from anyone's faces. Nobody moved out. Dante nodded. "Good. Let's mourn my father this week. Thank you for coming."

People slowly shuffled out of the room, not muttering, not discussing anything. Morana watched as Leo Mancini, Maroni's younger brother, gave a bitter look to Dante before walking out.

"He's going to be a problem," Morana commented once everyone had left.

Dante got up from the chair and walked to stand at the window, looking at the people outside. While Dante was back to being dressed perfectly, he hadn't shaved completely since he'd come back, and the scruff suited him. His profile looked severe, harsh, and a little intimidating, if Morana was being honest.

"I know," he said, his eyes outside. "Leo has always been hungry for power and wanted to step out of my father's shadow. I'll take care of him."

She didn't doubt that.

Morana looked at Tristan, to see him watching Dante with a slight frown.

"So, what's the plan?" Morana asked with extra enthusiasm, trying to lift the energy in the room a bit.

"Do you want to run a mafia family?"

Morana blinked at the question. "Um, no. Not particularly."

Dante finally smirked, turning to look at her, leaning against the window. "Are you two getting married?"

Wait what?

Morana looked at Tristan with wide-eyes, not knowing how to answer that question. Tristan shook his head. "Not until we find Luna."

Dante nodded, his gaze pensive. "You know, there's a reason why the Alliance flourished so long under those three. My father and Gabriel handled the business, and your father handled the information."

"I can handle the business in Shadow Port," Tristan's voice came from where he was seated. Dante chimed in. "And I can handle the business in Tenebrae."

Morana nodded, catching on. "And I can handle the information."

Dante walked to his father's, now his, desk and brought out a crystal-cut bottle of vintage scotch, pouring it into three glasses, handing them both one.

"To the Alliance," he raised the toast.

"To finding the missing girls," Tristan matched.

"To the future," Morana clinked glasses, looking both men in the eyes.

They were her family now.

And they had a long road ahead of them.

EPILOGUE

Tristan

*F*uck.

Tristan watched the strand of dark hair flutter as the woman beside him exhaled, making it float before coming to rest against her soft skin. Sleeping like this, she was subdued. Fragile. Reminding him of the little girl who had once smiled at him.

Any moment now, she would awaken and he would see the fire that lived inside her in those burnished eyes. Those eyes had always done so much to his insides. As a boy, he hadn't understood what the heaviness in his chest had been. As a man, he was learning. She had looked up at him with her claws bared to the world, her hate, her heat, and now her heart, all his for the taking.

She unmanned him, this little woman with the soul of a warrior. He was a smart guy but her brain was unlike any he had ever known, and it occasionally made him feel like an idiot. He didn't mind that one bit.

He traced a finger gently over her shoulder, marveling at the softness of her unmarred skin, down to her stomach, his lips curving. He knew she sucked her stomach in sometimes, trying to flatten out the little belly she had. She didn't know, didn't understand that she could gain inches and she'd still be the most beautiful thing he'd ever seen.

And for such a smart woman, it still left him floundering that she'd chosen him over and over again. Him.

She'd kissed his hands bathed in blood, touched his scars earned in pain, and looked at him to see only the man. She'd always been that way, his Morana. And though he'd never been able to give her anything, he tried every day. If she ever regretted her choice, he didn't want to examine what he would do closely.

His phone beeped on the side.

She stirred, making a cute little noise of irritation before settling comfortably in the crook of his neck, her breaths warming his skin. He smiled, checking the message.

It's here.

Contentment like he'd never thought he would find settled over him like a comfortable blanket, warming him from the inside. Pressing a kiss to her forehead, he untangled himself from her and got up to go.

"Whereyougoing?" the words smushed into his pillow.

Fuck, she was cute in the morning.

"I have something for you."

He saw as curiosity got the better of her and she opened one eye before groaning. "It better not be sex because I will kill you, Tristan. You come anywhere near my pussy for a week and I will murder you."

His lips twitched before he could help himself. "I didn't hear you complaining last night."

"I did," she argued, moving up, light hitting her neck and he saw the marks littering her skin. Satisfaction slammed through him. He liked that. He liked that a lot.

Shaking his head, he pulled up the blinds, bathing the penthouse bedroom in sunlight.

Morana narrowed her eyes before falling back on the pillow, groaning. "I can't move. I'm sore."

Tristan bent down, picking her up in his arms, sheets and all, and carried her to the spacious bathroom. Setting her down on her feet, he pressed a soft kiss to her swollen lips, half sure she would bite his tongue off if he deepened it. He didn't think she had any idea how much she amused him, the emotion something he'd never been very familiar with until her.

His chest lighter than it had ever been, he ran her a bath, knowing he had been too intense last night. But then, he'd had a good reason.

Pouring in some of the bath salts that were now stacked on the shelves, he gave her another soft kiss, looking into her supremely satisfied, languid eyes.

"Come find me after you're done," he murmured against her lips and left her in peace to soothe her body. Stripping down the dirty sheets, he made the bed, humming a little tune and stopped as he realized he was humming.

Was this what happiness felt like?

Shaking his head, he went to the guest bathroom and showered and shaved, getting ready for the day. As had become routine with them, he went to prepare breakfast while she got ready. Not many people knew about how much he enjoyed cooking. There was something so satisfying about creating something delicious from simple raw ingredients.

Feeding Morana though? It was almost a high he craved. He loved reading her face. From the very beginning, he had fed her and known exactly how she'd enjoyed his food. Seeing her eyes close and her breath catch, as she took that first bite, always got him a little hard. But more than that, it was the joy of connecting with her, knowing something he was doing was giving her happiness. He craved it.

Whipping up some eggs together, Tristan wondered how things were going to change now. Last night had been a party to officially announce Morana and him taking over the Shadow Port mafia business. With the death of both the leaders last week, things had been a little turbulent, to say the least.

After talking things through, Dante was taking things over in Tenebrae while Tristan needed to handle Shadow Port. This would be a new Alliance, a new era, between brothers. It was perfect, really. Tristan had never loved Tenebrae, the city roiled with too many memories for him that he would rather put away. And Morana loved this penthouse in Shadow Port, loved the city if he was honest. She especially loved that his bike was here, as she'd told him after he'd taken her out on it a few nights ago.

This building was already his but now it would become the mafia headquarter of the city. He needed to get staff, get security, and amp the place up. If they were going to make their life here, he needed to rest knowing it was as safe as he could make it.

Beating the eggs, he let his thoughts drift to Dante, slightly worried about him. He was fond of the asshole and lately, he'd sensed something darker in him than ever before. He'd tried to talk to him about him, tried to get him to open up about what had happened when he'd gone underground, but Dante was tight-lipped about it. And with Amara in the wind, Tristan was worried – not just for her, because he was fond of her too, but also for Dante.

The sound of footsteps made him look up at the woman who had been his reason for existence for so long he didn't know where he began and she ended anymore. He put himself in Dante's shoes, wondering what he would do if she disappeared without a word now.

The glass in his hand shattered.

"What the fuck!" she exclaimed, running down the steps to him as he breathed through his nostrils, numbing his pain by sheer will and looked at her. Her hair in a messy bun on her head that was slightly lopsided, her rectangular glasses perched on her nose, her body in a simple flowy dress with flowers on it, she took his breath away.

"Does it hurt? Shit!"

Taking a hold of his cut right hand, she turned on the tap and cold water ran through his palm, cuts stinging momentarily. Tristan looked down at the only woman who had ever cared if he hurt and pressed his lips to her head, trying to contain everything he was feeling. Some days, he felt like he would explode with the emotions she pulled from his once-dead heart.

Clueless about the turmoil inside him, she took his other hand and was about to put it under water as well when she saw the tape on his finger.

He hadn't planned on showing her until later but as she looked up at him with curious, beautiful eyes, his wildcat who just purred for him, he felt something in his chest melting.

"I'm cynical, Morana," he told her, holding her hand and her attention. "I don't believe in marriages. I don't believe in men who wear their rings with their wives only to take it off later. But I believe in loyalty. I believe in commitment."

He saw her eyes shimmering, knew she'd already figured it out. He wasn't surprised – sometimes she knew him better than he knew himself. She was his gift for a fucked up life, this woman of fire that warmed his chilled, lonely bones.

"I can't marry you," he told her, "not until I fulfill the promise I made to my sister."

She nodded in understanding.

"But I never, ever want you to not walk into a room and know that every part of me, fucked up man and the lost boy, belong to you."

He could see the effect his words were having on her. Her lips trembled as she broke their gazes and looked down at his hand. Taking a deep breath in, one that pushed the bite he'd given her on her cleavage into stark relief, she traced the tape on his left ring finger with shaky hands.

And then she peeled it off carefully, seeing the small tattoo he'd gotten two nights ago.

He looked down at it himself, pleased with the curvature, the one word loud and clear.

Morana.

"Oh shit," he heard her gasp before she looked up at him, openly crying now, her tears making her eyes squint in an adorable way. Though he was certain she'd kick him if he said so.

"I'm so fucking in love with you, Tristan Caine," she blubbered, attacking his chest with her face and pressing kisses against his pounding heart. He tamped down the immediate disbelief he felt at her words and breathed deeply, accepting that she – beautiful, smart Morana Vitalio who could do a million times better than him – loved his damaged ass. Too bad he was never going to let her realize that. She was fucking stuck with him now.

He pressed a little kiss to the top of her head, enjoying how small she felt against him. He forgot sometimes, with how fierce she was, that she was tiny.

He wanted to tell her he loved her too.

And he didn't know how to tell her that, how to verbalize that.

Maybe one day he would. He hoped someday he could. Until then, he could just show her.

※

He took her out on a date to *Crimson*.

It felt fitting, given everything had begun there. He ate the food, then took her to the bathroom and ate her out because she was too sore to take him and he couldn't help himself. But he liked that look in her eyes, the one right after she came down from an orgasm. She looked at him with this dopey smile that made something rumble in the hollow of his chest. He was going to keep her high on that shit just to keep getting that particular smile every day of his life.

Now, standing in the parking lot of their penthouse, he watched as she looked at his gift.

"You've got to be shitting me!" the woman beside him jumped in excitement, giving him a smile so bright it fucking knocked his breath out.

The three guys behind him chuckled. He wasn't entirely fond of them yet but they had followed him to Shadow Port from Tenebrae for their own reasons and one of them, Vin, was actually pretty cool with knives. Dante trusted him implicitly and that was good enough for Tristan. While he set up the system in the city, he had wanted to have a few familiar faces he could trust with him.

Right now, the only thing that kept him from punching them was the fact that they could all see the little hickeys Tristan had left on the back of her neck last night. They knew she was his. That pleased him immensely.

Fuck, he really was the caveman she called him where she was concerned.

It had been exactly this primal need to claim her, to show her she was his, after the party last night that had led to the entire night of sexual marathon that had drained him of every last drop of cum and sweat. He had attacked her the moment they had entered the penthouse, fucking her against those damn windows she loved so much, on the kitchen counter, on the stairs, before finally moving into the bedroom. To say he had been exhausted by the end would be an understatement.

He watched as she stared at the red '69 Mustang, an exact replica of her old car, her hand touching the metal of the car. He knew she missed her old car, knew she'd been attached to it.

He indicated for the guys to leave them alone, and stepped forward to where she stood.

"You like it?" he asked, needing to know his choice wasn't in vain. She nodded.

Before he could say something, she took his hand in her small ones and pulled him to the elevator, hitting the button for home.

"Thank you for the lovely first date, Mr. Caine," she looked up at him from behind her glasses. He traced her swollen lips with his eyes and turned to see their reflections in the mirror. It never got old. The first time he'd leaned back against the wall and watched them together, that first night she had stayed in his territory, something had fluttered inside his chest, seeing her tiny form beside his.

She looked just the same but she smiled more now. He didn't think she even realized it but he caught her biting her lip more, talking more, moving her hands more as she talked. She was more alive and seeing her that way made him feel so fucking good. He knew he was damaged. He knew he would never completely be able to give her everything she deserved. But he liked to fucking try and every time she smiled, it was his reward.

It was exactly what her father had made him promise with that dying breath.

'Take care of her,' the man had said and Tristan, in that one moment, had connected with him. They both knew the pain of losing everything they held dear, both knew the hope that kept them clinging to the brink of sanity. He had seen the man over the years a few times, every time he had been stalking his daughter. Not that he would ever tell her the depth of his obsession. No, that wouldn't do.

The doors slid open, bringing him back to the moment, and like a beacon, she went straight to the windows, looking at the spectacular night view as thunder crackled in the sky.

She took off her heels and threw them to the side, sitting down in front of the window, the room dark just as it had been the night his life changed.

She pat the space beside her, looking up at him with bright eyes.

And he followed like the besotted moth he was, ready and willing to burn in the pits of hell as long as she looked at him like that.

"I have something for you too," she told him softly, opening her black clutch and handing a plain envelope to him.

Tristan looked down at it, confused.

"I met the airport guy today," she explained and Tristan felt the tightening in his gut like he always did whenever another man was mentioned. Although he tried to keep it contained, fact was he knew the kind of men who lived in this world – men with no morals and no scruples and no decency. They would see her and steal her without a thought to her wishes. The one thing that kept her safe, as much as it irked her, was his reputation. They would steal her but they wouldn't cross him.

He still didn't like it. Fuck.

"I'd made a deal with him so I told him a little of what he wanted to know and he gave me that," she continued, completely oblivious to the possessive fire running through his blood.

Tristan stared into her eyes for a long minute, reading each fleck of olive over the light brown, her heart bared for him to see. Fuck anyone trying to take that light from him. He would rip them apart with his bare hands. Taking a small breath, calming down his territorial ass, he looked down at the envelope in his hands and ripped it open, taking out the single scrap of paper.

It was an address.

His heart thumped louder than it had in a long time as he stared at the simple hand-written address, a location five hours out of the city, and looked at her.

"I've already had the address checked," she told him, her voice shaking as she knew what this could mean. "It's a house. We're going tomorrow."

He wanted to thank her, to tell her what she had done for him, was still doing for him made him feel like the luckiest bastard on the planet. The words, as always, never made it out his lips. But she understood. She always fucking understood.

He wanted to tell her that love was too tame a word for everything that happened inside him where she was concerned. She had shifted him, realigned him from the inside out. Like a planet that suddenly pulls a moon into its orbit, she had bound him to her, given him direction for longer than she knew, gave him purpose to exist.

She was his gravity, his fucking planet, and he was lost without her.

With pasts bathed in death, with foundations bathed in blood, he had found something so precious he wondered sometimes if he wouldn't go through all of it again just to find her.

The rain came down on the windows outside, thunder rumbling, and he leaned forward, telling her everything with his lips the only way he could. She held on to him.

She always held onto him.

And with one woman he loved beside him, searching for the other he had lost, Tristan felt loved, accepted.

Whole.

And he would go through it all, over again, just for her.

*The Dark Verse series continues with the story of Dante and Amara in **The Emperor.***

I hope you enjoyed Tristan's and Morana's journey. Though it is not the end and you will see them again. Please consider leaving a review/ rating before hopping on to your next book adventure.

ACKNOWLEDGMENTS

Writing was not something I ever thought I'd do, not until a few years ago when my mental health took a nosedive and storytelling became my refuge. For that reason, my first thanks will always go to the amazing people who have been with me since the beginning, my fandom family who has supported me with their love the likes of which I've never known. You're the reasons I discovered who I am and you make me strong every single day.

Secondly, to my parents – I wouldn't be who I am without you. You've made me believe that I can fly all the skies, dive in all the oceans, fail or succeed, and you would love me just the same. You are my pillars, no matter where I am in the world, and I am lucky to be yours.

I also want to thank the entire book community that has accepted me with such open arms. To all the bloggers and bookstragrammers who freaked out with me and celebrated my book, thank you. Sharing my own love of all things romance, seeing the talent in your edits and photos and simply talking to you has been such a gift. To all the friends I have made in the community who make me smile and aww. Thank you for your love. You don't know what it means to me.

And to Nelly. My amazing, talented, visionary friend who so generously told me yes when I asked her if she would design the cover for my book. You are a gem and I thank my lucky stars every day for you. Every time you create something, it blows my freaking mind. I don't think I'll ever be able to verbalize the love I feel for you and how damn grateful I am every day for you tolerating my ass. Thank you. I couldn't have imagined anyone else doing this story justice the way you have. There was no choice to make.

To my friends, you know who you are. Thank you for being so patient with me when I disappeared for days and was a shitty friend basically. I love you so damn much.

To my tribe of readers, the gifts you have honored me with leave me speechless. The abundance you shower upon me fills my life every damn day. Thank you so, so much. You make my world a better place.

Most importantly, I want to thank you, my reader, for picking up my book and choosing to read me. If you've made it this far, I'm eternally grateful to you. I hope you enjoyed it but even if you didn't, thank you for choosing it. I appreciate you taking the time so much. Please consider leaving a review before jumping into your next bookish world.

Thank you so much!

CONNECT WITH RUNYX

Newsletter: https://runyx.kit.com/newsletter

Reader Group: https://www.facebook.com/groups/runyx/

Facebook: https://www.facebook.com/authorrunyx

Instagram: https://www.instagram.com/authorrunyx/

Website: https://runyxwrites.com/

Turn the page for an exclusive extract of ENIGMA ...

DEATH SMILES . . .

Unknown Girl,
Mortimer University

The girl stood on the edge of the cliff.

There was no moonlight for anyone to witness her demise, not a concerned soul around to make her question herself, not a sound beyond the sea and the whispers of her own moral decay.

Oh, she was of sound mind and judgment. Yet, she stood on the cliff on that moonless night, walking to her own destruction, an invisible gun of her own making to her head.

Maybe, things would have been different, could have been different, if she just had the courage. The world thought she was brave. They would remember her as such. There was nothing to indicate otherwise. Would this be a murder or a suicide or an accident? Would she become the girl on the news pushed by invisible hands, or a girl who jumped of her own free will? Or maybe, they would speculate a tragic fall of a girl who wandered too close to the edge. Literally, metaphorically, who knew?

The wind whistled around her, blowing her dress up and whipping her hair over her face. To anyone watching, she would have painted an ethereal, haunting picture.

Picture. Photographs. Memories.

She had so many of them.

She didn't want to stand on that cliff.

But she had to. There was no other choice, not for her.

Not when they were watching.

And they were always watching.

Even as she stood weighing her decision, her choices, her mortality.

Even as she stepped closer to the edge, her body shaking, resisting the directives of her mind.

Even as she closed her eyes and took the plunge, the wind rushing in her ears, the silence shattered by her scream piercing for a split second before cutting off abruptly.

They were watching as she lay on the dark sand on a dark night, and died.

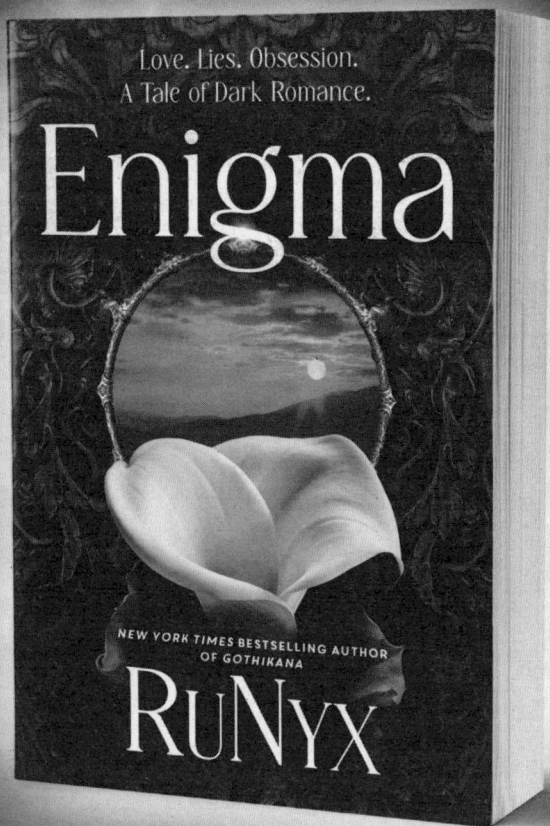

DISCOVER THE MOST LOVED
MAFIA ROMANCE SERIES

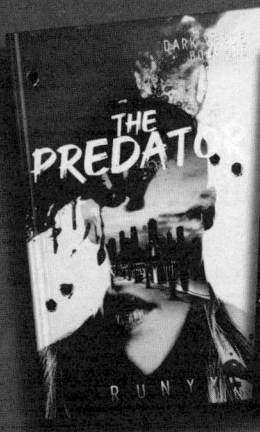

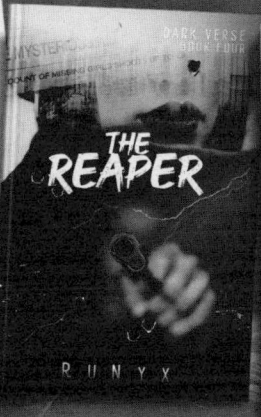

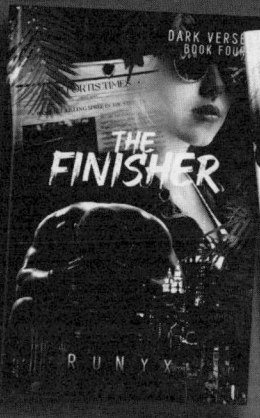

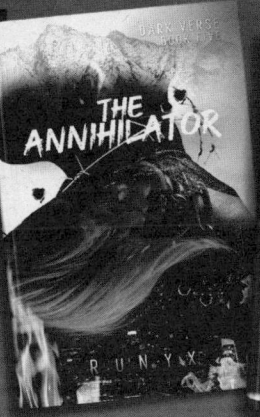

THE PREDATOR

DARK VERSE

R U N Y X

THE REAPER

DARK VERSE
BOOK FOUR

R U N Y X

THE EMPEROR

DARK VERSE
BOOK THREE

R U N Y X

THE FINISHER

DARK VERSE
BOOK FOUR

R U N Y X

THE ANNIHILATOR

DARK VERSE
BOOK FIVE

R U N Y X

THE SYNDICATER

DARK VERSE
BOOK SIX

R U N Y X

On a station platform, with nothing to read,
and a four-hour train journey stretching ahead of him...

That's where the story began for Penguin founder Allen Lane.
With only 'shabby reprints of shoddy novels' on offer,
he resolved to make better books for readers everywhere.

By the time his train pulled into London, the idea was formed.
He would bring the best writing, in stylish and affordable
formats, to everyone. His books would be sold in bookstores,
stationers and tobacconists, for no more than the price
of a ten-pack of cigarettes.

And on every book would be a Penguin, a bird with a certain
'dignified flippancy', and a friendly invitation to anyone who
wished to spend their time reading.

In 1935, the first ten Penguin paperbacks were published.
Just a year later, three million Penguins had made their
way onto our shelves.

Reading was changed forever.

—

A lot has changed since 1935, including Penguin, but in the
most important ways we're still the same. We still believe that
books and reading are for everyone. And we still believe that
whether you're seeking an afternoon's escape, a vigorous debate
or a soothing bedtime story, all possibilities open with a book.

Whoever you are, whatever you're looking for,
you can find it with Penguin.